THE RIVEN CHRONICLES

THE
FALLEN
PRINCE

 CHRONICLES

THE
FALLEN
PRINCE

AMALIE HOWARD

Sky Pony Press
NEW YORK

First Edition

This is a work of fiction. Names, characters, places, and incidents are from the author's imagination, and used fictitiously.

Sky Pony Press books may be purchased in bulk at special discounts for sales promotion, corporate gifts, fund-raising, or educational purposes. Special editions can also be created to specifications. For details, contact the Special Sales Department, Sky Pony Press, 307 West 36th Street, 11th Floor, New York, NY 10018 or info@skyhorsepublishing.com.

Sky Pony® is a registered trademark of Skyhorse Publishing, Inc.®, a Delaware corporation.

Visit our website at www.skyponypress.com.

10 9 8 7 6 5 4 3 2 1

Library of Congress Cataloging-in-Publication Data available on file.

Cover illustration by Steven Wood
Cover design by Sarah Brody

Print ISBN: 978-1-5107-0170-0
Ebook ISBN: 978-1-5107-0173-1

Printed in the United States of America

For my mom,
who never believed in labels
and who told me to be myself
no matter what

CONTENTS

PROLOGUE

THE FLARE OF blue fire is blinding. Then again, it's gone so quickly that even if you were staring right at me, you'd blink and it'd vanish. The emissions from the process of eversion—shifting between universes—are unavoidable. However, I try to be careful, everting in concealed areas away from people, and away from the eyes of the Faction and the Guardians. They're always watching for those who break the law—those who don't remain where they belong.

Me, more so than ever.

I belong in Neospes, a domed city in a parallel dimension to the Otherworld. But I'm here in pursuit of a man who everted over a year ago. A man who nearly destroyed my world in his quest for power. A man so consumed with retaliation that to let him loose in either world would be a colossal mistake.

And so I hunt him. I've *been* hunting him—across thirty states and always a step or two behind. He's clever, brilliant, and a master strategist.

After all, he's my father. And he's my *creator*.

I may look like an ordinary girl, but I'm far from one. It's something I'm still coming to terms with, ever since I learned the truth. I am a product of genetic experimentation and advanced robotics. I am the girl with nanoplasm for blood—the perfect combination of human and machine, an aberration of nature—and yet, its greatest creation. I am the only one of my kind.

My name is Riven.

And I am a killer.

1

DEEP IN THE OTHERWORLD

STOOPING TO LACE the untied shoelace of my combat boot, I meld into the crowd at Grand Central Station in New York City. It's strange to think that once upon a time in my world, infrastructure like this could have existed. Pre-Tech War, that is. Not that I would know—I was born in a dome where the tallest building is a castle three stories tall.

But my people often recount tales of grand mirrored spires that rose to defy the skyline, and thriving metropolises with skyscrapers that'd dwarf the ones in this world. Our historical records talk of buildings that were twelve times the size of the Empire State building I've just seen, and of hovercraft that flew between the towering structures on aerodynamic super-highways.

Everything was computerized, automated.

The offshoot of civilization on my version of Earth saw the human race building machines that superseded the rules of our own programming. We invented metal monsters, reveling in our superior brilliance, so much so that we didn't see it coming. In the end, when the artificial intelligence we'd built became self-aware and turned on us, *we* became theirs—vast cities of human slaves, caught in a nightmare of our own making and bound by the very electronic shackles we had created.

Our citizens rebelled—and eventually won—but only at enormous human and environmental cost. Ten long years of devastation in a war against our android captors saw our oceans gone and entire populations decimated. Surviving cities are covered by huge glass domes; ones built to protect the people within them from the unpredictable elements and volatile temperatures beyond.

While extant pockets of humanity claim the unburned plains of my world, the rest of it is ruled by the Reptiles—half-organic, half-android hybrid scavengers. They're the worst things surviving in the Outers beyond the city walls—amalgamations of animal and human parts in various states of decay, coupled with robotic operating systems. Some of them live in packs, others are more solitary, but they are all intelligent . . . and they're lethal.

Feeling the rush of bodies passing beside me, I glance upward at the artistically etched ceiling of the station, admiring it for a brief second. There is nothing like this in Neospes. Not anymore. But even though my world is a shadow of what it once was, we are rebuilding beneath a new king with new hope.

My pulse thrums at the thought of Caden. The boy—now king—who had stolen my heart without my knowledge, and the one I'd had to leave to make sure he and the people of Neospes would be safe. It's been so long since I've seen him, almost a year. I wonder if he looks the same with his too-long hair and his intense green eyes—eyes that I vividly remember, even now. Eyes that could always see right through me.

Awareness prickles along the back of my neck, and I tuck my head below my arm, scanning the area behind me. The Guardians had closed in before I'd shaken them off in Boston, jumping on a bus outside the city. I'd considered everting, but the electrical displacement leaves too much of a trace. And the Guardians are nothing if not vigilant, particularly after the influx of Vectors under the last King of Neospes's rule.

The Vectors were a soldier army created by my father—reanimated corpses fueled by nanoplasm—the very same nanoplasm coursing through my veins. And because of the microscopic nanobes in my body, I run hot—way hotter than any normal human. Suffice it to say, I'm as easy to track as the Vectors are. I set off the Guardians' eversion detectors like clockwork.

Standing cautiously, I duck around the circular information booth and peer over my shoulder. It's clear. I flatten myself against the window, trying to get a look around the other side, and catch a glimpse of a green jacket that seems vaguely familiar. I shake my head. I'm overreacting. Green is a popular color.

"Ma'am?" a voice says. "May I help you?"

I meet the impatient stare of the clerk sitting on the other side of the window. "What? No."

"Then, kindly make room for those who are waiting."

"Um, sorry," I reply.

Stepping away, I feel the prickly sensation again at the edge of my consciousness, and I crouch to fiddle with my boot. Precious seconds fly by before I see them—two men and a woman scanning the area. Looking for someone. Looking for me. I narrow my eyes, the nanobes in my retinas running a brief threat analysis. To anyone else, the three people seem ordinary, dressed in dark pants and dark shirts, but the advanced weaponry holstered out of sight on their belts suggests otherwise. So does the careful, methodical way they're casing the area. My jaw clenches. There's no mistaking it—they're Guardians. How did the Faction catch up to me so quickly?

I take a breath and make a run for it, skittering among bodies and ducking beneath a couple holding hands.

"Stop her!" the woman shouts. "She took my purse!"

A thousand eyes pivot in my direction as I dodge the two NYPD officers rushing grim faced toward me, and dart down a long poster-plastered hallway. The policemen are hot on my heels. Glancing over my shoulder, I count the two officers and the three people I'd seen before. Two more guys in army fatigues and really big guns join them. I curse under my breath and pick up the pace. Now's no time to play it safe. If they catch me, my father will disappear for good.

Gritting my teeth, I let the nanobes in my blood take over. Within seconds, my body receives a jolt of adrenaline so powerful that it makes my back arch with the force of it. Everything inside of me electrifies as my internal programming responds to my commands, my legs pumping like well-oiled pistons. I throw another look backward to my pursuers, hearing the broken static of two-way radios and shouted directives. The distance between us is now considerable.

Shoving the jacket cuff off my wrist, I engage the nano-suit beneath it, tapping manual commands into the console. *Defense.*

The suit's armor solidifies against my skin, just as I slide across a railing leading to an underground staircase, taking the stairs six at a time. I weave in between columns and double back up another staircase to the previous level with the giant posters on the walls. A sign above my head indicates I'm near Forty-Seventh Street, but that's too obvious an exit. They'll expect me to go aboveground.

Instead, I swing right in the wide passageway near the escalator, darting up yet another narrow staircase a few tracks down. A loud beeping announces that the waiting commuter train is about to leave. Without a second thought, I slip through the doors as they close. While the tinny voice of the conductor announces the stops, I take an empty seat, hunching down near the window, and pulling my hood over my head. Connecticut is as good a place to crash as any.

I calm my labored breathing. That was too close. Although, I'm not entirely sure what would happen if the Guardians *do* get their hands on me. Era Taylor, the leader of the Faction, knew that I'd be coming after my father. I'd made no secret of it once we found out that he'd everted to this world. There's no way I can let him get away, not after everything he's done, and knowing everything he is capable of. My father is a scientist at heart, one driven by the demands of his ego. There's no telling what he'll do with any technology at his disposal, and I can't afford to take the chance that he won't attempt to re-create another monster like me.

I consider my options. I could evert, but who knows where I'd end up—in the Outers, or somewhere way worse. The only safe eversion spot that leads directly back to Neospes is in

Fort Collins, Colorado, and I'm two thousand miles away. I'd everted once out of desperation with the Guardians hot on my heels in Nevada, and had ended up in the midst of a Reptile nest back in my universe. I'd escaped by the skin of my teeth. With my luck, I'd evert from this train and end up in the deep end of an acid swamp. No, I'll take my chances here.

I slouch down in my seat as the woman and the two men from earlier burst through the staircase entrance to the platform, steely glances combing the windows of the departing train. For a second, the light falls on one of the men, and I blink. A face shimmers into my memory of a boy I haven't seen in months—Philip, Era Taylor's son. But it can't possibly be him. The facial structure is similar, but that's where the resemblance ends. This boy is taller, broader, and bearded. I'm imagining things. There's no way Philip would be in New York. For all I know, he died that day we faced the Vectors *en masse* . . . right before Shae did.

My heart skips a beat at the memory of my sister. She'd died to save Caden and me, and everything she'd ever done had been to protect us. My jaw aches from clenching it so tightly. That's another thing my father will have to pay for—because he'd made her into a monster, too.

The train picks up speed on its way out of the station, entering the darkness of the tunnels, and I heave a sigh of relief. I'm sick of running from the Faction when all I want to do is find my father. Every time I get close, he manages to slip away. It's frustrating. If I didn't have to keep an eye on the Guardians every infernal second, maybe I'd have caught him by now.

I pull a thin tablet from my backpack and punch in a sequence. The facial recognition software that's been my breadcrumb trail runs in the background. This world may not have the advanced technology of mine, but some of the software is remarkably useful. I've patched in to the FBI database, bypassing their security with a mimic program of my own design. To them, I'm just another field agent accessing their internal database.

I tap on the screen and a pattern of red dots shows up. My father has been busy. The trail has no rhyme or reason—a handful of dots along the east and west coasts, with the majority of them located in central Colorado. My best guess is he's looking at zero-gravity eversion points because whatever he's planning has to be connected to Neospes. His last known position was here in New York City but, as always, I'd been a hair too late. It's almost as if he's toying with me, leading me on a wild goose chase just to prove that he can.

Six months ago in Los Angeles, we'd come face-to-face in a nightclub with only a six-inch-thick glass partition between us. It had spanned the room, separating the diners from the bar, and in the precious seconds it would take to get around it, I knew he'd be gone. Without the stupid barrier, it would've been so easy to reach out and lodge my ninjata through his traitorous heart. Instead, I'd stood there powerless, in furious silence.

"Riven," he'd said coolly as he leaned back in his chair and placed his tumbler on the white table. "You've been following me. Why?"

"To take you back to Neospes to answer for your crimes."

He cocked his head. "You and I both know that's not true."

"To kill you, then."

"Why?"

"*Why?*" I choked out. "You murdered Shae. And after what you did to me . . ."

He took a sip of the amber liquid in his glass, his insouciance making me feel like snapping those slender fingers, cupping the tumbler, one by one. "I made you stronger. I made you better. You're untouchable, invincible."

"You put tech in me when I was an embryo. You could have killed me. You could have killed Aurela."

"But I didn't," he said. "And your mother knew what she signed up for. You are the future, Riven. *We* are the future."

My fists clenched against my sides. "Don't you get it? There *is* no we. You have no future, Danton. I will hunt you to the ends of any universe, and I will kill you. Next time, there won't be a wall between us."

"So fierce, and yet, so foolish," he said, smiling as he indicated the seat on my side of the glass wall. "Sit. Chat a while."

A part of me knew that I should have walked away. Engaging with him was dangerous. He knew how to press every one of my buttons. But I couldn't bring myself to do it, not when he was right there.

I sat, rigid. Paralyzed. "Let's talk, then. What are you doing here?"

He shrugged, waving a careless hand—his gesture simultaneously elegant and ugly. "I should think that would be obvious. I'm saving our dying world."

"How? By destroying this one? We aren't meant to be here. We had our chance, and we blew it. You can't just take something from one universe and put it in another. The Faction won't stand for it."

"How is darling Era?" he said with a laugh. "The Faction is useless and obsolete. The only way for Neospes to survive is to take what we can from this world. Help ourselves to its vast resources. The people here have more than enough, after all, and they don't care for half of it. They are on the same path of destruction that we were."

My tone was laced with sarcasm. "So, you're trying to save them?"

"I am simply offering our people an alternative, and they will thank me for it."

"You're wrong."

"You never could see the big picture, could you, Riven?" He finished his drink in one swallow, and we both stood. "You'll come to heel soon enough."

"I'm not a dog."

"Aren't you?"

I shoved my chair back, punching into the transparent wall and watching tiny cracks branch outward in the tempered glass. "And still so predictable." He nodded to the two burly bouncers behind me. "That will be your downfall."

I'd shoved past the two men who were double my size, sending them skidding across the floor, then rounded the wall to the now-empty table where my father had been sitting. The only thing left was an empty tumbler with the imprint of his lips on it. I'd hurled it at the wall in frustration, and made a hasty exit.

Ever since then, I've been chasing a ghost . . . always several steps behind. And now the Guardians have upped the ante, closer on my trail than they have ever been.

Suddenly, the train lurches to a stop, the last carriage still touching the platform. The conductor's voice filters through the train car. "Please be patient. We will be on our way shortly."

Maybe it's a coincidence, I think. Mechanical trouble happens all the time with these commuter trains. But deep down, I know there's no way that I'm going to be that lucky—the Guardians will be on the train, searching it car by car. Pocketing my tablet and keeping my head low, I stand and make my way forward until I'm in the front car. Now there's nowhere to go but out— or stay and fight, risking the lives of innocent commuters in the process. I've never been a fan of collateral damage.

I unsheathe my ninjatas from their holster. The swords shimmer with incandescent blue lights as their microchip technology connects to the nanobes in my body. Several passengers hightail it out of their seats to the far end of the train car, eyeing the weapons with terrified expressions. I rap on the door of the conductor's box.

"Open up," I tell the man inside.

"I can't do that."

I eye him through the narrow window. "I don't want to hurt you, but I will rip open this door if I have to."

"You're just a kid. The police are already on their way." He glances at my blades, and then at my face as the nanobes rush there, flushing my cheeks with bluish fire. His eyes widen, but before he can move I crash the hilt of my blade into the handle and jerk the door open so hard that the metal tents outward. The conductor is trembling as I reach past him to grab the keys latched to his belt.

"Thank you."

"What are you?" he whispers with round eyes.

Ignoring him, I stoop down near the doorway to unlock the emergency release. One of the door panels slides back and I toss the conductor his keys before hopping onto the dark track. I have minutes at most to make my way out of there, a split second to decide whether I head into the darkness or back the way we'd come and risk running right into them. Then again, I'm never one to shy away from a challenge.

Re-sheathing my ninjatas, I backtrack through the narrow space between the train and the grime-covered tunnel walls. I'm careful not to step on the rails. With my luck, I'll electrocute myself and everyone within a five-mile radius. Voices filter from the third car, shadows moving past the windows as the search continues. I shimmy by silently, hoping the train won't start moving. I'm almost to the platform, home free, when I hear heavy feet thudding on the tracks behind me.

Time to run.

With a burst of strength, I leap onto the steel railing and haul my body over the lip of the platform, scanning the area. There are twenty-odd armed officers milling around. No civilians in sight. Smart. They've evacuated the area. I smile grimly. Works for me.

"That's the perp!" one of them shouts. In half a heartbeat as eyes and guns converge on me, I slam in the commands on the wrist panel of my suit—*offense*—feeling it shimmer responsively against my skin. I calculate the odds of getting out of this jam with minimum casualties.

"Stop, or I will shoot," a nearby officer barks. I note the stripes on his uniform and nod. A captain. He's the one in charge. "Hands up."

"If you say so." In slow motion, I raise my hands, crossing them behind my head.

"On your knees."

I offer an apologetic smile. "Now that, I can't do." With a swift movement, I grasp the hilts of my ninjatas and, again, pull them from their sheaths. The captain's eyes widen in disbelief—confusion, even. My grin widens. "What? You've never seen a sword before?"

"Nonlethal force!" I hear a muffled voice shout from the depths of the tunnels behind me. A female voice that sounds familiar, but I can't turn to see who it is as five of the men rush me at once.

"You'd be better off with the guns," I tell them, dropping to my knees and striking out on both sides. Two of the officers go down with identical incisions through the fatty flesh of their thighs. I don't want to kill them. My objective is to incapacitate. I dispatch two others—one with a jab to the temple with the hilt of one of my blades, the other with a reverse kick to the jaw. The nanobes are doing their job, rushing to the surface of my skin and flickering a hazy blue as they provide a dizzying jolt of speed and adrenaline.

The captain watches me with narrowed eyes before raising his automatic rifle and pointing it directly at my chest. I can see him considering not following the nonlethal force orders. "What *are* you?" he snaps through his teeth.

"Is 'your worst nightmare' too cliché?" I answer. My wisecrack falls flat, so I shrug and point to the gun. "That's not going to help you. Your best bet is to let me through. I don't want to hurt anyone."

"Like them?" He jerks his head at the four uniformed soldiers on the ground, clutching their injuries. "You think you're going to just walk out of here after assaulting four police officers?"

"They attacked me. I defended myself."

The man's mouth tightens. "Drop the swords." The remaining officers move to surround him in a semicircle, watching me and waiting for their orders. "I *will* shoot."

"So shoot," I say. "It isn't going to change the outcome."

"Of what?"

"Of you putting more of your men in danger, and of me leaving this platform. You're only delaying the inevitable."

"She's just a kid," one of the policemen mutters.

"No," the captain says, not taking his eyes off me for an instant. "She's not."

I grin and heft my swords, anticipating the furious volley of bullets. With inhuman speed, I bend sideways and feel them whizz past my head and torso, swinging into a crouch at the last moment before somersaulting toward the captain. The bullets lodge into the cement walls behind me, the sound like thunder in the eerie silence of the evacuated platform, but I barely notice. My blade is at his throat before he can squeeze off another round. Kicking the backs of his knees, I force him to the ground.

"Back off," I warn the rest of his men. "I don't want to kill anyone, but I will if I have to. Your CO's blood will be on your hands."

The remaining officers are watching me with varying degrees of shock and surprise, their guns locked and loaded. "Stand down," an authoritative voice says from behind me. "I'm Special Agent Fields. We'll take it from here." The officers don't move, watching their leader for confirmation. He nods against my forearm, his pulse racing on my skin. He's nearly twice my size, but no match for my strength. With obvious reluctance, the officers back away, but three hooded soldiers dressed in distinct red uniforms are quick to replace them.

The Faction's muscle.

The Faction has their own special brand of brawn. They've been highly trained in martial arts, and I know from experience that these guys mean business. Divesting the captain of his gun, I release him and shove him out of the way. I sigh and brace myself, my ninjatas at the ready, but the Faction warriors remain immobile, watching me . . . waiting.

"Riven," the same female voice from earlier says. "We just want to talk."

I freeze at the sound of my name, and slowly turn. "Charisma?"

It's the quiet girl from Horrow, whom I'd saved from a group of drunken boys nearly a year before. She doesn't quite look the same as I remember. Her brown hair is in a businesslike knot and she's dressed in black trousers with an armored vest over her shirt. Her face is unsmiling and rigid. Charisma looks all grown up and in charge. My eyes flick to the tall bearded man at her side, the ever-present tablet in his hands. I hadn't been wrong earlier. It *is* Philip—he must have sprouted five inches in the last year.

"I thought you were dead," I say to him.

"Obviously not," he replies.

"How's mommy?" I ask. His jaw tightens. "She know you're here?"

"Yes."

"What do you want?" I say rudely.

"We want you to come back with us," Charisma says. "To Colorado."

"I'm afraid I can't do that." I'm starting to sound like a broken record. "Things to do, places to see." My eyes narrow at the thought of her working for the secret group of world leaders who police inter-universe activity. "So, are you with the Faction now?"

"No, not exactly," Charisma hedges.

Keeping a cautious eye on the red-clad ninjas, my hands slide to my sides, still gripping my blades. "You either are or you aren't."

"I'm not. Philip's a Guardian."

"Wow, *officially*? No way. Congrats." I fight an all-too-teenage eye roll. "None of that has anything to do with me."

"That's where you're wrong," Charisma says. "I volunteered to come with Philip to find you because I knew—I *hoped*—you'd listen to me. We used to be friends, remember? I'm begging you to come back with us. Please, Riven, just hear me out."

Something in her voice tugs at me. Besides Caden, she was the closest thing to a friend I had during my stint at Horrow High School. I sigh. Being in this world has softened me more than I care to admit. "Fine. Out of respect for our two minutes of friendship, you have two minutes to convince me."

"I only need two seconds," she says. "Caden's there."

All my breath and bravado peels away. "What did you say?"

"Caden's there. And he needs you."

2

NEGOTIATION

THE INTERIOR OF the private plane is plush, with cream-colored leather and shiny chrome accents. I could enjoy it if the Faction soldiers weren't glaring me down as if they expected me to go full 'borg on a tiny aircraft twenty thousand feet in the air. I shake my head and stare out the window, watching the landscape drift by in stripes of brown and green. It looks nothing like Neospes. From such a vantage point, my world would be nothing but ash and red dust. No shimmering blue ocean, no lush green rolling hills—just blackened char from a decade of war.

My mind goes blank, drowning out the thousand questions buzzing there like gnats. After Charisma dropped her bomb-shell, I'd gone with them willingly—the hour-long ride to the small private airport in upstate New York spent in charged silence. Neither Philip nor Charisma had offered up any infor-mation, and I bided my time. If they're lying, they'll pay the price, former friendship or not. If they aren't . . . well, I'll have bigger things to worry about, like why Caden isn't ruling at home in Neospes, where he belongs. And why he's risked everything we've fought for to evert back here.

"Here's some water," Charisma says, placing a glass on the armrest of my seat. She sits across from me. I watch the drink for a second, sunlight reflecting off the ice cubes, before draining the contents in one gulp. If she wanted to kill me, she'd had other opportunities before we boarded this plane. And if she wanted to poison me, well, the nanobes running rampant in my blood aren't just good for strength. They'd identify and annihilate any foreign toxins in seconds.

"Thanks. So, are you going to tell me why Caden's here?" She nods, her eyes finding the men standing guard near the exit points. At her inaudible command, they melt out of sight to the rear of the cabin. I purse my lips. "Bet that would have come in handy a year ago."

"What?"

"Intimidation skills."

Charisma smiles. I see some of the unaffected warmth I'd remembered. That girl is still there, hidden behind whatever horrors have forced her to grow up in the space of fourteen months. "That seems like a lifetime ago."

"What happened?"

"Ten months before," she begins, "the school was attacked by a crazy gunman. Everyone—the news reporters, even—thought it was some guy with a death wish. But it wasn't. Philip told me later that the man was there for Era." I raise my eyebrow at the mention of his name, and Charisma pauses, flushing faintly. It's none of my business, but the thought of Philip getting romantic with anyone makes me cringe. Charisma and

Philip. Last time I'd seen Philip in physics, he'd been disheveled, nails bitten to the quick—a far cry from the confident guy he is now. But still, it's *Philip*.

"Speaking of Philip—you missed me so much senior year that you two started dating?" My half attempt at a joke falls flat.

Charisma smiles softly. "We took Advanced Physics together. I guess he felt comfortable with me. Things . . . evolved."

"Bet Era didn't like that." I snort.

"She was reasonable."

I lean back in my seat. "When did you find out about who they were—he and Era, and the Faction, I mean?"

"He had his tablet at my house." Charisma's flush deepens to a dull red. "I didn't mean to spy, honestly. It looks like every other tablet out there—shiny, touch screen. It started beeping and Philip was in the bathroom. But when I picked it up, it went berserk, flashing for a pass code as if it was going to explode right there and then if I didn't enter it. Philip came running out looking as white as a ghost, punched in the code and, before he could turn it off or hide it, a bunch of holograms popped up—ones of multiverse theory and geographical data of a place that looked like it'd been burned."

"Neospes?"

"It sure didn't look anything like Earth, but that wasn't what got me." She stares at me with intense, dark eyes. "It was the photo of you. A recent, *dated* photo tracking your positions between two obviously disparate worlds layered one on top of the other."

"Tracking me?" My eyebrows snap together. "When was this?"

"Few months after school started."

I shrug off the urge to toss Philip off the plane. I should have known he'd be tracking me. "So, Philip told you everything?"

"Most of it—the parallel worlds, the Guardians, what happened with Neospes's false king. I had to be cleared by Era before I got the rest. You were classified until recently when I asked to help."

"You knew what those soldiers were when they attacked."

"Yes, but only in theory. I'd never seen one until then. I was with Era at the school working on a project. The man had those . . . soldiers with him, dead ones."

"You can say it—Vectors."

"Vectors," she repeats. "I mean, I'd read the files about them, but up close, they were so inhuman. The Faction guard that Era had stationed at Horrow was no match for so many of them. They seized her." Charisma takes a long breath, as if to steady her nerves. "We got Era back before they everted, but at a huge cost. We're down to twelve Guardians, almost a quarter of our original numbers."

"Who do you mean, *we*? The Faction?"

She grimaces. "Yes."

"What did they want with her?"

"Information, I suppose. She was imprisoned for months."

But by whom? My father? He has his own reasons for capturing Era—negotiating diplomatic immunity or his return to Neospes. But I know that there's no way my father would let Era go if he were able to get his hands on her. The Faction has many enemies in both universes.

"Do you know who took her?" I ask. "Any confirmation?"

"Era didn't know. She never saw or heard any of them. She said that they were constantly moving."

My eyes narrow. "That's odd. She had to have heard something. Birds, people, cars, *something*."

Charisma shakes her head. "Nothing."

"Where is she now?"

"Home." I blink, thinking back to when Era Taylor's house had been overrun and destroyed by a thousand Vectors hot on our heels. As if reading my mind, Charisma clears her throat. "The Faction rebuilt it. The facility was too valuable to lose."

"But the location is compromised."

"Not necessarily. The Vectors have been decommissioned. And the security has been quadrupled."

"Whatever." I shrug and lean forward. We've danced around long enough with backstory. "Why is Caden here?"

"I can't say." Charisma swallows, her fingers twisting together. "I don't have clearance."

"Clearance? You seem to have plenty of clearance based on everything you just told me. What am I walking into, Charisma?"

"Nothing," Philip interrupts, striding over to us, his face impassive. I stare from one of them to the other, from his expressionless face to her visibly anxious one. They're hiding something, withholding a critical piece of information. Walking blind into a situation is not how I operate. Time to reevaluate my strategy.

I cross my right leg over my left, swirling the water from the melted ice in my glass. "You know that those guards can't stop me from leaving this aircraft."

"You're not going to jump out of a moving plane, Riven," Philip scoffs. "If you haven't noticed, we're thousands of feet in the air."

"Aren't I?" I tap on the silver cuff that's barely visible beneath the sleeve of my leather jacket. "Don't for a second forget what I am, or what I can do."

"Everything has a kill switch," he says. "Even you." He shrugs, eyes derisive. I frown. It seems that Philip hasn't quite forgiven me for nearly killing him and his mother in their secret underground lab when I activated four of their Vector test subjects. But it's more likely that Philip's ego is bruised because he hadn't realized what I was from the get-go. Then again, no one had. Not even me.

"Is that a threat?" I ask.

"Fat lot of good those nanobes are going to do when you crash into the ground at two hundred miles an hour."

Charisma's eyes are wide as she places her fingers on Philip's arm. "That's enough."

I smirk. "Better listen to your girlfriend, Philip. Bet the only reason you made it as a Guardian was because of her. Or is it that the ranks are so depleted, the Faction had no choice but to upgrade you? You and I both know how you react when facing hostile Vectors. You run like a little coward. No wonder Era was taken."

Philip's fingers curl into fists. "Shut up, Riven."

"Or what?"

"Or I'll make you."

"Brave words from someone holding a tablet," I jeer. "What are you going to do—throw it at me? I'm shaking with terror."

Philip bares his teeth in a mockery of a smile, the effect startling on his dour face, and shoves said tablet under my nose. "What do you think is flying this plane?"

Charisma leans forward, one arm pushing Philip back into his seat, the other tasked with appeasing me. "Will you two stop? We have to work together on this and bickering like a couple of idiots isn't going to help Caden, or anyone else."

At the thought of Caden, my irritation evaporates. I nod grimly, and Charisma's hand flutters to her side. Philip's mouth tightens, but he leans back and places the tablet in his lap. I take a breath. "For the last time, I am going to ask you—why is Caden here?"

Charisma sighs. "All I can tell you is that *he* found *us*. He everted here on his own. He wouldn't talk to anyone but you. That's why we went to New York. It was"—she glances at the tablet balancing on Philip's knees—"your last known location. The Faction wanted to keep an eye on you."

"Let me guess. I'm their best hope to find my father? Well, I found him, in New York, but you knew that already." My voice is scathing. I don't like the idea that the Guardians have been keeping tabs on me this whole time. No wonder it'd seemed like they were always on my back. My eyes focus on Philip's tablet. "How *are* you tracking me? I don't have a chip, even if you could track the implants from Neospes citizens."

Philip's lips curl into a smug smile that makes me want to smack it off his face. "We *can* track those," he says in a mocking tone, "but for you, we use your blood. Specifically, your DNA. It's special, you know."

I ignore the sarcastic emphasis. "Where'd you get my blood?"

"From a poker."

I frown. "A what?"

"Metal rod," he snaps. "Sometimes you use it to stoke a fire. Other times, to hit manipulative, lying hybrid cyborgs in the head."

A vague memory of Era Taylor hefting the blunt metal instrument before leaving me trussed up at the mercy of the Vectors runs through my brain. She hadn't known what I was then—only that I'd been allied with the Vectors.

"You took some blood. So what?"

Philip stares at me as if I'm an imbecile. "Your *blood*. As in advanced geno-robotics? You know, for a supposedly super-advanced cyborg, you're a little slow."

"The nanobes wouldn't survive without a live host."

His patronizing expression makes my hybrid blood boil. "AI evolution. You give artificial intelligence a chance at life and it'll take it any way it can. Even at the expense of the host. You guys learned that during your Tech War, didn't you? Androids," he adds with a dark look at me, "can't be trusted."

"What do you mean AI *evolution*?" I ask, staring from Philip to Charisma. She meets my eyes calmly. Too calmly.

She clears her throat. "By the time the scientists isolated the sample, the nanobes had consumed most of the remaining host blood cells. They'd recalibrated to briefly exist on their own, separating from your genetic coding."

"Recalibrated?" A shivery sensation pools in the pit of my stomach, making the hairs on my arms prickle. That's the thing with self-aware robots—they'll do anything to survive—

including self-repair. I shiver again, the sensation turning me into a block of ice. Or maybe I'm just being paranoid.

"Yes." He's enjoying my shock. "They wouldn't have lasted without a fuel supply, so we gave them an artificial one. Our scientists ionized them with an infrared laser and replicated their frequency, which is tagged to yours. Essentially, they created a receiver to track your movements. It's not a hundred percent accurate but, well, there's no one else like you on this planet. Even with a fifty percent success rate, it still works."

"Quantum coherence," I murmur.

I recognize the technology. My father had tried it once as a trace measure to keep track of the Vectors—using a mix of wave and radio frequency identification technology. It'd been unstable, the wireless frequency not meticulous enough to identify each Vector. But I can see how it would work with me. I am, after all, unique.

I swallow, frowning. "Show me."

Charisma nods at Philip, and after a long moment, he leans forward to the tablet laying on the table between us to swipe at an application. The lights in the cabin go dim and a hologram appears in the middle of the aisle showing a map of the East Coast. Blue dots mark various positions on its surface. I glance at the city names, visions of each of them flashing in my memory. They'd missed a couple, but the tracking device had worked well enough to capture the general pattern of my movements over the past year. A blinking light in the corner of the hologram catches my attention. The blue dot, unlike the others, is moving. That dot is me. Here, right at this moment. On this plane.

My eyes narrow. "Is the device on now?"

"We're always tracking you, Riven." Philip smirks and signals to one of the guards standing at the rear of the plane. The soldier carries over a thick black case. Philip swishes his hand across a touch pad on its front, infrared light pulsing for a minute across the vein network of his palm, and the case clicks open.

I'm holding my breath as Philip gently lifts opens the top. Icy white clouds steam outward. "They work better in the cold," he explains, watching my expression. "Too hot, and they'll explode without host body temperature regulation."

Inside the case, a slim, recessed cylinder becomes visible as the haze of dry ice clears. The cylinder is hooked up to what appears to be an intertwined Lithia fuel system and a mini-computer. The outer system itself is also intricate—no doubt constructed with technology from my world. There's no way the Guardians would be able to build something like this without using a Neospes cheat sheet. Funny how they don't mind bending the rules when it's to serve their own ends.

I swallow the cynical remark that rises to my lips as a glimmer of blue snaps inside the cylinder. The components inside the tube are invisible to the naked human eye, but not to me. Add it to the perks of being a cyborg—cybernetic genes that can turn your eyeballs into full-on electron microscopes. Squinting, my nanobes heighten the sensitivity of my retinas, magnifying my vision a millionfold.

Time slows as I study the rogue nanobes. *My* rogue nanobes. Tiny microscopic robots circle each other in a concentric pattern as a handful of other electrons swirl around their outer orbit. Small sparks of electricity bounce between them like an electrical storm in a teacup, surging in response to my proximity. Mesmerized, I stare in silence, the infinitesimal blue streaks of lightning growing more violent by the second.

"Enough," Philip grunts, snapping the lid shut.

The neurons inside of me fire, a blue haze rushing to the surface of my skin as I reach for the case. There's no way I'm going to leave a device like that in the hands of people who, given the chance, would decommission me in a heartbeat.

"Give it to me."

"No."

My mouth tightens. "I'm here with you now, so it's not like you need to track me. Plus, we both know that this tech doesn't belong in this world. Either you give me that case or I take it."

The barest whisper in the air alerts me to movement as the four Faction guards take up offensive stances. One of them steps forward to take the case from Philip. I reach for my ninjatas, but they're not there. Of course they aren't. They're across the cabin *behind* the row of guards. I stand slowly, everyone tensing in anticipation. The positioning system on my suit indicates we're just south of the airfield in Loveland, Colorado, and ten minutes from our destination.

"Riven." Charisma's voice is a plea. A twinge of concern makes me pause, but she's a big girl. She signed up for this on her own. I confirm that she's strapped in before taking matters into my own hands.

Without moving, I focus on the black case, my fingers curling into fists. The nanobes in my body leap into action until all I feel is heat licking at my insides. An electric blue radiates off my body as the soldier struggles to hold on to the now rapidly vibrating case. I would have preferred destroying it in a safer location—*not* ten thousand feet above the ground—but beggars can't be choosers.

"Riven!" Philip grunts. "What are you doing? The only thing keeping the nanobes stable is that electromagnetic field in that box. They're going to explode."

"I know."

His eyes widen. "You *know*?"

"Better strap yourself in." I propel my body forward, kicking the torso of the soldier at the exact moment that the case bursts into blue flames, launching them both against the side of the cabin. The explosion rips out two passenger windows. With a sucking sound, the soldier's body disappears through the hole along with fragments of the case. Wrapping my wrist around the end of the seatbelt, I'm nearly flipped off my feet as the plane shudders, the rush of air sucking one more soldier out of the compartment.

Two down, two to go.

The red lights in the cabin flicker on and off, a parallel row of white exit lights snaking their way down the middle of the plane. I glance behind me. Charisma is grasping the sides of her seat, her hair ripping free from its knot and whipping into her face, but at least she's buckled in. Philip, too. Alarms are shrieking madly as Philip slams his fingers against his tablet, struggling to stabilize the plane as we begin a nauseating nosedive to the right. Releasing my hold on the belt, I settle my weight against the seat on the other side of the aisle and engage the technology on my suit.

I can feel it calibrating against me, taking into account the velocity of the wind and the pull of gravity beyond it. Almost immediately, the suit tightens and anchors me to the floor of the swaying aircraft. Step by careful step, I make my way to where my ninjatas have been stored, flicking open the lock with a quick snap of my boot. I keep an eye on the two soldiers watching me with baleful glares and holding on for dear life. Like the others, they hadn't been strapped in so, to stop me, they'd have to let go. Neither seems so inclined. I wink and edge my way against the far wall to the gaping opening.

"You're just going to leave us?" Philip screams over the roar of the wind.

"You should have given me the case."

A sob breaks from Charisma. "Riven, please—"

I shake my head. As if I'd leave two innocent, albeit annoying, teenagers to die. I'm cold, but I'm not *that* cold. With a sigh, I tug against the overhead bin, locating a thickly wrapped, padded bundle. Just before I leap from the belly of the plane, I pull on the red tab and jam it against the opening, watching as the bright yellow plastic unfurls and molds against the gap, blocking the outflow of air. The portable raft will hold for now, stabilizing the plane . . . at least until they land.

I'm freefalling backward into thin air, hurtling toward the ground like a stray bullet. I glance at the sensor on my wrist— the suit calculates my odds of survival at about thirty percent, seventy percent if I land in water. Not bad odds, considering I've just leapt out of a plane with no parachute.

3

KEEP YOUR
FRIENDS CLOSE

MAYBE THIS WASN'T such a good idea.

My body is careening toward the ground at an alarming pace with the wind pulling back my cheeks and hair with brute force. My suit is going crazy, trying to calculate survival ratios and measure my rocketing biometrics. It's not exactly designed to save me from a seven-thousand-foot free fall. Thirty percent odds in a state that has more fields than lakes aren't that great. But there are also a few big reservoirs, and if I'm lucky—really lucky—I can land in one of those.

Scanning the area, I see a tiny shimmer of light. From my vantage point, it seems to be more of a pond, but anything's better than hard-packed earth. I glue my hands to my sides and steer my body in the direction of the glittery surface. Just before I hit the water, I curl myself into a ball and pray that it's more than twenty feet deep with no rocks at the bottom. My prayers are answered to a degree.

I enter the lake with the force of a meteor, only to find myself lodged to the waist in slick, oozing mud. I groan, but at least

I'm alive. It takes me the better part of an hour to get free from all the muck, and my suit is already malfunctioning from the moisture. I strip it off in a nearby abandoned shed and wring all the water out, but it's no use. My suit's on the fritz. Designed to counter every possibility *but* submersion, thanks to the lack of water in Neospes, the suit refuses to even power up.

Great, I think. The last thing I need when going up against a bunch of overeager Guardians and the Faction is a malfunctioning suit. Taking a deep breath, I disengage the neural connector and power down the suit completely. I'll take my chances without it, and try again when it's dry. Right now, I need to get to Caden.

It's not the easiest thing to hitch a ride looking as if I've just mud wrestled my way across the Midwest, but I manage to get one heading north to Fort Collins. The inside of the beat-up truck isn't much cleaner than I am. Its owner is a young guy dressed in cargos and a T-shirt with a baseball cap perched atop a head of unruly, fire-red curls. I'm guessing he's a college student working here over the summer. Before Caden had found out that he was the long lost prince to a parallel dimension, his plan had been to attend the local Colorado State University. Funny how things change.

"You okay?" the driver asks.

The last thing I want to do is make conversation, but I am grateful for the ride. "Fine," I mumble. "Thanks for stopping."

"You go to CSU?" he asks after a minute, staring at me out of the corner of his eye. "You look familiar."

"First year agronomy," I improvise, stifling a laugh. Then again, I'm half-covered in mud so I could look like anyone. "I was out testing soil samples. Summer intern for the USDA."

"Wow, that sounds pretty cool for a freshman," he says, reaching over to toss me a tub of wet wipes from the center console. "I'm a junior. I'm working to pay off some of my student loans since I couldn't afford to go back home. Are you staying on or off campus?"

"Off."

"Where?" he says. "I can drop you, if you like. It's not like I have anywhere to be for another forty-five minutes. Name's Bass, by the way."

"Riven," I reply, debating whether I should let Bass drop me off in an area that will be heavily secured. I probably have a better shot of getting there faster with him than without him. "Okay, sure. Head to southwest Frontage Street."

We ride in silence most of the way, with me murmuring directions across town, but Bass exhales loudly when we pull up to the forbidding wall and black gates. "Fancy," he says.

"Not my place," I say. "My boss's. Thanks for the ride."

Bass flushes. "Hey, um, do you want to get a beer sometime?"

"I don't drink."

"Coffee, then?"

I shrug. "Don't do that, either. See you around."

Bass drives off, his expression slightly miffed. Maybe he thought we'd had a moment in the truck, but I'm not here to make new friends, even if he seemed like a nice enough guy. I wait until the dented rear fender is out of sight before walking up to the towering iron gates on the outskirts of the town. I stare right into the security camera on the stone column to the left.

Before I can even open my mouth, the gate swings open on well-oiled hinges. I start walking up the paved driveway, but haven't made it a few yards before two men dressed in red and wielding machine guns meet me. More Faction soldiers, carbon copies of the ones I'd left on the plane with Charisma and Philip.

"Boys," I acknowledge as they fall into step beside me. Stony-faced, they don't say a word the entire trek up to Era Taylor's old house. I'm not intimidated, even though my suit's out of commission. If anyone wanted me dead, I'd already be dead. The way I figure it, the Faction needs me more than I need them.

The fact that Caden is here makes that more than obvious. I clench my jaw. He shouldn't have come back here, even if this world had been his home for most of his life. Caden is an anomaly like me, a product of two disparate universes. A long time ago, his mother accidentally everted to Neospes and the then-King had married her. When the king was assassinated, she fled back to the Otherworld with her son after discovering another plot to murder them both. The royal clone, Cale, assumed the throne so as not to cause panic, and sent in his most ruthless General to kill the true prince. Only, the General had failed, falling for the prince instead.

I sigh. Those days are long gone. I'd been Legion General for all of a few months before Cale sent me to kill Caden, only to discover that my own sister had been protecting him. My gut twists as I think of Shae. She, too, had been a casualty of Cale's twisted vendetta. He'd given the order to make her into a Vector to punish me, and I'd had to destroy her. I swallow hard, burying the emotion deep. This isn't the time or place to display weakness.

"Weapons," one of the men grunts at the entrance to the house. I look up to take measure of the rebuilt structure looming ahead of me. Before it'd been destroyed, it had been imposing but tasteful. Now, it looks like a giant square hunk of rock with a ten-inch thick steel door and no windows. As if I'd give up my weapons entering a building that looks like *that*.

"Negative."

"Weapons," the man insists, raising the nozzle of his gun as if that's going to make me do anything but knock him to the ground.

"Point that thing at me and you better be prepared to use it."

"Stand down, soldier," a sharp, familiar voice says through the door. "General Riven doesn't like to be told what to do, nor does she like to follow orders."

"Era," I say to the stern-faced woman sitting just out of sight. "I haven't been a general for a long time—you know that."

"Old habits die hard," she says, pushing the door wide. "Please, come in."

As I step over the threshold, I try not to let my surprise show on my face. Era Taylor is in a wheelchair—one that looks like a super advanced mini-hovercraft—but a wheelchair just the same. The last time I'd seen her, she'd arrived in Neospes like an avenging angel with an army of Faction guards ready to take down Cale. This frail woman is a pale imitation, but I know the last thing Era would want from anyone, much less me, is pity.

"Nice wheels," I tell her.

She waves her hand at the chair. "One of the bonuses of the job."

I push aside the twinge of compassion. If the situation were reversed, Era, or any of the Faction, wouldn't be mourning my debilitated physical state. Plus, Era's mind is probably still as sharp as a tack. My hand rests loosely on the hilt of a dagger tucked into my belt, the threat subtle. "So where's Caden?"

"No need for any of that," she says, her black eyes flashing for a second, before entering a command on the armrest console and steering the chair down the hallway. "He's here and safe. Philip told me what happened on the plane. They're okay, if you were wondering," she says over her shoulder.

"I wasn't."

"You weren't at all worried that you left my son and his"—she breaks off and clears her throat before continuing—"Charisma stranded on a plane, about to crash?"

I grin, unable to let the opportunity pass. "You can say it, you know. His *girlfriend*. Tiny little Philip, all grown up."

My grin widens as I savor the pissed-off look on Era's face. She must hate that she's no longer the only woman in Philip's life. He's a quintessential mama's boy.

When I first met Charisma, she was a party girl—one who drank to hide her insecurity and shyness—and let people take advantage of her. That all changed when I'd saved her from being hurt by a group of date rapists. The Charisma I've seen today is leaps and bounds ahead of the girl she used to be. She's strong and smart, and far too good for Philip.

"He should count himself lucky, you know," I say. "That girl has loyalty in spades. She's one of the few people I liked here."

"The same girl you were willing to let die?"

My exhalation is long and loud. "Era, you and I both know that that plane is equipped with vertical landing gear. I verified the specs the minute I got on board." I tap the side of my temple. "It's all in here. So, there was literally no chance of them crashing or crash landing. Or dying."

She stops the chair. "In that case, you chose to jump out of a moving aircraft that would have brought you to the exact place you are right now."

"I have trust issues," I say, shrugging. "Plus, we don't exactly have the best history of being honest with each other. How do I know you're not leading me to the gallows?"

"I see you haven't lost your sense of drama," she says archly, and I stifle a smile. Just like old times—playing her cards close to the vest. Era Taylor may well be one of the most mysterious and secretive people I've ever met. Who knew that a high school physics teacher would hold the keys to two connected parallel dimensions? I study the rigid line of her profile. Even in captivity her spirit hadn't been broken. They'd ravaged her body, but not much else. Looks are deceiving, hers more than most.

Era guides the chair to the end of the hall. I follow in silence with the two gunmen trailing my steps like shadows, aware of the cameras tracking my every movement.

The house looks nothing like it did before. The interior is a giant maze, bordered with shiny floors and metal walls. Everything about the space feels cold and clinical, and for a girl who grew up in her father's advanced robotic labs, that's saying a lot.

My eyes narrow as they fall on a series of black dots along the walls.

Era follows my gaze. "Laser security. But you knew that already."

"Neospes tech. Can cut a man to ribbons. Isn't that against the law?"

She eyes me coolly. "So were the Vectors sent here to capture me."

"What did they want?"

"They didn't say."

Her obsidian gaze settles on me with an odd intensity. I look away first. I don't even want to know what they did to her. It wouldn't have been pretty. The Vectors have no empathy and operate on programmed commands. Whatever torture she underwent would have been brutal. My eyes slide to her emaciated, motionless legs, and I quickly look away. I swallow hard. Now that I've opened myself up to human emotion, it's as if I can't stop feeling every little thing. Especially compassion.

I squirm. "I'm sorry."

"For what?" she shoots back, a half smile breaking the tight line of her mouth. "I'm here and alive." Her smile widens and she tips her head in a small birdlike motion. "Despite the reports, empathy from you is unexpected."

Squelching the stupid emotion, I roll my eyes. "Why? I'm a real person with real feelings and everything."

"And nanoplasm for blood."

She has a point. I shrug and decide to change the subject, gesturing at the space. "You did a little remodeling? Didn't feel like moving?"

"Something like that," Era says with a dismissive wave.

The Guardians had rebuilt the facility from the top down after the Vectors destroyed it while chasing after Caden and me. However, the fact that Era hadn't chosen to relocate to a safer, unknown area makes me wonder: *what's so important that the Guardians would decide to remain here in plain sight?* Unless it was some kind of stance—some show of strength that the Faction would not be cowed.

I almost crash into the back of the chair as she stops in front of the elevators at the far end of the hallway. She leans into the side panel for a retina and biometric scan, the red lines from the device distorting her face. I'll bet anything it's more Neospes tech, which makes me even more convinced that they're hiding something valuable here. I'm pretty sure the advanced security is not because this is the home of the esteemed Faction leader. There has to be more.

Era swings around as the partitions to the elevator slide apart, dismissing the two men walking behind us with a curt nod.

"Catch you later, boys," I say with a wink as the doors hiss shut. "Maybe you'll actually get to use those toys the next time we see each other."

"Level Six," Era says in a loud clear command after a glare in my direction.

"What? I have a rule. Point a weapon at me, be prepared to use it."

The elevator begins a slow, smooth descent. The last house didn't have any subterranean levels I'd known about—just the lab on the first level, and the upper floors. But this makes sense—on the defensive front, lower floors are more difficult to access.

"How far down does this go?"

"More than six levels," Era says.

I kneel down, resting my elbows on the armrest of the wheel-chair. Era flinches slightly at my nearness, but covers it up with a loud sigh. "You know I could make you tell me, right?" I say.

Era's gaze could incinerate stone. "Regardless of whom you think you are, Riven, I am the leader of the Faction, and you will address me with the proper respect."

I smile and stand. "Just checking to see if you were still in there."

"Despite what you may have heard, I am quite intact where it matters. Now, come along," she says as the elevator slows to a stop. It opens to a floor that looks exactly like the first, only there are a few more doors along the wide hallway, and two more soldiers waving big guns in my face. Now I understand why she dismissed the first two. Era ushers me toward a second elevator at the far end.

"I didn't know about what happened to you until recently," I admit, watching as she undergoes another security scan. "Charisma told me." I lower my voice as the elevator doors shut. This time it swishes to the side, and then down before coming to a smooth stop. "What did they do to you?"

Era's face twists, shifting with the memory of something hideous before recomposing into its formerly serene, yet stern, state. The monotone words she throws over her shoulder do little to conceal the weight of the emotion behind them. "They did what they had to do. They wanted information. I resisted, so they tried to make me comply by peeling the skin from my legs while I watched."

I try to cover my revulsion, pressing my lips together. "Who were they?"

"Vectors."

"But, sent by whom?"

"That is the question."

We travel in silence down another hallway before Era opens the door to a large office with a long, oval table and a wall-to-wall video screen displaying the feed of a rust-colored dead landscape that looks eerily like the Outers in Neospes. The room isn't empty. Five men and women occupy seats around the table. The rest of the Faction, I'm guessing. Era meets my eyes, and wheels her chair around to a space at the right of the head of the table, gesturing for me to sit in the empty seat across from her.

"I'd rather stand."

"Do as you like." She waves a hand around the room. "These, as you may have already deduced, are the five leaders of the Faction. Once the Lord King of Neospes everted here for help, they were convened at my request." I think of Cale before realizing that she's talking about Caden, *not* the clone responsible for nearly killing him and taking over the throne. She turns her attention to me. "You are here for two reasons. One, the Lord King requested your presence, and two, there is an imminent threat, and not just to Neospes. To us all. The Vectors who attacked me had a purpose. We need to find out what it is."

The tension in the room soars. I make a big show of taking the seat she had offered and lounging back, arms crossed over my chest. "And I can help you, how?"

Era's answer is a punch to the gut. "You were their leader."

"You think the Vectors sent here were Danton's?" I watch her expression, but she gives nothing away. There's a good chance they *could* have been my father's—after all, there's no one else who knows them as well as he does. He'd designed and built them from nothing but a line of code. But why would he attack the Faction *here* on their home turf? Or capture Era and release her? It doesn't make any sense. "Why *did* they let you go?"

"They didn't let me go," she says. "I was rescued by the Guardians and Faction soldiers. They found me and saved me from certain death."

I shake my head slowly. "Era, if the Vectors didn't want you found, you wouldn't have been found. If they wanted you dead, you'd be dead. There are no gray areas with them. Only orders." For a second, I think of the big Commander Vector I'd destroyed in Cale's quarters and shiver. It had been a new kind of self-aware android—one that could circumvent orders based on its own assessment of a situation. Yet another law that my father broke to serve his own interests. I take a breath as the attention in the room converges on me. "You weren't rescued, Era. You were released. The question is, why?"

"We'll have to disagree on that. The Vectors fled the minute my men discovered my location." I want to push the point, but remain silent. Vectors don't flee—ever. But I wasn't there, and what she believes has no bearing on why I am here right now. I have two objectives: kill my father and keep Caden safe. And Caden's more important—he's the *only* important thing at this moment.

"I want to see Caden. The Lord King," I amend after the stifled gasp farther down the table. "Now."

After a beat, Era clears her throat, ignoring my rudeness. "I think your father everted here for a reason, and not because he wanted to deliver a lethal blow to the Faction by targeting me."

"He's not after the Faction," I say tiredly. "He wants me."

"You?"

I frown at her, and lower my voice so only she can hear. "Didn't Aurela explain when I left Neospes? Danton wants my genetic code so he can replicate it. It's why I everted the minute he did. I left Neospes to find him and kill him first."

"You can't kill him, Riv," a deep and utterly familiar voice says from behind me. "We need his help."

I turn and all the strength leaves me at the sight of the boy—no, the man—standing there. Breath and bones desert me. Era disappears, as do the others—even the table and the walls fade to white. Time stills, and it's only Caden and me in the room. Every moment from when I'd first met him to when I'd left him standing crowned a king on the parapet of the castle in Neospes races through me like a violent summer storm, leaving me wrecked in its wake.

His hair is longer than I've ever seen it, brushing past his collar in messy waves. Like me, he's dressed in regular clothing from this world—dark jeans, T-shirt, leather jacket—but he looks every bit a king. There's power in his posture, in the strong curve of his jaw, in the glint of his eyes.

I want to throw myself at him, wind my fingers in his hair, feel every inch of his body crushed against me, inhale his scent, and feel his heartbeat. But, instead, I stay glued to my chair. It's only been a year, but it feels like there's an eternity of time between us. He's had to be a king, and I've had to be . . . me.

If it weren't for the stampeding reaction of my heart, we could be strangers. Remembering etiquette, I stand as Era and the others at the table already have, and attempt an awkward bow.

"My Lord King," I murmur.

But instead of responding with the protocol return greeting, a half smile flits across his face before he covers the ground between us in three long strides to gather me in his arms, oblivious to anyone in the room but me. He stares at me for a second with those green, green eyes as if trying to reconcile my face to the one in his memory. Greedily, I do the same, drinking in his features—the straight nose, the strong jawline, the wide parted lips that I want to lose myself in.

Caden's eyes meet mine, his fingers wind into the hair at my nape, and he yanks me against him, the blood in my body replaced with liquid fire.

"Riven," he whispers once, his voice husky.

I swallow hard. "Cade."

Something flares in his eyes at the sound of his name on my tongue. And then I can't even speak because his mouth is crushing mine in a kiss so fierce that my toes are lifting off the floor, and all I can feel is him.

4

POLITICAL AGENDA

"AHEM."

A discreet cough breaks us apart, and reality is swift to return once I step out of Caden's embrace. His face is flushed, as I'm sure mine must be. I try to compose myself, knowing that we have an audience, but it's a near futile effort as Caden's thumb brushes back and forth on the soft flesh of the side of my arm. The connection between us is as voltaic as ever, perhaps more so. Every cell inside of me—android and human—is wired and alive and combustive at the fierce, possessive look in his eyes. I lick suddenly dry lips, and something dark flashes across Caden's face. His fingers tighten compulsively on my arm. Although we are no longer kissing, we could still well be.

Someone in the room clears his throat. I try to move back to my seat, but Caden hauls me firmly up against his side as if he can't stand to let me go just yet. Fighting the urge to grin like a lovesick idiot, I focus on the faces in the room, instead. I'm not surprised to see their deadpan expressions. No one—not even the Faction—would dare insult a king, regardless of their personal opinions. Except for one person. I pause at the sight of the polished, smartly attired man at the far end of the room who is staring at us with unconcealed amusement. I feel like I've seen him somewhere before, but then again, he has one of those classic looks—dark hair swept away from his face, deeply set, dark eyes, average build—that are a dime a dozen in both worlds. I'm certain I've never met him before.

The man's gaze meets mine, and though he inclines his head in a universal gesture of greeting, he arches a groomed eyebrow, an obvious commentary on my scandalous behavior with the Neospes king. My eyes narrow. His too-familiar attitude is grating.

"Madame Chancellor," Caden says, addressing Era, and my attention flicks back to him. "Please continue with the introductions."

"As you wish, my Lord King," she says, bringing up a hologram of this world in the middle of the table. Like most of the others, her face is blank, betraying no emotion despite her obvious feelings about me. I'm certain that she, of all people, disapproves of the relationship between Caden and me.

After all, I'm the thing that she fears most. I'm walking, living, and breathing artificial intelligence bred into a human host. A conscious, synthetic life form—and an abomination of the worst kind. I'm hardly anyone's choice for a royal consort. It's not like the fairy tales of this world, where the servant gets to fall in love with the prince and become his princess. The reality is that no prince wants a clockwork princess. He wants a real-life, breathing girl—and I'm the furthest thing from that.

I'm slow to realize that without a single word Era has effectively demolished me with that careful mask. I breathe in sharply, and step away from Caden. To my surprise, he escorts me to my seat before assuming the empty one at the head of the table to Era's left. I try to keep up with the introductions, but I'm too fragmented.

"Lastly," Era says, gesturing once more to the hologram, "the gentleman at the end of the table is Cristobal Marx. He represents Latin America, and—" She breaks off with a glance at me, and then at Caden who nods briefly, his hand slipping down below the table to catch mine. I stare at our intertwined fingers for a second, dimly waiting for Era to continue. "And the corresponding parallel city of Avaria."

I bolt upright in my seat, my attention riveted on Era, everything else forgotten. Slack jawed, my palm slides from Caden's. "Wait, *what*?"

"Avaria," she repeats.

"Another city?" I ask. "But the only other survival colonies are the Artok tribes to the east." I frown, jabbing a spot on the world topology that marks the European continent, my finger sliding down to the southern hemisphere. "Down here, there's nothing south of Neospes but ash."

She eyes me. "Apparently not."

I hear what she's saying, but my brain refuses to process the information. All I know is what I've been taught, that we are the only human survivors and that the lower hemisphere of my world is uninhabitable. But now, those are both wrong. There are other survivors. A whole other *colony* we hadn't known about.

"But we sent drones. Scouts. There's nothing but wasteland down there. Why would they hide from us?"

Cristobal clears his throat and drums long fingers on the tabletop. "It's one of their defense systems—holo-imagery. You see what they want you to see." His voice is velvety, the soft trace of an accent rounding out the vowel sounds of his words.

"But *why*?" I repeat. "We could have traded, made connections. If they needed help or shelter, we could have provided that."

"Perhaps they did not want or need your help."

"Are they in a dome, too?"

Cristobal nods. "Of sorts, yes."

"What does that even mean? Either they are or they aren't. They can't survive without one. No one there can."

His smile is irritating, and I have an immediate urge to smash those white teeth into next week. "It means yes and no."

I half rise out of my seat, fists clenching, but Caden places a warning hand on my shoulder and leans in. "Sit," he whispers against my ear. "That's not why I'm here. There's more you need to know."

I comply, my gaze flitting from Era to Cristobal to the other four watching me like I'm a ticking time bomb . . . which is close to reality. Even if they don't know the truth of what I am—Aurela had made Era vow to keep it a secret—my reputation as a ruthless Vector general is probably worse. The only thing keeping me in check is Caden.

He stands to address the table. "As you know, I have come here for your help. Neospes is under attack."

"From who?" I say, stunned. I'm batting a thousand here. First, the bombshell of another city, and now, Neospes is in

danger. I've been so focused on finding my father that everything else has faded into white noise.

Lines furrow Caden's forehead. "More like, from what—the
Reptiles."

"Reptiles," I repeat. "Since when? They've never attacked
the city walls. They're scavengers, not assailants."

He nods. "They've grown braver. More aggressive. They're...
organized. Parts of the dome have been compromised. We've
been forced to shut down entire sectors to contain the threat.
We're running out of places to hide and people to fight."

I frown. "Why didn't you tell me? I would have come back
to help."

"You stopped returning to the castle. We waited, but then
we had to act or risk losing more lives." Caden rubs his chin.
"We were too late, anyway. The Reptiles infiltrated Sectors
Three and Five. We've had to shut them down to seal the
breach."

I'm frozen in shock and horror. The food sector and the
defense sector—both would be a huge blow to the people
inside the dome. My thoughts shift to my mother and her first
in command. "And Aurela? Sauer?"

"They're fine, but they lost a lot of men. We're considering
evacuating the city to the Peaks through Sector Seven."

I think about the underground mountain sanctuary where
my mother had hidden an entire rebel army from my father
for years. "There's not enough room there for everyone. It was
crowded enough with the rebels."

"At least they'll be safe," Caden counters. "It'll only be for a
short time until we can get reinforcements or, at least, under-

stand how the Reptiles are able to breach the walls in the first place. They've never left the Outers, until now."

"Caden," I say in a low voice. "If we leave the city, and they take over the dome, we'll have nowhere to return to."

He watches me, his eyes grim. "That's why I'm here." He glances at Cristobal, and then at each of the others in turn. "To negotiate with the leaders of Avaria to provide asylum to our people, should it come to that. But that's a last resort. I won't lose our city. I'll do anything to defend it to my last breath."

Suddenly, all the pieces come together in a rush. "That's why you need my father's help. You want to reboot the Vectors."

"Yes."

A muscle ticks in my jaw, my fists curling. "No. There has to be another way."

"We don't have much choice," Era interjects. "We've considered all alternatives. Short of evacuating the people of Neospes here, it's the only way we can save them."

"So let's evacuate them."

"They wouldn't survive this environment, Riven," Era says. "You know that. Their immune systems wouldn't be able to withstand this planet's allergens and infectants. They would die." My eyes flick to Caden. He'd lived here, breathed this planet's air for years after his mother had everted with him as a child. She'd died. He'd survived. The people of Neospes would likely share the same fate as his mother.

I massage at my temples. "What about Avaria? You said that was an option?"

Cristobal leans forward. "It is a possibility, once we have concluded diplomatic negotiations." At my frown, he explains. "A diplomatic liaison is the only answer."

Diplomatic liaison?

Caden suddenly seems more interested in dissecting the carved designs on the table than meeting my gaze. A sour feeling builds in my stomach, and I swallow. Even I'm not so naive that I don't know what that means. I've only just gotten him back, and already they're talking about taking him—no, *giving* him—away.

I study the curve of Caden's collar, my words a whisper: "When were you going to tell me about your . . . union with someone else? Before or after you kissed me?"

His voice is gentle when he replies. "It's a possibility, Riven. And one I have to consider for the sake of our people."

"Our people," I mutter bitterly.

Hardly. The people of Neospes could never be *our* people—I would never be their queen, standing at their king's side. I've been deluding myself all along. I never should have let this relationship continue after Caden's coronation. I should have just cut the ties between us. He's a king now, and he shouldn't be saddled with a liability like me.

Caden stands, pulling me to face him, and positions his body so that I'm out of view of the table's occupants. His hands slide against my elbows. "Riv—" he whispers.

"Stop. Let go."

Instead, his fingers tighten. "You know how much you mean to me. I've been lost without you." He bends to let his forehead rest against mine. I hate that we have an audience, especially now, when he's saying words that obviously mean nothing. My heartbeat slows, deadening inside. "But I have to do this. I have to figure out a way to keep them safe. Your mother. Sauer. All of them. It won't come to that if we can get your father's help. We won't need an alliance. If we can save the dome, then none of this matters."

"It's always going to matter," I say, disengaging myself from Caden's grasp. I don't look at him—I can't look at him. If I do, I'll lose any resolve I've managed to scrape together in the last ten seconds. I turn away to address the Faction, my voice dripping with sarcasm. "So, you think giving a madman free rein to reengage an army of Vectors is the solution?"

"It's our best bet against the Reptiles," one of the other leaders says. "Fighting tech with tech."

"And what about Danton?" I ask. "You think he's going to build you an army, let you use it, and walk away feeling happy about his good deeds?" I stare them down one by one. "I know him. I know what he's capable of. He'll do as you ask because it serves his ends. You'll let him return to Neospes. He'll have an army at his disposal, and he *will* use it to kill every one of you."

"We'll contain him," someone—the same man, perhaps—says.

"How?" I bang my fist so hard on the table that it rattles. "Like you contained him in Neospes? The Faction let him do whatever he wanted. He answered to no one then. You think he's going to follow your orders now?"

"Unless he threatened the connection between the worlds we were not bound to intervene," a tall, heavily bearded man says. "This time will be different."

I laugh—a long, slow, hollow sound that echoes in the room. "Then you are only deluding yourselves. You want to fight one evil with another. My father can't be trusted. He and his creations are going to turn on Neospes—and this world— the minute your puny little war with the Reptiles is over." I glance at Cristobal, my lip curling. "Your precious Avaria will be plundered, and you won't be able to hide, not from him."

"I agree." Era stands, her obsidian stare finding mine. "Which is why we want you to lead them. The Vectors."

The room almost spins out from beneath my feet and I clutch the table for support. I can feel the nanobes rushing like a violent tide inside of me, making the edge of the table buckle beneath the pressure of my fingers. A single word escapes my lips. "No."

"You've led them before, Riven. You were the youngest general in Neospes and you commanded legions of Vectors."

She doesn't have to remind me. The thought of going back to who I used to be fills me with an emotion I can't bear to accept. Dread, maybe. The Vectors killed without conscience— kills that I sanctioned as their leader. But I'd been Cale's puppet then. "I can't."

"You can." Her face could be carved from stone.

"What makes you think I'd ever agree?" I say, bristling at the not-so-subtle threat in her voice. The tension in the room is knifelike, stabbing from all sides.

Era leans in, her voice a stinging caress against my ear. "Because you're one of them, Riven, and because you are bound to your king." She clears her throat and speaks in a normal voice. "Neospes needs you."

Because you're one of them.

Era's words are like manacles. Of course. How convenient to bring up what I am when she needs my help. And yes, I am bound to Caden—in more ways than one. But what she means is that I am his servant. Nothing more. I close my eyes and take a deep breath, removing my heart from the equation. He is a king. In days of old, this is how alliances were forged during times of war—with political liaisons. I swallow the hurt that rises up with a bitter taste. Feelings have no place in my world anymore. They never have.

"As my king wishes," I say in a dead voice.

"Leave us, please," Caden commands, and although the Faction doesn't answer to him, they depart at a nod from Era. As her wheelchair swishes past me, I swear I feel the gentle, reassuring pressure of fingertips against my wrist, but it's gone so quickly I must have been mistaken. Era doesn't look in my direction.

"Riven," Caden begins. "You know I wouldn't ask you to do this—"

"Yet, you did."

"—if it wasn't important."

I blink and say nothing. Caden shifts to stand in front of me, his hand moving to slip through the strands of hair above my ear. I let him, the desperate desire to hold on to him for as long as possible overshadowing duty, and everything else. His palm cups my cheek. A thumb slides along my bottom lip. I hold myself like a statue, not daring to breathe because I know the minute I exhale, I'll fall into him.

"You don't know what you're asking," I manage, my voice hoarse.

"I do."

I shake my head as Caden tips my chin up, forcing me to meet his eyes. What I see there is my undoing—what it has cost him to even ask for my help. He would never have considered this without exhausting every other possibility.

I exhale and nod, voicing the question tearing apart my insides. "What about the other thing? The alliance. Have you met your . . . bride-to-be?"

"Riven—"

"Don't make this any harder than it has to be, Caden. Just answer the question."

"No."

"Good." I shrug and force a smile. "Well, here's to hoping that she has warts and can't fight to save her life."

A startled grin transforms his face. "Come to think of it, I did hear a rumor about some particularly large warts. And I don't need another warrior when I have you."

I allow myself to bask in the warmth of his smile, the tender look in his eyes, for a brief moment. "This is surreal. I can't imagine you *marrying* anyone." Anyone else, I amend silently.

"It's an alliance, not a marriage. And it won't come to that if we can get the Vectors. I trust you more than anyone else to do this. Think of it as a mission."

"That's the thing—it isn't just a mission. It's . . ."

Caden's other hand slides against my neck to cradle my face. "It's what? You can tell me. I'll understand, I promise."

"You *can't* understand, Cade," I whisper. The fear behind the words nearly chokes me. "None of you gets it. That isn't who I am anymore. I don't . . . want to be anything like the Vectors. And I'm scared that if I'm around them, I'm going to lose myself. The human part of me." A strangled sound escapes my mouth and I turn away, jerking my face out of his grasp as the memories rise up. "Oh god, Shae . . ."

The thought of my sister—of her dead Vector eyes—fighting me to the death, obliterates everything in my head. Suddenly, I'm on my knees. My father made her into a *thing* to punish me. And I'd been forced to destroy her. Sobs rack my body, the pain battering me on all sides. How do I explain that every time I see a Vector it has my sister's face?

And now they want me to lead them.

Caden wants me to lead them.

He kneels beside me, drawing me into a strong embrace and, once more, I let him. He strokes my hair and kisses the dampness from my cheeks, his breath feathery against my skin. "I'm so sorry. I didn't know. You don't have to do it, Riv. We'll find another way. We'll figure it out, somehow."

I turn my cheek to find his lips, tasting the salt of my tears on them. Caden kisses me back, his mouth slanting wide as my fingers wind in his hair, dragging his face closer. I memorize the scent of him, the taste, the shape of his mouth, and then I pull away, breathing harshly. It's the last time I'll ever kiss him as the girl I am now. With a fingertip, I trace his eyebrows, around his cheekbone, across his mouth. I stare at those expressive green eyes, shadowed with passion and sadness.

"I love you, Caden." I don't know why saying it sounds like good-bye.

His eyes widen. "I love you, too, but that's not why—"

I press my hand to his mouth. "I know. I'll do it. It's the only way to stave off the Reptiles without more human loss. The Faction's right. My father can rebuild a strong line of defense. We have to try. I'll do what Era wants."

"Thank you." Despite his earlier avowal, Caden's relief is palpable. It does nothing to assuage the sense of desolation I feel. "What your father did to Shae was inexcusable, and he will be punished for his crimes, I swear to you."

"I know."

Now that I need to look a murderer in the face and negotiate with him, I have to put away all emotion—cleanse it from my brain. Maybe my father has been right all along—emotion is weakness. I glance at Caden. Love is . . . only pain. He sees me watching and bends toward me. I slip away in a smooth motion, putting as much distance between us as I can manage. Hurt flashes across his face.

"What's wrong?"

"You need to lead the people of Neospes, and I need to do what I do." I smile, forcing back the dam of tears threatening to break. "We'll figure us out later."

"But that's not what I want."

"You're a king," I say. "What you want comes after the needs of your people."

"Riv—"

"I can't, Caden," I blurt out, gesturing to the space between us. "I can't feel all of this, *and* lead a Vector army. If you want me to be the soldier, I'll be the soldier. But I can't be both. Tell the Faction my answer is yes."

It's not until I'm out of the room and out of the mansion that I let the tears flow at full force. I wipe them away with shaking hands. It's the last time I will cry.

For myself. For anyone.

5

FRACTURE

I END UP on Caden and Shae's old street in front of what used to be their house. Instead, there's a brand new home in its place with a perfectly manicured lawn, looking as if it'd always been there. No one would suspect that a year ago, I had been the one to detonate a cleaner device in this exact location so that we could escape the four Vectors on our tail. Caden's home had been blown to bits, and June, a friend of Caden's mother, had been an unexpected casualty of the explosion. It seems like a lifetime ago.

"Excuse me? Can I help you?" I turn toward the voice. A woman sits on a bicycle in the driveway—obviously the house's new owner. Her face is apprehensive, and I can imagine how I must appear—disheveled, dirty, and covered in dried mud—a homeless, angry waif standing in front of her home.

"No," I say, managing a bleak smile. "I used to know the people who lived here. We went to the same high school."

"Horrow?" she asks in a guarded tone, eyeing me as if I'm about to rob her house in broad daylight. "We moved in the spring."

I nod. "It's a great neighborhood," I say lamely and cross the street. I can feel her eyes on me until I get to the end of the block. I don't know why I went back. Maybe it was to remind myself of who I used to be when things were simpler—when I was a soldier following orders, and Caden had been nothing more than a target. Now, he's the one issuing the orders . . . orders I must follow.

A horn honks behind me. I recognize the truck and its owner immediately as it slows by my side, but I frown and keep walking, tucking my hands behind my back just in case. "You know, Bass, if I thought you were the stalker type, I wouldn't have gotten in your truck."

"Not stalking, I swear," he says, driving at a snail's pace beside me. "Finished my shift and was heading home."

"On this exact road?" I respond drily.

He runs a hand through his unruly curls. "Well, not this exact road, but I saw you crossing a couple streets back, and did kind of follow you. Sorry. Too stalkerish?"

"You think?"

"It's just that you stand out a lot. . . ." His face turns the ruddy color of his hair. I glance down at my clothing and shrug. It's a small town, and I do stick out like a sore thumb. "So, you need a ride somewhere? Or how about a soda?"

"No," I say and then add in a gentler voice. "Maybe some other time, Bass."

His smile is overly bright, as if he's trying to hide his disappointment. "Okay, I work at the Engineering Center most nights if you're ever on campus doing your soil stuff. Near the Oval?"

"Sure, I know where it is," I tell him. "I'll see you around."

"You sure I can't give you a ride somewhere?"

"No, it's okay. I need to walk. Clear my head."

I watch as Bass's taillights disappear at the end of the street. I have to chalk it up to a coincidence. I mean, I'd been with Caden, Era, and the Faction for hours, and Bass's truck would have stood out on Era's street. I don't know why I didn't go with him to get a soda and take the edge off. Anything would be better than wandering aimlessly around a town that I'd left behind a year ago. But I can't be with a boy right now—especially one who is clearly giving me signals—not after what happened with Caden. I sigh. Or maybe that's exactly what I need . . . a distraction.

"Get it together, Riven," I growl at myself, disgusted by my desire to punish Caden for something that he didn't ask for in the first place. It's not his fault that he has to figure out the best way to save everyone—that's what leaders do. They have to put their people before their own needs. Still, I can't quite curb my bitterness at the thought of Caden and this unknown princess together . . . laughing, and kissing, and god knows what else. My fingers curl into fists, and I take several gulps of air to keep my raging jealousy at bay. "Stop acting like a selfish, infatuated idiot," I mutter. "Complete the mission."

The sound of car wheels slowing behind me makes me pause, and I whip around ready to tell Bass that if he doesn't back off, he isn't going to like the consequences. But it isn't a truck, and it isn't the face I expect. My fury drains away.

"What do you want?" I ask the driver of the silver convertible.

Charisma glances at me and then leans over to open the passenger door. "Get in."

"How'd you find me?" I ask after a minute, tossing my backpack to the floor of the car. I slam the door as hard as I can without breaking it, and she winces. "Your boyfriend have another fancy nano-tracker that I don't know about?"

"No," she says. "I had a feeling you'd be here. Or at Horrow."

My lips twist at her perceptiveness. Horrow would have been my next stop. "So, where're we headed? Back to the ranch?"

"My place," she says, shifting the car into drive. We ride in silence for a while, until she turns off the main road to a curving side street with charming cookie-cutter houses adorning its perimeter. She parks the car in a driveway at the far end of the street in front of a modest two-story house. "My parents are at work. I live on campus," she adds. "The existence of parallel universes doesn't do anything to curb parental expectations. I'm enrolled at CSU."

"Let me guess—you're studying applied physics or computer science?"

She shoots me a wry glance before rummaging in her purse for her house keys. "Biochem."

"That's interesting. I would have thought Philip or Era would have dictated your courses, considering you're now in the proverbial fold."

"I like understanding how the body works," she says while unlocking the front door. "Come on. You look like you could use a long, hot shower."

I follow Charisma inside the foyer, taking in the details of the neat living room and kitchen before tracing her footsteps up the staircase. The photographs above the steps are artfully arranged, showcasing a happy family—mom, dad, Charisma, and another dark-haired girl. "Nice pics," I say.

"My mom's a photographer." Charisma grabs a towel from a nearby linen closet and shows me to a bathroom. She looks at my clothes. "I'll find you something to wear while I put your stuff in the wash."

I glance at her tall, willowy form. There's no way anything of hers will fit me. "I'll just keep what I have on."

"Gross, Riven." She wrinkles her nose, and I almost grin at the brief glimpse of the girl that I remember meeting senior year. "You smell like horse manure. I'll find you something, don't worry. Now go."

I close the bathroom door and squat down in front of my backpack, pulling my Vector suit from its depths and hanging it over the towel rack. The self-cleaning function has already done its job. I unhitch the harness from my shoulders and place my ninjata blades on the floor before removing my soiled clothing piece by piece—cargo pants, shirt, underwear. Charisma's right. They do stink. I empty the pockets of my pants, removing all the random gear I'd stashed, and shove the pile of clothing outside the door.

I stay in the shower far longer than I'd planned, letting the scalding hot water wash away the layers of dust and grime. After shampooing my hair and scrubbing my skin raw, I remain under the spray until the water starts to turn cool. I wrap myself in a fluffy towel and brush my teeth with a new toothbrush that Charisma had placed on top of the towel. The face reflecting back at me in the mirror is tanned and healthy, eyes bright. A shimmer of blue radiates up my cheek. You'd think that a year on the road would have taken its toll, but not on me. The nanotech does a good job at keeping my human cells in prime operating condition. Running a comb through my tangle of dark hair, I pull it through the strands until my hair is a gleaming black curtain. It's longer than I've ever worn it, making me look years younger and more girlish.

"But you're not a girl," I say softly to my reflection. "Are you?"

With deliberate precision, I heft one of my ninjatas, running my thumb across an edge that's sharp enough to cut through metal wiring, and slide it across the curtain of hair. By the time I'm finished, the girl staring back at me is androgynous and fierce. Her mouth is a slash across her face, her cheekbones almost as sharp as the blade in her hand. This girl won't let anyone close. She'll die doing her duty.

A knock on the door jerks me out of my thoughts. "Hey, take your time, but when you're ready, I put some clothes in the bedroom across the hall. Yours are still in the dryer."

"Thanks."

"I'm going to make us something to eat," Charisma says, her footsteps echoing down the hall.

I pause for a beat, staring at the closed door and wondering about her angle. She's obviously on the inside with Era and the Faction, and she knows exactly what I am, but out of everyone, she's the only one I trust. Or maybe it's the old Charisma I'm trusting.

Shrugging, I clean up the mess, scooping up clumps of hair and dropping them into the garbage. I lift up my Vector suit, fold it, and place it back into the backpack, along with the items

I'd emptied from my pockets. In the bedroom, Charisma has left a worn pair of jeans and a long-sleeved T-shirt. They're not hers—maybe her mom's? Or the other girl I'd noticed in the photographs. I shrug and pull on the clean clothes, pleased at the near fit, and make my way downstairs, depositing my gear in the hallway.

"Tuna, okay?" Charisma asks me. Her eyes widen as she takes in my textured, shorn hair but, to her credit, she doesn't say a word.

"Sure." Having been on the run for so long, I've overcome my distaste for all manner of organically sourced fare. The engineered food packets I'd brought with me from Neospes had run out by the fourth month. I had to learn to eat this world's food or starve. I like fish the least, but I'm not about to complain. I sit at the breakfast island and bite into the sandwich. Charisma sits opposite me and takes a dainty nibble of hers.

"Thanks for the clothes," I say after chewing my mouthful.

"Stephanie. My sister's."

"I didn't know you had a sister. Younger or older?"

A look of anguish crosses her face. "Younger. She's sick. Lives in hospice. We found out a couple of years back that she had some kind of invasive heart disease." I stop chewing and stare at Charisma, a painful lump forming in my chest. She swallows. "I'm sorry. You don't need to be burdened with any of this."

"No, it's okay," I say. "I want to hear. How is she?"

"Not good. I kind of lost it junior year after she went back for a more aggressive round of treatments. There was a real possibility that she was going to die, and nothing I could do about it. I started spiraling downward. I didn't want to think, so I did really dumb things. That's when we met." She pauses, and I know we're both thinking of the time she'd nearly been killed after being drugged by a group of strangers. "It should have been me, not her. She was always the one who wanted to do things—travel, get married, have kids." Charisma smiles through a sheen of tears. "She had a bucket list when she was nine."

"I'm sorry."

"After the incident at Horrow with you, I told my parents what was happening, and decided to get some help. I knew the way I was acting wasn't helping her."

"What are the doctors saying about her prognosis?"

Charisma takes another bite before answering, her face strained. Considering she never told me she had a sister, it wouldn't surprise me if she clams up. For a second, it seems like she's going to do just that, but then she takes a deep breath as if it's a burden she needs to get off her chest. "She's not responding to the new treatments. She needs another transplant, but it's not like there's an endless supply of donor hearts lying around. Her body rejected the two she's had."

"I'm sorry," I say again.

"It's so unfair," Charisma murmurs, her mouth twisting. "You think that technology will make things easier, but it doesn't always work that way. Right now, Stephanie's in an induced coma—she doesn't have much time left. Her heart's going to fail, and there's not a damn thing anyone can do about it. I can't imagine life without her." Charisma's voice breaks. "Philip told me about what happened with your sister. I'm sorry, too."

I shrug, refusing to allow thoughts of Shae to filter into my mind. I keep my voice monotone and the conversation focused on Charisma. "Is that why you're studying biochemistry?"

Her eyes meet mine as if she can see right through the deflection in the conversation. "Yes. Molecular biology and immunology."

"For your sister?"

"Something like that." Charisma's face contorts as if I've touched a raw nerve. From what she's said, it sounds like there's no way her sister will survive long enough for anyone to help. "Philip says your medical technology used to be way advanced before your Tech War."

My eyes narrow with understanding. "Is that why you got involved with him and Era? Because you think they can help your sister?"

"I saw the Vectors, Riven. I know what your people are capable of. Your medical tech is far better than anything we have. Is it too much to hope that maybe Steph could survive there, in your world?"

"Maybe," I say gently. "But it's not likely. Our environments are too different."

"But Caden's here." Charisma's voice is quiet, pleading. "You're here."

"Caden's a product of both universes. He was genetically predisposed to live in both worlds and his body adapted more easily than anyone else's could have. And me"—I allow the blue light to flicker across my irises—"well, we both know what I am."

Her eyes widen at my theatrical display. "Amazing," she breathes.

"I'm not amazing, Charisma. I'm a cyborg. A thing engineered with human DNA and cybernetic wiring. There's nothing amazing about any of it. My lunatic father experimented on himself and on me. I'm the product of that. Nothing more."

"You really have no idea how lucky you are," Charisma says. "So many people would kill for your ability to self-heal."

I take another bite of my sandwich and chew slowly. "I'd take my chances to be normal in a heartbeat."

Charisma busies herself making two cups of tea. Something about her body language seems off, but maybe I'm reading too much into it. We're both tired and wound up. She turns back to me with an unaffected smile that makes me relax. "Until New York, I wasn't sure exactly what you could do. I don't even know if I believed it, until I saw you jump out of a moving aircraft. Like, *X-Men* style. It was kind of insane."

"That was dumb," I admit, returning her grin. "But, then again, I tend to leap first and think later."

"And you weren't hurt?"

"Not a scratch," I say and then add "lucky," after the look of wonder on her face.

She shakes her head. "Era was right. She said you were something special."

I blink, surprised that Era has had anything good to say about me. After all, I've caused the Faction no end of trouble with my vigilante antics trying to find my father over the past year. Then again, considering I now have to find the man and beg for his help, it's no surprise that she'd be on my side. "What'd she say?"

"You were the future."

"The future of what?"

"People, maybe?" Charisma shrugs, drawing her lip between her teeth, working through something in her head. "So, the nanobes in your blood protect you? They rebuild broken cells?"

I look at her sharply. The question is nonchalant, but together with the rest of the conversation, alarms are going off in my brain. She avoids my eyes. "Charisma, I don't know what you think you know or what Era or the Faction told you, but my DNA can't be replicated." I pause. "It can't help your sister."

"You don't know that. We made the tracker with your blood. Maybe we could synthesize it."

Crap. I exhale and pinch the bridge of my nose. This has been Charisma's endgame—learn more about the cyborg and figure out whether my nano-blood could heal her sister. But what she doesn't understand is that it'd take a miracle—more than a miracle. "The nanobes are tied to my DNA. Even if we tried, your sister would reject my blood, and the nanobes wouldn't be able to work, anyway."

"What about taking her there? To Neospes? To one of your medical facilities. You could do it."

I stare at Charisma, hearing the desperation in her words. She wouldn't have confided in Philip—he would have run straight to Era. And Charisma would have been cast out, her security clearance revoked. "You don't understand, I can't."

"But it could be possible, couldn't it?"

I want to ease the pain brewing in her eyes, but I can't give her false hope. The price for unsanctioned eversion is death, even if her sick sister *could* make the jump. "Charisma, even if it were possible, the Guardians would stop you. That's what they're there for—to prevent unauthorized breaches. Just as the people in Neospes would kill for your resources, people here would do worse for our technological assets. Your sister would get a new heart, but the cost would be her life. And yours."

"It's a cost I'd gladly pay." A resolute look comes over her face, the same one I'd seen back in the tunnels in Manhattan. She eyes me, her soft tone at odds with her calculating expression. "But I understand. Finish your sandwich."

"I'm really sorry, Charisma. I wish I could help," I say, finishing the meal in a few quick bites. She doesn't respond, watching me and nodding twice. An odd sensation flowers in my stomach. "We should be getting back. Caden and the others will be waiting."

"Don't worry; we're good." She pushes a cup of steaming tea toward me. "I told Philip that we were stopping off for a shower and a change of clothes. Let me go check on the dryer. Your stuff should be done by now."

As Charisma disappears from the room, my unease at her sudden change in disposition magnifies. I push the cup of tea away and swing off the stool to secure my backpack. My instincts have served me well in the past, and I'd do well to listen to them now. Desperation drives people to do many things, but it's Charisma, for god's sake. It's not like she can force me to take her sister to Neospes or do anything the Faction hasn't sanctioned. She has too much to lose.

I sense motion out of the corner of my eye and lurch to my knees, but it's only Charisma holding a pile of my freshly laundered and neatly folded clothes in her arms. She glances over at the island. "You didn't want your tea?"

"I'm not really a tea girl." I tuck my ninjatas in the backpack's sheaths. "Sandwich was good, though. Thanks. I'll get changed and we can roll."

A shadow flickers across her face, but it's erased by a bright grin. "Sounds like a plan." She thrusts the clothing at me and I reach forward to take it. My senses flicker, but I'm too late to react as I spot the shiny tip of a hypodermic needle beneath the pile. Charisma jams it toward my exposed wrist. "I'm so sorry."

Defense, I think automatically and jerk my hand away. But I'm not wearing the Vector suit that would have hardened in an instant, preventing the needle from piercing my skin. Instead, a cold sensation slithers along my veins as Charisma drops the empty syringe and backs away with wide eyes.

"What did you do?" My voice sounds thick. I stumble, my backpack falling from my rapidly numbing hands to the floor. I try to focus, to force the nanobes to do their job—attack whatever poison she injected into my system. But nothing is responding. My own harsh breathing is the only sound in the room. I struggle to shape words with my lips and focus my eyes on Charisma. "What the hell did you do to me?"

"You'll be okay, I promise," she says in a small voice. "It's an anesthetic with a neurotransmitter inhibitor so your brain can't relay messages to the nanobes. They've been disabled by a flash electromagnetic pulse. And you can't move because there's a paralyzing agent in the mixture."

She couldn't possibly have come up with the elaborate concoction on her own. I can only manage one word. "Why?"

"Isn't it obvious?" she whispers. "I need to help my sister. Can't you, of all people, understand that? If you could have saved Shae, wouldn't you have? Wouldn't you have done anything to help her, even if that meant breaking a few laws?"

I'm unprepared for the hot stab of pain at the mention of Shae. Now that I'm not in control of my impulses, it's as if the carefully constructed compartments in my brain are becoming unglued—the ones keeping thoughts of my dead sister safe and buried. I inhale deeply, willing my pulse to even out and my rage to subside. "You don't understand. It's not possible, Charisma."

"He told me it was."

Her words sound like faint echoes rumbling over a vast distance. I wait for them to make sense in my head, but they're quickly overtaken by an icy, instinctual fear, one that my gut senses long before my impeded brain can catch up. "Wait, *who* did? Who told you it was possible, Charisma?"

Before she can answer, my eyes are drawn to movement in the doorway of the kitchen. A familiar figure enters the room as the abyss yawns beneath my feet.

"I did," my father says. "Everything is possible. Isn't it, my dear?"

b

POWER PLAY

I AM POWERLESS. Rage pulses through my veins, and I inhale through my nose, willing myself to calm down. I have to keep my wits about me, especially with him here. My father moves closer, waving a light across my retinas from a metal wand he's holding. It records my vitals on a holo-screen along with some other empirical data that likely has to do with the nanobes. He smiles in satisfaction and pockets the device.

"You are in excellent health, daughter."

"Don't call me that!" My hand itches to slash my ninjata right across his throat but, of course, it's an action that my body can't execute because of the paralysis. "You lost that right years ago."

He smiles. "Fine, General."

I don't rise to his provoking response. Instead, I turn to Charisma who is staring at me with a pleading look on her face as though begging me to understand what she's done. My eyes harden. Her motives, while justifiable, won't regain the trust she's broken. "Why don't you ask him how many men he killed trying to replicate my blood?"

"She's dead without him, Riven," Charisma says in a small voice. "He says your nanobes can rebuild the defective parts of her heart."

I laugh, a sound that comes out like a wheeze. "Is that what he told you? That my *magic* blood will make everything okay? He's a liar who makes promises he can't keep. My blood will kill anything that's a threat to me, including your sister. All you've done is given her a death sentence."

Charisma shakes her head, her glance darting to my father. "He built an electronic lung for the old prince of Neospes. He can do the same for Stephanie's heart."

"Then you're a bigger fool than I thought you were. Where do you think he's going to get the equipment to build a heart? The Faction will never let you use that technology, not for your own gain."

"The Faction doesn't have to know."

"They always know."

Charisma's desperation is clear. When she discovered the existence of a parallel world with medical advancements that could save her dying sister, I'm sure it'd become the driving force in her life. Now I understand why she'd gotten close to Philip. A part of me wants to empathize with her. After all, I know what it's like to watch your sister die.

I think back to the moment in the cave before Shae sacrificed herself to the Vectors that were hot on our tail. If I had known what she was about to do, would I have acted differently? Would I have tried to stop her?

Probably not.

In Neospes sacrifice is necessary. That's why we're taught not to form attachments—not to love. It causes duty to fragment into shades of gray. If you're faced with a choice between saving the one you love and saving thousands of nameless others, you'll always be compromised. My thoughts shift to Caden. Maybe it's better this way. With what we're about to tackle, I can't afford to have my attention divided.

Inhaling a calming breath, I focus on the task at hand. My father.

"Release me," I tell him.

"I can't do that, Riven."

"You know that I'll kill you for this."

"I know you'll try," he says. "But for now, we have to be friends, don't we?"

I glance sharply at Charisma. She must have told him that the Faction needs his help; of course he'd think that he had something to negotiate with. It's just like him to work every situation to his own advantage, and now he has me exactly where he's always wanted me. He's so close, I can smell the spice of his skin—a special cleansing oil made just for him. One that is accompanied by a sudden unwelcome barrage of memories:

Me, competing at the Winter Games as he stands proud on the sidelines. . . . Me, deciphering complex coding program puzzles. . . . Me, sitting in his lab and watching him work on the Vectors.

Just as he'd worked on Shae.

The violent surge of anger makes something spark deep in my cerebral cortex, and I hone in on it, willing the nanobes pooling there to reboot. Those memories are lies. Danton never cared for me. I was an experiment—his pet science project. My father feels nothing, just like the Vectors he creates. No wonder he loves being around them so much. No one could be so clinical and cold without already being dead inside.

Ice slithers through my brain, dousing my thoughts and bringing me sharply back to the present. "Just because the Faction needs your help to defend Neospes doesn't mean that you and I are friends, *Danton*. We all know that, for you, everyone is disposable, even your own daughter."

His dark eyes glitter, a smirk twisting his lips. "Shae wasn't *my* daughter. She was your mother's Artok mistake."

Shae wasn't a mistake, you bastard! I want to rail at him. My mother's tribal heritage has nothing to do with why he'd destroyed Shae. True, she wasn't his blood, but he'd been the only father she knew. I bite my lip hard. "Only a monster would kill another man just because he coveted that man's wife. She was already married, and yet you wanted her."

"Your mother was a brilliant geneticist. A prize. And, yes, I wanted her. So I took her."

"She wasn't a thing to be taken. Neither am I." My voice shakes slightly. "Neither was Shae."

He smiles, cocking his head and studying me, as if thrown by the bitterness I can't seem to conceal. His expression is calculating. "Shae betrayed you, Riven. So did Aurela. They left you with me when they defected because they knew you belonged with me." His voice takes on a conciliatory tone as he moves closer and blocks Charisma from my line of sight. "You still do. Think of what you could accomplish . . . what *we* could accomplish, together. I built you to be great—to usher Neospes into an era of greatness—and you want to throw that all away for some boy." His fingers move to push the hair off my forehead, a gesture meant to be paternal, but that only makes me flinch. "I tried to show you what would come of that connection, but you chose to ignore my warning."

He is referring to the programming code he hardwired into my DNA as a defense mechanism against anyone but him getting too close to me. Months before, when I admitted that I loved Caden, my body went into overdrive and shut down. When it rebooted, I had only scraps of memory of who I was. My mother had been able to counteract the programming . . . saving me, and any others targeted by the rogue code in the process.

"Aurela fixed that."

"She *broke* you. She made you weak. Vulnerable."

"You're the one who breaks people."

Danton smiles. "I could reprogram you. Make you stronger than you ever thought possible. You'd be invincible. We could take Neospes back together."

I laugh in his face—an ugly humorless sound. He backs away, his mouth curling in distaste. "Come back to you?" I gasp, barely able to breathe through my pained laughter. "You stupid, arrogant ass. I'd rather become a Vector corpse than *ever* come anywhere near you. You're going to pay for what you've done to me and to Shae."

"Always back to Shae," he laments. "Shae was nothing, Riven. She would have led you astray. The Artok"—he pauses, disgust furrowing his forehead—"are a cancer on our society. Those fools don't understand what you're capable of."

"That's where you're wrong. They know exactly what I can do."

"If that's true, why aren't any of them here to save you?"

With a resigned sigh, he gestures to two people in the hall. My eyes widen as one of the figures steps into view: Bass. What's he doing here? Why is he with my father?

My mouth sets into a hard line—either Bass has been tailing me on my father's orders since the minute I got back into town, or he's one of Era's spies. *Time to find out which.* "Who's your lackey?"

"My research assistant."

"Research what?"

"Oh, haven't you heard? I'm the new visiting professor of quantum mechanics at Colorado State University." He winks, and then shares a glance with Charisma, who hasn't said a word since trying to convince me that her intentions were honorable. "Imagine having my very own laboratory, here of all places. It's obsolete technology, but better than nothing."

My stomach sours at the thought of my father in any kind of lab, even one with limited tech. "How'd you make that happen?"

"I can be very persuasive. And, of course, who else would be brilliant enough to demonstrate that the many-worlds theory is more than just conceptual, and that multi-universe travel is possible? To tell the truth, I see myself fitting in quite well here. My students love me, Bass in particular." There's nothing in Bass's expression to indicate he's surprised by any of this. *Is he a student at all?* My eyes narrow.

I keep my focus centered on my father as he nods to the second burly man who steps forward with a slim silver case. "You don't belong here."

"Neither do you." His voice is hard. He pulls a tablet from his pocket and consults it. "We only have a few minutes before those pesky cells of yours start to refire." He shakes his head in a self-congratulatory sort of way. "Let's get down to business, shall we?"

Danton's going to draw my blood and there's not a damn thing I can do about it. We don't break eye contact as he hefts the metal barrel of a syringe from the silver case and slams it into my body with a grunt of satisfaction. Charisma gasps loudly but Bass doesn't make a sound. I barely feel the needle as it slides into the thickest part of my arm.

Blue-edged crimson fluid pools against the syringe's clear window. The burly man reaches in to take the full vial from my father, placing it back into its case, and disappears from the room. Bass follows, casting a thoughtful look at me over his shoulder. I ignore him. He's a pawn, nothing more.

I focus on the slight sensation of feeling returning to my fingers and toes. Whatever it was they'd injected me with is already starting to wear off. I concentrate on the nanobes, feeling them rebooting, sluggishly at first, but then with more vigor.

"Is that all you need?" Charisma's voice is hopeful.

"For now." My father's toothy grin makes me want to vomit. "Now that you have fulfilled your part of the bargain, I shall endeavor to fulfill mine."

Their exchange is interrupted by the sound of the front door blowing inward off its hinges. My father's eyes go wide as he looks over his shoulder, then snaps his stare back to me. "What'd you do?"

"Nothing," I say with a grim smile. "You disabled me, remember?"

"I underestimated you."

"You always do."

I don't hesitate as my hand crashes into his face, launching him across the room. As my body comes alive, I enjoy the twinge of pleasure I get from seeing the bright smear of blood on his mouth and the bruise already flowering on his cheek. I advance on him, grasping him by the scruff of his well-groomed neck and holding him off the ground so the rest of his face turns a matching shade of purple.

"If I didn't promise the Faction that I'd keep you alive, I'd rip every bone from your body. For now, this will have to do." With a flick of my wrist, I hurl him straight into the wall behind us, smiling grimly. When he wakes up, he'll have one hell of a headache.

"Riven, please."

I glare at Charisma who is wringing her hands as if she thinks she's next. Like I'd ever hurt a defenseless girl whose only mistake was letting herself get played by a practiced liar. I make sure my voice is calm when I say, "I don't care what you promised him, but if you ever do anything like that again, Charisma, it won't end well for you. You get a pass this time because of your sister, but do not for one second think we're friends." I clear my throat. "That man has betrayed everyone he's ever made promises to. For your sake, I hope you're the first one he doesn't disappoint, but I wouldn't hold my breath."

"Are you going to tell the Faction?" she asks. I study her for a moment. I should let the Faction know that there's a traitor in their midst, but something stops me. Maybe it's the fact that I have little loyalty to anyone, or the fact that she's nothing more than a chess piece . . . like me.

"It's your secret to tell, but remember that secrets have a way of getting out and becoming currency for people like him."

Without another word I walk past her to greet an army of Faction guards at the door headed by Era herself. "What happened?" she demands. "We got a wireless SOS transmission. Was that you?"

I nod and jerk my head over my shoulder, meeting Charisma's gaze. "Charisma managed to contact my father and trick him into coming here." Era narrows her eyes and I shrug. "She suggested we use me as bait. It worked."

"Danton Quinn," Era murmurs, walking into the room and eyeing the unconscious figure in the corner. "You are now held under the authority of the Faction." I smile at hearing my father's ridiculous names said out loud. He's always fancied himself better than everyone else, insisting on two names when everyone else in Neospes only has one. He certainly has an ego double the size of any normal man.

"Well done," Era says to Charisma as the guards escort my groggy father outside.

She flushes—guilt and pride look the same. "It was really nothing."

"Were there others with him?"

"Two men," I answer. "One large and older, and the other, possibly a student at CSU. Red hair."

"Sebastian," Era says nodding. "Bass. He's one of ours. He's been undercover for months."

"Undercover?" I frown, my eyes darting to Charisma. She hadn't known, either. "If he's one of yours, you're saying that you knew where my father was all this time?"

"Yes."

"But why? You could have brought him in yourself."

Era exhales, pinching the bridge of her nose. "It's . . . complicated."

My jaw slams shut. *Complicated* is a word in this world that I'm starting to have a real problem with. "If you want my help, you're going to have to be straight with me. I'm not one of your minions. Either you tell me what's really going on, or I walk."

"Calm down, Riven," she says, unsurprised by my outburst. "Our intelligence tells us your father was working on something important. We needed him to finish it."

"What's more important than getting him to help rebuild the Vector army?"

"A vaccine."

"A vaccine for what?"

She goes quiet for a long moment. "An immunity vaccine."

Era can't possibly mean what I think she does. "An *immunity* vaccine, as in a vaccine to survive this world?"

"Yes. I'm not sure what Danton's endgame is, but Sebastian's confirmed that initial tests have been successful. Your father's been here the better part of a year with no ill effects."

"He's been using an untested drug on himself?" Then again, that's nothing new for my father. He'd experimented on himself before I was conceived.

"We still need his help to rebuild the Vectors, Riven," Era says. "This is a backup plan for the backup plan. One we need in case all other options fail. Neospes has been breached and Avaria's allegiance will depend entirely on Caden. And you."

I hate thinking of Caden having anything to do with Cristobal's ridiculous diplomatic liaison. But Era has nothing to worry about. I'll behave. "Understood," I say. "Why do you need a backup plan? Do you think Avaria won't take us in?"

She pauses before answering. "Their society is a closed group. It's the reason they chose not to be found or seen before the alliance. The people of Neospes—you in particular—are a risk to them and their way of life. Cristobal—"

"What about Cristobal?"

"He's not a supporter of the alliance."

"Why is Caden even going there if they've already decided they won't help? What's the point?"

Era takes a deep breath. "You know Caden. He won't give up. Not even when the odds are stacked against us."

"So your plan is to bring our people here? Make them all evert?"

Deep lines appear at the corners of Era's mouth. "If Neospes falls to the Reptiles and Avaria won't take us in, then we have no other option. There's no way I can sacrifice so many lives on my watch. We have an alternative—one that's viable thanks to your father. I'm willing to explore that scenario."

"But what about what you said? About maintaining the barriers between worlds? We're not meant to cross between them. Look at the Plague—millions died here because of those who everted. We'll be bringing risk to this universe."

"It's a chance I'm willing to take so that countless lives can be saved." She pinches the bridge of her nose as if the words are difficult. "Condemning people to death because we aren't prepared to take a chance isn't the answer. At least they'd *have* a chance. With Danton's vaccine, integration could be successful." She pauses, watching me. "I know what your father did to you, but this could help so many."

"You don't know anything."

None of them get it. My father is a genius—a brilliant scientist. But he doesn't care about the *cost* of his work. He just wants to prove the theory, no matter what it takes. He experimented on me, his own unborn child, without a qualm. All that ever mattered was the research.

Era rubs her face with her palm. "I know that his advancements will give the people of Neospes a fighting chance. Surely, you see the value in what he has achieved."

I study the implacable leader of the Faction, seeing her in a new light. I never imagined that she would be someone who'd circumvent laws the Faction had put into place, but when your back is against a wall, sometimes you have to make impossible choices. "Does Caden know?"

She shakes her head. "No one knows except you."

"Why?"

"Because if the vaccine doesn't work, they're all dead anyway. This is a last resort if Neospes falls and Avaria will not help. We can't let it come to that, Riven. You have to promise me that you'll do everything you can to defend the people of Neospes. This is what you were born to do. I know you have your differences with your father—and trust me, I understand—but we need him. We need you."

Era Taylor is not asking for my help—she's pleading for it. Regardless of my feelings, I've never let my father impact my decisions, and I'm not about to let him do it now. I lift my hand to my chest in a formal fisted salute and square my shoulders.

"On my life, Madam Chancellor."

⅂

BRAVING THE OUTERS

THE EVERSION TEAM heading back to Neospes is spare—Caden, me, my father, Bass, and a few Faction soldiers. Era is standing off to the side, but she won't accompany us. Her frail condition won't allow it. Sauer and Aurela will meet us in the Outers, not far from the rebels' old home base. I haven't been back to Neospes in months and I feel an odd tingle at the base of my spine. I glance at my father. His face is expressionless. I'm sure he's thrilled to be going back home to be under his wife's thumb. I almost grin.

I watch as they inject the blue serum—the one that Shae and Era developed together that allows human bodies to make the transition between universes in a non-zero gravity spot without adverse physical effects. I don't need it. The nanobes in my blood defend my cells during the transition, so I can evert from anywhere at any time without issue. I'd learned that the hard way. The last time I'd taken the serum, the effects had taken a nasty toll on my system, nearly getting Caden and me killed in the Outers.

Cristobal had left the day before to prepare everything on his end. If things had gotten worse in Neospes, Avaria would be our next stop. The plan was to deliver my father to Aurela, and have him re-engineer the Vector program. Although the Vector tech had been decommissioned and removed from their human hosts after the Faction exiled Cale, the actual bodies weren't destroyed. They'd been stored in huge, contained, underground bunkers because Caden hadn't known what to do with them. And now, because of him, Neospes has an army ready to be reanimated.

We only have to trust an egomaniac scientist to reboot them.

"On my mark," Era says.

As agreed, I'll be the last to go. We've timed it so that we arrive before the blistering Neospes sun climbs into the sky. But, just as it is impossible to predict eversion exit points due to the constant rotation of both worlds, it's impossible to determine exact times of the sun's high points. Everyone is dressed in protective gear, special suits designed to withstand Neospes's volatile temperatures while also regulating bodily functions.

Watching as the first group shimmers into the fabric of gravity and space—here one second and gone the next—I consult the panel on my suit's sleeve and enter the coordinates for eversion. According to the Faction's schematics, the jump will put us close to the Peaks—the impenetrable volcanic mountains of Neospes and the only place the Reptiles can't access. The electromagnetically charged bedrock in the mountains is so powerful that it messes with my circuitry, but with everything going on, entering the dome via the Peaks is certainly the best—and least conspicuous—option.

Caden meets my eyes and I give him a noncommittal nod. Under other circumstances, Caden and I would have everted together. But we can't afford to let our feelings dictate our choices. For Caden, the people of Neospes must come first. He has to be focused. I have to be focused. We both have jobs to do—jobs that will determine whether people will live or die.

"See you on the flip side," he says with a soft smile. I can see the tension in his features, in the frown lines between his eyebrows. Eversion is tough on human bodies, and sometimes, the stress is more mental than physical . . . part of the whole brain-body phenomenon. Everting can make you lose your mind, literally.

I don't smile back. "Remember to take a deep breath before you evert. Exhale it slowly, focusing on each second. It'll help with the transition."

As the last two people disappear behind Caden and his two Faction guards in a blue haze, I take a breath and hit the coordinates on the keypad.

Era's eyes meet mine. Even in a wheelchair she still looks fierce. "Remember your promise."

I'm not sure whether she means my promise to not get in the way or my promise to defend Neospes with my life. Maybe they're one and the same. "I remember."

I hit ENTER.

The wind sucks at my gut, pulling me in toward my belly-button as if every part of my body is dissolving and coalescing into that one point. I keep my eyes open for as long as possible, watching time elongate on all sides before the wormhole breaks me into a million pieces. The nanobes harden around my cells, making them impervious to the gravitational changes in pressure. For a second, I feel invincible.

Unbreakable.

At the midpoint of the transition, all is silent, like being in the center of a storm before things start picking up. I'm snapped back together again, disparate cells rushing together toward the whole. As I exit the jump, everything explodes into motion at once.

Voices are coming at me from every direction—screaming and yelling. My ninjatas are out of their harness and in my hands before I can blink. The hot glint of metal reflects off the bodies surrounding us, the sour scent of rotting flesh filling the air. Reptiles—hundreds of them. We're in the Outers. The Peaks are less than a mile away. How did they know to be here, at our exact point of egress? I squint toward the Peaks and see three hazy human outlines running toward its base. Hopefully, they're ours.

Disoriented, I wonder if Caden's among them, but my heart sinks as I see him a dozen yards away, an ocean of putrid Reptile bodies between us. He's slashing wildly, his face sprayed with blood, gore, and who knows what else. I try to make my way toward him, but a hideous-looking raptor with metal spikes arcing the length of its back swings a pike into my belly. Grunting, I hit the ground hard. It leaps at me, jaws gaping. Its foul stench fills my nostrils and I kick both legs into its midsection, while somersaulting upward. I scissor my ninjatas across its nape, severing the wiring there. The light in its eyes fades.

But my victory is short-lived. I'm swarmed by six more creatures. I've never seen this many of them in one place before.

As if they'd been expecting us.

Setting my suit to offensive mode, I let the nanobes take over my brain and my body. My arms are a blur as I duck into a crouch, slicing methodically, bodies collapsing around me as I leapfrog over a bull-sized Reptile, fisting my hands into the folds of flesh at its neck. The head comes off with a wet sucking noise, hanging by a few gore-covered connectors. Its single robotic eye centers on me before I rip the wires from its body.

"Run!" one of the Faction guards is shouting to Caden. "Toward the Peaks. Follow the others. I'll hold them off."

"No. I won't leave you."

I scowl. That boy can be so stubborn. I dispatch two more Reptiles and head toward Caden and Bass, who are standing back-to-back and have already taken out at least a dozen creatures between them. The bodies of at least three of the Faction guards have been ripped apart, their blood soaking into the dusty earth. I hop over a severed limb just as a Reptile snatches it up. Nothing goes to waste in the Outers. I slam my ninjata into the middle of its skull and twist.

"You good?" I ask them.

"Yeah." Bass gasps. He, too, is drenched in brackish, pungent fluid. "But we need to get the Lord King to safety. Now. These things are coming up out of the ground."

"What happened?"

"They were waiting. They surrounded us, as if they knew we were coming."

"That doesn't make sense," I say, stabbing a Reptile swinging human arms embedded with serrated saws toward me.

I shudder and make quick work of it, not even wanting to know whose arms those once were. Likely, one of the people murdered in a raid on the sectors in Neospes. "Where're Sauer or Aurela? Were they here?"

"Our positioning was off," Caden says, breathing heavily. "We came in on the wrong end of the Peaks. By the time we realized it, we were already under attack."

"Where's Danton?" I search through the human bodies strewn across the ground for my father. As much as I hate him, I don't want him to be dead . . . not when he's the reason we've all risked our lives in the first place.

"He took off for the Peaks with two guards," Bass replies, slashing at a hawk-bodied Reptile, complete with its own set of ratty wings.

Of course he did. My father is the master of self-preservation. I can't help feeling a sense of relief. At least he's safe for the moment—the Reptiles won't go near the Peaks. Now, I just need to get Caden to safety.

Bass, Caden, the last remaining Faction guard, and I form a thin line of defense against the remaining Reptiles. It's us against at least forty. Bass is right—they seem to be materializing as fast as we kill them. I frown. And they seem to be operating under a similar directive. They aren't behaving like scavengers at all.

"Caden, we need to make a run for it. Something's not right. These things are too organized. It's abnormal for them." I glance over my shoulder. We're at least four hundred yards away—the length of four football fields. I calculate the odds. We can outrun some, but not all of them.

"When I say go, run like hell!" I leap into the middle of the pack, swinging my ninjatas in a bloody arc. Severed limbs litter the earth like shredded paper. "Now!"

I don't look behind me to see whether they've complied. Instead, I focus on the task at hand—destroying as many of the Reptiles as I can. My nanobes rise to the occasion, making me speedier and more responsive than ever. I locate and eliminate the faster Reptiles—the runners. They're the ones who will bring the prey down for the rest of the pack to finish off. The clumsier ones won't be half as quick. With a roar, I dislodge myself, kicking and clawing my way out of the mêlée, before I start running toward the range of looming volcanic mountains.

Caden and the others are halfway there already. I pump my legs, pushing them to go as fast as they can until I'm flying over the ground. And then my body fizzles mid-motion—interference from the Peaks causes me to stumble and hit the ground hard. All the breath is knocked out of me in a painful *whoosh*, my body twisting head over heels as rocks cut into the exposed skin of my cheeks and hands. My ninjatas sail from my grip as I skid to a brutal, bloody halt.

Scrambling to my knees, I don't even have time to get all the way up when a monkey-like beast jumps on my back. Before I can react, something goes fuzzy in my brain. I feel a sharp pain in the corded tissue between my neck and shoulder. *Defense*, I think automatically, but the lights on the arm console of my suit flicker and fade. It's definitely the Peaks—the magnetic elements obstructing the operation of the nanobes in my blood. Good for the humans, but not so much for the Reptiles or me.

My vision blurs, the mountains winking out of sight for a brief moment. I don't see Caden anymore, which means, hopefully, he's already in the Peaks. And safe. I reach around my head and dig my fingers into the creature's sides, getting a vicious bite for my efforts. Diving for one of my fallen ninjatas, I know I only have a few moments before the rest of the horde catches up.

The monkey-thing bites me again, and I stab repeatedly over my head until I feel my blade plunge into wiry flesh. The Reptile screeches and starts flailing, catching me in the side of my face with razor-blade nails. Warm blood oozes down my cheek, and I do the only thing I can. I throw myself on my back trying to crush the thing with the weight of my body. I manage to dislodge it, but it crawls away before I can subdue it.

The buzzing in my head is growing louder, making it impossible to think clearly. My suit's connected to my cortex. I rip it off and start running woozily toward the mountains. At least I'm no longer being followed. I can see a blurry line of Reptiles howling in rage. They can't come any closer without going into system failure—I'd forgotten how potent the Peaks were. With a harsh breath, I collect my remaining ninjata, wincing at the fiery agony in my limbs. With my nanobes inoperable, I'll have to push through the pain, at least until I get to the mountains.

My vision starts to blur. I force my legs to move faster, but with my failing eyesight, I no longer have any sense of direction. I could be veering back toward the very pack of beasts I'd narrowly escaped. Something furry burrows sharp claws into my leg and, without thinking, I kick down and stomp on the creature's skull, feeling it collapse beneath my boot. I don't even stop to check if the Reptile monkey is dead. I keep moving, hoping I'm going the right way.

"Riven! Over here!"

Instinctively, I turn toward Caden's voice, running the last few yards completely blind before crashing into a warm, solid, human body. I'm heaving, trying to catch my breath. "Easy," Caden says into my ear. "You're safe." He grasps the side of my face, his thumbs gentle across my eyelids and temples. I blink, but there's nothing but darkness.

"I can't see," I gasp. "One of those shitheads bit me."

"Language, darling," someone else says, and my body twinges with recognition. I can't see her, but I'd know that expressive voice anywhere—my mother's. I feel another set of hands on my face, softer ones, as her gentle fingers slide down to the wound on my shoulder. "She's been poisoned. Let's get her inside."

"I can carry her." I don't immediately recognize the voice, but it must be Bass.

"No, I've got it."

"My Lord—"

"I've got it, Sebastian." Caden gathers me in his strong arms, and instead of resisting, I lean into his body. I'll allow myself to savor these precious few minutes before I have to pretend once more that we're nothing. My body rocks against his in tune with the rhythm of his steps. My failing robotics quiet as we enter the cool interior of the mountain, and all I can feel with my very human senses is Caden's strength. The familiar scent of him curls around me and, of their own volition, my arms cinch tighter around his neck. I don't have to see him to know that he's smiling.

"Stop grinning," I whisper up to him.

"How do you know what I'm doing? You can't see, remember?"

"I know you."

His head dips down to mine. "I can't help it that I like when you're all vulnerable and need me to ferry you around. I like protecting you."

"It's my job to protect you."

His breath feathers against my cheek. "And you did. Now be quiet and let me enjoy this moment."

I shut my mouth, pressing my forehead into his neck and feeling his pulse quicken at the sliver of skin-on-skin contact. He's like a drug—the more I know I can't have it, the more I want it. *It's only for a second*, I tell myself. Moving my head backward, I let my nose drag against his bare skin and inhale deeply. My lips are quick to follow, brushing back and forth against the hollow of his throat. Caden's sharp intake of breath has me smiling against him. Good to know that he's as unaffected as I am.

"Over here," Aurela says.

"But the clinic is this way," someone else says.

"She needs more than the clinic."

The shared moment is over all too quickly as Caden follows Aurela and lowers me to a cot. Voices surround me once more, then fade. I feel heat illuminate my face and body.

"You okay?" Caden hovers just above me, his breath warm on my temple.

"Fine."

"I'll be right outside." He presses a soft kiss to my cheek, one that ends up sliding toward the corner of my mouth, before leaving the room.

Warmth fills my body, and this time, it's not just because of Caden's touch. I can feel my nanobes firing. We're in the one area in the Peaks where communication is possible. The composition of the rock is different here than the rest of the mountain's electromagnetically charged volcanic glass. In this room, I'll be able to heal myself from the inside out.

"It's just me," my mother says, gently rolling down the material of my suit. "These cuts look deep. The ones on your face aren't so bad. Not infected. That's good. You'll be able to self-repair in no time."

My throat is parched, but I force out the words: "What is it? The poison from the Reptile?"

"Blinding agent in its saliva, probably to slow down and confuse its victims." She swabs the injured area and I wince, nearly jerking off the table as she plunges a needle right into the center of the bite.

"Ouch," I growl, forcing myself to stay motionless.

"Sorry about that. It's an antidote to counter the effects of the toxin. It'll feel worse than the bite. Looks like there are a few metal shards embedded in your tissue. I'll have to take them out. It's going to hurt because of the inflammation. Try to stay still."

I nod and brace myself. With the nanobes only recently active, I'm a long way from feeling back to normal, but they'll take away the sharpest bite of the pain. "You still keep this facility operational?" I ask, my fingers gripping the sides of the cot at the pinching sensation of the tweezers on my exposed muscle.

"We didn't, but now with the breach in Neospes, we've had to resume activity. We've reallocated all remaining weapons, too, the ones we managed to salvage from the defense sector. I wanted Caden here for safety, but he refuses to leave the castle and the people."

"That's Caden for you, always looking out for everyone else." I suck in a harsh breath as she removes a particularly large and deeply lodged shard. "Any news on why they attacked? The Reptiles?"

"No." I can hear the strain in her voice. "It's the same as when they attacked Neospes. Waves and waves of them. It doesn't make any sense. They seem—"

"Mobilized."

Bright light makes my eyelids flutter as shapes come into focus. It's only minutes before the antidote does its job and I can make out my mother's face. There are a few more lines around her eyes than when I last saw her, and her silver eyes are shadowed.

"Seems like it," she agrees. Aurela waves a hand slowly from side to side, watching as my pupils follow the movement. "Glad that worked. Any blurriness?"

"No, it's clearer by the second." I pull myself up to sit and catch a glimpse of my reflection on a screen across the room. I'm covered in grime and all manner of bodily fluid, some of it mine.

Aurela steps forward and pulls me into an embrace, ignoring the filth caked on my skin. "It's good to see you, Riven. You had me worried."

"I know, and I'm sorry." I hug her tightly and ask the question burning on my tongue. "Did you see Danton?"

"Yes." There's so much pain in that one word that it feels like a physical blow. It must be hard, seeing him after so many years—after everything he's done to her.

"Do you think he can do it? Rebuild a Vector army to go against the Reptiles?"

Aurela hesitates for a long minute before answering, doubt sliding across her face. "It's not a question of whether he *can* do it. It's whether we're putting our hope and trust into a man who has killed to get his way, who has proven that he cares about no one but himself, and who has betrayed us all before." Her voice goes quiet. "What's to stop him from doing it again, only this time with an army of Vectors at his back?"

"We'll stop him," I say.

"How? You know what he's capable of."

My eyes are steel. "Because when this is all over, I'm going to finish Danton Quinn once and for all."

8

THE BREACH

THE RAVAGED SECTORS of Neospes are even worse than I imagined. The food sector has been demolished and the defense sector stripped of weapons. It's a miracle that Aurela managed to save any at all, or that the dome hasn't been structurally compromised. As it stands, the outer dome is intact, which means that we can resecure the perimeter and salvage what's left of the two damaged sectors.

Most of the citizens of Neospes are hidden away in their homes. An occasional pair of curious eyes peeks out from behind closed windows. The people are scared, and rightly so. This is not the bustling community it was the last time I was here.

"Did you locate the breach?" I ask Sauer, my mother's right-hand man.

"Yes. It's been fortified. And we've separated the sectors within the dome until we can decontaminate the area."

"Contamination?" My eyes narrow.

"Residual gases. We lost twenty more men after the attack before we realized that the Reptiles had left behind some kind of acid contagion."

"That's inventive," I comment.

"Tell me about it. It's nothing we've ever seen before."

I follow Sauer, my mind racing. The pieces aren't adding up and I can't help feeling I'm missing something right in front of me. "Show me where the Reptiles infiltrated Four."

I follow Sauer past the line of soldiers standing between the food sector and the defense sector. I frown wondering why the guards are so heavily armed, and Sauer explains: "We've done a Reptile sweep, but we keep finding them. Some are as small as beetles. They're spies." Sauer sighs when he sees my expression. "It's only a hunch. I know you've talked to Aurela and the other sector leaders. I just don't think it's a coincidence that our two most critical sectors were attacked simultaneously. It was a tactical move." He runs a hand through his Artok-blond hair and shakes his head. "I've planned enough of them to know."

"I'm listening." Sauer's speculations make sense. But his theories on Reptile behavior aren't in line with how the creatures have been known to act. They scrounge for parts. They don't attack in collaborative, *tactical* waves, and they don't act as spies.

"Riven, they knew exactly where to attack." He eyes me, letting his meaning sink in. "As if they'd been informed where to go. Then—this is the worst part—they didn't take anything. They torched both sectors, destroying everything. It wasn't a raid. It was an assault. A coordinated assault meant to weaken us where it would hurt most."

"But how, and by whom?"

"Someone who wants to see the dome destroyed . . . to see Neospes destroyed." Sauer pauses. "At first, I thought it was Danton, but he couldn't do this from the Otherworld."

"Maybe they're simply getting more aggressive. They are artificial intelligence, after all, and those were the same machines that started the Tech War. The dome is like a candy store full of goodies."

"What's a candy store?"

"A place in the Otherworld where you can buy sweets," I begin, then shake my head. "Never mind. The city is like a feeding trough for the Reptiles."

Sauer shoots me a doubtful look. "I know what you're suggesting but, at best, these are drifters, Riv. Strays. They're nothing like the advanced machines from the War. Something or someone's leading them now. Hang on one second."

Sauer stops to talk to a soldier, while I continue toward the towering metal barrier now separating the two sectors. The guard nearest the opening to the quarantined Sector Five eyes me and moves to block my way. A heavy protective mask obscures his face.

"No entry to civilians without a pass."

"Stand down, soldier," I say.

"I have orders not to let anyone through. The gases inside are toxic. And you need a pass."

"General Riven doesn't require a security pass," Sauer says, catching up to us. The soldier's eyes widen behind his mask and he steps aside. My reputation hasn't faded one bit. Sauer nods at me, punches in a code, and bends forward for a retina scan. The door slides open as he dons a clear, face-hugging mask.

"What about her mask?" the guard stammers, unsure whether he should address me again.

"We'll take it from here," Sauer says as the sliding panel closes behind us.

In mute horror, I stare at the devastated area of the sector. Black ash covers most of the ground between half-collapsed buildings. All of the human casualties have been removed and disposed of, but layers of dried blood cake the ground. Oozing black puddles of tar and the noxious odor rising from them make me wince. Definitely poisonous, and definitely lethal to humans. It's a wonder that anyone was able to survive.

My hands resting firmly on the hilts of my blades, I follow Sauer between two still-smoking warehouses. Inside one of the buildings, movement catches my eye. It's probably a trick of the light.

"Over here," Sauer says. "And be alert. Some of these things are still alive."

Maybe it wasn't a trick of the light. The hairs on the back of my neck stand in warning as I slide my ninjatas out and hold them flush against my thighs. Something skitters in the shadows of the building and my breath catches before I realize it's only a rodent.

I catch up to Sauer, the feeling of being watched fading the farther I get from the building. He's standing near the far side of the dome. I recognize the location, of course.

Cale and I used to dare each other to go outside the dome as kids, knowing we'd get into trouble if we were ever caught. Leaving the safety zone had been illicit and thrilling. It had been our secret spot, a tunnel in the bedrock carved by a long-dried underground stream when Neospes had fresh running water. I stare at the old access hole, now filled with titanium, as the memories rush back.

It was the first time I'd seen a Reptile. Cale had just turned eleven. Thinking himself braver than ever, he'd dared me to accompany him on an early morning adventure beyond the dome. As much as I hadn't wanted to go, he was my responsibility.

"Come on, Cale. This is far enough. We need to get back." We'd turned around only to see a horse standing between our secret exit and us. Only, it wasn't a horse.

"What is that?" Cale had whispered.

"Cale, get behind me."

"No way." He'd stamped his foot. "I want to see."

Steam had blown from the creature's distended nostrils, and then it had charged.

I remember the rotting smell and the chunks of flesh hanging off its wired frame. It was also the first Reptile I'd ever killed.

Cale became obsessed with Reptiles after that. He would lure and catch smaller ones, keeping them in cages. He studied the creatures, torturing them—ripping them apart and piecing them back together. I'd always thought his morbid fascination was odd, but, in hindsight, it was understandable. After all, he was a clone with a failing body, searching for a way to reconstruct himself.

But Cale is dead. He'd died months ago in the Outers. And anyone could have found this passageway—even a Reptile.

"We filled it in once we discovered where the breach in the dome was," Sauer is saying. "It must have been here for years."

"Looks like it," I say. "Is it secure?"

"It is now."

I'm not sure why I don't tell Sauer about Cale. I should have reported the information immediately, but he was the king's son and I was bound by his orders. Maybe this whole attack could have been avoided if I had said something.

I clear my throat. "I knew about it."

Sauer's gaze meets mine sharply. "What?"

"Cale and I used to sneak out here when we were kids. I'd forgotten it even existed until now."

"And you didn't think to say anything?" Sauer snaps.

"I was a child," I respond in an even tone. "And bound by the command of a prince. Did you ever find Cale's body after he was exiled?" It's a rhetorical question—no bodies are ever found in the Outers.

He shakes his head. "You think that he was alive and tried to come back?" Sauer asks. "And maybe one of them followed him?" Sauer's eyes widen. "Come to think of it, there were reports of missing supplies, but we thought they'd just been miscounted. Maybe it *was* him."

"Could have been," I agree, and gesture at the ash-covered earth around us. "But then, where is he? Nothing human could have survived the blast or the residual toxins."

"Then they killed him?"

"Maybe."

It makes an incongruous, though logical, sort of sense. A group of pack-hunting Reptiles could have easily followed a starving man back to the dome. I think of the human arms on the Reptile I'd fought in the Outers and suppress a shudder. Could they have been Cale's? And, if so, where had the rest of him gone?

"Come on. We should let Aurela know," Sauer says. "Perhaps she'll have a different theory."

We make our way back, each caught up in our own thoughts, when the sensation of being watched again makes the hairs rise on the back of my neck—it's the same building as before. Stupid rodent's probably still scrabbling around in there. I peer into the shadows, exhaling in a wild rush as I'm greeted by silence. I'm being paranoid. But as I step forward, an animal roughly the shape of a dog leaps from the darkness at my head. I react instinctually, blocking it with my right forearm, and skewering it in the same motion with my left. Two of its paws drop to the ground as its limp body slides off the serrated edge of my blade. Sauer races back to my side.

"Reptile." I watch as it tries to crawl back to the shadows of the dilapidated building on its severed legs. I stall Sauer's hand as he lifts his knife to kill the thing.

"But it's not dead."

"I have an idea, one you're probably not going to like." I sever the head from the body with a quick stroke of my ninjata and heft the remaining part on the blade's tip.

"What are you doing?" Sauer asks, his tone incredulous.

"We're taking it with us."

"No. We're not."

"Sauer, I don't want to pull rank on you, but I will if I have to. This is the only way for us to figure out what these things want."

Understanding dawns in his eyes. "You can't possibly mean to tap in remotely to that thing's brain. Aurela won't allow it."

"Aurela can't stop me. If this turns out to be a calculated breach, as you suspect, they'll attack again, and we need to be prepared. At the very least, if we're lucky, these things would have only been following a food source."

"And, if not?"

I grimace. "Then grab a shovel because we'll be in deep shit."

Sauer and I make our way back to Sector Two. Soldiers give us a wide berth, eyeing the twitching skull on the end of my sword with a mixture of fear and disgust. Luckily, the Reptiles weren't able to breach my father's old lab, which would have made what I'm planning to do much more difficult.

Sauer and I enter the elevator to the underground bunker. He glances at me. "I don't have clearance," he says. I frown at him, surprised. "Aurela thought it would be best . . . because of Shae," he explains.

The sound of her name makes my stomach clench, but it's nothing compared to the naked pain slashing across Sauer's face. He and Shae had been in love, and he, too, had seen her as a soulless Vector. Understanding courses through me. This lab is where my father would have made Vector-Shae. I take a deep breath, find Sauer's hand, and squeeze hard. The biometric scanner passes over my entire body before the green light in the elevator panel clicks. I select the lowest level and the elevator descends smoothly.

Neither of us speaks until the elevator stops and the doors open. "This way," I tell him, realizing that it's the first time he's been down here. Sauer peers beyond the glassed-in corridor, taking in the rows and rows of decontaminated human bodies—decommissioned Vectors—awaiting robotic programming.

My father is busy in front of a giant screen rebuilding the code that he'll download into each Vector's operating system.

My mother is overseeing his work. She'll read through every line of code to make sure that he hasn't built in anything unexpected. She's right to do so. I don't trust the man as far as I can throw him. But he's all we have.

Clear cylinders of nanobes are lined up in neat rows in an adjoining room. For now, they aren't online, but they will be once the programming code has been initiated. Staring at the translucent bodies of the hosts, I feel a weird sensation. I used to think that I was one of them, but, of course, I am so much more. They're dead. I'm alive. They're preprogrammed robots. I'm making my own choices. I once hated what I am, but I've come to realize that being a cyborg has its advantages.

Like what I'm about to do.

I walk into the lab without knocking, effecting a frown from my father. I stare him down before tossing the Reptile's oozing skull on his table.

"Brought you a present," I say with a grin.

"It's a Reptile. So what?"

"I want you to hardwire it into me."

"Riven, no." My mother storms into the glass office, slamming the door shut behind her. "It's too risky."

My father smiles and leans back in his chair. "Such a great family reunion. I have to say, I've waited for this moment for so long."

"Shut up, Danton," my mother says in a low, fierce snarl. His eyes widen and his mouth snaps shut in surprise. He's seeing my mother in a whole new light—I don't think he likes being bossed around.

Aurela turns to me. "No," she repeats.

With a brief glance in my father's direction, I recap what Sauer and I discovered earlier. "We need to know for sure whether they're following a directive or whether the whole thing was just chance. This is the only way."

"The Reptiles are nothing but common vultures," Danton says. "Of course it's not under a directive."

I shoot him down with an icy glare. "Remember Dorn?"

His eyes narrow, but we both remember the soldier that infiltrated Neospes years before, looking totally human. Turns out that he'd been a machine on the inside, with secret orders no one could decipher. Of course, I hadn't known what I'd been then.

"Just plug me in." I exchange another look with my mother, warning her not to go anywhere, not while my father's poking around in my head.

He rises and walks over to the severed head. Red robotic eyes roll around in the skull's sockets. Turning it over, he digs a scalpel into the top of the creature's metal-hinged spine, wrenching out a square drive. It's covered in decaying gray ichor. I watch as he cleans the drive and removes a paper-thin device the size of a watch battery. Frowning, he places it on a disk reader. Gibberish comes up on the corresponding screen.

"Do it," I tell him, sitting on his desk and leaning forward.

I wince as he cuts a swatch of skin above the nape of my neck, and peels back the flesh from the base of my skull. He connects a long cable from the reader to me and I blink as my brain starts to process the information being relayed from the Reptile's core. Most of it I don't understand—a rush of inde-cipherable data flooding in all at once. Frustrated, I rip the connector from the back of my neck, my nanobes rushing forward to suture my skin back into place. Then, I hop off the desk.

"Did you get anything?" Aurela asks.

"Nothing so far," I say with a frustrated sigh. "It's unreadable." I turn to my father as something occurs to me. "If it's encrypted data, can we decode it?"

"Probably."

"How long will it take?"

"A couple hours."

"You have one," I tell him. "We need to find out for sure whether we even need to activate an entire Vector army."

"And what do you want me to do with all of these," Danton asks, gesturing to the neatly lined-up bodies ready for reanimation.

"We need to find out what's on that drive. If we launch a counterstrike against the Reptiles, we could lose a lot of these anyway."

"Isn't that the point?" Danton asks. "They're disposable. Inconsequential."

The cavalier way he is speaking makes something inside of me snap. It's exactly how he'd thought about Shae when he made her into one of them. She was something to be used and then discarded. "They weren't inconsequential when you tried to use them to take over the monarchy," I shoot back.

"What's the matter, Riven? Sounds like you care about the Vectors after all."

My mother draws me aside, as if sensing my impending outburst. "Are you sure waiting is wise?" she asks quietly. "We're down thousands of men. The Vectors are our last hope to defend the city walls. Without them, we have nothing. And the sooner we get them to destroy the Reptiles in the Outers, the better . . . the *safer* we will be."

"It's your call," I say. "But we're launching a counterattack in anticipation of something that could turn out to be an anomaly. We could end up wasting valuable resources. Instead of sending the Vectors out to take out Reptiles, they should be used to clean up Sectors Four and Five. We should use them to rebuild, at least until we have proof."

"Maybe you're—" My mother's sentence is interrupted by bright amber flashing lights going off along the walls. I meet her eyes just as Sauer bursts into the room.

"Perimeter alert," he says grimly.

"Which sectors?" I say, bringing up a hologram of the dome in the middle of the table. Sauer moves the grid around, centering on the alarms.

His face tightens. "All of them."

"Looks like you're going to get all the proof you need," my father says.

Sauer pulls up a real-time video feed off the security devices on the west quadrant and another on the opposite side. Color drains from his face.

"Are those—?" Aurela's voice trails off in horrified silence.

"Reptiles," Sauer whispers. "An army of them."

I connect wirelessly to the cameras stationed around the dome, confirming what Sauer is seeing on screen. The Reptiles are back, this time *en masse*. And they've surrounded the entire city.

9

THE ART OF WAR

THE LINE OF Reptiles is ominous, but it's been an hour and they haven't moved. We've summoned the remaining legion commanders and assumed battle positions at various posts within the dome. The first wave of Vectors has been reanimated and is ready to go. Hopefully, they'll be enough. Staring at the seething line of snarling Reptiles, I'm not so sure. War, at its core, is a numbers game, and the odds aren't in our favor. I calculate roughly six Reptiles to every soldier—human and Vector—in this city.

Sauer puts a rectangular-shaped device to his eyes. I telescope my vision outward, the nanobes in my retinas working to magnify the landscape. Shimmering bands of gaseous rivers undulate on the scorched red earth. The heat of the mid-morning sun is already a blistering one hundred twenty degrees and rising. And yet, the creatures aren't even attempting to find shelter. No living creature—including the androids—willingly takes on a Neospes sun at full mast, not when daytime temperatures can soar high enough to melt metal. But there are at least a few hundred Reptiles braving the heat. I can see them pawing the ground and butting into each other. They're chomping at the bit, as if waiting for some signal.

None of this makes sense.

"Have you ever seen this many Reptiles?" Caden asks Sauer, making me jump. He's standing next to me on the lookout point, his face tightly drawn, sword in hand. He tugs on the titanium armor covering his chest and arms. It's coated in Reptile fluids from the last time he defended the city. Caden looks entirely too comfortable in gore-spattered armor—every inch a king heading up the front lines.

"No, my Lord King," Sauer replies.

"What are they waiting for?" I ask, my own gaze focused on the unmoving line. "They're just sitting there."

"I don't know, but we need to be ready if, and when, they start to advance."

Caden signals to Aurela. "Order the Vectors to line the perimeter. Fire up the lasers and prime the graviton reactor."

"I'll be right back," I say.

Sauer stares at me. "Where you are going?"

"If they move, do not engage." I swing myself down off the parapet.

Caden leaps down beside me and grabs my arm, pulling me around to face him. "I'm coming with you."

"Your place is here. I'll be fine."

He eyes me suspiciously. "You're not going to do anything rash, are you? Like confront that mess on your own?"

"No." I hold his gaze, willing him to believe my lie. I'm not exactly going to confront the horde, but what I'm planning does slip into borderline-rash territory.

His mouth moves into a sardonic twist, and I sigh. So much for being convincing. Caden jerks his head in Sauer's direction. "Go with her. Don't let her out of your sight."

"You do know that I'm not a child, right?" I say drily.

"Yes, but you're stubborn and have crazy ideas. We need you here." Caden pauses, clearing his throat. "I need you . . . to stay alive."

His soft words ignite something in my chest, but I keep my tone blasé. "You know that I'm part robot and can take care of myself just fine. I don't need a babysitter."

"Hey," Sauer says, insulted.

"No offense, but you'll just slow me down."

"Riven—" The sound of my name on Caden's lips halts me in my tracks. His face is pure steel, and holds an expression I haven't seen before. Unyielding. And undeniably *hot*. I suck in a breath and shake my head to clear it as the warmth in my chest detonates. Seriously, we are on the brink of annihilation, and all I can think about is dragging that unbending, autocratic face down to mine until neither of us can breathe.

"Fine," I say in a ragged voice, pointing to a stern Vector waiting at the stone steps. "I'll take that guy." This is why love gets people killed. They can't focus on anything but the other person, even in times of crisis.

"I'd prefer you take the commander."

"And I'd prefer you let me do my job," I say sweetly.

This time I don't wait for Caden's reply. If he insists that Sauer join me, I'll have to temporarily incapacitate him, and I'd rather not do that.

"Stay close," I command the Vector as we race through Sector Seven.

The streets are empty—most of the citizens have been evacuated into temporary underground shelters. Aurela isn't taking any chances, not after what happened in the other sectors.

I catch up with her at the surveillance post and ignore the thunderous look on her face. She already knows—via Sauer or Caden, or both. "Where are you going?" she asks, hands on her hips, blocking the entrance to the Peaks.

"I need to confirm something."

"Riven, I am not moving until you explain what you are doing and where you are going. Caden may be intimidated by you, but I most certainly am not. Are we clear?"

"Crystal," I say, my mouth twitching. She is my mother, after all, and Shae used to say that I got my stubbornness from her. "When we everted earlier, a Reptile attacked me. I need it."

"That's going to be long gone."

"Not where I left it. It would have been brought down by the electromagnetics from the Peaks, and nothing else will come close to retrieve it."

"Why?"

"A hunch. I think these things are receiving orders, and we need to find out where they're coming from. That's where we should focus our attack. We don't have the numbers to hold off this many."

She studies me, her forehead creasing. Her gaze drifts to the silent Vector at my side. "You know that thing's not going to work near the Peaks." It's not a question. I nod. "Take Arven and Rafe, then." She nods to two men a few feet away.

That's two more backs I'll have to look out for. I shake my head. "It's too dangerous. I need five minutes. I'll be fine alone."

"I don't like it."

I grasp her shoulder and squeeze gently. Her fingers slide to rest on top of mine, the soft touch releasing a swell of emotion. "I know, but you're going to have to trust me."

"It's not that I don't trust you—those things are unpredictable. Everything we know about them is no longer accurate. And there are so many. . . ."

"I'll be careful." I swallow and do something completely out of character for me—I give in. Maybe it's the fear I can feel beneath her fingers. Something about the look on her face tugs at me—she's already lost one daughter, and she doesn't want to lose another. "Fine, I'll take your men if it will make you feel better."

"It will. Wind at your back, my daughter."

"And at yours."

In the next moment, I'm racing into the underground tunnels that lead to the caves beneath the Peaks. As anticipated, my inner circuitry shuts down, but the rest of my body works just fine. I grin, and enjoy the feeling of the hard, dusty earth beneath my soles and the harsh cadence of my breath. Sometimes, it's nice not to feel so superhuman.

I run as fast as possible, glancing behind me just once. Arven and Rafe have no trouble keeping up with me, which is a credit to them both. Even without my extra cyborg advantages, I'm pretty swift on my feet. After a mile, the underground terrain shifts and we start to move upward. I can feel it in the muscled tension of my calves.

At the entrance, I can make out the faint outline of the Reptiles, but they are too far away to get to me. The one I'd left is still there, a shiny metal dot laying on the barren landscape. I nod to the men behind me. Arven and Rafe both have weapons drawn—long-range crossbows loaded with electromagnetic arrows—just in case.

"Cover me."

After a deep breath, I take off at a full sprint toward the remains of the creature. I can feel the collective consciousness of the line of Reptiles center on me, but, to my surprise, they don't move. That's a first—normally they'd be rushing toward anything that looks like prey. Things are getting stranger and stranger, but I don't have time to dwell on it. I heft the metal skeleton in one hand. The frame has been picked clean by the carnivorous nocturnal worms that live in the Outers. They'd have no use for tech parts, and the Reptiles couldn't get close enough to sift through the remains.

I make it back to the Peaks, where I study the prize I've collected. There's no movement. Like me, the creature's circuitry is disabled.

"How far is the Peaks control room from here?" I ask Rafe.

"Not far."

We retrace our steps to Aurela's central command room—the one with the working communications—and I feel the nanobes in my blood start to reboot. But they're not the only thing rebooting. The head in my hand quivers, two red pools of light flaring. Repeating the process I'd seen Danton use earlier, I find the coin-shaped disk in the creature's head. "This won't be pretty," I warn a stoic-faced Rafe.

I reach around the back of my head and use a scalpel from Aurela's connecting lab to cut away the flesh. Wincing at the sharp sting, I feel my way to the panel and slide in the disk. I blink against the sharp pressure and the rush of data flooding my brain. Complex processes and jumbled data stream in front of my eyes. My stomach sours. Although I can't translate the code, it's exactly the same as the last Reptile.

Exactly the same.

"Come on. Let's go," I say to Rafe after removing the Reptile's brain and destroying it. "I have one more thing to do."

We take off again into the shadowy darkness of the tunnels but, instead of veering right to the path that leads to the interior, I go left, heading away from the mountain range. Once more, my cyborg senses become sedated by the power of the underlying rocks so that I have to rely on an innate sense of direction to make my way toward a small pocket of clefts high in the ceiling. Caden and I had fallen into one of these the first time he everted to Neospes. It seems like an eternity ago. The image of Caden's grim face on the parapet flits across my thoughts. The boy he'd been then is long gone.

So is the girl who brought him here.

"Where are we going, General? The path to the city is behind us." Arven pants, hooking a thumb in the opposite direction. We're standing in a large underground area with multiple offshoots. These tunnels web for miles. You could get lost in them and never be found.

"I know. I want to get a closer look at the Reptiles and what they're doing. Maybe we can see through one of the fissures."

Arven nods. He's a seasoned soldier—Aurela's second-in-command. He was the man who'd caught Caden and me unawares our first time in the tunnels. His mouth purses as if he's weighing the odds of following me against heading back to Aurela. But then he kneels and runs his fingers through the dirt. His eyes are closed; his body is still, as if he's listening. I frown, but remain quiet. From what Aurela has told me, Arven was born an exile and knows these tunnels like the back of his hand—he has no need for holographic subterranean maps. Everything he does is based on instinct.

"How far out do these tunnels run before reaching a fissure that's wide enough for me?" I ask as he stands, dusting his hands on his tunic.

"A few hundred paces that way."

"Okay, let's do it."

With a deep breath, I follow him and sprint down the narrowing tunnel until he stops, peering upward. My skin tingles and a rush of nanobe-blue sweeps the darkness of the tunnel. We're far enough away from the mountain's magnetic rock, which means I'm back to full operational power. The panel of my suit flickers and turns on. I consult it—we're about a mile away from the Peaks, which should put us close enough to see what the Reptiles are doing . . . and to figuring out why they're not attacking.

I pull the hood of my suit up, feeling the sharp snap as it connects to my brain. Algorithms and data flicker through my vision as the suit calibrates to my biometrics.

"Give me a boost, will you?" I say to Rafe. He nods and braces himself against the wall, making a bracket with his hands for my foot. With a grunt, I push up off his hands and then his shoulder, wedging myself into the narrow opening. The smell of sulfur and heat seep down into the cooler air of the tunnel.

I inch upward, hauling myself onto a ledge before leaning down to swing Arven up, and then Rafe. The crack is just wide enough for our bodies to fit through, but not by much. I feel the sharp push of rock against my back. Placing my finger on my lips, I switch the hologram to display the surface topography.

I bite back a gasp. The black line of Reptiles on the holo is at least ten bodies deep. There are far more of them than we'd guessed. I need to get a closer look—we won't have this opportunity again. The Reptiles are far enough away for me to slip unnoticed out of the fissure. Nodding to the two men beside me, I pull myself up and out, rolling to my stomach and bracing myself against the blast of heat.

Pulling their hoods over their faces, Arven and Rafe do the same. They're covered head to toe in protective gear similar to my suit, but not as technologically advanced. They've been trained in stealth; we barely lift a cloud of dust from the ground. My suit immediately mirrors the burnt-red color of the landscape. The thermometer on my sleeve indicates that it's a balmy one hundred thirty degrees. If I didn't have my suit's protective covering, water would be evaporating from my eyes as quickly as I could blink.

I zero in on the Reptiles, confirming what the hologram had displayed in the tunnel: there are *thousands* of them. My eyes rove toward the middle, my enhanced vision providing a clear view of the different shapes and sizes. Some look more animal, with visible flesh parts. Others are metal husks. I swallow bile—there are even a few human-looking ones among the mass. My stomach sours as my gaze falls on what looks like a small boy, until I see the wiring around its rib cage and the half-rotted brains leaking out the side of its skull. It's the *head* of a small boy mounted on a metal spike. Rafe gags beside me. I'm not far from doing the same.

Focus.

I take a deep breath and reassess the line. There are runners, hunters, and trackers, all standing together . . . all *working* together. I've never seen the likes of it. My gaze snaps to what looks like a tall human standing in the very center of the column. The other Reptiles are a foot or two behind him. For a second, recognition flickers in my brain and I blink. When I look back, the human is gone.

Seeing the young boy earlier has made me paranoid. I must have imagined it. There's no way a human could survive out here, so what I saw couldn't have been a person at all. The rest of its body is likely metal just like the child's.

A slow, measured touch on my leg makes me inhale quickly. I meet Rafe's eyes. They are wide with fear and focused on a point over my left shoulder. Moving slowly, I twist backward and come face-to-face with two Reptiles that look like huge scorpions hovering over us. Before I can move a muscle, Rafe is snatched up and ripped into several pieces by the two creatures.

Blood and gore splatters us, and Arven and I dive out of the way as one of the Reptiles hurls its spiked tail right where we'd been lying. I face off against the closest one. It's standing above the crack, and the only way back down is past the enemy. I grit my teeth and draw my ninjatas from their sheaths.

Offense, I command the suit. It hardens against my body just as an iron-spiked limb crashes into my side. The force of the strike knocks me flat on my back, but I vault to my feet, lashing out with my blades. Black fluid spurts from the creature's severed leg, and I dodge another attack from the thing's barbed tail. A shivery sensation prickles my skin as I glance over my shoulder.

We've drawn the attention of the Reptiles closest to us, and unlike last time, they're advancing. Swearing sharply, I look to Arven who's handling the smaller Reptile with a finesse born of years of training. He's gotten in a couple good hits with his crossbow and, although the Reptile is still moving, it appears to be blinded. Arven hefts a cleaner—a golf ball–sized detonation device—in his hand and leaps onto the thing's back.

Dodging another strike from the scorpion facing me, I skid under the Reptile and slide my swords along its belly. Black ichor gushes out and the thing shrieks, drawing even more attention from the advancing horde, before collapsing onto its side. Seizing the opportunity, I slash my blades across its tail and chop it off before lodging a second stab deep into the thing's skull. Without stopping to think, I slit my finger and jam it into the creature's skull. The nanobes rush forward, propelled by my command and wirelessly join with the creature's command center.

Everything in my brain goes blank as I sync with the creature twitching beneath me. I gasp. Turns out it's not just with this one—I'm wired into every Reptile in the Outers. I feel their collective hunger and sense their communal mission. They're going to destroy the dome. A command snaps into my brain and I go rigid.

HOLD

Something flickers in my memory—another voice issuing commands—one so similar, but so *foreign*. I recoil against it. The creature spasms beneath me as my human eyes register that the line of Reptiles breaking toward us has fallen back. They are connected to one entity—the one giving the commands. The wireless order morphs into a second directive that makes every cell in my body shudder.

YOU CANNOT WIN . . . RIVEN

My body is numb, and I can't breathe from the excruciating weight pressing upon my chest. I rip my finger away from the Reptile as the echo of mocking laughter resonates through my brain.

"General! We have to move."

My mind feels sticky as I disconnect from the scorpion. I nod numbly at Arven, who is precariously perched atop the second Reptile. He yanks on the arrow lodged in its eye before tossing the cleaner into its gaping jaw and leaping down.

We slip into the crack, the explosion shaking the earth above our heads. Bits of red rock crumble around us as Arven tumbles past me. Vaulting into the narrow chasm beside him, I see that his leg is broken and blood is dribbling from another injury at his temple. I grab his body and run, using every bit of tech at my disposal to get us out of the rapidly collapsing tunnel. Before communication winks out, I send a message to Aurela telling her to meet me in the control room.

By the time we get back, I'm winded, and an unconscious Arven falls from my grasp. He is whisked away by a few of Aurela's men.

"What happened?" she asks, her eyes flashing fire as I stop to catch my breath. Sauer looks concerned, as does Caden. I frown in his direction—I didn't ask for either of them to be here. But I'm sure they would have seen our little scuffle in the Outers.

"Turn on the holo," I grind out. The table comes to life. I close my eyes and push the data from my brain into the hologram's receiver. The wireless transfer is swift, and images pop up in the middle of the table. I step forward and use my fingers to adjust the image, zeroing in on the line of Reptiles. "There are more than we anticipated. They're organized. They're being commanded, and they plan to attack."

"Commanded?" Sauer repeats in a disbelieving tone. "By whom?"

I filter through the image, my thumb and forefinger separating the holo into a fragmented starburst. Any number of people in Neospes had known me, knew who I was. The owner of the voice could be anyone—I've exiled enough traitors to the Outers.

I find what I've been searching for—the man I thought I saw. I tap on the image, bring it into focus. There he is staring boldly at me, crossbow in hand, with a smirk on his very human lips. The only difference is the shiny metal that now brackets half his body. My gaze flicks to Caden's.

The silence in the room is deafening as we stare at the leader of the Reptiles.

Cale . . . the fallen prince of Neospes.

10

SURVIVAL INSTINCTS

HE'S ALIVE. OR whatever counts as being alive in the Outers. Even pixilated on the holo-screen, Cale's face is the same as I remember. Rugged, angular, and entirely unforgiving. The skin of his temple has been partially peeled back, revealing the glint of dull metal. We exiled him to the Outers to die, yet here he is, standing strong with an army of Reptiles at his back.

I should be surprised, but I'm not. Cale has always been a survivor. I suppose that when you're created to die, you learn how to survive as a default. Even if it means becoming something loathsome—part man, part creature. The thought of it makes my blood curdle. Cale wanted to be king of Neospes. He'd almost succeeded in erasing Caden. And now it looks like he's a king after all . . . King of the Reptiles.

Sauer clears his throat. "This is unexpected."

"Understatement of the century," Caden mutters. "Guy's like a cockroach, you can't get rid of him."

My mouth twists. "Stubborn genes." Caden has never been known to run from anything. Stands to reason his clone would still be fighting for what he thinks is rightfully his. "Coupled with a strong survival instinct. Take everything you know about yourself and multiply it by meaner, harder, and tougher."

"Thanks," Caden says. "My uber-evil doppelganger sounds awesome."

"You can see that he'll stop at nothing." I glance at my mother whose face is ashen, glued to the hologram. "Even uniting with the Reptiles to take back Neospes—in bones and ashes, if he has to."

Sauer pulls up some schematics on another section of the screen. "They've got the entire dome surrounded—that is, any part not bordered by the Peaks."

"So, we're protected here?" Caden says. "We should evacuate everyone to this area, at least until Danton can reactivate the Vector army to defend the city walls. They'll be safe."

"Yes and no," Sauer responds, studying the line of Reptiles. "If the Vectors are unsuccessful, then we'll be stuck in a death trap. There's nowhere to go but the Outers, and with dwindling supplies, it'll be a slow death by starvation and dehydration."

"But the rebels lived here for years. Right, Aurela?"

My mother turns slowly, snapping out of her fog. "Only with regular supply shipments from Sector Seven. If the dome is breached . . ." She doesn't have to finish her statement. If the dome falls, we all fall.

"How many of them do you think there are?" I ask Sauer. "The Reptiles? A few thousand?"

He nods. "Four or five, maybe more. We have no idea if this is all of them. The Lord King—my apologies," he says flushing, with an embarrassed look at Caden. "*Cale* was a master of strategy." Sauer jabs at the images on the screen. "It's possible this scene is only what he wants us to see."

"The tip of the iceberg," Caden murmurs.

Sauer frowns. "The what?"

"Iceberg," I explain. "In the Otherworld, it's a giant float-ing piece of ice that is dangerous because the bulk of it rests beneath the ocean's surface. The Lord King is saying that we have no way of seeing what's hidden."

"How many Vectors do we have?" Caden asks. "If we were to launch an offensive?"

Aurela marches to the table, her earlier emotion replaced by determination. At one point, she'd cared for Cale as much as I did. I'll admit that seeing him out there surrounded by Reptiles had been painful for a sharp second, but I'd said my good-byes to Cale after he betrayed me. And that thing out there isn't Cale. Not anymore.

"Not enough to sustain an offensive," she says. "Defense, only." She presses a series of numbers, opening a communications line to my father's lab. His face pops up on the screen, eclipsing all the other data for a second. Aurela wastes no time. "Danton, how long before the first line of Vectors is up and running?"

Ignoring her, Danton peers at me through the two-way comms screen. "You look terrible, Riven. Had fun on your little expedition?"

"Answer the question."

"Hours," he says, his eyes fixed on me. "Less."

"We need them now," Aurela snaps.

"Aren't we demanding? Fine." He waves a careless hand. "Give me a few minutes to test that the programming is online

and functional, and you'll have your army." His eyes narrow
and move from me to Aurela, before taking in the rest of the
room. "Why the sudden urgency?"

"Because you were wrong," she says. "We *are* under attack."

I frown, watching my father's face—nothing indicates surprise or shock. My memory flits to the Reptile soldier, Dorn,
whom I'd mentioned earlier in the lab. My father had tried
to conceal that man's programming when he'd infiltrated the
dome. Danton had said it was for my safety, but maybe he'd
known all along what the Reptiles were capable of.

"It's Cale," I say. "He's the leader."

Danton's gaze swerves to mine across the video feed. "Cale,"
he says in an intrigued voice. "Wasn't he exiled?"

"He was. He's a Reptile now."

My father blinks. "He always was . . . driven."

He says nothing more so Aurela disconnects the call and
turns back to us. "We don't have many options. Even if Danton
completes the first wave, we'll only have a few hundred Vectors
to face off against thousands." She rakes her fingers through
her hair. "The dome may hold against a prolonged siege, but
our defenses will falter."

"How long?" Caden asks.

"Two weeks, maybe. Three, max."

We stare at each other, with only one option viable. We have
enough time to make it to Avaria and return with reinforcements. The distance between the cities is about five thousand
miles. Still, the conditions aren't friendly and we have no idea
what to expect between here and there.

I clear my throat. "By hovercraft, we could be in Avaria in three or four days. Come back with help."

"That's three days of straight driving," Sauer interjects. "And that's if we don't run into any trouble."

"We could do it in shifts, and it's not like we have any other choice. We either go for help, or stay and hope that we can hold Cale off." Given the numbers, Sauer and I know that that's a long shot, even with the Vectors.

"Wait, can't we just evert there?" Caden suggests. "You know, go to the Otherworld, then take a plane and head to South America—it's the same geography—and then evert back? That'll only take a few hours, and that's how Cristobal does it."

"It's not that simple," Aurela says, waving a hand to bring up an atlas showing the topography of Neospes and its surrounding environs. Swishing her fingers together, she condenses the map and overlays it with another—a map of the Otherworld. The outline of the landmasses are similar, but they don't line up exactly when you look closely. There are huge pockets of eroded zones, which means there is a lot of room for error . . . and death. "Without Cristobal with us, there are too many unknowns. You could evert right into an oil swamp. Our only option is to go by ground on this side, as Riven's proposed. Take our chances with whatever's out there."

"We need a team," Sauer says decisively. "Caden has to go to formalize the liaison. Riven, you should probably—"

"I'm going," I say, staring him down. "You won't last a day without me. And there's no way I'm letting Caden go to a strange city on his own, diplomatic *liaison* or not. We have no idea why they'd choose to form an alliance now when, by all accounts, they have a secret paradise. You have to wonder what they want from us in exchange."

I don't miss the look that Caden and Aurela share. My eyes narrow. "Wait. You already *know* what they want."

She nods. "Your father."

"Danton?" I collapse back into the seat behind me, my brain adding together the missing pieces—they want him because of what he knows, what he can do. Because of *me*. "That's why Era was so intent on finding him. It wasn't the Vectors. It's because you need him for the agreement you have with these people. Don't get me wrong. I hate the man, but you know what he's capable of. You're just going to hand him over to them?"

"It was their only stipulation," Aurela says gently. "He'll be treated well, Riven."

"I don't care if they starve him," I snap. "He is a liability." Not to mention a brilliant robotics scientist with an uncanny knack for manipulating his way out of any situation, and one who just happens to have an intimate knowledge of all Neospes's secrets. "Caden, this is madness. You can't—"

"It's done. It's the only way we could save Neospes."

"Aurela, Danton knows too much." I take a breath and hold her stare. "What about what he knows about me?"

"Riven—"

"The man's a psychotic egomaniac, but he is our asset," I argue. "We're not just unleashing him on them, we're giving a society we know nothing about a weapon to use against *us*. We're vulnerable enough. How can we trust them?"

"They're giving us their sovereign in return," Sauer says. "Trust me, we're getting the better end of this deal."

"Sounds like a great trade." I can't keep the sarcasm out of my voice. I refuse to look at Caden or my mother. Call me a skeptic, but something is off. And it's not because I'm jealous—though I am. The thought of handing my father over to strangers bodes well for no one. I take a deep breath, placing my hands flat on the table. "Fine, but for the record, it's a shitty idea. Get the team ready, we leave at nightfall."

I exit the room without a backward glance. My robotics flicker out the minute I leave the room. I need space, away from everything and everyone.

I don't realize where I'm going until I'm halfway across Sector Three and heading toward my old house in Sector Two. My father's house. From the outside, it looks the same as the last time I saw it, except the flowers that once bloomed around its base have become nothing but brown clumps of dead leaves. I study the minimalist white abode. My father had caught Caden and me making out here. I feel a faint flush rise up my neck, and shove it away. No use thinking about Caden or any of that now. In the next few days, he'll belong to someone else.

I glance up to the cameras dotting the landscape and make an obscene gesture, knowing *someone* will be watching. The symbol is from the Otherworld, but I'm pretty sure they'll get the message.

Navigating the treacherous rocks edging the gorge at the back of the house, I swing myself down off the lip to find the hidden zip line in a shallow cave. I can't believe it's still there. Then again, titanium alloy is basically indestructible.

Grabbing the small metal lead hooked into the stone, I kick my feet out and take the leap. Exhilarated, I close my eyes as my body flies over the rocky gorge, the wind blowing in my face as the stone face of the other side rushes to meet me. To an onlooker, it would appear as though I was about to crash into the far side of the gorge, but it's all part of the illusion I'd built to deter prying eyes. Despite the knowledge, the rush is the same—the feeling of danger making my heart trip seconds before my feet kick past the material mimicking the rock around it, and I land safely in the cave beyond.

Automatic motion sensors power up, illuminating the roughly hewn space with soft white light. It's connected to a solar panel hidden above a rock shelf on the cliff face. One good thing about Neospes—we get plenty of sun, which means lots of solar energy. A compact bedroll is tucked away in the corner along with a store of dried food and portable hydration packs. A collection of odds and ends litters the side of the cave—weapons, games, and childhood treasures. This cave had been my hideaway. My refuge. Feeling safe for the first time in months, I lie back on the bedroll and close my eyes.

But what seems like minutes later, I'm awakened by a scrabbling noise that has me on my feet in a hot second, ninjatas at the ready. Blinking the sleep from my eyes, I take a few breaths and force myself awake. Approaching the mouth of the cave that's covered by the holo-screen, I listen carefully. The scraping is getting louder—something is out there, and it's heading right toward me. I flatten my body against the cave mouth and raise my swords just as something presses into the side of the curtain. The canopy is pushed to the side, a shadowy mass blocking the light. I pull my blade back, ready to deliver a killing blow.

"Riven? You in here?"

"Caden!" I gasp and withdraw my weapon, dragging him inside, and letting the screen reseal to the rock face. "You fool, I nearly killed you. What are you *doing* here?"

"I followed you," he grunts.

"How'd you get over here?" He's sweating and his breathing is labored.

"Climbed."

I stare at him. "It's fifty feet on either side."

"What can I say? I'm determined."

"Or you have a death wish. You could have fallen and broken your neck. And then where would your precious alliance be?"

"Well, I didn't fall, did I?" He shrugs and studies my cave. "I always wondered what it was like inside when you pointed it out to me last time. Cool."

I'm quiet as I watch him. I'm not sure that I have anything to say, not after the earlier heated exchange in the Peaks.

"So no dolls, then?" He grins.

"I played with weapons, not dolls."

"I see that." He examines my eclectic collection of items. "What's this?"

He's holding a book my father had given me after the Games of my seventh summer. I'd forgotten about it. I take it from him. "My father gave it to me. It's a collection of poems. A chapbook, he called it, left over from the war, from some anonymous person."

Caden's eyebrows launch into his hairline. "Danton Quinn likes *poetry*?"

I shrug. "He wasn't always a jackass. He used to like other things before the science took over. Before the power got to him. There were times, glimpses really, where I could see that he was proud of me. Not me, the thing. Me, the kid." I exhale slowly. "But whatever, it meant nothing. It's a valuable relic, that's why I kept it."

I pass it back to him. He runs his finger along the worn leather of the binding and leafs through the brittle, yellow pages. He's quiet for a while, studying the inked words. "These are amazing. Maybe they were his way of telling you what he felt."

"Those poems are about love, Caden. If they were written in programming code, maybe I could believe that."

He turns to a well-worn page, and I flush. It's a poem I know by heart. "Why does your heart hide," he reads, "when it knows only the obvious comfort of a love fully returned, so beautiful it renders the world tearful . . . and I, as silent as you."

I look away, biting my lip, even though the words are seared into my brain. Suddenly the cave seems smaller, suffocating. I snatch the chapbook from his hand and snap it closed, my breath hitching in my throat. The combination of Caden's presence, the poem's meaning, and the look in his eyes is unraveling me thread by fragile thread.

"They're just stupid poems about nothing."

"Riven—"

"Want to do something fun?" There's a bright, desperate edge to my voice that I can't quite conceal.

"Sure."

"How good is your boarding, as in skateboarding?"

He frowns. "Decent."

I rummage around the back of the cave, and hand him a curved steel board, hefting a similar one under my arm. "Ever try hoverboarding?"

"Where . . . out there on the half pipe from hell?" His eyes flare with excitement at the sleek-looking hoverboard.

I nod and raise an eyebrow. "It's a rush like no other."

"You've got to be kidding."

"Come on, don't be a chicken." Pressing the power button, the board comes to life in my hands. "It's easy—the board will stay about a foot off the ground, but the rocks make it interesting. Just don't fall," I yell over my shoulder as I leap onto the deck and carve my way sharply down the stony canyon face.

"And you call me the one with the death wish," Caden yells. But he doesn't let fear of a bone-crushing fall stop him, and follows, showing off with a shaky ollie on the topside of the gorge's lip.

"Fancy moves get you killed," I say zooming past him.

"Says the girl with no game at all."

I grin, and tip my toes forward on the hoverboard's nose to increase my speed. I do my version of a kickflip on the far side, watching the board oscillate beneath me before landing firmly back onto its deck. "Beat that!"

I'm too busy boasting and not looking where I'm going. The hoverboard tilts off a particularly large rock and the sudden imbalance has me struggling to stay upright. It's a losing battle. I brace myself as I tumble into the unforgiving side of the ravine. My arms whip around my head to protect it as I roll to a final, brutal stop, gasping for breath.

"Riven!"

"I'm fine," I croak, but even speech causes my ribcage to hitch painfully.

Caden swoops to my side, leaping off his hoverboard, his brow furrowed. "Can you move? Should I call Sauer? Your mother?"

"No." I grimace, wincing at the sting radiating up through my back. The nanobes are rushing around trying to repair the damage, but it's extensive, and I know it will take a while. "Help me back to the cave," I grit out. "I have a medkit."

Caden lifts me gently, but even the smallest movement has me flinching. I'm lucky that I didn't crack my skull open. Half splayed on Caden's hoverboard, we make our way back to the cave. The hoverboard powers down and I roll onto the cot.

"Where is it?" Caden asks.

"In the back. Near the book. Silver. Syringe."

The meds will take the edge off, and hopefully the nanobes will do the rest. Doesn't help that I feel like throwing up. *What was I thinking?*

Caden slides the needle into my leg and I immediately feel the cool rush.

I flinch. "That was dumb."

"But you get points for sheer awesomeness."

"Thanks," I manage, my face hurting from trying to smile. "I don't think the rock missed a single inch of me. I got worked."

Caden kneels near the bedroll. "Here, let me." His fingers slide along my back, releasing the catch of my suit.

"What are you doing?"

"You're bleeding. It could get infected."

"It won't."

"Can I just check, or are you going to talk the whole time?" His fingers are feather light against my neck, sliding the zipper down along my spine. I'm wearing flimsy undergarments beneath the suit, but it's not like I was expecting taking it off in mixed company. The suit works better when it's attuned to me with no extra layers in between. I blush and meet Caden's eyes, but the only thing filling them is worry.

"How bad is it?" I ask.

"Pretty bad."

"Use the stuff in the clear bottle from the kit," I say. "It's a tissue repair agent. It'll help. The nanobes will get the rest eventually."

Caden is incredibly gentle as he swabs the liquid onto a cloth and applies it down the length of my back. "I'm going to turn you around, if that's all right," he says in an oddly tight voice. I nod and help maneuver my body around so my back is against the floor with Caden crouched over me. His fingers peel the rest of the suit off my shoulders and down my torso, exposing my serviceable bra, before they skip down the sides of my ribs. He pauses, his fingertips skimming my skin, coating the wound with the liquid repair salve. He sucks in a breath.

"What's the matter?"

"Nothing. It's just . . . amazing." His eyes meet mine, full of wonder. "I can see the robotics working beneath your skin, healing from the inside out. It's incredible."

"Perks of being a cyborg."

"You're incredible," he whispers, as if I hadn't spoken.

I clamp my lips shut, acutely aware of his achingly tender touch on my bare skin, not to mention that I'm half-naked with the boy I love with no one around to remind us of who we are and what we should or shouldn't be doing. The meds are working faster than I expected, eclipsing my pain with things

I shouldn't be feeling. Not now. Not anymore. I want to stop him, honestly, I do. But I can't . . . not when he inches the suit over my hips and down each leg. If his ragged breathing is any indication, I know he's feeling as unhinged as I am. A butterfly touch caresses the inside of my sole and flutters up my calf before brushing the side of my thigh.

"Caden . . ."

"Shhh, just let me enjoy this for one second," he says, his hands continuing their journey over the tops of my legs, the backs of his knuckles sliding across the thin material to the hard, exposed ridges of my stomach.

"Enjoy what?" I manage.

"You being at my complete and utter mercy." Half-stooped over me, Caden's hands are grasping mine now, lying just over my head.

A breathless sound escapes my lips. "I'm not human, remember? I'm not at anyone's mercy, least of all yours."

He bends his head to brush a kiss across my cheek, holding my hands in place. "You look pretty human to me," he says right before his lips settle on mine in an exceedingly possessive kiss, one meant to remind me of exactly how human I am. I open my mouth and sigh, giving in to the sweetly coaxing demands of his lips.

Before I know it, we've twisted on the bedroll and I'm lying flush on top of him, his hands kneading my backside and my lower back. I have no idea where his shirt went, only that we're skin to skin, and his pants are undone. In a smooth motion, Caden flips me over, his lips following the hot path of his hands and then nibbling their way upward back to my mouth.

Pain forgotten, I'm awash in a sea of blissful sensation, one that's flooding me from head to toe, until the only thing I feel is this boy.

The Lord King of Neospes.

The thought is a swift, brutal dose of reality.

"Caden, we can't," I say against his mouth, struggling to gather my thoughts and rein in my racing pulse. I slam my palms against his bare chest, feeling his pulse leap wildly at my touch. "*I* can't."

He pulls away. Understanding shimmers across his face as he brushes a strand of hair off my cheek. I can tell he doesn't want to stop, but he's not the kind of boy to force himself on anyone. I can see the dark blush of passion in his eyes and I can feel it in his body against me. I don't want to stop either, but I'm scared, and if I don't end it now, I won't be able to. Getting lost in Caden is an all-too-easy proposition and there's so much on the line . . . so much to lose.

But staring up into his face, my entire future flashes before my eyes. And it's bleak. It's empty without him. Life is about taking chances. It's not tomorrow when we're on our way to some strange city. It's not in a year from now. It's today. It's now. I don't want to lose him, not yet, not when I have him here right now with me. In *this* moment, he's mine. As I am his.

Caden doesn't have to say a word. I know he'll do whatever I want. I slide my fingers up his chest to his neck and through the fine hairs above his temple, feeling his heart thudding harshly into mine.

"What are you thinking?" I ask him.

"That there'll only ever be you for me."

"What about the alliance?"

"It's an alliance." He taps his head. "That's here." His hand slides to his heart nestled between us. "You're here. Just you."

I swallow hard. Instead of responding, I pull his head down to mine, and run my palms down the sides of his muscled back, hooking a knee upward to tug his pants down with my toes. The position makes us both gasp.

"Riv," he whispers. "Is this what you want?"

"Yes. I've never been more sure of anything."

"Are you okay? I mean, you're still hurt."

I grab his chin with my free hand, this time locking both legs up around his waist with a wild, unrestrained grin. "Perks of being a cyborg."

11

PREPARATION

THE SUN HAS just set beyond the desert plains of Neospes, casting long shadowy fingers across the face of the Peaks. It seems like days have passed since Caden and I had been in my cave even though it's only been a few hours. Two, to be exact. We'd reluctantly rejoined the Sector after ignoring three successive calls on each of our communications devices. It wouldn't take a genius to figure out that the Lord King and I had disappeared together. The thought makes me flush. Not that I care what anyone thinks, but I'd like to keep some things private.

I glance at Caden who, like me, is outfitted in special gear designed to brave the harsh elements beyond the dome. Our eyes meet, and the electricity between us is so tangible, you could power the room with it. I look away. After we left the cave, we'd gone our separate ways to change and assemble our gear.

I needed space . . . and clarity.

Being with Caden makes me forget everything—that we're at war with enemies who will do anything to destroy us. And, worse, what I am—a weapon built to defend and protect. I'm not meant to love or be loved. I wouldn't change what happened between us, but I recognize it for exactly what it is . . . a single, suspended moment. A gift.

Now, with lives on the line, we both have a job to do. I have to let him go, for the sake of everyone else, and for my own.

"Riven." The soft voice interrupts my thoughts. "A word."

"Of course." I follow Aurela into a small room. She closes the door behind us. "What is it?"

She eyes me for a long moment. "Is this going to be a problem?"

"What?"

"You and the Lord King."

I can't help the slow rush of mortified heat that floods my cheeks. Of course she knows. "No."

"Good." Her voice softens and she leans forward, her fingers brushing my hair in an oddly maternal gesture. "Are you well?"

My blush intensifies, along with my sudden dependence on monosyllabic answers. "Yes."

"You needn't be ashamed, my darling. It's a natural thing."

"Maybe for the Artok," I mumble. "Not for me."

"But you are half Artok, and when we love, we love with everything within us," she says. "I know how you feel about Caden and, well, I suppose it was to be expected." Staring at her, I don't know if I'm going to bolt or throw up. The thought that my mother has guessed what happened between Caden and me is utterly and excruciatingly embarrassing.

"Have you had your regular physical since you've been back?"

And now she's talking about our annual standard medical exam, which includes a mandatory vaccine for population control to prevent conception. I swear my cheeks feel like flaming neon beacons. "Yes," I stammer. "I mean, no. But Caden has. We're fine. Seriously, can we *not* talk about this? It's not like you're going to be a grandma to little hybrid babies, or anything."

"Of course not," she says with a half smile. "Nonetheless, I wanted to make sure that you're all right and, also, that what happened between the two of you won't affect your judgment out there."

"It won't. Duty, and all that." The words are harsh, edged with a pain that I can't quite conceal from her despite my flippant words.

"Riven."

"Don't, Mom. It's fine. I'm fine. I let him go before, remember? A year ago, when I left to find Danton. I can do it again."

"Riven, about your father." She draws a harsh breath. "I'm not defending him and what he's done, but he's trying."

My eyes narrow. "Trying what?"

"To make amends."

"How can you even say that? He can never make up for what he did to me. To Shae." The pain is like a blow to the face. "He used you, abused your research on genetic coding. He lied to us, abandoned us. There's nothing he can do to *make amends*. He made me a monster."

Her fingers feather along my cheek. "You are my daughter, and what's in here doesn't make you any less so. I know you don't trust him, but your father has . . . changed. Is changing. I think he's finally understanding what it means to be a parent."

I gnash my teeth, remembering his cold smirk and words at Charisma's house. "Then he's got you fooled like everyone else."

"I know you're angry. You should be. The man's an arrogant, selfish ass. But deep down, I believe he always cared for you. You, more than anyone or anything."

I snort, but then remember the chapbook. I shove the thought away ruthlessly. "Danton cares about Danton, and that's it. We're nothing but expendable test subjects."

She doesn't argue, and maybe it's better that she doesn't. My father can't change. He's a heartless, calculating bastard who wouldn't know the meaning of the word *father* if it hit him in the face. I study my mother. Despite her strength, she's always had a forgiving heart—her Artok heritage, I suspect—and a part of me can't fault her for looking for the redemptive qualities in others. It's what makes her an exceptional leader. My father, however, is another story. He *can't* be redeemed. Ever.

"Riven, one more thing. Be careful out there, okay?" Aurela pulls me in for a long embrace. "I've lost enough daughters for a lifetime."

I hug her back, letting her warm scent curl around me. It's so strange to me that something as simple as an embrace can fuel your desire to live and make you feel invincible. It's a fleeting thing, of course, but I've learned to accept it for what it is. Aurela once told me *to accept love gives strength and to give love takes courage.* I'm working on both.

"I'll take care of the Lord King," I say gruffly. "And keep us both alive."

When we rejoin the others, I close my eyes and breathe out, letting the tension in my body dissipate. The brief, albeit awkward, conversation with my mother had, strangely enough, helped me to put things into much needed perspective. Thoughts of my father aside, I've brought myself clearly into the present, compartmentalizing the past where it can't affect my choices. I turn my attention to Sauer and my mother.

Sauer has assembled a six-person team: himself, Caden, me, two of Aurela's trusted soldiers—Arven and a woman named Sylar—and, lastly, Bass.

I frown. "Shouldn't he remain here to keep an eye on Danton?"

"Bass's experience is in the field," Sauer says. "It's why he was sent to the Otherworld. He's an asset, quick on his feet, and remarkably adaptable."

I stare at Bass and he returns my gaze with an even look. He'd seemed so unassuming, so under the radar in Colorado. Now, dressed in tactical gear, he looks every bit a Neospes soldier. It's amazing I didn't see it before. Guess he does blend in with his surroundings. Still, I find it hard to trust anyone who'd spent any considerable time with my father, no matter what my mother thinks.

"Fine, but he better not get in the way. And what about Danton?"

Aurela nods. "He stays here. We can't risk Avaria reneging on their promise once he's in their hands. The trade will occur once the threat is contained. I'll keep an eye on him, don't worry," my mother says. "We'll hold down the fort until you return."

"I know what you said earlier, but stay alert."

"I will," my mother says. "I've got the only shutdown codes for the Vectors, and I've verified all the programming code." I nod, satisfied. "Wind at your back."

"And at yours."

We approach the waiting hover, and stop dead in our tracks. I've never seen its like before. The forbidding vehicle is half tank and half spaceship, with huge propulsion jets on either side, and heavy-duty plasma weaponry up top. Those plasma cannons could level a small city. Heavy titanium plates plaster the exterior of the hover, making it look like a giant shiny armadillo, and a retractable glass shield covers most of the cabin area. Like the dome, it's designed to convert and store solar energy. Two all-terrain scouting hoverbikes are strapped to the back, and the hull is jammed to the brim with enough artillery to start a war of our own. The transport looks mean and fierce, and definitely not human-made.

"Where'd you get this?" I ask, but my words are lost in the hum of conversation.

"Did you leave room for food?" Caden jokes, studying the propulsion jets on the side. "It looks hard-core. I've never seen one of these in Neospes before. Does it work like the other hovercraft?"

"Yes and no. Ever see *Star Trek* in the Otherworld?" Bass asks, eyes twinkling.

Caden gasps. "No way."

"Relax, Sulu. We're not going to be flying off into space, or anything. But you know how those engines used antimatter as their energy source? Well, this hover is built with something similar—a matter/antimatter drive train."

"Whoa. I didn't think those existed. Not in real life, anyway."

"It's volatile technology."

"Why?" Caden asks.

"Where'd you get it?" I ask more loudly.

Bass pauses, but answers Caden first. "The engines are unpredictable. We got the idea from the Machines before the War. That's how they powered the huge war hovers they used to burn our cities to the ground." His gaze slides to me. "And I can't say where we got it, that's classified."

"Classified?" Caden frowns. "As Lord King, I'm declassifying the information right now."

Sauer clears his throat. "It was saved after the War. It's been underground—no one knew what to do with it, so your great-grandfather decided that it would be best to hold on to it. To study it. I think everyone kind of forgot it was there, to tell you the truth."

"Wait, are you telling me that you've never *used* one of these before?" My voice rises with every word. "And that it's a *Machine* ship?"

"Yes, it's been field-tested. It works just like any other hover."

I shake my head. "No. There's no way that we are going in that thing."

A muscle ticks in Sauer's jaw. "Riven, it's two or three times faster than any other hovercraft we have, and its defensive and offensive capabilities are off the charts. It's our best shot to get to Avaria and back, quickly *and* safely." His voice turns hard. "You can stay or go, but this is the vehicle we're taking. The Lord King's well-being is my responsibility and I won't put him at risk, not even to appease you."

We stare at each other in the charged silence. The last thing I want right now is a standoff with a senior ranking officer—one of my mother's most trusted men—and, least of all, with Sauer, who has become a friend. "I don't mean to challenge you," I concede. "It's just that you're putting Caden in a hover-craft designed by the Machines. It seems counterintuitive."

Sauer nods. "Perhaps, but it is our best option."

"Fine, but if we blow up, that's on you."

Night's fallen by the time we say our final good-byes. We're planning to leave via the Eastern quadrant, which has the most direct route through the Outers to the mountain ridges on the far side of the desert. We'll have to fight off some of Cale's Reptiles, but hopefully the dark will provide enough cover.

"Wait!"

We all turn at the sound of the voice. It's my father, walking toward us with something in his hand. Four armed guards escort him, but everyone tenses the minute he's within arm's reach.

"I designed this for you," he says to me. His face is emotion-less, but something flickers in his eyes for an instant. I can't put my finger on what it is.

Is this his way of making amends? I frown—Danton Quinn doesn't deserve any benefit of the doubt. "I don't want anything from you."

"Trust me, you'll want this."

I stare at him as he thrusts a folded garment at me. It's a suit—a Vector suit. The material feels silky against my fingers, and is lighter than any Vector garment I've ever worn. "What is this?"

"New suit I designed. It's thinner, more responsive, and fitted with some new technology—radiation sensors, hazard alerts, that sort of thing."

"And, thanks to your sick sense of humor, it's going to shut down mid-battle and get me killed?"

"I wouldn't do anything to jeopardize your life, Riven. You should know that by now. You're my daughter."

"You're a sperm donor, nothing more." I see that same emotion flicker across his face. Remorse? Sadness? Regret?

He inclines his head. "Be that as it may, I would never hurt *you*. Anyway, I heard that you ran into some trouble with your last suit, and thought I could help."

"Bit too late for the Daddy-of-the-Year award, isn't it? Plus, my suit's been repaired. I don't need a new one," I say coolly.

"This one's better, more advanced. I made it with your DNA, the sample I took from you in the Otherworld. It's designed for you, Riven, crafted to be in tune with your singular . . . skills."

"You can take your super suit and go right to hell."

He nods, as if anticipating my response. "Consider it a peace offering."

We eye each other in stony silence—demonstrating a mulishness that I suppose I inherited from him in the first place. Or maybe I get it from my mother. Glancing at her impassive stance, I square my shoulders and evaluate the facts without emotion. This suit would be an asset and I'd be a fool not to take it, especially since the repair job on my own was rushed and it still feels slightly glitchy. I'd stashed some extra standard-issue Vector suits with the rest of my gear as backups. A brand new suit—and one designed specifically to work with my DNA—would come in handy. But, how can I trust anything my father does? Even his motives have motives.

"If Aurela clears the suit, fine. But don't for a second think that there's peace between us. You're a criminal, and you'll pay for your crimes one way or another."

"As you say."

We wait in silence as Aurela nods and has two of her advanced robotic scientists examine the proffered suit. They take it away and return a few minutes later.

"Clear," one of them says.

Aurela consults with them and returns to our group. "Looks fine. No embedded backdoor codes, and he can't access it or you remotely. It's clean."

"Of course it's clean," he says mildly. "The suit is hyper-responsive to you and the whole thing's a—"

I cut him off. "Don't you have Vectors to reanimate or people to kill?"

Without looking back, I toss the suit into the hull and climb into the hovercraft.

Inside, Sauer is explaining the controls to the rest of the team—we'll all be required to drive at some point. It seems pretty simple, but I can't suppress the unease winding through me as we start moving. I rake my hands through my hair and sigh.

"What's wrong?" Caden asks. "Is it Danton?"

"No." I hesitate. "It's just something Aurela said, but that's not what's bugging me. Apart from using a hover that I've never seen before, I think it's weird that the Reptiles haven't struck yet. Cale has to know that we won't attack first. But they're just standing there. What are they waiting for?"

"Maybe it's a scare tactic. Psychological warfare—defeating the will of the enemy as a precursor to an assault."

Of course. Cale always was a master manipulator, scheming against the monarchy for years. It makes a sick sort of sense that he'd wait until the last moment, hoping that the sight of so many Reptiles would send the people of Neospes fleeing for their lives, begging for mercy. But what Cale doesn't understand is that every last one of us would die before ever yielding the dome to him.

"You better hope Avaria comes through," I mutter. Caden doesn't answer, but a muscle starts to tick in his jaw. "Strap in, we're about to reach the Reptiles."

Bass leans over. "We may not have to. This thing has stealth mode. That's how the Machines were able to hit so many cities undetected."

I frown. "We'll still have to go through the Reptiles."

He winks at me, and I don't miss Caden's irritation. "Not if we go *above* them."

"Above? The hover gear won't go that high."

"This beast has vertical propulsion jets. The hover technology conserves energy when necessary, but we could fly all the way to Avaria if we were sure that the fuel would last. I don't think the commander wants to push it, though."

The blood in my veins runs cold. Flight technology was outlawed after the war when the Machines took full control of everything that was accessible online. And now, here we are on one of *their* ships.

Caden and I both watch as Sauer enters a sequence of numbers and everything but the backlit navigation panel goes dark. "What, exactly, is stealth mode?" he asks.

"We mimic our surroundings," Bass explains. "Kind of like the Vector suits mirroring the environment. It's like a giant smoke screen. We hide in plain sight."

"Won't they hear us coming?"

"Not in this baby. One thing those android pieces of shit knew how to do was build the perfect attack ship—triple threat of stealth, silence, and death."

I'm not convinced, but sure enough, we glide right over the Reptiles. We're all holding our breath, but as Bass had explained, even if one of them were to look up, it would only see a shadowy gray sky. Maybe Sauer's right that this is the best way to get us to Avaria.

"If this ship is so advanced," Caden asks. "Why can't we use it against Cale and the Reptiles?"

Sauer's response is grim. "If we force his hand, we have no idea what he will do to retaliate, and Neospes is vulnerable as it is."

"You should get some sleep," I tell Caden, pushing a glowing icon on his seat panel that reclines his chair. "We don't know what we'll be up against out here. Rest now while you can. I'm going up top."

I engage my suit and slip outside. In typical Neospes fashion, the night air is freezing and frost has already crusted on the underside of the cannons. I grab one of the chairs and take up watch position. Sauer insisted that the aircraft has advanced attack detection capabilities, but I don't care. I have more faith in my own eyes and ears.

"Want some company?" Bass is dressed in a similar insulating suit. A clear mask protects his face.

"Sure."

He grabs the empty chair and props his feet up on the weaponry, looking as comfortable as if he were sitting at the Winter Games watching an exhibition match. We sit in companionable silence for a while, the shifting landscape flying past. Once again, Sauer was right—we are moving faster than any hover. We'll probably get to Avaria in two days if we're lucky.

Bass drums his fingers. I can't see his eyes, but I can sense he's watching me. I don't really want to talk, but I have questions. "What were you doing back there? In the Otherworld with my father? What was he working on?" I give Bass a warning look. "If you tell me that it's classified, I'll throw you off this ship."

He grins. "Wow, I don't remember you being this feisty. Or, maybe that's what I liked about you."

"Stop dancing around the subject and answer the question."

"He was working on a lot of things."

"Like the immunity vaccine?"

Bass shoots me a look. "You know about that?"

"I know a lot of things. Is the vaccine for real?"

"Yes, but it's not one hundred percent effective against all Otherworld infections. Just some of the major ones."

"What made you take the mission to work with him?"

Bass sends me another sidelong glance. "You don't remember me, do you?"

"From the Otherworld?"

"From this one." He sighs and clasps his hands behind his head. "You were young, about five. We'd been testing the first round of reanimation for the Vectors and you sneaked into your father's lab. One of them attacked you."

The memory is as real as the day it happened—the feel of that giant, brutal hand winding in my hair and those dead, milky-white eyes. I shake it off. "You were there?"

"I was one of the assistants."

I squint, scanning the lab in my memory and recalling the figure of a skinny boy cowering in a corner. He must have been new, not much older than me. His face had been as terrified as mine. I nod slowly. "The boy in the gray intern suit. You were about twelve?"

"Ten. It was my first real job in the Sector. I tested off the charts for robotics." He pauses. "*And* hand-to-hand combat. Your father thought it was a win/win for him—brains and brawn. I advanced quickly through the ranks of his assistants."

"I never saw you with him." I'd certainly never come face-to-face with Bass until we met in the Otherworld.

"That was part of my job. Being invisible."

"You did it well."

"When the Faction approached me, they had been watching me for a while. Let's just say that Danton Quinn has a unique way of expressing his appreciation and gratitude. My entire family—mother, father, and brother—were killed in a freak factory accident in Sector Three. Only, it wasn't a freak accident. Turns out someone had tampered with one of the chemical reactors." He pauses. "It was never confirmed, but I always suspected foul play. Danton wanted my total focus. The rest is history. When Era asked me to spy for her, it was a no-brainer."

I shake my head in disgusted sympathy, my recent uncertainty about my father's motives disappearing. He'll never change. "How do you stop yourself from just throwing him off a building? It would make both worlds better."

"Trust me, it's hard not to," Bass says with a laugh.

I frown. "Why did he let you go on this mission? Wouldn't he be suspicious?"

Bass's smile is brilliant. "That's the beauty of it—me going along was *his* idea. He thinks we're keeping an eye on them, and you."

My father isn't easy to mislead, yet Bass has somehow managed to pull off this deception. I feel a glimmer of respect. "He hasn't suspected anything after all this time?"

"I'm good at what I do, Riven."

Suddenly, I'm grateful that he's one of the six on this ship. He's a survivor. He's loyal. And now I know he has a blood debt to collect.

12

HOSTILE TERRITORY

"WE HAVE A problem."

My eyes fly open and I'm off the cot in a flash. Sauer's already beside me. I scan the ship and then remember that Caden is up top with Sylar. We're taking three-hour shifts for now—two on watch, two on drive duty, and two resting.

"Report, Arven," Sauer commands. He walks over to the instrument console, where Arven is standing with Bass.

"The scanners are picking up interference. I think we're being followed, but every time I try to get a lock on it, the signal disappears, almost as if it's anticipating *our* tracking."

Sauer's eyes narrow. "How long?"

"Since we left the edge of the Outers, at least," Bass says. "At first, we thought it was radioactive interference, since this is uncharted territory for us, but it's too consistent."

"Same frequency?"

"Yes."

Sauer goes silent, mulling over the possibilities. There's no way we can afford to lead a tail straight to Avaria. The consequences could be deadly. I consult the panel on my suit. "Sun's up in a couple hours. We could try evasive action while we still have night on our side."

"Not sure that would work," Bass says. "They're locking into some kind of homing signal on the vessel. Even if we took evasive action, they'd still be able to locate us. We'd have to find the beacon on the ship and destroy it."

"Then we search every inch of her," Sauer says.

"We don't even know what we're looking for, Commander," Arven interjects. "It would be a futile effort."

I try not to send an *I told you so* look at Sauer. Of course this machine would have homing signals that only other Machines could lock onto. I exhale, frustrated, just as something clicks in my brain.

"Wait," I say slowly, "maybe I can locate it."

"How?"

"Like I did with the Reptiles back in the Peaks. I can patch in to the ship manually and try to override it."

Bass nods. "That would buy us some time. If whoever is tracking us tries to get a line of sight once the signal goes out, we can take care of them. It's worth a shot."

"What's going on?" Caden pops his head through the hatch. "Why'd we stop?"

"We're being followed," Sauer explains. "Arven will relieve you—we need your station battle ready."

"But—"

"My Lord King, I must insist." Sauer nods at Arven. "Tell Sylar to be on alert. Do not hesitate. Do you understand me?"

"Understood."

Arven climbs out, and I nod to Caden. "Guess you should strap in just in case things get rough." I turn my attention to Bass. "Let's go."

"Wait, where are you two going?"

"Engineering."

"I'll go with you."

I shake my head. "You're staying put."

"Riven—"

"My Lord King, your safety is paramount. You're better off here with Sauer. Bass and I will be fine."

Caden arranges his expression into an unemotional mask. His eyes flick to Bass and then back to me before he nods. If it weren't for the muscle ticking wildly in his jaw, I'd believe his performance. But Caden is angry. More than angry. I can see it in the rigid slope of his shoulders and the frigid glint in his eye. He doesn't trust Bass—especially when it comes to me, but I'm a big girl and I can take care of myself.

Bass quickly follows as I lower myself through the engineering hatch. The space is narrow and lined with sleek-looking access panels. At the far end, I study the antimatter/matter generator warily. It's a ticking time bomb, the magnetic storage rings of the device glinting as it separates antimatter from matter, awaiting the command to combine the two and create the propulsion energy powering the craft. Antiprotons are mighty things—and dangerous enough to obliterate this entire ship.

"So, what's up with you and the king?" Bass asks, making me jump.

"None of your business. Make yourself useful and ensure that that generator doesn't make a peep while we're down here."

"I don't think he approves of you being down here with me," Bass comments.

"What makes you say that?"

"He looked pissed. I mean, you guys looked pretty cozy back in the dome. Seriously, what's the deal? Are you shacking up with the Lord King of Neospes?"

"You have some nerve." I turn to lay into him when I see the panel above his right shoulder. Bass is waggling his eyebrows suggestively, and I shake my head. "You have a sick sense of humor, and no one's shacking up with anyone. Now move."

I tap on the panel, watching it slide back to reveal a blue-hued command board along with some hardwired ingress ports. Engaging my suit, I sync the operations panel on my wrist to the one on the ship before plugging in the lead connection. Within seconds, I'm patched into the main operation controls of the ship. Information is flowing faster than I can process it—operating parameters, mechanics, flight data, maintenance, and finally, tracking capabilities. I isolate the data and zero in on the various frequencies, trying to find the one that's transmitting out. The androids developed a tracking system for all their ships so they'd be accessible remotely, no matter the location. Late in the war, once a ship found a rebel pocket, scores of fellow ships would home in on the outbound signal to annihilate the threat.

I'm surprised that this one hasn't been disabled, given how long the previous king had it after the war, but maybe our engineers hadn't even realized it was functional. Or maybe the magnetics of the Peaks deactivated it and no one realized the signal was there in the first place. Now, it's broadcasting to whoever's listening.

"Did you find it?" Bass's voice sounds like it's coming through a tunnel.

"I think so. It's some kind of repeater. Hold on a sec."

The outbound signal is small, barely discernible, but I find it. Time to shut it down before it does any real damage. I enter the kill script on my suit panel, but suddenly the screen fades to black.

"Shit."

"What happened?" Bass asks.

"Stupid piece of—" I power down the suit and repower it, watching it boot up and feeling the swift responsive surge in my nanobes. "Give me a sec. Suit's on the fritz. I fell while hoverboarding."

Bass grins. "Heard about that."

I glare at him. "Seriously, is everyone in Neospes a raging gossip?"

"Only when it's really juicy." Bass smirks at me, and I roll my eyes.

"Asshat." The suit comes back online, but the kill command hasn't worked. I unplug the device. "Looks like I'm going to have to do this the gross way."

"Gross way?" Bass looks confused until I pull back the sticky flap of skin on my scalp and shove in the metal lead. His face turns a pale shade of green.

Blue lights shimmer along my skin as my brain connects with the ship's computer. I smirk at him. "You'll be fine, princess."

This time, when I enter the kill connection script directly into the computer controlling the ship's wireless frequencies, it processes the command immediately. I disconnect from the computer and slump down against the opposite wall.

"You okay?" Bass asks, looking wan. "Did you get it?"

"Yes, and I'm fine. All that operating system information is overwhelming. I need something to eat—that usually helps."

"Riv?"

"Yeah?"

"That seriously was the nastiest thing I've ever seen."

I laugh. "In all your years working with Vectors, me plugging in a little old wire into my brain is what sends you scurrying?"

"Because you're a girl. I mean you look like a girl."

"I *am* a girl." I grin wolfishly. "Just one who can slice open her skull."

Bass makes a puking noise. "Yeah, well, you could have warned me or something. Seeing that almost made me lose my breakfast." He shudders theatrically. I'm grinning as we climb back into the hull. "There's payback in your future, you know."

"Just try it." Bass lunges for me, swinging me over his shoulder. My head narrowly misses the ceiling. His fingers tickle my ribs, and I'm laughing so hard that I start snorting upside down. "Quit it," I gasp, thumping his back. "Or I'll electrocute you."

"You can do that?" he asks, lowering me, his hands still around my waist.

"No, but I can do this." I crouch and swing one leg out, catching Bass in the back of the knees. He goes down like a sack of stones, at the last moment catching hold of my vest. I lose my balance and tumble forward, sprawling right on top of him, my head crashing into his. "Ouch," I say wincing. "That didn't go as planned."

"Did I get you?" Bass asks, brushing his fingers across the tender spot on my brow.

I squint, feeling the nanobes beneath my skin rushing to the affected area. "Your head is like rock. I may actually have a concussion."

Bass smiles up at me. "I might have a remedy for that."

In that moment, I'm all too aware of him lying beneath me, and the expression on his face becomes intense. Suddenly, the playful mood evaporates.

"Bass, I'm not—"

"What's going on?" Caden interrupts, watching us with narrowed eyes.

"Nothing." I scramble to my feet and notice his frown. "We were just playing around. Bass never saw me plug in. He freaked out like a baby seal, and wanted to prove his manliness."

"Did not," Bass protests.

Caden doesn't respond, but his hostile expression speaks volumes. There's no explanation I can give that won't cause a scene, so I say nothing. We have a bigger situation to deal with, and it doesn't include pacifying two testosterone-fueled boys.

Ignoring the skyrocketing tension, I move toward Sauer and give him the thumbs-up. "It's done. Now, for Part B."

"Part B?" Caden growls, his scowl threatening to go supernova.

"We wait until whoever is tracking us shows up, and get rid of them."

"But you got rid of the signal."

"Doesn't mean they aren't close. They could still be tracking us. We need to find out who or what they are. Sauer, what's the game plan?"

The sun's about to come up and we're in an uncharted area. It's not like we have many options, and we could probably out-run our pursuers if we tried. But I'm of the opinion that it's better to find out what we're dealing with—whether it's Cale or a harmless rogue signal. It looks like Sauer feels the same. He brings up a holographic map in the center of the room. A blue dot in the middle shows our position about a thousand miles south of Neospes. Doesn't seem like much, considering how long we've been gone, but I'm guessing Sauer doesn't want to push it on the first day.

He jabs at a thin range of mountains to the right of our loca-tion. "We could head to this ridge and trap them. It's not too far off our course, and looks like there may be canyons for cover. Lure them in and take them out. An hour tops. Arven? Riven?"

"Sounds good to me," I say. Arven agrees.

Sauer points to Arven. "You and Sylar will stay on the ship with the Lord King." He glances at me. "Riven, you take the west quadrant. Bass, you're going to be here." He stabs at a loca-tion opposite where I'm supposed to be. "You'll take the hover-bikes."

It doesn't take long to make the detour to the crest of moun-tains. It's a perfect spot. Sauer was right—the weird U-shape of the range will be good cover, and once we trap our hunters, they'll have nowhere to go as Bass and I herd them toward the ship.

"Do you see that?" Sylar's voice is thin through the com-munications headpiece. I remember that she's still up top on watch. "Looks like grass, or moss, or something."

"That's not possible," I say, bringing up the landscape on screen. But Sylar's right. It does look like vegetation, which would mean an available water source. I study the lush under-growth. Water hasn't flowed on this world's surface for years—in Neospes, our treatment plants dig deep, scouring the bed-rock for residual aquifers.

Sauer shrugs. "There used to be hidden underground springs. Maybe this is one."

But something seems off to me. The mossy area is only con-centrated in one spot, and around the foot of the mountain the area is gravelly and dusty. If there were actually water, wouldn't the rest of this region be flourishing, too? And if it were safe, wouldn't there be a colony of *something* living here? I shake my head—much like the Outers, nothing is as it seems.

"I'll be right back," I say. "Need to change. This suit's mal-functioning and I don't want to take any chances with what-ever's out there."

Caden follows me into the narrow lavatory at the back of the craft. I let him. "What's the matter?" I ask, shimmying out of my suit and pulling a clean, unripped Vector suit from my stashed gear.

"What's going on with you and Bass?"

"Nothing." I lower my voice. "Caden, I don't know what's up with you, but you need to get it together. We both agreed that what happened wouldn't affect us."

"I know, but seeing you with him . . . he's too familiar with you."

"Bass isn't being too familiar with me. That's how it is in the legion. We're friends, nothing more." I snap the fastenings of the suit in place, blinking as it comes online. It feels different from my other suit, like an extra layer of skin—not as user-friendly, either.

"You were on top of him."

"I fell."

"I didn't like it."

I turn to face Caden. "What does it matter? In a few days, you're going to have your hands full, and I'll be the one feeling jealous."

Caden's eyes narrow in frustration. "What are you saying? You're doing it purposely?"

I turn to stare at him, bristling at his accusation. "Doing what? Distancing myself? Cade, I have to. You know what's at stake. I can't afford to let my emotions get in the way of doing my job. To keep you safe, not make you jealous." I take a breath, softening my words. "You have absolutely nothing to worry about with Bass."

"He's into you."

"But *I'm* not into him. Caden, please. We agreed to let each other go, right? Don't make this harder than it has to be."

"You're right. I'm sorry." He reaches for me and I slip under his arm to exit the space. Letting him touch me will disrupt all my carefully compartmentalized thoughts.

"I can't."

His hand flutters to his side. "Be careful out there."

"I will."

"And Riv, for the record, I never agreed to let you go. Those were your words, not mine."

I nod mutely and climb outside. Bass is already unloading the hoverbikes. I don't want to think about Caden's parting words and what they mean. I inhale deeply to clear my head. He doesn't think sometimes—he says what he feels.

He'll *have* to let me go in a couple days, whether he wants to or not.

"Bass," I say into the comms device built into my headpiece before hopping on the bike. "Keep an eye out for that green stuff. It doesn't look right."

"Got it."

We zoom off in opposite directions and I watch as the ship hovers into stealth mode, mirroring the stone face of the mountain behind it. With my enhanced vision, I can see the slight haze of its outline, but if I didn't already know it was there, it'd be undetectable. After stashing the bike on the far side of a large boulder, I crouch down and wait. The instrument panel on my wrist says it's nearly a hundred degrees and climbing, but the suit does its job, wicking moisture away from my body and keeping me cool. I scan the horizon, but there's nothing but hazy bands of heat flickering through the morning sunlight. I finger the hilts of my ninjatas. Something is off. It's too quiet.

"See anything?" Bass's voice buzzes in my ear.

"Not a thing."

"Me, either."

"Weird, right? I mean, you'd think we'd see *something*. A beetle or a bug, but it's all gravel." I glance down at a small round orb and prod it with my toe. It rolls to the side and three gaping holes stare up at me. It's not gravel. It's a skull.

Add bones to the list, I think as a similar white sphere catches my attention—this one slightly bigger than the first. Frowning, I squint through the reflection of the sun and kick at the pebbles beneath my feet. A dozen more skulls roll out along with limb bones of all sizes—all picked clean.

"Bass—"

"Wait, my sensor's picking up something. Whatever it is, it's fast. On your ten o'clock. I'm sending you the coordinates now."

Bones forgotten, I focus on the area Bass has highlighted. I count five seconds before a shape comes into view, then two shapes. I recognize the saucer-like discs immediately. They're trackers, sent out to collect and remotely return information. But for who? Cale? Or something more ominous tied to this ship?

"On my mark," I whisper.

Bass leaps out at the same moment I do, brandishing a staff with blades at either end. He takes out one of the trackers with a swift strike. I unsheathe my ninjatas just as the ground trembles below my feet and something else appears . . . something big, and not a tracker at all.

The Reptile that bursts from the earth behind us is like a giant arachnid, red and black and shiny metal. I swipe at its legs but it's too fast, hopping out of the way and slamming down a barbed-wire, hairy limb on top of me. Bass isn't faring any better as the thing shoves him into the side of the mountain with one jab of a leg. Rolling out of the way, I barely get to my feet before it spits a sticky net of webbing toward me. I twist to the side, but I'm not quick enough as the glob glues half of me to the ground. Hacking at the viscous webbing with the ninjata in my free hand, the Reptile spider hovers above, ready to deliver its deathblow.

Then, before I can blink, something green snakes into the body of the beast from the right, and then another from the left. Confused, I look up toward where the ship should be, expecting to see laser fire bursting from the cannons, but nothing is there. Another green tentacle wraps around the creature's body, dragging it to the ground, not two feet from me, pulling it into the maw of green moss.

And what a maw it is, full of jagged teeth! The Reptile tarantula disappears, hissing and screeching as limb by limb the tentacles feed it to the hungry, gaping mouth in the ground. Green shimmers with red for a minute as the last of the Reptile is consumed before the remnants of metal and bone are ejected to the side . . . just like all the other skulls and skeletons littering the gravelly earth.

Hacking off the last of the webbing, I shudder and scramble out of reach. The moss is alive—some kind of organic monster, luring in its prey with its luscious promise of water and food. Bass was lucky he didn't get thrown in that direction—he would have been devoured in a second.

He staggers to my side, staff in hand, and slightly dazed. "Did you see that?" he gasps. "Swallowed that thing whole."

"Carnivorous moss," I mutter. "Who would have thought? Did you get the tracker?" Bass nods. We should be able to get some good intel on what it was recording and sending back to whoever is watching. "Take it back to the ship. I'll take care of the other one."

"No, it's too dangerous."

"We can't afford to leave it."

I watch as Bass gets on his bike, the first tracker in tow, and heads back to Sauer. Movement catches the corner of my eye and I spot the second tracker, lurking on the west side of the mountain. It must have been recording everything that happened, feeding it back. Sheathing my ninjatas, I pull the electromagnetic gun from my belt and line the tracker up in my sights. As much as I prefer ninjatas, guns can be quite useful at times.

Crouching, I take my time with the shot—missing now would cost us more than we are ready to lose—and pull the trigger. My aim is true and it's only moments before the tracker falls to the ground, completely fried. Pushing to my feet, I pocket the gun and head toward my hoverbike when something snakes around my ankle and smashes me to the hard ground. Dazed, I see stars. Sharp rocks and bits of bone cut into my skin as I'm dragged along, my fingers scraping futilely for a hold. A glistening strip of green winks into my peripheral vision, just before a second tentacle winds around my left wrist, burrowing into my flesh.

I'm moments away from being swallowed.

13

PREDATOR

GNASHING MY TEETH, I sink my heels into the hard earth, trying to fight against the creature's pull, but it's far too strong. That Reptile spider was six times my size and it hadn't stood a chance against the thing. Twisting painfully as I'm dragged along the ground, I struggle to get my free arm around my back to grasp my ninjata, but it's no use. I can't even signal Sauer for help because my comms piece has been ripped out of my ear and is lying out of reach.

Defense, I tell the suit.

It hardens immediately, offering some protection against the sharp stones and bits of bone stabbing into me. I try to turn my body onto my stomach so that I can grab my harness, but the constant yank of the beast is making it difficult to get any leverage. For two seconds, I'm flung onto my side, my right arm aligning with my thigh holster. I don't hesitate, grabbing the gun and firing at the ropy vine, freeing it for a brief moment. The beast answers by thrusting two more tentacles in my direction—one reattaching to my ankle, and the

other winding brutally around the hand with the gun. Even
with the suit, I can feel the creature's strength. I cry out as
the bones in my wrist shatter and the gun falls from my limp
fingers.

This is it. This is how I'm going to die.

But I'm not going down without a fight. I kick out and wrap
my uninjured hand around the vine, digging my nails into its
clammy, snakelike membrane. It tightens more, making me
gasp. I let go—I don't want any more broken bones. If, by some
miracle, I'm able to get free of it within the next ten seconds, I'll
need a working arm to kill this creature.

I see Bass swing around on the hoverbike, heading in my
direction, and I shake my head wildly. He'll get himself killed.

But if he sees me warning him off, he gives no indication.
He skids in on the bike and vaults off, his staff spinning. The
dynamic blades on the ends have been replaced with spikes and
he doesn't hesitate as he slams one end into the tentacle that's
crushing my wrist, and then rotates the staff to rip through
the vine squeezing my foot. A third spin frees me completely,
green ichor spraying from the severed tentacles. The smell is
fetid—rotten meat and bile—making me gag.

"Thanks," I yell out, scrabbling backward.

"Don't thank me yet," Bass shouts.

Several more vines shoot out and I vault to my feet, grabbing a sword in my good hand. The nanobes are doing their
best to heal my body, but my entire right forearm has gone
numb. Bass and I hack at the tentacles as fast as they come,
but the thing is like a mythical hydra in the stories from the
Otherworld—we cut down one vine and ten more sprout from

its place. The beast shrieks—a hair-raising sound that makes both Bass and me slam our palms to our ears.

"The only way we can kill this thing is with the ship's lasers," I pant. "We need to make a run for it so Sauer has a shot." Bass nods, his staff spinning, warding off yet another thrust from the creature as I locate my comms unit. "On my mark. One, t—"

The word is snapped from my lips as a huge vine snakes around my waist, crushing the breath from my body, and a second binds the arm holding my ninjata. A third grabs Bass by the leg, and he goes down hard. He is out cold and blood is pouring from his ear. My eyes snap to the rising hover ship and I wave my arms wildly. I wouldn't put it past the moss monster to pull the whole ship down if it came anywhere within reach.

"Shoot it, Sauer!" I shout into my mouthpiece. "Shoot it now!"

"We can't," he replies. "You're both in the kill zone. We could hit you."

"It's going to kill us anyway. I'd rather die without being digested. Shoot it!"

"Hang on, maybe we can get closer."

"Don't! We don't know how far this thing can reach!" But even as I scream the words, the air is already filled with greedy, grasping vines. We're forgotten for the moment—though still held fast—as the beast focuses on larger, more dangerous prey. "Sauer, pull up. *Pull* up!"

"What the hell!" Sauer's shout rings in my ears. One tentacle wraps around the tail end of the hovertank, jerking it downward just enough so that two more can hook onto the underside. The situation couldn't be worse. Watching this attack is like seeing something out of one of Caden's science fiction movies—a monstrous green beast latched on to a spaceship, about to ingest it whole.

"Sauer," I call desperately, "you have to fire, or we're all done."

"Stand down, Commander—" The voice is Caden's. I sigh in exasperation. I knew he wouldn't be able to separate his emotions from executing what needs to be done. I'll pull rank on Caden if I have to.

"Do *not* stand down, Sauer. Do your job! Fire."

"Riven." Caden's voice is calm, controlled. "We will fire, but only when I give the order. Can you get to Bass?"

I frown. He's only a few feet away. "Yes."

"Okay. Do it."

Kicking my legs sideways like I'm swimming underwater, I crawl to Bass's side. He's still unconscious. "What do you want me to do?"

"Are you able to use your free hand?"

Of course it has to be the injured one. I wiggle my fingers and wince. "Depends on what you want me to do."

"I want you to evert with Bass. We'll shoot, and then evert back in thirty seconds. Do you understand?"

I open my mouth and close it. I have to hand it to Caden— it's a crazy idea, but it just might work. I take a breath and punch in the parameters for eversion on Bass's wrist pad. I enter mine remotely—via wireless command—and sync the two, before closing my eyes and throwing myself over Bass's body. Then I press ENTER.

Everything around us disappears into mist as the wind sucks at my belly button, pulling me into the wormhole and then ejecting me on the other side in the Otherworld. I fight the nausea, soil filling my nostrils and wind whipping against my face. You'd think I'd be used to everting by now, but every time it feels like your body is being turned inside out. It's enough to make a grown man puke, just as Bass is doing right this minute. I look around, getting my bearings. Looks like we ended up on top of a small hill in a rural area. Could be worse—we could have everted right into a crowded mall or somewhere just as conspicuous. Hard to explain materializing out of thin air.

"What happened?" Bass croaks, wiping his mouth with the back of his hand.

"Everted. You passed out and that thing had the ship. You okay?"

He gives me a sidelong look. "How did you know I'd taken the serum, and it was safe to evert?"

Crap. I hadn't even thought about that. But he'd had to or he'd be a liquid human mess at my feet. "I didn't."

"I take it every day, just in case."

"Isn't that bad for your organs?"

Bass stands, clutching his staff, and touches his injured ear gingerly. "Danton improved it. We both took it in the Otherworld in case we needed to evert in a flash. Where are we, anyway?"

"I think Texas." I blink, reconciling the map of our world with the one in my head. "Somewhere near San Antonio."

"Maybe we should move away from this spot so that when we evert back, we don't end up in a puddle of green guts."

Bass's quip forces a grin to my lips. "That is a *great* idea."

We limp down the hill. Bass is already inputting the coordinates for us to evert back to Neospes, and after a few minutes, he gives me a thumbs-up. "Ready?"

I nod, linking remotely to him. "Just hope we don't evert right into that thing's stomach."

But luck is with us when the wormhole spits us out a few feet from where we'd been trapped. Instead of the moss monster, there's only a blackened crater, green and brown muck splattered everywhere, and it stinks to high heaven.

"Good to see you." Sauer's voice chimes in my earpiece.

Bass and I hobble to collect the hoverbikes. "Good to see you survived," I reply.

"Thanks to Caden's quick thinking, we all survived. How's the wrist?"

I flex my fingers and curl it around the hover's handlebars. "Nearly healed."

Bass shrugs and turns over his engine. "Wish I could say the same." He swipes at the crusted blood on the side of his face. "I'm going to need a medkit and a couple of very steady hands."

"You got it," Sauer replies.

A short while later, we're back on the hovertank, bikes strapped in place and again on course to Avaria, but everything feels strangely anticlimactic. I've been lying down—Sauer's orders—to get some rest, but I can't sleep. Every time I close my eyes, all I see is green flesh-eating moss. I glance over at Bass who's said nothing since we came back on board. He's resting quietly on a nearby cot while Sylar's very expert hands tend to the wound on his ear. Her training as a field medic is already being put to good use.

"Stop fidgeting," Bass says to me.

"Can't sleep. I keep thinking about being eaten alive. What do you think that thing was?"

"Some evolved terrestrial life form, I expect."

"Do you think there are more of them out there?" I stifle a yawn.

"That, and probably worse."

I yawn again, despite being wide awake, and prop myself up on my elbow before addressing Sylar. "Where's Sauer? Up top?"

"Yes, with the Lord King."

At least Caden's in good hands. His eversion plan had been a stroke of brilliance. But if our positions were reversed, and it'd been Sauer out there instead of me, I would have fired without a second thought—soldiers should be prepared to sacrifice their lives for the sake of the mission. Getting Caden to Avaria is the first—and only—priority.

That said, I'm grateful to be alive. Bass, too, I expect. I messed up big time. To be honest, once Caden gave the order to evert, I hadn't completely thought it through since, with my nanobes, I'm used to everting on a whim. Truth is we'd gotten lucky. Without the serum, Bass would have been pulverized.

Squashing my guilt, I squint at Sylar. "Do you know if they got anything on the tracker?"

"The commander wanted to wait until you were back on board, just in case we had issues accessing the tracker's information."

"Did the moss beast do any damage to the hull?"

Sylar shakes her head. "We've run a quick diagnostic and everything seems fine. It'd probably make sense to land and run a more thorough analysis when we can do so safely." She pauses, looking at me grimly. "Though out here, you can never tell if it's going to be safe. One of those vines hooked into a propulsion jet, but I think the hover gear is fine for the moment." She eyes me as I cover my mouth, suppressing another wide yawn. "You really should try to get some rest. I'm just about finished with him."

Nodding as she leaves the cubicle, I will my body to relax, starting with my toes and working my way up. I engage the nanobes, sending out a command for them to go into hibernation mode. I inhale deeply, then exhale a few seconds later, making my mind a blank slate where there's no moss, no monsters, and nothing but an empty void. My heart rate slows; my body stills. Everything fades to black.

In the darkness, I see Cale's face.

But it's not the Reptile Cale. It's the boy I used to know, beckoning me. "Come on, Riven. I have something to show you." He's younger, maybe fifteen or sixteen. In my dream state, I follow him to the dungeons of the castle, grimacing at the sewer smell. I've never been to this part of the castle before, but obviously Cale has. He's navigating the twists and turns of the dark passages as though he knows exactly where he's going. Cale stops. "Close your eyes. I have gifts for you," he says with a gleeful smile. I obey, and feel his hand on my arm, leading me down steps into an area that smells even worse than the rest of the dungeons. "Open them now, Riven."

Bile rises, clogging my throat. Some kind of desert feline is inside a wire cage. It stares at me with baleful eyes, snarling at

Cale for a minute before turning away. I see a wound on the creature's side. Bloody and ragged bits of threaded tissue wind around shiny pieces of metal. It's a clockwork cat. "Where'd you find it?" I ask, repulsed.

"I built it," young Cale says, puffing out his chest with pride. "Do you like it?"

"*Built* it? How?"

He rolls his eyes and stares at me as if I'm an imbecile. "I caught a stray cat sniffing around Sector Five outside the dome. Then I gutted it and hooked it up to another Reptile. Before long, the Reptile—I don't remember what it was—started taking over the cat. It was so cool to watch."

"That's sick."

A gruesome smile overtakes Cale's mouth, making his childish face look sinister in the dim light. I take an involuntary step back, and feel the slimy wall of the dungeon pushing against me. The entrance has disappeared. A shudder ripples through my body. "Don't be afraid," Cale says. "Come. I have another gift for you."

What could be worse than a gutted animal? My feet move like leaden weights as I walk past the cat to another room with another cage. I retch into a dank corner of the cell.

"Do you like her?"

In this cage is a girl . . . a girl with my face.

Only it's not a girl—it's a Reptile. She could be my clone, down to the slanted gray eyes and dark, choppy hair with its blue braid. She's holding two swords, watching me with a feral stare. Her head cocks to one side, a slow snarl pulling up the corners of her lips. I swallow hard, looking from a satisfied Cale to this creature with my face.

"Where'd you get it?" I snap, finding my voice.

"Your father's garbage," he says in a smug voice. "Didn't you know he was trying to clone you? Guess it didn't work. Out you went with the trash. But you're lucky I found you. Isn't she beautiful? She does anything I want." He studies me with a crude, meaningful expression that makes my breath come fast.

I swallow hard. "Get rid of it," I manage to say.

"Why? She's perfect. You're perfect."

Suddenly, Cale morphs from a boy into the form I'd seen out in the Outers, his single red eye glowing. I want to run, but my feet are glued to the floor. I can't move a muscle. Every part of me is dead, unresponsive.

"She's not me," I mumble.

Cale's next words, slid in so smoothly, jolt my subconscious. "Where are you going, Riven? You think those people are going to help you?" He leers, a laugh bursting from his lips. "Oh, you think I didn't know? I know everything. You will fail. Join me where you belong. We will take Neospes together."

"Never. I'm nothing like you."

"Aren't you?" His voice is mocking. A metal finger glides down my cheek, down my shoulder, to my arm. It hooks into the side of my ribs and pulls. I gasp, staring down at the coils of wiring protruding from me. "They made you, just like they made me. You're a thing, not a person." The words are like bullets.

"I'm going to kill you," I growl.

"With what? You're unraveling. Look at yourself."

Cale's voice goes hollow, and I glance down. My legs have disappeared. I'm nothing more than half a torso on the filthy floor. Cale's laughter echoes throughout the dungeon as the robot girl approaches. She grins, kicking at what's left of me with her metal foot, and leans down until we're nose to nose.

"He's right, you know." She even sounds like me. "You hold yourself back. Give in to what you are. It's inevitable. *We* are inevitable."

"The only thing that's inevitable is your death." I take my ninjata and stab robot-me right in the throat, nearly cleaving her head from her body. She disappears in a haze as I splutter through a mouthful of blood, and wonder why my ninjata is lodged through my neck and why the ground became a slippery pool of blood.

"I give you a choice," Cale says. "Join us or die."

I wake in a cold sweat, the sound of mocking laughter echoing in my head, and grasp at my neck. It's still in one piece. My breathing is ragged and I take a minute to calm my racing heart. Bass is still asleep in the cot next to me.

Something flickers in my brain, filtering information. I fly off my cot waking Bass who leaps off of his own, staff in hand, blinking wildly. "What's wrong?"

"Arven," I yell, "get Sauer. I need to see that tracker right now."

"Now?"

"Yes."

Arven puts the craft into autopilot and engages stealth defense. Once Sauer's in the hold, we surround the tracker and I enable it. A single yellow point glows brightly at its center as it boots up. Disabling any inbound and outbound remote access capabilities, we connect the tracker to the ship, letting the information feed directly to us.

Sauer stares at the screen, frowning. "There's nothing here. It's wiped."

"Hang on," Bass says, narrowing his eyes. "There is something there. See that dot blinking in the lower left corner? Looks like some kind of message icon."

Always cautious, Sauer runs an analytic check first. It comes back clean—the file is a picture. He taps in a sequence and a hologram opens on the screen. I stop breathing, my hands clutching the edge of the console.

It's a photo of a cage in a dungeon—the exact replica of the one in my dream.

"What is it?" Caden asks.

"A message from Cale. That tracker has been operational this whole time, programmed with a subliminal encoded message meant for me."

"Wait, how is that even possible?"

"I have microscopic computers in my brain, Caden."

He frowns. "Cale would need your DNA to develop something like that."

I shrug. "Plenty of my blood was spilled in the Outers during the Reptile attack when we everted. It wouldn't have been hard to collect some. Remember that frequency Philip and Charisma used to track me? It's sort of the same idea, like sending a mental email."

"Can he hurt you?"

Without thinking, I run my fingers across my neck. "No."

"What did it say?" Sauer asks. "The message?"

"He knows that we're trying to get help. He's going to take back Neospes." My eyes meet Caden's. "And he wants me to help him do it."

14

BLOOD AND BONES

THE HOURS PASS in a tense but monotonous cycle—watch, drive, rest, repeat. I'm on the driving shift. Bass and I have paired off in the rotation, which Caden isn't too thrilled about, but I don't know how many times I can explain to him that Bass and I are just friends. He's acting like a stupid, jealous teenager. And the truth is, being around Bass puts things into perspective. I'm focused. And I have to focus on what needs to be done if we're going to survive—like figuring out what Cale meant with his cryptic message. What's he planning? Who's he working with? Who are his spies?

I try to calm my racing thoughts by focusing on the blacks and grays of the landscape sweeping by, highlighted with an occasional spark of scarlet where fissures in the planet's surface have widened enough to display pools of molten lava. So far, most of what we've driven through has been deserted—all dust and cracked earth—a desert surface similar to the Outers, punctuated by grottos dark as pitch. Those are my least favorite—they make me feel claustrophobic. I've managed by day, but I'm not looking forward to moving through them at night, when things seem to get exponentially worse.

Caden commented earlier that the land reminded him of the bottom of the Grand Canyon, but was way less pretty. I'd seen it once when I was chasing after my father, but I really hadn't had the time to appreciate it. As the hovership maneuvers its way through a series of steeply sided canyons, I can see what he means, though.

I squint through the dashboard as a huge cliff comes into view, noticing a number of holes in its face. For a second, I wonder whether anyone lives there, and then shake my head. There's no way anyone could survive out here. Without a dome moderating the volatile temperatures, it would be next to impossible. Then again, the rebels had been able to survive in the Peaks, and evolution is an amazing thing.

"You think anyone's over there?" I ask Bass. "Humans, I mean?"

"Maybe." He rises and squints, staring at the line of holes. "I don't think I want to find out. I've heard stories of ultra-evolved apelike beasts that live in cliff burrows like those, and they're definitely not friendly."

I press a button on the console and scan for life forms as we pass. A sea of red dots fills my vision, confirming my suspicion that the holes are inhabited. Entering a command into the sleeve of my suit—my last functional Vector suit—I analyze the life form and run it against the database of known organisms. It's close, but not human—something called a goraken. The image that pops up shows a large, muscular, blue creature with six arms and a distended jaw full of jagged teeth. The limited data says that they're nocturnal and live in the dark, but have a keen sense of smell. They can track blood over a mile away. And Bass is right—they don't look friendly.

"What do you think we'll find down there?" Bass's voice is quiet.

"In Avaria?"

"Yeah."

I shake my head. "Not sure. From what Era said, it's in the middle of a jungle. Caden—the Lord King—said that Cristobal told him it was one of the only similarities this world has with the Otherworld. He called it the Amazon. Apparently, it's a protected rain forest. Can you imagine?"

"No."

"Me, either. All we have is rock."

"We had jungles once," Bass says. "I read about them when I was growing up. All the historical records say that they were completely razed during the war. Way back when, this universe was as lush as that one." He sighs, leaning back. "It's so different, right? Their Earth and ours? You kind of have to wonder what splitting point in history made us veer toward artificial intelligence." He eyes me. "You ever think about it? How many millions of parallel dimensions must be out there? And how it came to be that we found a backdoor between ours and theirs?"

"Sure."

He laughs. "Seriously, why did we get all the self-educating, power-crazed androids, and they get to live happy, peaceful lives in a thriving paradise?"

"Luck of the draw, I guess." I wouldn't exist if I didn't have cyborg technology in my DNA. But choosing between being a genetically engineered creature and living in a world untouched by machines is a no-brainer. Running water, grass, fresh air, and normal temperatures? I'd choose it in a heartbeat. "Would you do it if you could? Evert and live there? Say if Danton comes up with an effective immunity booster?"

Bass shrugs. "Maybe. Maybe not. I don't really fit in there."

"You sure looked like you were fitting in when I met you in your beat-up truck. Plus I thought you were the master of adaptation and deception."

Bass grins. "I meant inside. They're too different. I don't know how to explain."

"Softer, you mean?"

He nods. "Indulged."

"They just evolved differently. Their battles are different from ours."

"Yeah, we fight for our lives, and they fight to win popularity contests, or to see who has the bigger house or faster car." He shrugs. "Didn't you go to high school there for a while?"

"I did. It was . . . interesting."

"That's an understatement." Bass snorts. "They don't even know how to defend themselves. They have enough to eat and roofs over their heads."

For a second, I see a new side to Bass, but it's not an unfamiliar one. I'd felt the same way, once—judgy and superior. "Some do," I say. "And some don't. Poverty and hunger exist there, too. Civil and religious wars are rampant in parts. Androids aren't the only power-crazed species. Humans can be, too."

"I guess so."

My mind drifts to Charisma. I'd trusted her. At least, until my father got his hands on her and fed her a bucket of lies. Still, she'd always helped others, including me when I'd first arrived. "They're not all bad."

"If you say so."

I laugh. "Well, there was this one girl, Sadie. She hated me with a passion and . . . you ready for this? She was Caden's girlfriend."

Bass's eyes light up and I bite back a grin. It's amusing how much he loves gossip. "So, that must have been fun," he prods.

"There may have been a bathroom incident. Not one of my proudest moments."

"What'd you do?"

"She tried to push me into one of the stalls, so I flushed her a little," I say defensively. Bass laughs so hard that he almost slides off his seat. I shake my head. "Stop, I'm serious. I feel really badly about that. No one, no matter how mean, deserves to be dunked in toilet water."

He chuckles. "I'm sure she survived, and hey, I'd take running water any way I could get it."

"Speaking of running water, that's what I miss most about being in the Otherworld," I say with a sigh. "Showers . . . all that water. It was heaven."

I watch the look of ecstasy on Bass's face. I know exactly how he feels. The first time I'd taken a shower in the Otherworld, I had no clue what to do. I'd stepped in fully clothed and gotten drenched. I'd sat on the stall floor for nearly an hour until the hot water started going cold and my skin had gotten all pruney.

"Did you ever go swimming?" I ask Bass.

"No. I always imagined what that would be like, but then I couldn't bring myself to do it. Maybe I was afraid. Baby steps."

"I know what you mean. I did find a great reservoir with Shae, though. If I ever get the chance, I'd swim there. *That* was heaven."

"I'm sorry about what happened with your sister," Bass says quietly.

I swallow hard, heat pricking my eyelids. "Were you there? When my father . . . when Danton . . . when he . . ."

"Yes." Bass doesn't hesitate, and a part of me respects him for that.

"Thanks for being honest."

"Riven, I—"

"I know it wasn't you. None of that was your fault. You're a pawn in all of this."

Something flickers across Bass's face, and he opens his mouth as if he's going to say something more, then shuts it again. I'm grateful that he does—I don't want his pity. Thinking about Shae brings a heaviness to the pit of my stomach, and thinking about what my father did to her makes me so furious that I can barely focus. I force myself to calm down, counting backward in my head, until my breaths are slow and even.

I don't even notice that Bass has gotten up from his chair and is standing beside me, his arm around my shoulders. "What are you doing?"

"Giving you a hug?"

Suddenly, an odd desire to hug him back overcomes me. I blink, but my body does as commanded. Bass's eyes snap to mine as his hands slide around me. It feels right and wrong at the same time, conflicting emotions racing through me.

You want this.

I don't even know where the thought comes from, but it's true. Somehow, I want Bass's arms around me. I want more than that. I turn my face. He's inches from mine, when I hear the gasp behind us.

"Get your filthy hands off her!" Caden lunges forward to slam Bass up against the wall of the cockpit, his forearm pressing into his windpipe.

"Caden, stop," I scream. "You're strangling him."

Sauer and Arven rush in, pulling Caden off of Bass. "What's going on?"

"Why don't you ask his high holiness here?" Bass snarls, rubbing his throat. "Barging in where he isn't wanted. Last I heard, you were going to Avaria to get married. I wasn't doing anything she didn't want."

Caden's pained look slides to me, and I swallow. "Everyone needs to mind their own business right now, and back the hell off." I blink. Those weren't the words I'd been about to say. Even Sauer stares at me as I shove past him. "I need some air."

Up top, someone comes through the hatch behind me. I don't have to turn around to know that it's Bass. Sauer would have rotated everyone out—kept order. Bass takes his spot beside me. "So, that was intense."

"I don't want to talk about it." I inhale sharply. "I mean I do want you to know that that's not going to happen again. I was confused."

"Got it."

"Look, I'm serious, what happened was—"

"Riven, we're good. Forget about it."

Relieved, I nod. I don't know what came over me down there. One moment, Bass and I were chatting, and the next, I literally wanted to throw myself at him. I peek at him out of the corner of my eye, and cringe. I don't even *like* Bass, not in that way. And the betrayed look on Caden's face was devastating. But I'd initiated the almost-kiss, there's no denying that. The impulse had felt strange—like an order that I was compelled to follow. It didn't make sense. I shrug it off and focus on my ninjatas.

"Are those Artok?" Bass asks after a while, eyeing the blades I've been swinging restlessly in my hands.

"Yes."

"Nice."

I'm grateful for the mundane subject change. "Where'd you get your staff?" I nod at the weapon stored on his back. "The ends are dynamic, aren't they?"

Bass grabs ahold of the ebony-colored rod and twirls it in his hands, extending it to full length with a slight press of his fingers. "Yes. I designed it."

"Can I check it out?" He hands me the staff and I examine it. It's made of a silky-smooth material that's oddly responsive in my hands. "How do you make the weapons change?"

"Skin recognition—it's linked to my fingerprints," he explains, taking it from me. "A sequence of touches initiates a blade, or spikes, or a lance. Like this."

His fingers move swiftly across the middle of the weapon's midpoint and, suddenly, a wicked-looking curved blade—like a scimitar—appears at either end.

"Wow, that's impressive."

"That's not all," he says proudly. "If you, or any attacker, tried to take it from me, the staff has its own defensive response. It would cut your hand in half."

I frown. "How come it didn't before? When I held it?"

"Because I let you." He grins. "It only engages defensive mode when it's active."

"Good to know." I watch Bass compress the staff with a flick of his thumb and toss it over his back into its harness. It's an interesting weapon, to be sure, and obviously built with cutting-edge technology. Bass had mentioned that he was good at robotics, so it makes sense that he'd be able to design such an intricate piece of weaponry.

"We're coming up to another canyon." Sauer's voice in our comms pieces makes both Bass and I sit up.

"Copy," I say, straining to see in the encroaching darkness. I engage night vision on my visor and watch as the terrain comes into focus. "Are you seeing what I'm seeing?" I ask.

Bass exhales. "It's deep." Deeper than anything we've navigated before. And it's narrow, with polluted toxic marshes on either side.

"We're in the bone yard," Sauer says. "We'll have to go through."

"What the hell is a bone yard?" I ask.

"It's the Neck. The part that connects the two hemispheres," Caden answers, his voice is hollow and distorted through the communications earpiece. Residual guilt leaps in my stomach, but I shove it away. "Like North and South America in the Otherworld."

"It's nothing good," Sauer chimes in. "Get ready."

"Why do you look so nervous?" I ask Bass, who's priming his plasma gun.

"People who come to the bone yard disappear. It's one of the reasons we knew nothing of Avaria. The bone yard's a natural deterrent—few, if any, come out alive."

Great. Not like we haven't had enough of that crap storm already.

I follow Bass, getting my own cannon ready. Bass and I both have ours set to obliterate. We aren't taking any chances—not with living or metal threats.

"On alert," Sauer commands as we descend into the chasm.

I see where the canyon gets its moniker. Thick pillars of bone-white structures litter the chasm's surface. Sauer has his job cut out for him, maneuvering the ship around them. Shivering slightly, I can't decide if they look more like teeth or gravestones.

A shadow catches my eye and I look up just as a dark figure winks out of view.

"There's something up there," I mutter to Bass. My fingers are itching to get hold of my ninjatas. I'm far better at close range combat than I am with a gun, even one as powerful as this one. Bass looks up, but all that's visible is a bloodred moon shimmering in the inky darkness. "There!" I say, pointing to one of the pillars. "Saw it again."

"I don't see anything."

Homing in with the help of the nanobes, I zoom in on the top of the column, but nothing is there. I blink, and suddenly my vision is filled with a blur of something dark diving toward me. I pull back to normal mode, just as a stick-thin, wiry figure lands on the nose of the ship and sinks into a low crouch.

It's covered in what looks like white paste, with fierce black eyes and a red, snarling mouth. Mismatched fur covers its body, but as far as I can tell there's no metal. Not a Reptile—organic from the looks of it. The creature cocks its head, watching me for a second, before placing a lethal-looking dart into a pipe and bringing it to its lips. I can't shoot the creature while it sits on the ship, so I grab my ninjatas. A slim dart flies out of the pipe, and I instinctively duck sideways, the spike missing my shoulder by an inch.

Protection, I tell the suit, feeling it harden around me. It'll take more than a dart to get through the material.

"Riven, stay down!" Bass swings at the thing, but it leaps out of the way like a nimble monkey. "Where'd it go?" he asks, peering over the side of the ship.

"It jumped."

"Must be thirty feet to the ground."

"What's going on topside?" Sauer calls out on the comms. "There's movement all over the place."

"Something jumped on the ship," Bass yells back. "It's some kind of biped—only one. Where are you seeing movement?"

"All around us. I'm engaging the shield in five, so get down here. You are free to engage. I repeat, you are free to engage. Shoot to kill."

"Bass," I warn. A dozen more of the creatures climbed onto the hull, watching us with those same curious, birdlike motions. Bloodred markings are etched down the sides of their bodies. They each have a pipe—filled with the same projectiles the first one had shot at me—and they're blocking our entrance to the hold.

"We can't get past them."

I raise my ninjatas. Bass and I position ourselves back-to-back with weapons at the ready. I engage my suit's offensive mode and blink as it comes online. For a half second, I wish I were wearing the suit Danton gave me. But this one will do for now.

"There're so many of them," Bass says. "Where'd they all come from?"

"Riven, Bass, report," Sauer urges. "You're on screen. What are those things?"

"Some kind of primate," Bass says frowning.

"That's not possible," I say. How would they be able to survive outside at night? Unless they've evolved to deal with sub-zero temperatures. I glance down at the gauge on my suit panel to verify the numbers. I blink. The reading couldn't possibly be correct. It's nighttime—there's no way it could be seventy-one degrees.

"Bass, what does your temp gauge say?"

His eyes widen. "Seventy degrees."

"Sauer, do you copy? Do you show seventy degrees, too?"

"Correct," he responds. "Must be the Neck. I've heard conditions are all over the place because of the equator. Huge lightning storms around these parts, too."

That would explain our visitors' lack of covering . . . well, except for the sparse fur around their torsos. I look up and exhale slowly. Creatures similar to the ones in front of us are covering every inch of the tops of the pillars. They are alert, watching us, as if ready to swarm at any second. *What are they waiting for?*

"Are you seeing this?" I say in a low voice. "Sauer, what do we do?"

Arven's voice comes through the speaker. "I don't see any option but to blast wide, but we risk damaging the ship if any of these pillars collapse. If we engage the shield with you two out there . . ." Arven trails off. He doesn't have to explain what will happen once the shields kick in—anything touching the ship will incinerate in seconds. "You'll have to shoot through them."

"We can't just kill them," Caden breaks in. "I think they're defending their territory. Can't we stun them? Or freeze them?"

"One tried to shoot some kind of dart at Riven," Bass returns. "If it's a choice between them or us, I'm going to choose us. They engage, I engage. I don't think they're here to see us merrily on our way. There's a reason no one ever makes it through the bone yard. Obviously, it's these skinny white apes."

One of the creatures straightens into a near-standing position. It has a Mohawk of red spines crowning its skull and holds a vicious-looking spear in its hand. I stare at Bass and shake my head. "I don't think those things are primates. They look like . . ."

Static rushes in my earpiece. "Repeat, Riven."

I squint, focusing the nanobes in my retinas to take a snapshot of the creature with the red spines. I hold my breath, processing the data through my brain and running it against the database of life forms I'd accessed earlier. I blink at the response, and run it again. It's a one hundred percent match.

"They're not primates."

"What?"

"Those things are as human as you are."

15

THE ULTIMATE WEAPON

THE ONE WITH the crown of scarlet spines jerks his head at me and then down to my blades. He's the leader. I can't quite work out if they're friendly or if this is part of some war ritual before they try to take us down.

"Don't you dare drop those swords," Bass hisses, hefting his staff even higher.

"I wasn't going to."

The man speaks a guttural language, gesticulating at us and at the weapons in our hands. I'm very aware of the row of sharpened teeth in his mouth. If there's one thing I've learned about surviving in this world, it's that things with pointy teeth tend to be carnivores. These natives are hunters, and they don't want to *kill* us. They want to *eat* us. Out here, it's slim pickings. I'm pretty sure we're like a free-for-all banquet.

"What's he saying?" Bass whispers.

"Hang on."

The man gestures again, repeating his sentence. Running the language through my database, I find a match that performs an adequate translation. It's some sort of pig-Latin dialect. "I think he wants to know who we are and where we're going," I say. "Sauer, what do you want me to tell him?"

"The truth. That we are passing through."

"Are you sure?" I reply in a low voice. Just because these people speak a different language doesn't mean they aren't able to understand ours. "Maybe they don't want us to go past. We know nothing about them"—I inhale, scanning the surrounding pillars—"other than there are thousands of them and six of us. Somehow, I don't think they're just going to let us pass just because we're on a peaceful mission. I vote no."

"This isn't a democracy."

"You're not up here, Sauer. This isn't the time for peaceful tactics. Trust me."

"Stand down, Riven. You have your orders."

I grit my teeth. There's a reason these natives live here. There's a reason that no one makes it through the bone yard. And there's definitely a reason for my gut instincts going haywire. Those three things add up to nothing good. "Sorry, Sauer. I'm not putting the Lord King's life, or any of ours, at risk. I don't trust these things, and last I checked, I'm a General of Neospes, which means I outrank you." I ignore Bass's smirk, along with the silence on the other side of the comms. "Arven, on my mark, engage the shields."

"You know what you're doing, right?" Bass asks.

I'm not one hundred percent sure this is going to work, but we don't have many other options. If they swarm the ship, our whole crew will be in danger, including Caden. "Bass, I'm going to clear a path. The minute you have access to the hatch, you get down below."

"What about you?"

"I'll be fine."

"I'm not leaving you out here," he argues.

"Bass, don't be stupid. If one of those darts gets you, you'll be the first course." I almost smile when his eyes go wide. "See the red marks? Not paint. Blood. So, when I say go, you go. Are we clear?"

"Clear."

"One. Two. Thr—"

Before I can finish, the leader narrows his eyes and snarls, and a hair-raising shriek bursts from his lips. The shriek echoes from man to man, until all the natives are screaming in deafening unison. It's a war cry. I leap forward and swing my ninjatas, kicking the creatures closest to me off the ship. Half a dozen down, and for a brief second, the hatch is visible.

"Now, Bass. Go!"

He slams his fist into the access panel and slides through the entrance. With Bass out of the way, it's just these freaks and me. I swing my swords in a lazy motion.

"Leave my ship or die," I tell the leader in his language, the guttural words falling from my mouth with ease. He looks surprised, but bares his teeth and signals to some of his kinsmen who scramble down the pillars like insects, and then eyes me. I stare back, undaunted. "It doesn't matter if it's one or one hundred. I will kill every last one of you."

The leader hisses, and I take that as my cue, engaging my suit. Vaulting from the ship, I sense a flurry of motion behind me. Bass was wrong—the distance to the ground is more than thirty feet, but I land easily and roll into a crouch. The air is filled with flying white bodies following my descent. "Shields now, Sauer, and pull up! Arven, engage those propulsion jets and get above these columns."

I race away, weaving between the fat pillars. The leader and a score or so of his men are hot on my heels. They're screeching and shouting as though enjoying the chase. Darts bounce harmlessly off my suit, but I keep running until I know I'm out of the blast area of the ship's engines. Out of the corner of my eye, I see the ship flare blue and burst upward, tossing the burned bodies of the remaining natives off the hull.

I turn, facing off against hundreds. The leader with the red spines scuttles up a nearby column before giving the order to attack. His face is triumphant as the rest of the natives circle me, several bodies deep. I feel a bursting sensation on the inside of my skin as the nanobes in my blood surge. They're alive and firing at the challenge. Blue shimmers across my face in hot waves, my fingers tingling with strength and purpose.

Kill them all.

I don't know where the order comes from, only that it's there. Pulsing, hot, and powerful. And then I'm nothing but rage as an inhuman berserker force takes a hold of me, the adrenaline making my body vibrate with energy. I've never let go like this before. And now, I'm more machine than girl. I duck and weave, my swords flying faster than I've ever thought possible, until the air is ripe with the smell of blood. I don't stop, giving free rein to the robotics that so efficiently fulfill my commands. The rush is intoxicating . . . overpowering. I've never felt so free in all my life, so unfettered from everything. Conscience, even.

"Riven, stop!"

Caden's horrified voice is in my earpiece, cutting through the fog surrounding me. My vision refocuses and I exhale. The mound of bodies around me is staggering. I swallow hard, my breathing ragged, and look down. I'm drenched in blood. It's on my arms, my chest, and my visor. It's dripping from the edges of my ninjatas, and the dusty, gray earth is slick with it. Hundreds of dead bodies surround me, and I feel nothing but grim satisfaction—an order executed to perfection.

I raise a sword to the leader, still in his position at the top of the pillar. I can't see his face, but I imagine what it must look like. "There," I call out, wiping my blades on the sides of my suit. "You can eat for weeks."

I don't look back as I step over the bodies, making my way past them. No one follows me. I know they won't. I walk until my legs are burning, until all of the adrenaline fades from my system.

"General, there's an open space up ahead. We'll meet you there."

I don't recognize the voice—it could be Arven's or Sauer's— but I obey, one foot in front of the other, swords at my sides. Eventually, I reach the clearing where the rest of the crew is waiting. Caden's face is expressionless, but I see it in his eyes . . . the sorrow, and it guts me.

Sauer moves forward, but Caden stops him. "I'll get her," he says. I let him take the ninjatas from my twitching fingers, and then he hands them to someone behind him. Bass, I think.

I can smell the crew's fear. They're afraid of me—of what they saw me do, and I don't blame them. I'd be afraid of me, too. I remain silent until Caden and I are back on the ship in the tiny, but private, medical bay in the back. "Give us a moment," he tells Sauer. "Get us back on course. She's fine. She'll be fine."

Caden doesn't speak as he disengages the Vector suit from my body, peeling it off inch by inch. I let him, standing there like an obedient child. As my brain goes back to normal, I feel . . . like a ghost of myself. Caked blood flakes to the floor. Caden's hands are sticky from the wet patches as he pulls the suit down to my hips. He sucks in his breath, taking in the discoloration all over my torso and arms. I look down, following his gaze. The natives hadn't gone down without a brutal fight—every inch of my skin is covered with fresh bruises and bites. I hadn't even felt them. I still don't.

Opening a medkit, Caden dabs a salve to the injuries. He doesn't say a word, not until he's finished his ministrations and I'm dressed in a pair of cargo pants and a tunic. He sits me down on the bunk and hands me a water packet.

"Drink this," he says brushing my hair out of my face. It's probably the only part of me that isn't wounded. The visor did its job well. I glance at the blood-soaked suit lying in a crumpled pile in the corner. In defensive mode, the suit had stood up to more than expected.

I stare at the floor, my chest burning at Caden's tenderness. A rush of guilt overwhelms me along with the need to explain myself and beg his forgiveness. "I'm sorry about the thing with Bass. I don't know what I was thinking. I don't even *like* him."

"None of that matters. You're safe, and that's all I care about." Caden tips my chin up to face him. "What happened out there?"

"I . . . don't know." I take a sip of water and stare at the ground, trying to swallow past the knot in my throat. "I feel like I'm breaking into pieces—my brain tells me to do things, and I do them."

"I'm here, Riven, and you're safe." His fingers feather across my temple and all I want to do is press my cheek into his palm, so I do. It's soft and strong, just as he is. Caden slips his hand around the back of my neck and pulls me against him. "It just didn't seem like you."

I laugh, a raw guttural sound that has no humor in it. "But it *was* me. I killed all those people. I don't know what happened—I went into some kind of berserker battle mode." I sit up, retreating from Caden's embrace. "I could have led them away, but I *wanted* to fight. I wanted to end them. I wanted to punish them, and I did."

"You did what you had to do."

"Did I?" I raise bleak eyes to his. "Don't you see what I am?" I say with another ugly laugh. "I'm nothing but a Vector—programmed to kill, and that's what I did even though I could hear a voice inside my head screaming to stop."

"You're no Vector, not by a long shot. You defended us. You put yourself in the face of danger and you prevailed. There's something to be said for that, Riven."

"You're wrong; I'm a monster," I contradict hoarsely.

"If you are," he says, his eyes gentle, "then so am I. So is Sauer. So is every single person on this ship. We've all had to do things that we're not proud of, or things that go against every bone in our bodies. We do it for the greater good, and to protect the lives of others. We defend the weak when they can't defend themselves. And that certainly doesn't make us monsters, even though it may feel like it sometimes."

"I wanted to kill them."

"That doesn't make you a bad person, Riven. It makes you human."

I frown, meeting his eyes. "It makes me human to want to kill?"

"No, it makes you human to want to protect those you love. No machine can feel that." I shake my head, ready to argue, but Caden kisses my forehead. "You're more human than you believe. What you're feeling right now is regret. Vectors feel nothing. They're programmed to obey and kill, and they don't feel a thing while they're doing it."

"You don't understand . . ." I trail off, unable to explain how *good* it'd felt . . . how every life I'd taken made me feel stronger, made me feel invincible. It was as if the nanobes had thrived because they'd succeeded in completing the task that had been set for them—*kill them all.* It's hard to separate my sense of triumph from my growing self-loathing.

"Riven, look at me." Caden holds my face between his palms. "I can't imagine what it must be like for you, and I don't pretend to know everything. But I do know that you control those parts of you. You did nothing wrong. You have to see that."

"Do you really believe that's true?"

Caden rests his forehead against mine, his breath warm on my cheek. "Yes."

But deep down, I know he doesn't. He'd been against mur-
dering them. He's saying the right things now because he
knows I need to hear them. But Caden wouldn't have killed
those people, even if they were trying to kill him. He would
have found some way to save us and save them. It's the difference between him and me. Deep down, I am nothing but a
Reptile—a machine hampered by my own humanity.

Maybe Cale's been right about me all along.

At the thought of him, I blink, recalling the coldness of the
directive: *Kill them all.* And then I recall the one I'd heard with
Bass: *You want this.* Snatches of my dream tumble into my head
and the photo message that had been waiting for me on the tracker.

Oh my god.

"It's Cale," I whisper, horrified.

Caden's eyes narrow. "What do you mean, it's Cale?"

"He's in my head." My thoughts are frantic. "First the dreams,
then the thing with Bass, then those people. It makes sense."

Caden grasps my shoulders, his eyes worried. "Riven, what
do you mean he's in your head? I thought you said he couldn't
hurt you."

"He can't. It's psychical."

Caden doesn't have to point out the obvious—that despite
being subliminal, Cale has succeeded in getting me to follow
his directives to the letter. "Can you block him?"

I focus for a second, running a diagnostic scan. "Yes, now
that I know what he's been doing. I need to reboot my security
parameters, isolate the signal transmission."

I don't admit how violated I feel. Cale had been inside my
head. I'd let him in. He could have done worse—forced me to

attack someone on the ship or to hurt Caden. But he'd been playing me, just like with the photo of the cage. He *wanted* me to know it was him. But how had he initiated access? I frown. Maybe when I synced with the Reptile, he planted some kind of reverse connection. I rerun the security scan several times to be sure I've blocked Cale, but the taint of his presence remains.

"You should get some rest."

"Caden, I don't—"

He smiles, light firing in his green eyes. "As much as I don't want to pull rank on you, *General*, I am your king and I order you to rest."

Embarrassment heats my cheeks. "About that . . . Sauer must be pretty mad. I didn't mean to call him out like that. We were short on time and—"

"There's nothing to apologize for. You do outrank him, and he knows that." Caden pushes me gently down to the bunk. "Now, stop being so stubborn and just lie there for a minute. Let your body heal. Sleep."

"Caden?"

He turns back at the door, just before pressing the access panel. "Yeah?"

"You know I'd never . . . want to hurt you, right? With Bass, or anyone else."

"I know."

I inhale a slow breath. "And thank you."

"For what?"

"For being you. I'm not sure what would have happened if you hadn't stopped me before. Both times."

"You would have stopped yourself." Caden stares at me as if he wants to say more, but then decides against it. "Try to get some rest. We're almost to Avaria. We'll get help, take Cale out, and save Neospes. Then everything will go back to normal."

But as the door slides shut behind him and I'm lying in the darkness, all I can think is that things won't ever go back to normal.

I am a machine. This is what I was bred for. What I was made for. Danton *designed* me to be a soldier . . . to be the best soldier. To defend, to protect, to kill. It's in my DNA. Cale's wrong—I'm not a Reptile.

I am a weapon.

I close my eyes, the words filling my head until they're all I see in fluorescent blue lettering, like code. Everything becomes crystal clear. I've been holding myself back, pretending to be something I'm not because of my basic human wants. But human desires only sow seeds of doubt. I covet what I can never have—a life that belongs to someone in another universe. Oddly enough, *Cale* has made me recognize that.

Swinging my legs off the side of the cot, I examine my skin. Most of the wounds have already healed. I can see the slight bluish tinge of the nanobes under my skin as they rebuild tissue and remove infection. If I were human, I'd be dead or bedridden.

But I'm not human. I'm me. And I'm alive.

I grab my gear from the shelf, and rifle through the bag until I find what I'm looking for—the suit my father had made for me. The material is silky as if it's woven from gossamer. Unlike my previous suits, the neural connector is not at the neck. It connects to my entire spine from base to tip. It's not like anything I've ever seen and I shiver in anticipation.

I peel off every inch of clothing and slide on the tensile suit. Tiny sensor pads align to my bare skin, making it tickle for a second. I pull the material up and over my hips and back, feeling the connectors line up and sink between the discs in my spine. The nanobes react instantly to the probes, surging beneath my skin to link them to my brain. The suit's not even online yet and already I can feel my body responding. Attaching the final fasteners, I tug on my boots and stand. The material feels like a second skin.

With a deep breath, I power up the suit, everything in me firing in response to the tech. I can feel the metadata running through my brain, creating records of my biometrics, and aligning with my central nervous system. The suit connects to the satellites still orbiting the planet, and recalibrates its new location, sending me information of the ship's position. My brain is nearly overwhelmed with the upload of specifications, commands, diagnostics, and systems information. Within seconds, the sync is complete.

I stare at myself in the mirror. The suit is indigo blue, shimmering from the light of the nanobes beneath my skin. I string my harness with my ninjatas over my shoulder and throw on my beat-up leather jacket. I smile at the girl in the mirror, and she smiles back, supremely confident. Blue programming code ricochets off her cheek. This girl knows exactly who she is.

No Vector. No Reptile. No human.

Just *me*.

16

CITY OF WONDER

AVARIA IS NOTHING like I expected. Then again, we're not exactly in Avaria yet. We're on the outskirts of the city, waiting to be escorted in. The wall before us, looming like a forbidding slab, is fifty feet of pure reinforced steel, built to keep things out. And in, too, I suppose.

We're standing in a row outside of the hovertank. Bass is on one side of me, and Sylar and Arven on the other. Bass and I have fallen back into our usual routine, as if the cockpit interlude never happened. I'm grateful for small mercies. Caden and Sauer are two steps ahead of us. I can't help noticing that Caden has changed—he's dressed in official military garb. He'd noticed my clothing the minute I came out of the medical bay.

"Danton's suit." It wasn't a question, and Caden's tone had been guarded.

"Yes. I ran out. This is the last one left. I had no choice." But of course I did—I could have gone without a tech-enabled suit, and take my chances. The truth is, I didn't want to. "Aurela cleared it," I'd added.

Caden had forced a smile even though I could see the worry in his eyes—he didn't trust my father, either. "You look like Mystique."

"Who?"

"The mutant girl from *X-Men*. It's a movie. Not that you look like a mutant. That's not what I meant. You look fine. Better than fine. Never mind."

I'd caught Sauer's lips twitching, but he'd taken pity on Caden and outlined the mission parameters. I hadn't missed the satisfied grin on Bass's face, as if he was enjoying every second of Caden's discomfort.

My eyes narrow as I squint to see the reflection of something gleaming along the wall's length. It must be part of the holo-imagery defense mechanism that Cristobal had mentioned back in the Otherworld, the one that prevents anyone from seeing the colony. I frown and magnify the image. Upon closer examination, it looks too convoluted to be a hologram projector. It's some kind of laser weapon with image processing sensors; I'm sure of it.

Bass notices that I'm studying the barrier and whispers, "Sauer told me it's fourteen inches thick."

"And deadly," I say, jerking my head at the equipment lining the top, spaced in equidistant intervals. "They had to have seen us coming a mile away. I'm surprised they didn't try to fry us."

Bass's eyes widen. "So, you think the fence is live?"

"See the galvo-reflectors up top? They're using ultraviolet laser tech to eliminate threats." I pause. "Kind of like an electrified fence, only one that's hot enough to melt anything from a distance. They must have disabled it for us."

"Whoa, guess they really don't like visitors," Bass says. "I shudder to think what would happen if we *weren't* invited."

I nod toward a suspicious, human-sized pile of black ash on Bass's right.

"That's sick," he says.

"They must have a lot to protect."

We wait in silence as a central seam splits the giant wall open and Cristobal Marx comes strolling out. His smile is as I remember—white and impersonal. He's dressed in a simple, woven, cotton shirt and fitted pants, but he seems as dangerous to me as he had in the Otherworld. Every instinct inside of me screams not to trust him.

"Welcome to Avaria, Lord King of Neospes," he says bowing to Caden, who inclines his head graciously in turn. "Please allow me to escort you to the chief and your bride, who are both anxiously awaiting your arrival. You may leave your ship inside the gate—it will be quite safe, I assure you."

Caden nods at Arven, who pilots the craft into a hangar inside. The city side of the wall is no different than the outside—dusty earth and thin air. Cristobal leads us to a nearby tent. While we wait, we're served wrapped leaves with beads of moisture still on their surface. Sylar's gasp is audible. Watching Cristobal, we all do as he does, pressing the unrolled, cool surface to our faces. I almost sigh at the refreshing feel of the leaf against my cheek as my skin absorbs the moisture like a greedy sponge.

"Where do you get this?" I ask him.

He smiles at me. "Ah, General, it's good to see you again. I will be looking forward to seeing how you like our beautiful city."

I place the folded leaf into a nearby basket and lean back in my chair. "You mean the dome/no dome scenario you mentioned at Era's house?"

Cristobal's smile widens. "Yes! Now, come. We have much to do before the feast tonight."

"Feast?" Caden asks.

"The wedding pact, of course," Cristobal says, just as Arven joins us. He, too, is offered a leaf, which he stares at until Sauer explains how it's to be used. We follow Cristobal to a waiting hovercraft, and I glance over my shoulder to see the wall gliding shut.

"Is the wall laser enabled?" I ask Cristobal.

Surprise lights his eyes. "Yes. Near-infrared and ultraviolet laser technology," he says. "But you knew that already or you wouldn't have asked."

"I saw the equipment. Pretty big defense for a wall guarding nothing."

There's that smile again, but this time I feel like knocking it off his face. He smirks as if everything is a big secret, and spreads his hands wide. "You will have to see to believe."

I shrug, and sit in the back seat. Bass joins me. "What's wrong?"

"Nothing I can put my finger on."

"Heebie jeebies?" he asks and I fight the urge to grin. Once more, he has hit the nail on the head.

"Exactly."

We strap in as the hover moves forward, gliding away from the wall. Eventually, a dome comes into view, only it's not the same shape as the one in Neopses. It's more of a tube than an inverted bowl. A small army stands at the entrance. They don't need reinforcements at the wall—that's designed to defend itself—but the people of Avaria aren't taking any chances.

Cristobal slows the hover and passes a biometric scan at the first wave of soldiers. He performs the scan several more times before we gain entry to Avaria. It's a bustling city, much like the ones I've visited in the Otherworld, only with streamlined hover traffic weaving between tall, aerodynamic buildings that nearly scrape the dome's clear surface. Cristobal maneuvers the hover into the interchange and I force myself not to stare. What strikes me the most are the patches of green turf I see stretching between the streamlined structures.

"Is that real?" I breathe.

"Yes, that is real grass."

"But how—"

"You'll see."

This time, when Cristobal smiles, I feel a sense of wonder. Our trip through the glass city ends as we reach the far side of the dome. I frown. Are we going outside already? Cristobal passes through another series of scans and descends from the hover.

"No tech in this section," he says cryptically. "We walk."

Not wanting to attract attention, I power down my suit with a quick command and follow the others through the security checkpoint. We enter another glass tube—a second ring within the first—but this one is full of trees and dark, lush foliage. It's the opposite of the first domed ring, and unlike anything we have in Neospes.

"What is it?" Sauer blurts out, awed.

"It's a biosphere," Cristobal explains. "The early settlers wanted to protect the remaining flora after the Tech War. This was one of the more lush areas of our planet, and parts of it survived in spite of the Machines. Our forefathers built this as a garden of sorts, one to complement the city you just passed through." He waves a hand above us. "The dome was constructed to maximize the sunlight and to help the plants grow. In the beginning, the early Avarians did not understand how the plants were thriving until, one day, they realized that their city was built above an underground spring." Cristobal looks right at me. "That's when they started construction on the outer wall."

Of course. They'd do anything to protect a secret water source on a planet that was as dry as a bone everywhere else. I nod—if it'd been Neospes, we'd have done the same. The Machines had sucked the oceans dry to convert them into energy. Running water would be more valuable than liquid gold.

The sound of some kind of animal in the distance makes us all jump. "It's a chattera," Cristobal says. "Similar to the Other-world's monkeys. We have many species of animals living here."

"Pure?" Sauer asks.

"One hundred percent pure-born."

Sauer and I exchange a look. No wonder they'd wanted to remain unseen for so long. What they've accomplished here is a miracle.

We follow Cristobal deeper into the jungle. The occasional screech of a bird or bellow of an animal makes us laugh. I see pockets of open space with more grass and exotic, brilliantly colored flora. We stop for a while to smell the blooms—their fragrances are intoxicating.

"Come," Cristobal says as we near yet another checkpoint. We've walked in the garden for over an hour, though it's felt like only minutes.

"How big is it?" I ask him. "The garden?"

"The width of this dome is about five miles across, but nearly a hundred miles in circumference. Now we need a little help from the monorail. It would take days to walk."

At the checkpoint we board an efficient-looking elevated railway that operates off of a line attached to the inner glass wall of the garden dome. "I thought you said no tech," Sauer remarks. "Why didn't we take the hover?"

"A hover couldn't make it through here. In some areas the undergrowth is so thick it's impossible to pass. The monorail makes it easier to get from one side to the other."

"What's on the other side?" Sauer asks, his brows snapping together.

"You'll see."

But I can't imagine anything better than what we are seeing right now. Even the six fierce-looking guards who have joined us for the ride don't make me flinch.

"This is amazing," Bass says. His nose, like Sylar's and Arven's, is pressed to the monorail windows.

Something glittery grabs my attention below the track, and I blink. It can't be. But, sure enough, I can see the flash of running water. Running water that looks like it's flowing *under* the glass dome to whatever lies beyond it. But that's not possible. There are no rivers or waterways in this world.

I catch Cristobal's eye. "Is that what I think it is?"

"An aboveground river? Yes. It's man-made, but it serves its purpose. When the first chiefs realized that the plants had water, they dug and dug, until the underground spring was no longer below the surface. However, it was difficult to keep it contained. It was as if they'd unleashed a tsunami of life. The underground spring fed pools and lakes, and the forest blossomed."

"So, that's how all this happened?" Caden asks.

"No, my Lord King," Cristobal says, unmistakable pride in his voice. "That's how all *this* happened."

And before I can register what Cristobal is talking about, the monorail whooshes past the end of the dome, through an outlet, and to the other side. It takes me a minute before I realize that we're flying beside a canopy of thick, dense trees, and the monorail, once connected to the side of the glass dome, now rides upon widely spaced metal pillars. We are out in the open air, which is filled with strange sounds and invigorating scents. In the distance, I can see the tip of a purple peak breaking through a barrier of clouds . . . real, actual *clouds*! Now, I know I'm dreaming.

Caden's eyes are wide with awe. This is what the people of Avaria wanted to protect—and, no wonder. It's a miracle that a place like this even exists on this planet.

"This can't possibly be real." The words are mine, but it's Sauer who gives them voice.

"Given a chance, life will always find a way to endure," Cristobal returns. "A single seed will wait an eternity for a drop of water, protecting the life within it, until growth becomes an opportunity."

Sauer blinks as a flock of birds swoops past. "But *how* is this possible?"

"It's a self-aware, independent ecosystem," Cristobal explains. "Everything in here is interconnected."

"What about the temperature fluctuations?"

Cristobal nods. "That's the beauty of this place. We don't have the same instabilities that you see in Neospes. During the day, water evaporates into the air, and condenses into the clouds you see over there." He points to the thick haze near the mountain's tip. "And it rains."

"Rain?" Sylar gasps.

"With sunlight during the day and rainfall at night, the forest has flourished, growing even beyond our expectations and reaching farther than that mountain range. The dome has acted as a barrier of sorts, making it more humid during the day. With more plants, more water from the soil makes its way into the air. Solar radiation leads to more rainfall, more plants, more photosynthesis, and more life. It's a complete reversal. The planet is fighting back."

"How big is this place?" Arven asks unsteadily.

"Millions of acres. It backs onto a mountain range to the west. We never expected it to grow so rapidly."

"Is that why we can breathe so easily in here?" Sauer asks, inhaling deeply. "All the oxygen?"

"Yes."

Sauer's right. I breathe in, feeling the cool refreshing scent hit the back of my throat. Even the air tastes fresher. It's no secret that we synthesize oxygen in the domes to make up for the loss of terrestrial vegetation planet-wide. Over the years, the air has been getting thinner, and it's becoming harder and harder to breathe in the open spaces like the Outers. But, even though human bodies have evolved to survive with the decreasing levels of oxygen, it won't last forever. This wild, thriving forest may change everything.

I look up as the monorail comes to a stop and we descend to the bottom of the pillar. It's dark and moist here on the bottom of the forest. I can barely see through the canopy to the sky above, with some of the trees arching hundreds of feet above us, their trunks so thick it would take several people to link arms around them.

"Unbelievable that this is even possible," Bass says to me.

I smile, agreeing. "I remember studying rain forest ecosystems in the Otherworld. But nothing I read prepared me for this, here, of all places." I brush my fingers over the slick surface of a dark green frond, watching a bright blue amphibian leap out from beneath the bushes and hop away. "It seems so surreal. I mean, look at them—they're alive . . . not Reptiles . . . it's amazing."

"This way," Cristobal announces and we fall in line. I notice that six guards are bringing up the rear, rifles at the ready. I frown, studying the laser-sighted tranquilizer guns. Cristobal looks back. "Don't worry. It's for the forest dwellers if they attack. This, after all, is a wild place. The tranqs slow them down, but cause little harm. More gentle than stun guns." My frown deepens. The guards have those strapped to their legs, too. Those weapons, I notice, have more lethal settings than stun. If those guns are not for the animals, then who are they for?

"What kind of dwellers?" I hear Caden ask from the front of the procession. "More chatteras?"

"Yes, and other fauna that existed before the Tech War. More species are discovered each day." Cristobal smiles widely and waves a hand. "Ah, here we are. The home of the chief."

"Your chief lives out here?" Sauer says, incredulous.

"Yes. We live in the domes, but Lady Inka particularly enjoys being a part of nature. Best of both worlds."

The path we're walking on turns into a wider trail. I notice that the foliage has started to change as well—less underbrush and more floral vegetation. Bright spots of color fill the landscape with blooms of every variety, most of which I've only seen the like of in the Otherworld—in shades of every color under the sun.

"It's amazing," I breathe.

"This is only the entrance." Cristobal turns to smile at me, and beckons us forward. "Welcome to Avaria Proper, the jewel of our city."

Walking through the valley of orchids, the smell of them heady, we enter the clearing beyond. It's nothing I expected. Strung between rows of trees is an oasis in the sky, like a giant tree house—man-made, but built so cleverly that it could be a part of the rain forest. Smaller huts are connected to the central area by walkways high above us. Chatteras dangle off the rope bridges, prattling away. I can see human faces peering from the open windows in the adjoining huts, but no one comes out to greet us. Cristobal disappears for a moment, and we are left staring in wonder. Caden sidles over to my side, where I'm studying a blue flower shaped like a bell.

"This is insane, right, Riv?" he says, now that his diplomatic escort has departed. I hear the childish wonder in his voice, and almost grin at how much effort it must have taken to stay quiet in Cristobal's presence. "It's like a paradise you read about in books. No wonder they kept this place secret." He shakes his head, gently touching the edge of the blue flower with his fingertip. "The Reptiles would rip it apart."

Caden's right. If the Reptiles ever found this place, it wouldn't last a week. They'd scrounge for every usable body and pillage every resource.

But if the Avarian people have hidden the city for so long, why open it up now? Why trust us now? What do we have that they need? Besides my father—and what would they need him for, anyway? From the looks of the outer dome, they have all the tech they could ever need.

A group approaches us led by a couple. The man is tall and forbidding with a lined, hawkish face. Black markings cover his nose and cheeks, and his chin is pierced with thin pieces of wood. A crown of brilliant red and gold feathers spans his forehead. A thick silver necklace covers half his chest. His body is lean and muscled, and he's not wearing much beyond a loin-cloth. Similar black markings grace his arms and thighs.

My glance goes to the girl at his side, and my breath stops. Tall and slender like the man, her skin is a golden bronze that looks like it's oiled from within. Braids wind through her dark hair, dotted with flowers and jewels. Slanted brown eyes rest above sharp cheekbones, which slope down to a full, upturned mouth. Red markings streak across her cheeks and down her nose, but her face is unpierced. She's more fully covered, but even in her simple clothing, her legs are long and shapely, and her shoulders, erect and proud. Golden bracelets adorn her arms and neck and, surprisingly, a longbow rests comfortably against her side. Not only is she beautiful, without a single wart to be found, she's also a warrior.

And she's Caden's bride-to-be.

17

ALLIANCES

"GREETINGS, LORD KING," the man says. He bows, and everyone behind him follows suit. "I am Aenoh, and this is my daughter, Inka. We bid you welcome to the jewel of Avaria."

"Thank you, Aenoh," Caden says, striding forward to touch the back of the man's hand with his, and then presses the same hand to his chest in what must be their traditional greeting. I wonder if Cristobal instructed Caden on Avarian customs. And then I remember that Caden has been studying these people for months because of the liaison. Of course he'd know protocol. "We accept your gracious welcome and thank you for your generosity." He pauses before turning to Inka. She, like her father, bows gracefully. I notice that Caden doesn't touch fingers with her, but offers her a short bow. "My lady."

"Please, call me Inka."

"And you may call me Caden." He turns and introduces each of us. "These are my companions: Commander Sauer, whom you've met via visual comms; First Lieutenant Arven; Second Lieutenant Sylar; Bass; and lastly, General Riven."

Aenoh's eyes snap to me. A strange expression flashes across his face as he studies me, but he quickly masks it. His daughter's gaze flicks to me as well, full of curiosity. I return her look, keeping my expression blank. Aenoh claps his hands and several people dressed in tan step forward—one attendant for each of us. "You will be escorted to your private quarters before the welcome feast. Then we will head to the capitol for discussions of a more political nature."

Sauer pulls Caden aside, his voice low: "My Lord King, we really don't have time. Do you think this wise? Every second is essential."

"We risk causing offense if we don't go to their welcome feast, Sauer." Caden glances at me. "And I want to find out more about this place. About these people. What drives them." He pauses. "And what else we can learn about them."

"As you say, my Lord King."

A young, shy female is my escort, and I follow her to the tree house entrance where a narrow wooden staircase spirals upward. We climb two more sets of steps, and cross a couple of roped bridges before arriving at a small hut, nearly obscured by leaves and branches. She bows and points mutely to a washbasin and folded clothing on the cot. While I explore the small but meticulously constructed cabin, she waits outside, pulling a grass-screened door shut behind her. I stare out of a small window and see Bass one tree over doing the same. He waves and points down. After following his gaze, I almost wish I hadn't— we're suspended high in the air above a deeply carved precipice.

Stepping back, I approach the bowl on the other side of the room. To my surprise, it's full of scented, oiled water—water for bathing. I still have to get used to the fact that we are not in the Otherworld. After a lengthy sponge bath, I consider wearing my suit beneath the clothing waiting on the cot.

Regardless of how agreeable Aenoh seems, this is a strange place and we don't know a lot about what he or his daughter wants. I recall his odd look when Caden introduced me, and opt to wear the suit. Better safe than sorry. In the privacy of the hut, I bring the suit online, checking its functionality. It doesn't seem to be impacted by our surroundings. Even though we are deep in this new forest, I can sense power sources all around, as well as from the primary ring in the distance.

As my suit syncs to me, data rushes into my brain, and vice versa. I process all the information I've received since we first arrived in Avaria—fauna, flora, geography, topography, all of it. I pull up the map on a hologram from my wrist cuff. Cristobal hadn't lied. The forest is enormous, spanning thousands of miles. But what he didn't divulge is that the same steel wall surrounds it nearly all the way around. It must have taken decades and immense manpower to build.

I frown, circumventing the laser tech I'd seen on top of the wall. I'm careful not to dig too deep—I don't want my snooping to be caught by their security—but it's as I suspected. The lasers are programmed to eliminate any, and all, threats that bypass their hologram safety imagery. I hook into a satellite feed of the planet's terrain at my coordinates and, sure enough, everything I see is dust and burned earth for miles.

So, why would Avaria risk coming out of anonymity? The only thing I can think of is Vector tech, but that doesn't make sense. Their defense systems are virtually impenetrable. They wouldn't need Vectors.

A polite cough from the doorway has me yanking the Avarian dress over my suit. I retract the visor and engage camouflage mode, watching the suit turn the color of my skin. The long, bell-shaped sleeves of the pale green flowing dress flutter lightly against my skin. I remove my boots and slide my feet into a pair of leather slippers. I feel ridiculous—almost as ridiculous as I did in the dancing girl's outfit during the Solstice Games.

"May I assist with your hair?" the girl asks.

"My hair?"

"Please, allow me." She motions to a small stool and I sit. She strokes a brush through my choppy—and dirty—hair. I wouldn't be surprised if she finds some moss monster guts crusted in there. Her fingers move nimbly, weaving and pulling something between the strands. After a few minutes, she turns me to face her and smiles, holding up a small mirror. Tiny jade-colored flowers are entwined with beads in small clusters over the crown of my head, and my hair has been cleaned and plaited. Fluttery strands frame my face, the vibrant flowers making my eyes look like bright gems. "Does it please you?" she asks shyly.

"Yes, I like it very much. Thank you."

The girl's face flushes as she walks to the door. "Come, I'll take you to the feast."

We meet Bass along the way, and he, too, looks clean and well-dressed in a flowing top and loose pants. His red hair has been trimmed, and his stubbly beard, shaved. "Wow, Bass, you clean up good," I tell him, grinning.

"So do you. You could almost pass for a girl."

As I'm about to respond, I catch sight of Caden standing in the entrance of the main house. His clothing is similar to what he wore at his coronation—royal ceremonial dress—and the swift memory of that day has my knees weakening. How silly I'd been then to think he could be mine, and that I'd be the one to stand next to him on the castle parapet in Neospes overseeing the Summer Games.

Now he belongs to Inka.

She'd looked beautiful before, but now, standing beside him dressed in full ceremonial garb, the effect is stunning—and agonizing.

I swallow hard, my vision burning, and feel Bass take hold of my elbow. The sensation of his fingers brings me back to reality, and I send him a grateful look. He just nods. We walk toward Caden and Inka together, and both bow.

"General Riven. Bass," Caden says.

"My Lord King. Lady Inka," we both murmur in response.

Inka stops me as we walk past and leans in, her voice quiet. "I look forward to getting to know you better." Startled, I can only nod as we're ushered into the gorgeously tented hall where bits of colored fabric fan in the breeze.

Bass and I leave our weapons in an adjoining space. I'm not happy to be separated from my ninjatas, especially in unfamiliar territory, but at least I have my suit. Bass looks as troubled as I do to be leaving his staff behind.

The area is large, dominated by a huge, round wooden table, covered in all kinds of fresh fruit and foods, including standard Neospes fare. Aenoh sits at the head, and I greet him while Bass reports to Sauer.

"General," he says, his voice booming. "I've waited a long time to meet you. May I call you Riven? Please call me Aenoh. It means hawk in your language."

"Of course," I say. "Mine means to rip apart."

I can feel his gaze assessing me, his eyes narrowing before his lips part in a wide smile. "The daughter of Danton Quinn and the lovely Aurela. How are your parents?"

"My father is a prisoner of the Crown," I say, "and my mother is doing what she does best, defending Neospes from our enemies."

"It was such a pity to hear of your father's madness." Aenoh drains the contents of his mug. His eyes are bright, and I question whether it's the first drink he's consumed. I feel no guilt in pressing my advantage.

"Madness?"

"In his bid to take over your city by aligning with the crazed, fallen prince."

I make my voice as inflectionless as possible. "I wouldn't call it madness, my lord. I would call it avarice. My father wanted something that wasn't his to covet. He thought he would gain it by manipulating the then-prince."

Aenoh laughs a belly laugh. "Luckily for your little city, the real prince was crowned, and Danton's plot foiled."

I ignore his dig and incline my head. "Lucky for us, indeed."

He sips from his refilled mug. "And now you need my help."

"It appears so, my lord."

"Please, call me Aenoh. I insist."

I nod graciously and soften my next question with a bland smile. "Why *are* you interested in my father?"

"He has something I want."

Aenoh stands and claps his hands. Clearly, our conversation is over. I make my way to the only remaining empty seat, which, of course, is on Caden's right. His bride-to-be is on his left. I nod to Sauer, on my other side, and train my eyes on Aenoh.

He raises his cup. "Welcome to our guests on this auspicious occasion. Let us feast in honor of the upcoming nuptials and alliance between our two great cities."

Aenoh takes a swig from his mug, and everyone else follows suit. Servants uncover steaming platters. One offers me a cut of dark meat, and Aenoh bellows, "Roast boar. Caught it myself."

Having eaten in the Otherworld, I'm used to different kinds of food—so are Bass and Caden—but I have to bite back a smile when I see Sauer's queasy expression. After subsisting on engineered food that tastes like nothing and contains perfectly balanced nutrition, eating an animal or plant by-product in its organic form for the first time is daunting.

I chuckle and lean over. "Chew and swallow, Sauer. Come on, thought you were Artok. Didn't your family feed you Sector Seven's freshly roasted rodent?"

"I'm a soldier. We ate rations. Ones that didn't look like . . . this."

"Don't knock it till you try it." I ladle a few different dishes onto the large fig leaf on the table and put it in front of him. "Here, these are mostly vegetarian. Small bites."

"Thanks."

I take a huge bite of pheasant and watch Sauer turn a sickly gray. Grinning, I eat until my stomach feels like it's going to explode. I'm enjoying the meal, but eating also means I don't have to talk to Caden. I feel his glances fluttering in my direction, along with every restless movement of his body.

"So, General," a musical voice says, "what do you think of our forest?"

I turn to Inka, who is leaning forward to see past Caden. Up close she's even more striking. Her eyes, which I'd thought were brown are, in fact, an uncommon tawny color, flecked with gold. "It's beautiful," I say. "And please, my name is Riven."

"Caden tells me that your journey here was quite dangerous." My stomach jerks at the sound of his name on her tongue, but I force my face to remain blank. I must not be doing a good enough job, though, because something flashes in her eyes—understanding, maybe. "He said that if it had not been for you, your ship wouldn't have made it."

"I'm sure the Lord King is exaggerating. It was a team effort."

"I am glad you arrived safely." Inka pushes her chair back, and Caden rises. "Come, Riven. I would love to hear more of your city and your adventures in the Otherworld. Do me the pleasure of accompanying me to the veranda for some air."

Surprise flicks over Caden's face, but he nods courteously and bows. I can feel him watching as we cross the room. Aenoh frowns as we walk past him, his lips are pressed into a slash of obvious displeasure, but he says nothing to his daughter.

Only when we're outside does Inka speak. "This must be hard for you."

"I don't know what you mean," I say, startled.

"Your king. This alliance."

I stare at her, the suit tightening against me as it analyzes her eyes and voice inflection—there's no artifice in her words. "If this alliance will save my city, then it is in the best interests of all of us."

"But not you," she says gently. I don't reply, staring out into the dark green foliage. "Everyone knows of your . . . value to your king."

"I am a soldier," I reply, flinching at her choice of words. "That is all."

Inka sighs and follows my gaze out into the deep, dark forest. "I give you my word that we will defend your city. I will protect your king with my life." I frown at her odd choice of words. Her eyes slide back to the interior of the room and she bites her lip. She looks back at me. Her voice lowers. "Riven, I beg you, you must not—"

"Inka!" A loud bellow cuts her off as Aenoh strides toward us, his face wreathed in phony enthusiasm. "It is time for a dance with your husband-to-be."

"Must not what, Inka?" I whisper urgently.

"Later," she says as her father reaches us. "Of course, Father."

I gnash my teeth in frustration as he leads Inka inside. *What had she been about to tell me?* It had to have been something important.

After a few minutes, I compose myself and return to the hall. The tables have been cleared, and several women are performing a mesmerizing dance in the middle of the room. They sway and weave to the beat of drums, and then pull Caden and Inka to the center of the floor. After a while, even Sylar and Bass join in. I'm too wound up from Inka's comments to enjoy the festivities, declining several offers from Aenoh's people to join the dancing. Instead, I stand in a corner against a wooden pillar.

Sauer comes over to me. "What's bothering you?"

"I'm fine."

"You're not fine." He clears his throat. "I know this can't be easy for you."

"Sauer, I don't need a babysitter, and I don't know why everyone—you, Bass, even Inka—seems to think this is so hard for me. I'm pretty familiar with what my duty entails. If it means letting him go, that's what I must do. Just as *you* did with Shae." I watch the pain flash across his face—he'd been in love with my sister. They'd risked their lives for each other, but Neospes—and duty—had always come first for both of them.

"Doesn't mean it's easy." Sauer's hand slides across to grasp mine in a comforting squeeze. Surprised, I squeeze back. Despite being Artok, Sauer is not a demonstrative person. We stand in companionable silence, staring at the revelry for a while. "What did you mean when you said Inka thinks it's hard for you, too?"

In a low voice, I tell him about the conversation I'd had with her on the terrace. His face tightens. "Something's going on," he murmurs. "I've had a strange feeling since we got here, as if they're stalling or hiding something."

"Why do you think they want my father?"

He frowns. "Vector tech?"

"But why? Advanced imaging tech and automatic sensory weapons conceal this whole facility. It seems weird that they'd offer us help in return for his know-how in wiring cybernetic corpses."

"We'll get to the bottom of it."

"Before or after we agree to take their armies with us to Neospes?" The implication hangs heavy in the air—we could be trading one evil for another. Without understanding the objective of our allies, we're running blind. "It could be a Trojan Horse."

"A what?"

"It's an old Otherworld story. An old race of people called the Greeks used deception to enter the city of Troy and defeat them by hiding soldiers in a great wooden horse that was presented as a gift for their city, when it fact, it was the opposite. We are inviting Aenoh's army into Neospes for help. What if we're being tricked like the Trojans were?" I shake my head. "You're not the only one with a bad feeling, Sauer. We have to find out what Aenoh wants, and what Inka meant to tell me."

"You think he's planning something?"

"I don't know, but it doesn't feel right." I stare at Caden dancing with Inka, his hand on her waist, and my stomach sours. I can't help feeling that we're all pawns, being moved around by Aenoh. He's taking advantage of our vulnerability.

"I'll look into it." Sauer sighs. "But I hope you're wrong. We need allies more than anything right now."

"I know," I murmur, watching the dancers toss bright yellow flowers over Caden and Inka. Aenoh steps forward to bind their hands with red string—some symbolic ceremony that announces their engagement. Caden's eyes meet mine across the room, his feelings plain—fear, regret, sorrow, pain, love— and something inside of me snaps.

I retreat from the hall, lowering myself swiftly to the ground. The twilight sky above me is purplish-red and half-overcast as I disappear deep into the trees, the sounds of the celebration fading into the background.

"It's over," I say to myself. "Let it go. Let him go."

I close my eyes and focus on the voices of the forest, feeling my breathing calm with each slow inhale and exhale. The noises around me amplify, separating into distinct sounds: a chirp of some nocturnal bird; a low-pitched whistle; the creaking of boughs above. Something rustles in the undergrowth behind me. I turn, unafraid, and come face-to-face with some kind of jungle feline with bright purple rosette markings coloring its golden pelt. It's easily double my size.

The cat stares at me, yellow eyes glowing, its mouth gaping open to utter a soft growl. Lowering myself to a crouch, I study the creature. It's likely a carnivorous hunter, so I keep my motions smooth and unthreatening. Suddenly, a snapping noise above us has its forelegs bunching, and a snarl breaks from its mouth. It's poised to attack. Meeting it head-on, I lean forward, my mouth bared in my own snarl, and let blue lights flicker along my face in the same pattern as the creature's hide. The cat stops mid-motion as we stare each other down, the harsh huff of its breath the only movement between us, one killer facing another. We stay like this for what seems like an eternity until it flicks its head dismissively and bounds off into the jungle.

Strangely awed, I rock back onto my haunches with a thoughtful sigh.

Lesson learned—choose your battles.

18

LINES IN THE SAND

"WHAT DO YOU mean your army is not ready?" Sauer shouts, pounding his fists on the tabletop. We're in a large amphitheater in the first domed ring, seated around a table made of metal and glass, and enabled with all kinds of technology. We could be standing in a similar room in Neospes, with the same line of stern-faced soldiers positioned at the rear of the chamber. No doubt, they're part of this mysterious army that suddenly "isn't ready." I can understand Sauer's frustration, having come this far only to be told that we won't be getting the help we need—at least, not immediately.

"That is not what we agreed on," Sauer insists.

Aenoh crosses his arms over his chest. He's changed from his casual clothing to military gear, although the wooden piercings in his face still make him quite fearsome to look at. "Our army will follow in a few days," he says.

"How does that help us?" Sauer is irritated. "Every second we waste puts Neospes in jeopardy. We risked everything to make the journey here so that we could return with an army at our back. Instead, we'll have nothing. You gave us your word."

"And you gave us yours that we'd get Danton Quinn. Where is he?"

Sauer's eyes narrow. "He is in Neospes. Once the threat is contained, you will have your exchange. Does your bond mean nothing, then?"

"We honor our promises," Aenoh says, lips thinning at Sauer's insulting tone.

"Commander," Caden says, trying to defuse the mounting tension. "Let's hear what Aenoh proposes, and then we will walk through the plan again."

Aenoh clears his throat, and Sauer resumes his seat. I move down the table, recalling a few faces from the feast who are apparently Aenoh's advisory council, as well as Cristobal and Inka, seated a few seats down from her father. A fierce-looking woman is seated next to Inka, one I don't recognize. She's as statuesque as the princess, with coffee-brown skin and short, spiky hair. Perhaps she's Inka's guard, although from what I've seen, Inka seems more than capable of defending herself.

Arven, Sylar, and Bass are seated between the woman and me, and Caden is opposite Aenoh.

Bass hasn't said a word. He disappeared after the feast. When I asked him where he'd gone, he was evasive, muttering that he needed some air. I couldn't blame him. The whole song-and-dance routine is a little too much to handle when the people of Neospes edge closer to death. Even now, Bass seems preoccupied, his fingers drumming on the side of his chair as if he's somewhere else completely.

"You okay?" I ask him in a low whisper.

"Yeah."

"Do you have something to say, General?" Aenoh booms. All heads in the room turn in my direction.

"Yes, as a matter of fact, I do," I say coolly. "It seems counterintuitive to head back empty-handed. Perhaps you can spare some of your men, if not the whole army."

"As a matter of fact," he says in a mocking tone, "we have something better." He nods to a few of the people at the rear of the room. As they exit, he brings up a hologram above the table. It's obviously a weapon, a very compact machine about the size of an oxygen canister. It looks like some kind of enhanced electro-laser.

"What is that?" Sauer asks.

"It's a directed-energy weapon," Aenoh, says, flicking his fingers to make the hologram burst into separate fragments. "One designed to completely disable any robotics, including Reptiles. It's designed to be harmless to humans, but there is a setting that will evaporate any organic matter, should you so choose. The firing mechanism is built with pulsed electromagnetic energy."

"So it's a maser," Bass says quietly, his fingers still drumming. I'd forgotten that he's super qualified in robotics. "Amplified electromagnetic waves."

"Yes," Aenoh says. "You know of this technology?"

Bass nods. "They tried to build one of these early on in the War, but couldn't get it to be strong enough at longer distances. The Machines picked our soldiers off before they could even fire off a shot. They couldn't get the stimulated emission piece to work. How'd you do it?"

Aenoh smiles. "That, my boy, is proprietary."

Bass's fingers clutch the table, and a muscle jerks in his cheek. But Sauer gets to the punch before he does. "If that thing is going anywhere near my ship," he says in a firm voice, "then you better explain how it works. We have a highly reactive core and I'm not taking any chances with unknown tech."

If Aenoh's lips could get any thinner, they'd disappear entirely. But he concedes after a silent exchange with Cristobal, nodding at one of his advisors, a bald man with piercing blue eyes. "Matias will explain."

Matias stands and clears his throat. He expands the picture on the hologram, delving into its operating components. "We experimented with magnetic field compression within the device, using frozen hydrogen in the outer shell. As a result, the reactivity of the compressed core increased exponentially with a lower heat signature. We incorporated quantum processes, using gamma ray photons, to maximize the EMR or radiation burst." He takes a breath, canvassing the room. "We were able to harness the combination to develop a working prototype." Matias splits apart his finger and thumb to pinpoint a section in the holo, indicating the interior mechanisms of the weapon's core. "Lastly, we used a particle accelerator here to maximize the electromagnetic burst, creating a kind of megaburst."

Bass nods, and points to a series of concentric tubes. "So you're saying that you used the same electromagnetic waves to energize the electrons, and then push outward from a circular accelerator here to increase the blast radius and amplitude."

"Yes, that is correct."

Bass leans back in his chair and exhales. "Risky, but brilliant."

The man smiles at Bass's praise. "Despite the considerable risks, the result was beyond our expectations—basically, a deadly voltage surge from the changing electric and magnetic fields that would have a devastating effect on all electronic mechanisms, sensor components, and automated operating systems."

"So, there you have it," Aenoh says.

"What's the fallout?" Caden asks.

"Little or no effect on us, but all communications, electronic weapons, and the like would be knocked out. It's a last resort."

"Let me get this straight," Sauer says. "You're giving us this fantastic, *last resort* that will obliterate our enemies, but it will also knock out any defensive measures we have in place, leaving us vulnerable to attack."

"Attack from whom?" Aenoh says smoothly, spreading his palms. "You'll have destroyed your enemies. Isn't that what you want?"

He's so transparent. I suppress the urge to burst out laughing. I meet Sauer's eyes, thinking of our conversation about Troy. Using this technology would only serve the Avarians. Their city will be untouched, while Neospes will fall.

"Destroying our comms and defense is not an option," Caden says softly.

"You can rebuild." Aenoh points a finger at his daughter. "You are allied with Avaria. Our cities are united."

Sure, after you've plundered our resources. I frown. It would take years, decades even, to rebuild Neospes. We live simply, but much of our defense and food production depends on electronic technology.

Not to mention, me.

Sauer's face is tight, as is Bass's. I can see the tension in Caden's jaw as he analyzes the scenarios. If they detonate that weapon with me within range, I'd be just as affected as the Reptiles, and there's no way to predict what would happen. There's a good chance I would die.

More than a good chance.

But, of course, Aenoh wouldn't know that. There are only five people in this room who know the truth about what I am, and they're citizens of Neospes and loyal to the death.

But what if Aenoh *does* know? What if this is part of some elaborate plan to get rid of me? Era wouldn't have told Cristobal or any of the other Faction leaders, but things have a way of getting out. Philip and Charisma both knew about me, and well, I've learned that loyalties can be shifted with the right incentive.

"It seems we have no choice," Caden says in an even tone.

"The armies will follow, that I promise you." Aenoh pauses for dramatic effect, staring at each of us in turn. "Because Matias and I will accompany you on your return." Silence follows this announcement. The chief of Avaria coming back with us to a war zone, armed only with a deadly cannon and a weapons expert? "Matias is the only one who knows how to operate the weapon."

"I'm sure he can explain to Bass how it works," I interject. "In fact, that may be wiser, just as a precaution."

"Of course," Aenoh says, nodding to Matias. "We will leave in an hour, which will give us enough time to prepare."

Inka pushes her chair back and stands. "I will come, as well."

"No, daughter," Aenoh snarls. "We agreed that you would remain here as leader in my stead."

She glares at him, her body rigid. "*You* agreed." A fiery look passes between them, but Inka doesn't back down. "Your council can lead while you're away. My place, as you've decreed, is with the Lord King of Neospes, is it not?"

"Enola will go," he growls, indicating the woman at Inka's side. "Your place is here."

"Why? So you can throw her off the side of the ship? We both know how you feel about her, and so does everyone else in this room."

His words are a vicious hiss. "This is not the place."

"It's never the place, or the time, or anything. Enola and I are both going."

Aenoh's face darkens and he pounds the table so hard that the hologram flickers. "Inka! That is enough. You will stay, as will *she*." The venom in his voice has the hair rising on my neck. Apparently, there's no love lost between Inka's guard and her father.

"You cannot stop me."

His nostrils flare. "You are my daughter."

"And now bound to another."

It's like watching two brilliant swordsmen duel, neither giving in to the other.

Aenoh changes tactics, his voice becoming gentler as if he's suddenly remembered his audience. "Inka . . . I cannot worry about your safety, and the people need you here."

"The people will listen to what you tell them." Something flickers across her face—a silent threat, maybe—and her father blanches. I wonder if it has anything to do with what she'd begun to tell me at the feast.

The air is charged, but eventually Aenoh addresses the group. "The four of us will accompany you. Cristobal will update the Faction. Our armies will follow." He looks like he's going to explode. "Prepare their transport," he tells the soldiers at the back of the room. "We leave within the hour."

And just like that, everyone clears the room. Bass takes off with Matias, and Arven and Sylar head back to the ship. Sauer and I escort Caden back to his quarters in the Avarian dome. Cristobal accompanies us since he'll join Caden in briefing Era before we leave. As we're walking, I pull Sauer a few steps behind Cristobal and the Lord King, keeping my voice low to evade the cameras' built-in voice recognition analysis software. "I don't trust him."

Sauer's response is barely audible: "Me, either, but we don't have much choice. At least we have a weapon we can use against Cale if we need it."

"I don't have to tell you what will happen if we fire that thing . . . what will happen to me."

Sauer studies my face. "We just need to make sure you're out of range deep within the Peaks. You'll be safe. Arven knows those tunnels. We'll make sure you're there before we launch the weapon."

"What about Neospes? We'll be vulnerable without our defenses in place."

"We'll have to take our chances. And we need to figure out where Inka's loyalties lie. She knows something . . . something that Aenoh is willing to barter for her silence."

"I don't trust her, either," I say. "At least, not fully. Keep an eye on Caden. As much as Era trusts Cristobal, I think he's in on whatever Aenoh's planning. I'll catch up with you at the ship."

"Where are you going?"

"Need some air," I say. That, and I want to find Inka to finish our conversation. Sauer arches an eyebrow at the four guards trailing behind us. "I can handle them."

I take off to the right, watching as two of the guards veer off to follow me. I maintain a leisurely pace, jumping onto a short transport carrier that takes me to the edge of the primary dome, where the security team stops me.

"Identification."

"I don't have ID for your city. I'm one of your chief's guests."

The two men stare at each other and consult a tablet in front of them. "We cannot let you pass without a proper escort."

"I forgot," I say with a bright smile. "Here come mine right now." I glance at the two guards, both of whom had been in the session room earlier, and make a big show of waving them over. "They have Aenoh's clearance, and I would like to pass."

"Let her through," one of them says. "We have been instructed to stay with her."

"Yes, sir."

The open-air monorail sweeps through the indoor forest. This time, I see a flock of brilliant blue birds take flight, screeching loudly, and keeping pace with the monorail before swerving off into the trees. Despite my suspicions about their chief, what the Avarians have accomplished here is truly a miracle.

When the ride ends, I retrace my steps to the tent where the feast was held, the two men still trailing behind me. I don't see Inka anywhere, but I do see the girl who dressed me earlier.

"Hey," I say. "Do you remember me?"

"Of course," she says, bowing.

"Have you seen Lady Inka?"

"She was here a few minutes ago," she says. "She went hunting."

"Hunting?" I recall the longbow at her side the first time I met her.

"Yes, in the forest."

"Thank you," I say in a loud voice. "Will you escort me to the hut? I'd like to refresh myself before the journey and, perhaps, have a short rest." She nods, and we cross the roped bridges, reaching the hut in no time. My two shadows place themselves on either side of the door, and the girl shoots them a meek look. "Don't worry about them," I say sweetly. "They're here at Aenoh's request to make sure I'm safe."

I thank the girl so much that she's blushing as she backs out of the room. "Please do not disturb me," I tell the men stationed outside. "I wish to rest before we leave."

They nod. I'm sure they're wondering why a so-called ruthless general wants to sleep when she should be worrying about other things.

But I have no intention of sleeping.

I make my way to the window where I'd seen Bass and take a deep breath, staring at the precipice below. Inching through the window, I plant my foot firmly on a thick branch and lower myself until I'm flat against the side of the hut. The branch sways slightly, but holds my weight. I take a deep breath and swing my body down to the next bough, hanging for a millisecond before I feel bark beneath my toes. Maneuvering my way down, branch after branch, until I reach wider limbs, I jump to an adjacent tree and glance up. There's no movement on the bridges alerting others to my disappearance.

Once on the ground, I take off into the forest, using my tracking senses—a bent leaf here, a partial footprint there, the fragrance of an exotic flower just brushed by human hands. I engage my suit, pulling empirical data from the forest floor, running it against Inka's biometrics, and calculating the odds that the tracks are hers.

I speed up, feeling the wind whip through my hair. A group of chattaras screech above my head, swinging from branch to branch and keeping pace with me. Their colors blur as they leap together—russet, tan, gold, and black—wildly jumping from tree to tree and making odd barking noises. There must be almost twenty of them. I run faster, leaving them in the distance, and follow the tracking algorithm of my suit.

Exhilarated, I come to the edge of the river where the trail ends. I catch my breath leaning against a vine-covered tree, and breathe in the lush scent of the forest. I've never experienced anything like this, not even in the Otherworld. This part of the river is shallow, but I'm mindful of the suit until a message indicator on my retina screen catches my eye—*waterproof setting*. My father wasn't kidding—this is a pretty nice adjustment. I click on it, feeling the material shift against my skin, before removing my boots and stepping into the cool water. The stones feel heavenly against my bare soles. I let myself indulge in the sensation for a few moments when an odd sound catches my attention.

Wading across the river, I round a bend and pause in surprise. A long, thin waterfall descends from a steeply carved gulley. But that's not what makes my jaw drop. It's the woman standing beneath the plunging stream of water. I've found Inka, and, to be honest, I'm sort of wishing that I could un-find her right now. As if I needed to know that she has a perfect body, with not a blemish in sight.

I try to back away, aware that I'm invading her privacy but, of course, I'm not that lucky. Inka's shout makes me stop. She beckons me with a smile as she wades over. Without an iota of embarrassment, she steps out onto the mossy forest floor and slips into a cotton garment. I look away. If I looked anything like her, I'd probably have plenty of confidence, too.

"I was hoping you'd find me," she says, and then laughs, shaking some droplets from her hair. "Although, not precisely at this moment."

"Sorry," I mutter. "What do you mean you were hoping I'd find you?"

"I did leave quite an obvious trail for you," she says, arching an eyebrow. "If I didn't want to be found, you wouldn't have found me."

"Thank you for making it easy."

She grins and waves at the fierce woman standing guard on the embankment, her face, as always, expressionless. "Enola, come. I want you to meet the General."

I notice that Enola has changed from her leather gear to a cotton tank and sarong. Nonetheless, a row of deadly knives rides on a harness at her hip. I also see the crisscrossing layer of scars across her shoulders. Inka catches me staring. "Enola used to be a slave until I freed her. She had a terrible master with a great love of violence."

"A slave?" I frown. "I didn't think Avaria had slavery."

"We still do—it's an abhorrent part of our culture, one that I'm trying to eradicate. Unfortunately, changing lifelong customs is not an easy task. You remember the girl who escorted you to your changing hut? She is one of Aenoh's."

I see Inka in a new light. People who fight for others are easier to trust—they're not out for their own gain. "She was kind."

"When I am chief, I hope to be rid of the practice." Her fingers brush the scars that are visible on Enola's arm. "For now, Enola is my guard and my most trusted confidante. Now you can understand why my father reacted the way he did earlier. She was a slave, and is common-born. I don't care about such divisions. My father does, but he isn't always right."

I can't help but think of the parallel barriers between Caden and me. Our situation is far more complicated than a friendship between a princess and an ex-slave—and far more tragic. Thinking of Caden, I remember why I was seeking Inka in the first place. "What were you going to tell me at the feast?"

"You shouldn't trust Aenoh." She studies me as though I'm a fascinating jungle creature. "He knows about you. He knows what you are, and he wants you."

"Wants me? What do you mean?"

"He *wants* you."

I flush and laugh uneasily, the sound reverberating through the trees. "Well, he can't have me."

"He already does." I look at her, confused. "The Faction bartered your father's life in return for his assistance to your city. Aenoh offered your father the option of his life for yours. So now you have been given to him."

Knowing every despicable detail about my father, I never expected much from him, but this is a new low. "He can't do that," I whisper. "I don't belong to him. I don't belong to any-one."

"In Avarian culture, it is a father's right to arrange a match for his daughter."

"We are not Avarian."

"Not yet, but when the battle is over, and Neospes falls under our control as my father intends, you will be."

19

MAN OR MACHINE

I AM SEETHING. No wonder he'd seemed remorseful and had given me the suit like some consolation prize. I can't even think about the man without wanting to dice him into tiny, unrecognizable pieces and scatter him to the wind. But my greedy, soulless father will have to wait. Right now, I have to deal with being in close quarters with a man twice my age who wants me to be his little hybrid breeding toy. The ship is tight enough with six people, let alone ten.

We'd left Avaria on time. Inka made me swear not to share with anyone what she'd told me—at least, not until we reached the relative safety of Neospes. Her father has a way of making ugly things happen, and it turns out that Matias isn't just a weapons expert. He's also her father's right-hand man. He's trained in a full range of combat techniques and is particularly skilled at making people disappear.

"You'd be putting your king at risk," Inka had said. "Aenoh will stop at nothing to get what he wants. Even if it means regicide."

So I've kept my distance and held my tongue. I agreed to stay quiet for now because, frankly, the less Aenoh knows about what *I* know, the better. And I have no intention of marrying that old lecher. I'll electro-fry myself first.

I glance at Bass, sitting in his usual spot in front of the plasma cannon. Sylar and Enola are up top with us. I'm not sure what the new rotation is, but I think Caden is at the helm with Sauer and Inka. The other three are resting. It's an interesting dynamic, that's for sure. I'm positive that Sauer doesn't want three Avarians piloting the ship at any given moment. Other than the few words we exchanged at the waterfall, Enola hasn't said much. I trust her more than I trust Aenoh or Matias, though.

"Hey, Bass." I nudge him with my boot. "I feel like I haven't seen you at all in the last five hours."

He gives me a strained smile. "Trying to understand the maser contraption we have on board. Matias was . . . difficult."

"How so?"

"*Evasive* is probably a better word."

"But you know how it works, right?"

"More or less," Bass says. "As much as I could learn in a couple hours, anyway." He grins at my daunted expression. "I'm kidding. Have I ever steered you wrong?"

"No. Anyway, you owe me for saving your life when the moss monster attacked. I expect you to return the favor when you detonate that thing and I stay alive."

"That won't happen. You dying, I mean."

His tone makes me pause. "How do you know?"

"Because I do. Now, will you shut up for a second so I can enjoy my sliver of peace before we have to go down into the hell pit?"

I grin. "Sure."

Sauer's pushing our speed. My suit's information panel indicates that we're going over two hundred miles an hour, almost double the speed of our outbound trip. Either Sauer's become more comfortable with the Machine technology or he's worried about the mega-killer maser we have on board—maybe a combination of the two. If something goes wrong with that device, we could blow ourselves and half the planet into oblivion.

"The maser," I say in a low voice to Bass. "It's contained, right?"

"Locked down and only Sauer has access—" His words are torn from his mouth as—suddenly—a massive collision rocks the hover, nearly tossing us off. It's followed by another and another. "What the hell?" he yells, hanging on for dear life.

The hover lurches to a brutal stop. "Sauer, what are you doing?" I yell into the comms unit. "Why are we stopping?"

"Sensors show we're coming into some bad weather," he replies. "If a wind gust rips under us we could flip, and with that weapon on board I can't take any chances. Have to set down. What are you seeing out there?"

"Holy shit." Bass's eyes are wide as he stares at something over my shoulder.

I turn and my breath stalls. The dark cloud on the horizon is thick and ominous, roaring forward like a massive wave of earth. Lightning rips through its center as sand cyclones spit bits of debris over us—sand, gravel, and fist-sized rocks—

getting bigger by the second. The hull rattles as a huge chunk shatters at my feet.

"Sandstorm," I reply to Sauer as I decipher the information from my suit pinging back from orbiting satellites. "Coming out of the west, and it's big. Visibility is nearing zero. Rocks the size of bowling balls. Bass, we better take cover."

"That's not good," Bass mutters.

"What's a bowling ball?" Sylar asks.

"A big heavy ball about the size of my head," Bass says, opening the hatch and ushering her and Enola inside. I follow, sealing the entrance behind me.

We huddle together and watch the storm increase in intensity on screen, feeling the impact of gigantic pieces of rock pummeling the sides of the ship. "Sauer, we're not going to be able to withstand much more. One of those rocks is going to hit the hover gear, or worse." My gaze slides to the cargo hold where Aenoh's weapon is being stored.

"What do you want to do? We can't outrun the storm, not at its current velocity. We'd be lucky to last five minutes, if the wind doesn't flip us. We're sitting ducks."

"Not necessarily," I say, then pause, staring at Aenoh out of the corner of my eye.

"What do you mean?"

I don't answer. We're all going to die if I don't do something. "I can fly it," I say softly so only Sauer can hear me.

"Riven, you're not . . . qualified."

I glare at him. Technically, this ship was built for Machines *by* Machines, and I'm the closest thing to that. "I think I'm more *qualified* than most," I say firmly. "Everyone strap in.

You two, with me up front," I tell Sauer and Caden. I see Bass's surprised look—he's kind of been my wingman the entire trip. "Sorry, Bass, there are only two jump seats in the cockpit. I need Sauer, and the Lord King has to be with him. Plus, I want you out here in case anything goes wrong with that shit-cannon."

"What are you going to do?" Bass asks, narrowing his eyes.

"I'm going to fly us out of here."

Sauer shakes his head. "Riven, we don't know if the ship can take it."

Another collision makes us stagger. "The ship can't take much more of this. Either you give me the go-ahead or we stay here and get crushed."

"Are you sure?" he says, drawing me aside.

"This craft was built for . . . a certain kind of pilot." Like Sauer, I keep my voice low, even though I can see Aenoh straining to hear. "I'm pretty sure it's computerized, and I can sync the coding to my brain. The suit will do most of the work. I'm taking a gamble, but the alternative is worse."

"Do it." The order is from Caden. "I trust you."

"Don't count your chickens just yet," I mutter. "Now, strap in and do me a favor, Sauer. Close the bridge access panel, will you?" I'd rather work without any distractions or disturbances . . . like Aenoh obsessing over my every move. Sauer does as I've requested, sealing the bridge off from the rest of the cabin. I take a deep, calming breath, feeling the ship rock from the force of the wind.

I enter a few commands into the ship's computer and sync to it so I'm remotely connected to the operating system. As the ship runs its execution scripts, the rush of data is over-whelming.

Okay, Riven, take it slow, I tell myself as I engage. The engine reboots and the hover rises off the ground. *Slow and steady.* But my efforts are thwarted as a huge gust of wind sends the entire vessel spinning. I struggle to regain control, manually entering commands, but my response time is too slow. The ship sinks into a tailspin, putting us completely at the storm's mercy.

"Strap in, Riven," Sauer yells, panicked.

Collapsing into the command chair, I hit the safety button and the gel covering settles over me like a chest plate, harden-ing into place and holding me securely in the seat. An entire new array of instruments lights up on the dashboard, includ-ing two glowing liquid plasma orbs at the end of each of my armrests. I notice my vitals pop up on screen—heart rate, brain activity, blood pressure—the works.

"What's it doing?" Caden shouts.

"I think it's calibrating my stats to its operating system, making *me* its command center."

After a few seconds, the screen goes blank, and then two words glow: EXECUTE OVERRIDE? My fingers reach for the spheres of shimmering, white matter.

"Riven, no," Sauer says. "You don't know what that is."

I study the palm-sized devices. "It's a port."

"A port for what?"

"For me." I plunge my gloved hands into the shimmering orbs without a second thought and feel my entire body come alive. Energy fires through me, the entire suit electrifying and making blue starbursts leap from my skin. Sauer and Caden shield their eyes from the intense brightness. Suddenly, I'm one with the hover . . . no, not just one with it. I *become* the hover. It is responding as if it's an extension of me.

"What happened?" Caden asks.

"I think this whole suit is a neural conductor," I say. Danton must have anticipated that I'd be piloting this craft, and he engineered the suit to maximize uplink capabilities. "I don't know how, but I'm literally plugged into the ship. I'm inside its brain, or maybe its brain is inside mine."

Caden frowns. "That's not exactly reassuring."

"It's like an extra limb. All I have to do is tell it to move. I think it's how the Machines flew these ships—all through an autonomous mother control center. The suit has overridden it so it thinks *I'm* the control center." I close my eyes and feel the entire ship shudder as the propulsion jets come online. "Hold on. We are out of here."

Go.

The ship obeys like magic, rising sharply through the wind, rocks, and sand. I dodge oncoming projectiles and lightning strikes with ease, my brain at one with the ship's autonetics. I only have to think it, and my wishes are executed with flawless precision. Exhilarated, I keep ascending until all I see through the screen is a welcome crimson sky. Below us, the ruthless storm is a dark shape on a path of destruction.

Settling my hands on the orbs, I push forward, steering the craft with a flick of my fingers. We're racing through the sky at quadruple the speed of any hover. At this rate, we'll reach Neospes in hours. The invigorating sensation of being connected to the vessel's computer system doesn't wane, and I'm tempted to push it further to see just what it can do. I can't quite explain what it feels like—maybe like being on the inside of a giant robot. I lean right and the ship responds automatically, bearing right.

"This is amazing." I glance over my shoulder. Caden and Sauer are both watching me with twin expressions of awe. "What?"

"Nothing," Sauer says. "Well done."

"Everyone okay back there?" I ask on the comms. "Bass?"

"Yes. That was a little gnarly, but we're no worse for wear," he says. He snorts under his breath. "Matias might have thrown up a little."

I hear an indignant, "I did not!"

"Just kidding, man." I can tell Bass is enjoying poking fun at the unflappable Avarian. "Who knew you could fly a ship like this?"

"I'm thinking my father knew. That means you knew."

There's silence on the other end of the comms. "We hoped it would work. It's my programming."

"Figured. Seems like your style." Entering the coordinates of Neospes, I let the ship do the work. "Sit tight until we stabilize. We're not out of the woods yet."

For a moment, as the ship charts a course, responding to my thoughts, I wonder why I'd ever been opposed to using Machine-engineered robotics. It's superior technology, far beyond anything any human has ever developed. It's heady enough manipulating one of these things. . . . I can't imagine how a central control could have operated hundreds of them. Then again, the super computers had infinite interfaces. No wonder they'd taken over.

Piloting the ship, I feel energized. More than when I'd fought those cannibals in the bone yard. Then, the nanobes had given me strength to fight. Now, it feels like it's the other way around—like I'm giving them strength. Maybe they're getting stronger.

"Feel free to move around, but I'm not familiar with the atmospheric conditions up here. I'm going to take her down some, but it could be bumpy."

"You're glowing," Caden says, coming up behind me.

I turn to him. "What?"

"Your eyes, they're electric, like you're lit up from the inside."

"It's the nanobes," I say, and swallow hard at the look in his eyes.

It seems as if Caden wants to say something more, but then surprises me by leaning down and giving me a hard, upside-down kiss. Sauer turns away, embarrassed, and makes his way into the main cabin.

"Caden, you shouldn't be—"

"Don't say anything," he says, peppering my eyes, my cheeks, my nose with soft butterfly kisses. "Just accept it." He lowers his voice to a whisper as the door slides closed behind Sauer. "And that you're sexy as hell when you go all 'borg."

He captures my lips in another swift kiss. I don't know if it's because of all the nanobes firing inside of me like liquid adrenaline, or because of the strange position of his mouth, but every part of my skin feels like it's on fire. My lips cling to the warm wetness of his, the nanobes going into a supernova frenzy. The combination of the stolen embrace and the thought of Inka so near makes the moment even more heated.

What's five seconds? She'll have him for the rest of her life.

Yanking Caden forward, I kiss him back with a fierce desperation. The ship dips suddenly as I lose focus, and we break apart so I can regain control.

Out of the corner of my eye, I see Bass standing near the access panel. I wonder how long he's been there, and I blush. His face is shadowed, but he hides his expression well as he disappears from view.

"I need to concentrate," I tell Caden. "I can't think clearly when you're doing that. And you shouldn't be kissing me anyway. You're engaged to a girl on the other side of that door."

"Sorry," Caden whispers against my mouth. "I can't stop thinking of the perks."

"The what?"

"The perks of being a cyborg," he whispers against my ear with a grin.

Oh. *Those* perks. I feel the rush of heat intensify from somewhere deep in the pit of my stomach, rising up through my back to my neck. The ship makes a sharp swing to the left, veering madly off course, until I manage to get it back on track.

"Sorry, turbulence," I announce on the comms.

"Nice recovery." Caden smirks.

"You need to go or I'm going to crash this thing. This is why the Machines were excellent pilots—they had no emotions. Now, go check on your future daddy-in-law."

Caden places a hand over his heart. "That's just cold. Fine. I'm going."

"Will you send Sauer in? And Bass."

"Of course."

I shake my head at Caden's retreating back, my heart racing and lips tingling. That boy will be the death of me. No matter how much I try to be indifferent, my puny defenses are no match for him. Especially when he kisses like that. We'd both been caught up in the moment, and the truth is, I'd wanted the kiss as much as he did. His timing is terrible, but it could be worse. We could still be stuck in the middle of an angry rock storm. In the grand scheme of things, a kiss is pretty harmless. Or, at least, I think so until I see Bass's cool expression.

I ask Sauer to go run a diagnostic with Arven on possible hull damage. "See this area near one of the propulsion jets? I think it must have gotten hit. I'm sensing a slight drag, and I'm not sure what's causing it. Can you isolate? We may need to shut it down. I'm dropping low just in case we need to switch to hover mode."

Once Sauer leaves and I've launched the new lower flight parameters, I turn my attention to Bass. "Okay, spill it. What are you pissed off about?"

He eyes me and snaps, "You really think making out with the Lord King is the best idea right now?"

"Who're you? My keeper?"

"No, I'm your friend, and I don't want you to get hurt."

"I'm a big girl, Bass. I can take care of myself. And, frankly, that's none of your business. It's no one's business but mine and Caden's."

Bass's mouth thins. "And what about Neospes?"

"What about it?"

"What if everyone else gets hurt because of your actions?"

I shrug, frustrated. "It was a kiss, Bass. There's a lot you don't know about what's going on. And, honestly, things are probably going to get a lot worse."

He sighs, raking his hand through his hair. "I know more than you think. We need to be focused right now. In the field, out there, it's us against a highly motivated enemy."

I get where he's coming from, and I'd be concerned, too, if the situation were reversed. "Look, Bass, you're the last person I want to fight with. What I have with Caden is . . . complicated. There's history and, yes, I hate that he's bound in this alliance, promised to someone more worthy than me. But I swear, none of that will affect my judgment when it comes to Cale or defending Neospes. You have my word."

"She's not more worthy than you," Bass says quietly. "It's the other way around."

"Politics." I smile at him. "We cool?"

"Yeah."

"Okay, I'm going to need you to—"

My words are cut off as the ship jolts violently to one side. Piercing alarms start screeching and flashing red across the entire instrument panel. Sauer comes running onto the bridge, followed closely by Caden and Arven.

"What now?" Sauer asks urgently. "We should be near the far side of the Outers."

"I don't know. The sensors are registering ionized weapons attacking the ship. Something's going after the shields."

"Something? What? How?"

"From there," Bass says, bringing up a terrestrial view on screen.

A gigantic wave of Reptiles is firing active ion blasters at us. Sauer's right—we're at the edge of the Outers, the Neospes dome just visible on the horizon. We should have guessed that Cale would be waiting with an ambush. The enemies on the ground aren't the only assailants. Suddenly, the ship's display is full of interference from dozens of flying Reptiles. The hull shudders as another wave of attacks pounds the underside.

"Shields are at twenty-one percent," I say. "We took a beating during the rock storm, and they're using an ion pulse to chip away at it."

"Why?"

"I'm guessing they're trying to bring us down."

"Can we pull up and go around?" Sauer asks.

"Not with the damage to the engine. We could implode. If we can't flee, we have to fight." I glance at Caden, my eyes glowing blue. "Permission to engage while we still have a chance."

"Granted."

Closing my eyes, I focus on the target—the Reptiles with the ion cannons pointed at the ship—and engage our plasma weapons. It's like being plugged into a video game where my hands are the guns and my brain is the trigger. I exhale and start firing. Fire erupts where the plasma cannon makes contact, but the Reptiles keep shooting.

"Shields at eleven percent," Arven says. "Nine, and decreasing fast."

"We need a new plan," Sauer replies. "I say we risk the engine."

"Three percent."

I make the call, pulling up sharply. I'd rather risk exploding at fifty thousand feet than be swarmed by a group of carnivorous Reptiles. But it's too late. Our shields have failed completely, and suddenly we've lost all forward momentum.

"What the hell?" Sauer growls.

"Hang on!" I set the engine for the maximum acceleration and, for a minute, it seems like that's working—we start moving up. Then everything powers down suddenly. I lose the uplink and am booted out. For a half second, I wonder why we're not falling out of the sky. I try to reboot but the control panel has gone completely dark.

"This is not good," I mutter.

I try to resume communication, using emergency power to reboot and force the ship's computer to come online. All of a sudden, the vessel starts moving slowly backward.

"Can you see what's got us?" Sauer asks, punching in commands on the screen.

"Yes," I reply in a dull voice. "It's an energy field graviton net. That's why they wanted to take out our shields. Cale wants us alive." I sink back into the chair studying the cabin's occupants. "We should have destroyed that damned tracker."

"The one with the picture of the cage?" Caden asks.

Bass frowns. "Why?"

"That thing ran a full schematic on the ship. The photo message was a decoy. We were worried about decoding the message, when we should have realized what the tracker was really doing—luring us right into a trap."

"How?" Aenoh asks.

I stare at him for a moment before responding. Bet he didn't plan on this happening. "Bass, why don't you explain to the chief how gravity and quantum mechanics works?" I don't hide my sarcasm.

"It's all about mass, matter, and gravitational force," Bass obliges. "Energy field graviton nets have to be specifically constructed based on their targets, which is why they were unpopular during the War. The smallest change of mass on a metal ship would impact a graviton net's ability to hold a target immobile, much less manipulate it. However, if you had exact specs on hand—say from a tracker that just happened to be on board—such a net would be impossible to escape."

"Can we get out of it?" Aenoh asks.

"No."

"What does that mean for us?" Inka whispers, watching Bass with wide, but fearless, eyes.

Bass looks up, his mouth twisting. "It means we're royally screwed."

20

PRINCES AND PAWNS

WE STARE AT each other in silence, feeling the inexorable traction of the net pulling us closer to the Reptiles with every passing second. The tension is thick.

"We should use the device the minute we get on the ground," Matias suggests. "Eliminate them all, including your fallen prince. It's the only answer. There are thousands of those creatures and ten of us. We don't stand a chance." I notice he doesn't look at me when he makes his suggestion. Maybe he doesn't know.

"Thought you were the greatest warrior ever," Bass snaps, making Matias's lip curl. "A hundred-on-one are pretty good odds for a fighting man. Ask anyone here."

"Perhaps," Matias concedes, "but why waste time when we can kill them all in one fell swoop?"

"Matias, we do not detonate the weapon," Aenoh says in a clipped growl. "That is not an option. Not yet." I force myself not to roll my eyes. Of course, why would he want to destroy his greatest prize? He, too, would want us out of range.

"As you say," Matias replies.

"So what do we do?" Arven asks.

"We need to hide the maser," I say slowly. "Cale may have laid a trap, but he doesn't know what we have on board. I think he figured out we were going for help, but he couldn't have known we'd return with a weapon that could destroy his entire army."

"But where could we hide it?" Arven asks.

"In the med bay?" suggests Sylar.

I think for a second. "That could work, but my guess is they'd strip the med bay for supplies first."

"How about in plain sight," Inka says, chewing on her lip. "I mean, it looks like a canister, not a weapon. If you didn't know what it was, you'd go right past it. We could put it in the back with some of those oxygen tanks. The Reptiles have no use for those."

"It's a good idea, but they'll scan the ship," Bass responds. "They want weapons, and this weapon would be a huge asset against the Vectors."

Arven stands, excitedly. "We could put it inside the propulsion jet casing."

I'm shaking my head before he can get another word out. "No, Arven. The antiprotons are volatile enough. You really want that thing in there *with* those? If the whole thing goes unstable and blows, we're not just talking about killing a bunch of Reptiles. We're talking mass extinction."

"The engines are powered down, so the risk would be minimal," he counters. He takes a breath. "Just listen. According to the ship's schematics, it's designed with a sizable air pocket just inside the external shell, for cooling, I think. The radioactivity from the magnetic storage rings that separate the antimatter from matter should mask it, at least enough for us to bypass the Reptiles' scans."

I frown. "There's a reason for that outer casing."

"Wait." Sauer clears his throat. "Let him explain. Arven, are you sure there's no risk?"

"I can't say a hundred percent, but I'm sure that the Machines that designed this ship would have built in a fail-safe if the matter/antimatter drive train were compromised."

"It's the best idea we've got," Bass says in a low voice. "I'm with Arven. We're nearly on the ground, so we need to move."

"Okay, do it," Sauer orders after a long pause. I concede. As much as the solution scares the pants off me, we don't have much choice. That weapon is our one shot if things go south with Cale. "Arven, take Sylar and meet us back here as soon as you're done. Bass, get us geared up."

"I don't understand why we don't just stay on the ship," Aenoh says after they're gone. "The enemy can't get in and, if they do, we kill them one by one."

"Because, if I know Cale," I say, "he'll shut down the oxygen supply remotely. Then he'll threaten to burn us out."

"How do you know?"

My voice is cold, my face like stone. "When he was still human—when he had a soul—he ordered me to do the same thing with renegade soldiers who'd stolen a hover. We dragged their bodies out, blistered and burned, as a flesh-eating virus consumed them. The old Cale never cared about anything other than what he wanted. And now he's a thousand times worse."

Aenoh's mouth opens and closes. I stare him down, daring him to say more. He doesn't.

"So, what now?" Matias asks after a while, palming his gun.

"We defend ourselves. If we're going down, we're going to take as many of those Reptiles with us as we can."

"I don't get it. Why bring us down in the first place? Why not just shoot us out of the sky?"

"Precious cargo," I say.

"What?"

I shrug. "If I had to guess, I would say that Cale was here with so many of his Reptiles because he's anticipating our return with an army at our backs. A more likely scenario, though, is that the tracker transmitted the weight levels on the ship, and since there *is* no army and we are four bodies heavier than when we landed in Avaria, Cale wants to see who—or what—we have on board." I meet Caden's eyes. "Your clone is very cunning, always ten steps ahead."

"He's not so smart if he's a Reptile." Aenoh snorts dismissively.

"You don't get it, do you?" I snap. "Cale was exiled. The only thing out here in the Outers is death. He was clever enough to not only rebuild his failing organs, but to organize the *Reptiles*—who, for all intents and purposes, should have killed him—into a cohesive, deadly unit. No one has ever been able to control them . . . until now. So, you tell me if you still think he isn't brilliant. If I had to guess, I'd say he wants this ship"— I jab a finger at him, Inka, and Caden— "and whoever is on it."

"And you?" Aenoh says, mockingly.

"Especially me."

I don't know why I'm letting Aenoh get under my skin, but we've underestimated Cale enough. He wants this ship. With its offensive capabilities he wouldn't need to batter down the remaining walls of the dome—he could just blow the entire city into the ground, then fly to Avaria and do the same there. Nothing would stop him.

As far as taking me as a hostage—I'm not sure. Though Cale deceived me by sending me to the Otherworld poisoned by lies about Caden, in the end, he'd twisted his command into my betrayal because I'd chosen the rightful prince.

And Cale has always been one to hold a grudge.

Then again, so have I. And I have a score to settle with him.

Arven and Sylar rejoin us, and he nods to Sauer and me just as Bass walks in, arms loaded with weapons. "It's secure. What now?"

I take a breath. "Cale wants the ship intact. His army will only shoot at us at close range. Once that door opens, we fight like hell. Protect the Lord King"—I hesitate and swallow hard—"and Lady Inka at all cost." I'm relieved that my voice didn't waver, but I notice Caden's sidelong glance and Aenoh's offended look. "You have Matias," I remind him with a grim smile. "And right now, we are on Neospes's lands, and the Lord King is our priority. I suggest staying close to your man."

For a brief second, I imagine how easy it would be to send one of my blades back during the mêlée, accidentally striking him. I shove the thought away. For now, there's more at stake than Aenoh's debauched plans.

"Bass, you and I will take point. Sauer, you've got the rear with Sylar and Arven. The rest of you, stay central. Matias and

Enola, on the sides with Aenoh and Inka between you. We stay together and work as a unit. Do not, under any circumstances, separate from the group. The Reptiles will swarm you. Do you understand?"

I survey the nine people nodding beside me as the vessel abruptly stops. Everyone is armed. Bass has his staff, Inka her bow, and me my ninjatas. Everyone is dressed for the volatile temperatures of the Outers. The sun is dropping, but it's well over one hundred degrees out there. I bring my suit online, checking that everything is functional.

Oddly, I don't feel anything but absolute readiness. Fighting comes second to breathing for most of us. Glancing behind me, I notice that Caden is holding his saber and I wink at him. I'd rather have him fighting beside me than anyone else, including Sauer and Bass, who are both extraordinary fighters. My sister, Shae, taught Caden everything he knows, and she'd been the best single swordsman in all of Neospes. "Hope you haven't gotten rusty from lavish living in the castle," I say over my shoulder.

"Not a chance," he tosses back with a confident look. "Too bad we didn't have a chance to spar. I've been training with Sauer."

"Oh, well, there goes all of Shae's training."

"Hey!" Sauer protests. "Who do you think taught Shae?"

"Who's Shae?" Aenoh asks, irritated.

I glare at him. "She was my sister. Cale, you know, the one who you think isn't so smart? Well, he killed her and made her into a Vector. You've heard of them, right? Programmed reanimated corpses? Then Cale made me fight her in front of everyone and kill her all over again."

Aenoh pales, but says nothing more. I turn back to Caden. "Don't take any unnecessary risks, okay?"

Caden nods. "I won't. Wind at your back."

"And at yours."

"How many do you think are out there? A couple thousand?" Bass asks, circling his shoulders slowly. He, too, looks ready.

"Just about." My adrenaline spikes as something pries the access port open. They've overridden the security system and the power grid of the ship. "Here we go."

I engage both offensive and defensive modes on my suit, feeling it become one with my body, and smash my ninjatas through the first Reptile that comes through the door. Bass takes care of the next two, his staff lunging outward like a pike. We move as a single unit through the doorway, striking from all sides as wave after wave of Reptiles rush us. Even from the inside, Inka is fast with her bow, firing arrows designed with electromagnetic arrowheads that ignite once lodged, frying the target from the inside out. Enola has her hands full, but seems to be in control. She's also using a bow, but is nowhere nearly as fast as Inka.

"Riv," Bass yells. "On your left."

I turn swiftly, my blades flying as I make short work of the five dog-like Reptiles that have flesh dangling and oozing from their metal exoskeletons. I barely see the giant bear-creature rushing me, and its paw catches my shoulder. I go down like a sack of rocks, slashing blindly with my ninjatas. A head flies toward me. Caden's cleaved it straight off the creature's body. I stab the tip of my blade into the back of the skull and watch the neon yellow light in its eye fade to nothing.

"Thanks," I say, vaulting to my feet.

"No problem." He swings his saber, easily dispatching something that looks like the demon-spawn baby of a spider and a komodo.

"I swear, these things get uglier and uglier," I gasp, taking on two more. "They'll scavenge for anything."

"No kidding," Bass agrees, sidling up to my back. His staff is covered with gore. He kicks a Reptile in the face and slams the end of his lance into its head, twisting ruthlessly. I face off against two more, just as four attack Bass. I finish mine off quickly and turn to help him, but he doesn't need it. I've never seen his staff move so quickly, like a fluid extension of his arms. He spins it in a circle over his wrists, and decapitates the last creature with a flourish.

"Nice work," I tell him.

"You're not so bad yourself."

We write off another dozen creatures, and then, for a brief moment, the wave stops as if the Reptiles have received a remote command. Our crew huddles together warily, shoulders touching, a circle of ten surrounded by a leering ring of thousands. Hundreds of destroyed Reptile bodies separate us. Not bad.

"Everyone still alive?" Sauer asks.

We answer affirmatively, some more vocally than others. Enola looks winded, but unharmed. So does Sylar. Sauer is flushed, and has moved from guns to blades. So has Matias, who's run through his considerable supply of ammunition. Aenoh has a curved blade in his hand, and he's breathing heavily. I'll hand it to him—at least he didn't turn tail and run. Then again, he's a warrior, even if he is an arrogant ass. Inka seems to have an inexhaustible supply of arrows. Caden's covered in gore but doesn't seem to be injured. Apart from a few minor hits, we've taken the first wave quite well.

"Status?" Bass asks me.

I glance down at my body, registering the data from the suit. "A couple hits, but nothing major. You?"

"All good."

Not that that means much considering how many creatures are still standing, poised to attack. We've barely made a dent. I take a long breath just as a ripple shudders through their ranks. I raise my ninjatas, but none of the Reptiles advance. Their piecemeal bodies stand watching and waiting. A hush falls and they go preternaturally still.

"Ah, Riven, always fighting the good fight." The disembodied voice is somewhere to my left. My body tenses in response.

"Where are you, Cale? Why don't you come out and face me?"

"Did you miss me?" the voice taunts. "Oh, wait. Why would you? You sent me out here to die."

"You tried to kill us. You committed treason."

"Treason? I was defending my throne."

Caden tenses beside me. "It was never your throne."

There's a moment of silence before Cale speaks again. "Ah yes, I see you've brought the prodigal son with you. The perfect specimen, so to speak. Tell me, Riven, does my perfect self *do* it better?"

Heat flares up my neck. I can feel the eyes of the others— Bass, Aenoh, Inka, Matias—flick toward me. My ears burn.

Caden doesn't say a word, but I feel his shoulder lean into mine, and I take strength from it.

"What do you want, Cale?"

"You know what I want."

"No, I really don't."

Mocking laughter erupts from the Reptile crowd, sending a shiver down my spine. It doesn't even sound like him anymore. "I've really missed our games, you know, this lovely back-and-forth between us. You always were the one who knew me best."

"Why are you doing this?"

"Because you took my life from me. *He* stole it, and I want it back. I want it all back—Neospes, the throne, the crown, you. I want you at my side where you belong." His voice takes on a conversational tone. "You know, in hindsight, I never should have sent you to find him. The Vectors would have eliminated him eventually. You became his savior."

"Cale—"

"And left me to rot as soon as you had your happily ever after with him." Cale cackles loudly. "I heard a vicious rumor that he's bound to someone else now. A beauty, so I'm told." He pauses. "Ah, I see. The rumors are true—your bride-to-be is indeed lovely, dear brother. Can I call you brother? I feel, in my heart of hearts, that we could be brothers. On second thought, maybe *sire* is better. After all, I was created in your hallowed image." I give Caden a sharp look, hoping he doesn't respond to the baiting. I want Cale's rage trained on me. "Riv, it's really too bad that you weren't good enough. Don't you get it? You'll never be good enough for him. But, hey, if you're fine with being third-rate seconds . . ."

I wheel around, furious, but Bass beats me to it. "Why don't you show your face, you piece-of-shit coward?"

"And Bass," the voice drawls mockingly. "So much to be said of you . . . the turncoat's turncoat. You don't even know where your loyalties lie, do you? One day, all those secrets will come tumbling out, so be very, very careful."

Bass's lips thin into a hard, white line but, to my surprise, he doesn't respond.

I frown. *What secrets?*

"What a fun band of adventurers you've brought with you, and they've done a lot of damage. You, too, of course. But you know, nothing goes to waste in the Outers, so it's not a complete loss." Cale's laugh is long and slow, grating on my nerves. I exhale slowly, counting backward in my head. "Good to see you still know how to fight, Riven. I'm proud that your skills have improved with age. Almost like we could be back in the holo-dome during the elite trials, isn't it?"

"You mean when you were human?" I snap.

"Oh, I'm human," Cale says. "I've just made a few minor adjustments. Nothing to get all freaked out about."

"Then show yourself."

Everything goes quiet for a while, and I think that maybe I've lost him. Or he's finished talking. And then the line of Reptiles opens up and someone walks forward, stopping between the Reptiles and us.

Caden inhales sharply. There's the boy I saw on the hologram in the Peaks. The boy I used to know.

Only, it's not really him.

The leader of the Reptiles is tall and slender with dark hair and piercing green eyes. Make that piercing green *eye*. The other one is a dull red ringed with yellow. The hologram hadn't been that good on detail. At close range, I can see the tech melted between his bones, wiring running from his neck to his temple, metal shining through in patches. He looks nothing like the boy from whom he'd been cloned. A high-tech, advanced-weaponry crossbow is grafted to his shoulder. I don't have to look to know that it's trained right at Caden.

"So what's the verdict? Do I pass muster?" Cale's lips curl in a smile. "Do you like my enhancements?"

"Is that what you call them?" I ask. "You're nothing more than one of them . . . a Reptile."

"Semantics," he says with a careless wave of a half-metal hand. "I needed a new lung, and my wonderful sire standing beside you didn't want to part with his. I also needed half a heart, and a kidney. You wouldn't believe how resourceful these creatures can be." His hand slides over the head of a feline-bird beside him. The Reptile leans into his palm like a cat. "And loyal. *So* loyal."

"What do you want, Cale?" I repeat, tired of his games.

He steps forward until we're barely two feet apart, and lowers his voice. "I would welcome you back, Riven. I will always make you feel special, because you are special. You would never be second best. After all, you're not really *real* either." He grins. "Did you like getting my little electronic messages? If you weren't like me, how could you have received them *and* followed them to a T? We are two of a kind and you know it."

None of us is prepared for what happens next. Bass rushes Cale just as the crossbow goes off, the arrow flying toward Caden's heart like a flash of brilliant light. I don't know how I do it, but I grab the arrow mid-flight, nearly losing my fingers in the process. When I turn back, Cale has Bass in a choke hold, the metal fingers of his right hand holding him at least four inches off the ground. Bass kicks uselessly, his face turning purple.

"Let him go, Cale."

"Or what?"

"Or nothing," I say. "Take me instead."

Cale pretends to think about it and then shakes his head. "As much as I love watching my *maker* squirm, you and I both know that you have nothing to bargain with. But I'm in a generous mood." He releases Bass, who falls to the hard earth, coughing, clawing at his scarlet throat. "There you go. Feel better now?"

"Thank you."

"Now, with that out of the way, shall we discuss the terms of your surrender?"

"Our surrender? You're crazy."

"I thought you'd say that, so time for a little incentive." Cale signals to a Reptile toward the back of his line, and an inordinately large creature moves forward. It's carrying something . . . something I immediately recognize as human. The large Reptile lumbers closer, and the silvery glint of the person's hair nearly does me in. It's not her. It *can't* be her. But her features take shape as the giant nears, and my heart stalls.

With a cry, I lurch forward and grab Cale by the scruff of his neck, pointing the tip of my ninjata into the flesh there. He doesn't fight me, a glimmer of a smile hovering over his mouth.

"Riven, don't!" Sauer shouts, but the warning is dull, as if coming from miles away. The giant Reptile holds my mother high like some kind of grotesque trophy, and I release Cale with numb fingers, my knees buckling as I stagger backward.

"What have you done to her?"

Cale grins at me, his face bright. "Sometimes, dear one, in times of war, sacrifices have to be made."

21

THE REPTILE KING

AURELA'S FACE IS tranquil, and there's no blood on her clothing. My laser vision engages, checking for injury and recording her vitals. My mother is alive for now, but seems to be in some sort of coma.

"If you've hurt her, I will end you."

"Save your empty threats, Riven," Cale says with a careless toss of his hand. "She's alive. You would have been so proud. She traded herself for thirty hostages when we breached Sector Six. Quite a martyr, your mother, but I guess it was inevitable. I was forced to execute four children before she begged me to stop. Offered herself in exchange for the rest." A muscle ticks madly in my jaw, the berserker rage brewing in my stomach. "She's always had such a soft heart for the young."

I grind my teeth, trying to calm the anger that's nearly choking me. Sector Six housed most of our medical research facilities—I don't even want to think about what Cale would use it for. "She was good to you, you bastard. She always took your side, always saw the good in you, and *this* is how you repay her?"

"Casualty of war, my friend. And let's not forget that Aurela led the rebels against me for years—back when, you know, I was weaker."

"I am not your friend," I growl at him. "You lost that privilege long ago."

Anger flashes in his eyes before he recomposes himself. "As you say. We were discussing the terms of your surrender." He arches a dark eyebrow, awaiting my answer.

I swallow hard, my eyes flicking to my mother's inert form. The group shifts nervously behind me, but we have little choice. If we don't capitulate, she dies. "State your terms."

"Drop your weapons. Release your ship to me."

"No," Aenoh whispers sharply from behind me. "She's one person. We are ten. You cannot negotiate our lives, I will not permit it."

"Ah, yes, the stranger," Cale murmurs. "Do you have something to add to the discussion?"

Aenoh regards him with baleful eyes. "I negotiate my own terms, not those of some half-breed, self-crowned prince."

Cale's eyebrow arches so high it nearly disappears into his hairline. "Where'd you find this charming fellow?" he asks me before turning back to Aenoh. "You do realize that you're technically surrounded by half-breeds, don't you? And, for the record, the General isn't a half-breed. She's the future—everything we were meant to be, and more."

But, of course, Cale doesn't know that Aenoh has his own designs in mind for me. I'm not sure what game Aenoh is playing, but I know that he, too, is not to be underestimated. "Fine," he says. "Take her and release us."

"So you can raise an army against me? I think not." Cale turns back to me. "Where were we? Oh right—drop your weapons and give me your ship." His eyes wander over the craft greedily. "It's quite a beauty, isn't it? My father kept it hidden for years, wouldn't let me near it. He told me it was dangerous. Who knew it could actually fly? Its weapons system is like nothing I've ever seen. Some of these guys"—he waves his arms over the Reptiles—"remember these ships in action. Their collective memory is amazing—so much knowledge retained over the decades. It's like having infinite consciousness at your fingertips."

Cale's words trip over each other as if he has too many things to say at once, his internal system causing verbal overload. I frown, watching him carefully. He's always been just a bit erratic and his transition to Reptile seems to have exacerbated that. Noticing my look, he blinks several times as if trying to recalibrate himself.

"So, Riven, what say you?"

"What happens to the rest of us if I agree? What happens to the Lord King?"

"You have my word that he will remain unharmed, as will the rest of your companions . . . as long as they obey."

I narrow my eyes at him. He's too silver-tongued, too glib. "How can I trust you after everything you've done? How do I know that you won't kill Caden or any of the others the minute I agree?"

Cale offers me a smile that doesn't quite work with his unsettling nonhuman features. "You don't. But I want you to come home, Riven, where you belong. You and I have always been a team—the dynamic duo, remember? You were the only one who ever really understood me."

"Everything you ever said was a lie."

"Not everything."

The seconds tick by and I know I have to make a decision. The only cover is the busted ship behind us. Data flashes through my brain—the ship's back online. Auxiliary power seems to be working now that the hover's on the ground, which means we might have a viable means of escape. I run a diagnostic scan for security configuration. All systems have been rebooted and returned to default settings. I check functions; the ship could probably operate at hover level if push comes to shove but, at the very least, I can make it secure. Working quickly via uplink, I reset the cryptographic algorithm, reducing permissions to zero, and add a supplemental buffer. Heart racing, I execute the script.

"You tried to kill me, remember?" I say, trying to buy extra time while the script launches.

"I wasn't going to kill you," Cale says. "You needed to be taught a lesson."

"And what lesson was that?"

"Defying me has consequences. But I'm a forgiving man. I'm willing to forget your past transgressions if you behave now." He smiles again, impatience glinting in his eye. "Come now, you and I both know I can execute every last one of you. I'm being generous allowing you to surrender and save your . . . friends." He says the last word as if it's something distasteful in his mouth.

I don't trust Cale, no matter how much he professes to care about me. He kept me close because I was useful to him, just as I would be now in his conquest of Neospes. Cale only cares about himself. I swallow hard. Aurela would want me to fight—she wouldn't want me to sacrifice Caden for her. But I can't condemn her to death.

I'm considering lowering my weapons when a disturbance swells from the rear of the Reptile ranks. Interference flashes behind my eyes, and relief floods my body like a tidal wave as the encoded message comes across loud and clear.

On your orders, General.

A shadow crosses Cale's face, his mouth spiking downward as he receives a similar message from the army behind him, confirming what I already know.

The Vectors are here.

Cale turns around, and I glance over my shoulder at Sauer, the decision clear in my eyes. We're going to fight. He nods in silent agreement. Caden does, too. Bass taps his staff in the flat of his palm, his face grim and resolute. Cale's fingers have left deep red welts at his throat. My gaze reaches Inka, who carefully notches an arrow to her bow.

Engage at will.

I release the order, my heart racing with anticipation as the sounds of warfare echo across the Outers. The wall of Reptiles melts toward the battle behind them, leaving Cale and me in a standoff with a handful of creatures protecting him. Rage ripples across his face as he swings back to face me.

"This changes nothing. We are greater in number and the Vectors *will* fall."

"The Vectors are programmed to do one thing—destroy. You, of all people, know that. Every Vector will take down fifty Reptiles, and you'll have nothing."

"I can still kill your companions," he says. His Reptiles push closer, guns raised. "Yield and I will spare them."

I lower my ninjatas as if I'm about to submit to his wishes, dipping into a slow crouch to lay them down at the sides of my boots. "You were right, Cale."

"About what?" He's distracted now, worried about his advantage slipping away. I can see the tension in his shoulders and the angry set of his brow. His metal eye glints coldly.

"About me."

"How so?"

"I *am* the future." My grip tightens around the hilts of my ninjatas, but instead, I focus the nanobes in my brain to send out an intense frequency. The Reptiles closest to me fall to the ground screaming in agony. Cale clutches at his head, backing away. The Reptile holding my mother loosens his grip and falls to one knee. "Now, Bass!"

He dashes forward, grabbing my mother from the creature's slack grasp and drags her to safety. Caden and Sauer form a wall around her. I nod to Inka. She releases the arrow notched in her bow and it hits the creature in the head, where it explodes on contact.

"Go! Take her and get back on the ship!" I shout. "The Vectors will buy us time."

"But the ship is compromised," Sauer says.

"The auxiliary power is back online. Get Aurela and the Lord King onboard and seal the door. I've reprogrammed the security algorithms. Cale won't be able to open it this time, not without me." I blink, sorting through the push of information. "My brain is linked to the operating system. I was able to access everything once the uplink went live. I can't explain how I'm still connected to it."

Bass's face lights up. "It paired to you when you flew it before."

"We can't just leave you out here," Caden argues.

Fighting to maintain the outbound frequency, I take a long breath. "You're safer inside the ship. You're a threat, Caden. You always will be, and Cale's never going to let that go. Protect your future queen. Protect my mother. Go!"

"I'm staying out here," Bass says.

"No, I need you in there. You're the only one I trust to keep Aenoh and Matias in line. Please."

Bass stares at me for a long time before agreeing. "Don't die," he says thickly over his shoulder.

"I'll try not to. And, Bass—" But the words are knocked from my mouth as Cale's metal hand catches me square across my face. The frequency stops abruptly, and I pull myself to my feet, dazed, but swords in hand. I clear my head to seal the door shut behind Bass. He'll rush out like an idiot if Cale gets too close.

Thick, congealing blood oozes from Cale's ear down his cheek as he lunges toward me. "You bitch!"

"I thought you liked to play rough?" I dart out of the way, wiping the blood from the corner of my split lip. "Or is that only when you have others to do your dirty work?" I throw a sympathetic look at the giant, headless Reptile lying a few feet away. "Sorry about that one. He must have been really important."

Cale roars, detaching his crossbow from his shoulder. "Haven't changed a bit, have you? Sarcastic to the bone. Well, that won't be the case when I kill every last person on that ship, including your dear mother and your *lover*."

"You really need to let it go, Cale," I say, watching him as he circles me, the crossbow swinging from one hand like a club. "And, as you said before, Caden's not bound to me. He belongs to someone else now."

"That's true. Doesn't mean I won't enjoy hearing the sounds of the flesh melting off their bones."

I shake my head, smiling calmly. "Didn't you hear? *I* control the ship. You couldn't get past my encryption if you tried. Go ahead." I see his brow furrow as he attempts to access the ship's computer. Frustration flashes across his face, and his attention flicks to a Reptile with a giant cannon attached to its back. I offer an apologetic smile. "Oh, I disabled your graviton net, too. Sorry about that."

Cale snarls at me. "You think you're so smart, don't you?"

"Not really, and I kind of have you to thank for that." I watch his eyes narrow. "That's the thing about remote systems—there's always a chink in the armor, all these backdoor codes connecting them. When you were babbling about everything being connected, about all the sentient data from the androids, I tried to see if I could access them. How do you think I knew just what frequency to run? Or how to jam your weapons? You might want to up your security." I give him a disgusted look. "So this is it— you wanted me and here I am, just the two of us. Any last words?"

Cale laughs, a loud, chilling sound that makes the hairs rise on the back of my neck. "You can't kill me, Riven. You don't think I've taken precautions? You need me."

"Seriously? Those are your last words? They're a little predictable, even for you." I swing my ninjatas in a lazy circle. "Here's what's going to happen. I am going to end you. Your army is going to be destroyed, and that will be the end of your little coup. You have no more cards to play, and when this is all over, no one will remember your name or that you even existed."

"You think you can save your mother by hiding her in that ship?" Cale growls ferociously, a muscle ticking in his jaw. "I *let* you take her. Thanks to Sector Six, we've implanted a device over her heart. It will take over and replicate, making her one of us. It's a prototype I designed—self-replicating micro-robots. Nothing like yours, of course, but they're effective in their own way. They don't care too much for their human hosts, unfortunately. Not really symbiotic creations." He pauses with a dramatic flourish. "Once they finish with her, where do you think they'll go next? They feed on life like a virus, and you've just given them nine ablebodied hosts." I frown, searching his face to see if he's telling the truth. Cale arches an eyebrow daring me to doubt him. "It appears that I have one more card to play, after all," he murmurs.

I access the ship's computer, running a medical diagnosis on my mother's body. My stomach sinks as the final image becomes clear. Cale wasn't lying. A metal spider-like creature clings to her heart like a parasite.

"If you hurt her—"

"I know, I know, you'll kill me," he mocks. "Just like you killed me after Shae. You really should try to follow through on those empty threats, Riven."

My teeth are grinding together so hard it feels like my jaw is wired shut. My fingers curl around my weapons, my breath coming loud and fast as Cale continues. "I have to admit I enjoyed watching them gut and decontaminate your sister. It was oddly . . . pleasant. And seeing her dueling you was the ultimate prize."

My blood boils, the nanobes rushing in a mad fury, but I don't react to Cale's taunts. My focus is clear. I flex, feeling the suit undulate like a second skin, and access the internal programming. There are layers of code now that weren't there before—evolving, learning technology. I don't have time to wonder why my father built into my suit the same self-aware technology that had destroyed Neospes in the first place, but right now, the suit is adjusting to me . . . calming me as I focus on what to do next.

Cale's voice fades as I push outward, pinging the collective consciousness of the Reptiles, analyzing data, and searching until I find a vulnerable access point. I enter it with brute force, shutting down their security layer and mirroring the Reptiles' operating system with a proxy script. The Reptiles are loyal to Cale—that much is clear. I scroll through the source files and frown. Something's not right. Some of the commands are coming from Cale, but most are coming from a remote source—a central intelligence.

Obliterating Cale won't do a damn thing.

I glance at the boy standing in front of me, and exit my host, covering my tracks and erasing the log files. I take a careful, even breath. "What is it you want?"

"Call off the Vectors. Join me."

I blink, sending out a remote command to my Vector army, and obediently, they retreat. I sheathe my ninjatas. "Done. Take Aurela back to Sector Six, remove the bug, and you have my word."

A tinny noise echoes through the communications device on my visor. "Riven, what are you doing?" Caden asks.

We have no choice, I reply wordlessly, transmitting my responses to the ship's communications system. *You heard him. You're all at risk. I have to do as he says.*

"It's a trap."

Possibly. But I've analyzed all outcomes, and this option has the best odds for your survival.

There's a long pause. "Listen to yourself, Riven, who cares about odds? Trust your gut. You've always done that. Kill Cale. We'll figure out what to do with Aurela."

Negative. He dies, you all die, and I can't risk that. I pause, turning off ship-wide transmission. Making sure the connection is secure I send to only Caden's device: *There's something more here, something I can't put my finger on. It's the hive mentality that made me suspicious. Cale wouldn't have put himself in danger that easily if Aurela was his only insurance. There's more—a command center somewhere else that's controlling everything. We have to find out where and what that is before it's too late.*

"What do you mean?" he says in a low voice.

The Cale we're seeing now is only a piece of the whole. The bigger threat is elsewhere.

There's silence on the other end of the comms. The soft exhale of Caden's breath is the only indication he's still there.

Stay put, and keep this to yourself. We can't trust anyone.

"Do we have an agreement?" I say aloud to Cale. "Once she's safe, I'll do as you ask."

Cale nods and signals to the remaining Reptiles. A black beast resembling a horse with metal limbs and rotting flanks canters forward. "Riven, this is for the best. Surely you can see that. Humans aren't meant to rule. We're smarter, more advanced. This world—and the Otherworld—are ours for the taking."

He climbs onto the beast's back and lowers a hand down to me. I hesitate for only a second before taking it, pulling myself up behind him. We take off at a mad gallop toward the city. At my command, the hover activates and follows. Two separate armies march in unison toward Neospes—Reptile and Vector. I can't help thinking of the similarities between them, but I quickly shove the thought away.

Time to meet the real king of the Reptiles.

22

TACTICAL WARFARE

THE SMELL OF Neospes greets me before I see the actual dome. And when I do, my heart sputters to a near stop. Bodies litter the earth—left to rot and be picked apart by scavengers—humans and Reptiles alike. At least the city hadn't gone down without a fight. But for every dead human, there are at least four live Reptiles, snarling and pawing around the dome, watching me with savage eyes.

Aside from the bodies, the overall condition of the dome takes my breath away. Huge black spots coat the insides—the same poison that I'd seen in Sector Five—and plumes of dark smoke rise from within. The only untouched sectors are Seven, which I'm guessing is because of its proximity to the Peaks, and Two, where my father's lab is located. It may seem like a coincidence, but deep down, I know it can't be.

I keep myself upright in the saddle, but can't help pressing against Cale's back every time the stupid Reptile horse jerks.

Cale had laughed during our awkward ride. "You know you can put your arms around my waist," he'd said.

The thought of touching Cale made me want to vomit. "Let's not get ahead of ourselves, shall we?"

But, eventually, I'd had to brace myself against him or risk falling off. If I closed my eyes I could almost imagine that it was the old Cale sitting in front of me. But the sour odor of decaying flesh beneath his jacket was a constant reminder that the boy I'd known was dead . . . just as I'd known when I was fighting my sister in Vector form, that it wasn't really her. And so, I'd held on to the edges of his jacket above his hips, cringing each time my body collided with his. Every moment of the trek across the Outers had been torture of the vilest kind.

"Looks like you've already breached the city." I slide from the Reptile's back as soon as we're within walking distance of the dome's entrance. "Why do you even need my help?"

"We can't access Sector Two—there's some kind of electromagnetic grid around it and, well, you know about Sector Seven."

"The grid's new. Danton must have known you'd eventually breach the dome. Is he in there?" I already know the answer. I'd completed a scan of the sector the minute Neospes came into range. My father is in his lab along with a few dozen scientists. It wouldn't surprise me if he'd stockpiled food and water in order to withstand a lengthy siege. His survival instinct is the one thing that has kept him alive all these years.

I frown. "Why Seven? You know that I'm as affected as you are in there, so what's the point?"

"You're human. We are not. When our robotics shut down, we shut down. I need your help to secure the sector and the Peaks. We used bio-agents to weed the humans out, but there's no way of knowing for sure if it's clear. I've heard that the tunnels in the Peaks go on for miles and I don't want rebellion brewing again."

"Why are you even doing this, Cale? What's Neospes to you? You murdered hundreds of innocent people for what? A crown? You don't even need to live in a dome."

"It's *my* crown," he snarls and then, just as quickly, calms down. I'm getting used to his irrational bursts of anger. "You really have to see what I've done with the place. Come on, I'll give you the grand tour."

"First Aurela," I say firmly. "Then your tour."

"Fine."

The hovertank stops a few feet away. Shields are at a hundred percent. I relay a brief message to the ship, and lower the security parameters so that Bass can exit, cradling my mother in his arms. I contemplate leaving everyone else on the ship, but there's no way I'm leaving Caden unprotected with Aenoh, not even with Sauer there. Who knows what he's planning.

"We keep our weapons," Sylar says as she disembarks.

Cale eyes her but says nothing. I watch as the rest of the crew descends down the ramp, following Bass and Aurela. She looks like she could be sleeping. I stare at Bass. His face is tight, shadows dark below his eyes.

"What's the matter?" I ask him.

He lowers his voice. "Sylar did a medical probe after you ran your computer diagnostic. That thing on Aurela's heart is squeezing tighter and tighter, slowing her heart rate to unsustainable levels. She's fading with every breath."

I blink. My scan tells me that the odds of her survival are above fifty percent—good if we can get her to Six and successfully remove the clamp. "Let's go."

Be vigilant, I communicate via the open comms to Caden, who is sandwiched between Sauer and Arven.

Just before we enter the dome, a raptor Reptile dives in from nowhere, clawing Sylar's head right off her shoulders. She collapses, twitching in the dust.

"Sylar, no!" Sauer shouts, dropping to his knees beside her body. But there's nothing anyone can do. Blood pools around her. Carnivorous worms are already burrowing from below. Sylar is gone.

"That was a message," Cale says in a mild tone. "*I* call the shots."

Once more, the nanobes and suit work together to keep my roiling emotions in check. I feel an inhuman sense of calm despite Cale's brutality. I welcome the reprieve. The others aren't so lucky. Sauer's face is livid; Arven's is wracked with pain.

Shaken, we walk single file through the rubble. Despite his earlier spectacle, Cale isn't taking any chances. Several beast-like Reptiles trail behind us.

I try not to get distracted as we walk through the deserted sectors and past crumbling buildings and still-smoldering homes, bloodstained stones beneath my boots. It's hard to feel such grief for the lives taken and the city now lost. My fingers clench at my sides and, just as quickly, I feel my anger dissipate, leaving cool indifference behind. *That's weird*, I think.

No. It's evolutionary.

I blink, stopping in my tracks—tense—worried that the response was sent by Cale. But it's not a wireless frequency. The response is hardwired. And the only thing connected to me is my suit. *Danton's* suit.

"What's wrong?" Bass asks, nearly crashing into my back. He eyes me warily.

"Nothing. Keep going."

But my mind is racing. I pose the question remotely: *are you self-aware?*

Yes.

Who designed you? I ask.

Danton Quinn and Sebba.

I know the the first name, but not the second. I frown, running through the list of Neospes citizens and coming up with no match. I've never known a Sebba. Then again, I hadn't known Bass, either. Seems like my father was particularly adept at hiding brilliant young protégés whose talents he wished to exploit. *Who's Sebba?*

The one who built me.

I stumble, almost tripping over the legs of a dead soldier. I locate the rest of him and almost gag. He's been lasered in half, the remains of his torso charred and neatly cauterized. I steel myself—it won't be the first dead body and it won't be the last, not with Cale heading this attack.

Sector Six is heavily guarded. Two extra-large Reptiles stand guard at the entrance to the medical facility. They are primarily made of metal, like silver skeletons. One has arms that look like they've been taken from some kind of gorilla. The other has a half-human face. For a moment I wonder if the face belonged to the soldier I'd tripped over. I snarl in disgust—even if it's not his face, it's *someone's* face. I run my facial recognition software. Niall—a soldier who had served under me early on in Cale's regime. He is—*was*—the same age as me.

We follow Cale past the guards, feeling their eyes burning into our backs. I glance over my shoulder and notice that their gazes linger on Caden, and I regret my decision not to leave him on the ship.

The medical facility is relatively untouched. More skeletal robots occupy the inner labs. I frown, staring at one that is dissecting a human heart. Another is using laser repair technology to either rebuild or repair another organ that looks like a lung on a nearby table. Or maybe it's doing something far more sinister.

Cale signals to one of the robots. "Remove the clamp on the human in med bay three. And be careful. If she dies, I'll strip you to pieces and toss your remains in the Outers." He looks at each of us in turn. "You wait out here."

"Where are you going?"

"I have to check on a few things. Don't do anything stupid. Remember what happened to your friend."

"Wouldn't dream of it." I can't quite keep my sarcasm at bay.

I watch as Cale retraces his steps back to the lab with the Reptile and organs. Our escorts remain behind with us, weapons ready.

Caden looks horrified. "You know what Cale is capable of. Don't let it affect your judgment. Be vigilant." Sauer and I exchange a worried glance, and I tilt my head at the Avarians who seem composed for the most part.

I nudge Bass. "Any idea what that thing was doing back there? In that lab?"

His eyes narrow. "Tissue reanimation, maybe. Looks like they're trying to revive dead tissue with robotic technology. See the lines overhead?" He gestures to the barely visible tubing above the metal table, which is feeding shimmery blue fluid into the organ.

"But that's not new technology—we do that with the Vectors."

"No," he says with a decisive shake of his head. "Vector technology uses corpses as hosts. We remove all organs. Dead tissue isn't actually revitalized. Programming controls the bodies, but they're still deceased."

"I don't understand. What's the difference?"

Bass looks at me as if I'm missing the bigger picture. "Everyone wants to create the next you. Programmable, live human tissue is the logical next step in the evolution of robotics."

"Why?" I'm not deliberately being obtuse. I just don't get it.

"If you were leading a superior race and could figure out how to integrate robotics with living cells—program humans to do whatever you wanted—wouldn't you pursue it? It's what we do with the Vectors."

"They're dead, Bass. It's not the same."

"To the scientists, it's the best of both worlds. Maybe that's why your father wanted to replicate your DNA so badly. Cale was right—you kind of are the future."

"But even if it were possible"—I pause for a moment—"and say they were able to replicate me, I'm my own person. I don't respond to anyone's programming."

"Don't you?"

It's a loaded question. My gaze snaps to Bass's. "You heard about that?"

"The love program? Oh yeah, everyone in the lab heard about *that.*" He grins. "You have to admit it was outstanding. He wrote code based on you saying three words that he never wanted you to say to anyone ever, and it completely reversed your programming. Danton Quinn's an asshole, but he's a brilliant asshole."

"Glad you like him so much," I say drily.

Bass shoots me a look. "I hate the guy. Doesn't mean he isn't a genius."

"Whatever." I watch the machine working over my mother. I can't see what it's doing. It could be inserting something else into her body for all I know—some kind of poison that will go into effect the minute we leave. I wouldn't put it past Cale. After all, he just killed Sylar for no reason.

He has nothing to gain.

I jump at the sudden, omniscient voice in my head that's like a voiceless line of code. It's like having a freaky alter ego lurking in the back of my consciousness. I know I shouldn't engage—after all, this could also be me going slowly insane.

How so? I think back.

He wants your trust. He will not risk losing it by killing her.

What about Sylar?

She was expendable.

You're pretty smart for a computer.

I was built with your DNA.

Then you must know that flattery will get you nowhere. I almost power down the suit-consciousness, and then I realize I can put it to good use. *Can you remotely connect to the computers in here and get a closer look at what that thing is doing?*

Yes.

The rush of images is like a river, but I sort through the data and focus on the movement of instruments. My mother is fully under; her vitals look good. The procedure looks like open-heart surgery, but the incisions are so small that there's barely any exposure. Whatever that thing is doing, it seems to be following Cale's instructions. Guess it doesn't want to be shredded and sent to the Outers.

Eventually, one of the instruments is drawn out of the incision, gripping a bloody clump—the webbing that had been around Aurela's heart now clotted with blood. The machine discards the twitching net into a silver basin, and I gag at the nest of ripe Reptile eggs. All they need is a live host. The android lasers my mother's wound closed, and increases oxygen flow.

After a few moments, her eyelids flutter open and she sits up. Her eyes widen at the skeletal creature looming over her, and she skids off the side of the table, grabbing a scalpel in one hand. Without blinking, she ducks behind the Reptile, and lodges the blade into the back of the thing's neck. It shudders and goes still. Hovering over the creature's immobile body, her wild gaze meets mine through the window.

"Damn it, that was my best one," Cale says, coming up behind us. "You know how hard it is to find a Reptile with steady hands?" He eyes me. "Happy now that your badass mom is back?"

Cale rolls his eyes and the familiar comment snaps me back into a childhood memory. We'd snuck out of the sector, trying to get to the Peaks so we could check out the infamous Outers. A rogue Reptile had cornered us. Luckily, Aurela had the foresight to follow us, shooting the Reptile with an arrow from her crossbow before he could do much damage.

"You fools," she'd scolded. "You could have been killed."

Eight-year-old Cale had looked at the crossbow with huge eyes, his voice an awed whisper. "Badass."

A reluctant smile had replaced her anger as she handed him the crossbow. "Thank you, my Prince, but now you're both on lockdown for a week for breaking curfew and sneaking out without proper permission and escort."

Lockdown had been the worst punishment then—nothing but studies, work, and sector outreach. Cale had sailed through the penance without a second thought. The prize of my mother's crossbow had been worth the hours of isolation.

I remind myself that the Cale from years ago is not the same as the monster standing beside me now. Respect or admiration for my mother didn't stop him from putting that piece of shit on her heart in the first place. I shove past him into the room. "Mom, are you okay?"

"Riven," she says in bewilderment, clutching my shoulders. "Is that you? When did you get back? Did you get the army?"

I glance at Cale, but his expression is hard to read. "No." I lower my voice. "But Aenoh is here, as is Caden's bride. They're outside."

"Why?" she asks.

"Not entirely sure." I stare at her willing her to ask no more questions.

"Then why are *you* here?" she says, watching Cale with murder in her eyes. "There was a breach and an attack. I had to surrender. That's the last thing I remember."

"Cale put a Reptile in you," I say in a flat voice. "He took it out when I agreed to help him retake the city."

She clutches at her chest, the fresh red scars the only evidence of what I told her. "Riven—"

"I'd do it again."

Cale clears his throat loudly. "Not that I want to interrupt your tender family reunion, but we have things to do and traitorous family members to oust from their hidey-holes." He grins. "First, though, the grand tour. Shall we?"

"Stay close," I murmur to Aurela as we exit the facility.

Leaving the sector, we climb onto a waiting hover that's controlled by a Reptile covered in flat, rusted scales. We sit in silence, my breath rushing out as I realize that we're heading up to the castle in Sector One. This can't be good.

"Come on," Cale says. "I hope you like what I've done with the place." He directs the last part at Caden.

We enter the main hall and I stop short, wincing at the sour, rotting odor of decay assaulting my nostrils. The entire room is dominated by thick black cables, connecting into a hundred screens of different shapes and sizes. At the center of all the wires is a person.

No, not a whole person . . . half of a person.

I look closer, bile rising in my throat. It's a kind of distorted human with stumped limbs and a deformed head suspended in midair, held in place by metal leads that run from the creature's open skull all the way down its mutilated, oozing torso.

The creature's exposed, enlarged brain is plugged into the surrounding equipment. Ribs protrude from behind peeled back
tissue, exposing a shiny titanium spine leading up to a screen
above the thing's head. Mismatched computerized eyes focus
on us, and our images appear on the screens.

"Welcome home, Riven," it says.

The grotesque face is familiar. Too familiar. I stare from Cale
to the thing, and back again. A smile stretches across his face.

"I see you are making all the right connections," he says.
"Unfortunately, he's the product of what happens when you
try to make a clone from a clone. It doesn't quite work. The
risk of chromosomal imbalance increases. But while he
doesn't make a wonderful first impression, his brain more
than makes up for it." Cale smiles. "It is a very *special* brain,
after all. This is Sebba."

Sebba—the one who helped Danton with the suit. Has my
father been working with Cale all along? I fight the urge to tear
the suit from my body.

Is that Sebba? I ask the suit.

Yes and no.

What does that mean?

It is part of Sebba, but not the whole.

I frown. Is Sebba some kind of Reptile, then? *What is Sebba?*
I ask carefully.

The suit's words make my blood run cold. **Sebba is the
most advanced prototype of human and machine fusion
since you.**

"What have you done, Cale?" Aurela whispers, jerking me
out of my thoughts. "This is senseless, even for you."

Cale's lips curl with an ugly laugh. "It's nothing the monarchy hasn't done for years." He smiles triumphantly, his gaze sliding to Caden. "Sebba, why don't you bid an extra special welcome to our esteemed maker."

Caden falls to his knees, clutching his head and screaming.

23

DECONSTRUCTION

"WHAT ARE YOU doing to him?" I shout, dropping to my knees as Caden convulses helplessly. "Stop, or I will tear this place apart!"

"Among his other gifts, Sebba is a very gifted enhanced telepath. It's only the power of suggestion; he's not actually causing him any pain." Cale studies us, gloating. "Sebba can only control those who are open to suggestion."

"Caden," I say. "Look at me." I drag his face to mine, holding his cheeks between my palms. "You need to fight—it's only in your head. There's no pain. Do you hear me?" He nods, but I know he doesn't believe me. I slap him hard. He blinks, his eyes dilating as he focuses on the real pain of my strike.

I turn to Cale and his abomination. "Do that again, and you'll both regret it."

Sebba tries pushing into my head, but it's easy to block him out, like swatting at a bothersome gnat. For a moment, I wonder what enhanced telepathy actually means. Is Sebba's brain function augmented by genetic manipulation? Telepathy is an odd talent, but certainly not outside the realm of possibility. In an effort to build the strongest human possible, our scientists engaged in all kinds of genetic experimentation, including the development of telepathic abilities. In the end, telepaths were classified as less useful—cerebral rather than built for survival. And since the androids weren't susceptible to the power of suggestion, that area of genetic enhancement hadn't been continued.

Why would Cale need a telepath?

The answer lies in Aenoh's glazed eyes, and my breath hitches in my throat. Avaria's exact location isn't known except if you have the coordinates.

"Aenoh, don't let him in," I cry. "He's trying to access your memories, to figure out Avaria's location. You need to block him out. Focus on something trivial."

"Very good, Riven." Cale claps loudly. "I'd forgotten how perceptive you are."

Inka notches an arrow and steps forward. Our Reptile escorts point their weapons at her head, but she doesn't flinch. Her voice is low and implacable. "Release him or I hit your clone right between the eyes. Even if your soldiers kill me, they will not stop this shot from meeting its mark."

"I wouldn't mess with her," I say. "She's a crack shot." Inka's fingers tremble; the telepath has a hold on her now. "Focus," I whisper to her. "Focus on what you know to be true, and hold on to it." With a deep, fortifying breath, her fingers flatten and pull tight and, just like that, Sebba releases his hold on both of them. Aenoh slumps to the floor, gasping.

"Enough play, Sebba," Cale laughs. "We'll have time later. Come, Riven, let's put those new talents of yours to good use."

He pulls up something on a central screen—a grid of the entire Neospes network—and zooms in on my father's laboratory. "Disable it, whatever he's built to keep us out."

"What makes you think I can do that?" I say evenly.

"Disable it, or I forget my promise and kill them one by one, starting with her." He hooks a thumb to my mother.

"Threatening me isn't going to make me comply. You should know that by now."

He throws back his head and roars. "Don't posture, Riven. It's so beneath you. We both know how much you love these humans—how bound you are to them. Even when they abuse your abilities while claiming to love you back."

"You don't understand human relationships or what true love or empathy feel like. You never could because you don't have a heart."

Cale sneers and points at Aenoh. "Your new friends? This man wants to take you—in the most carnal sense. Sebba has seen his desires." My stomach dips a little, hoping that Aenoh hadn't also exposed the weapon hidden on board the ship, but I'm banking on the fact that telepaths can only access thoughts that are present at the forefront of the brain. Cale turns to Aenoh, eyes burning. "Don't try to deny it. That's why you're here, isn't it? Your army is never coming. Did you tell them that? You're here to plunder a desperate city and kill a man or two"—Cale's smile turns evil as he quirks an eyebrow to Caden—"and, perhaps, I should let you."

Aenoh backs away, Matias at his side. Sauer and Bass watch, surprised.

"What's he talking about?" Caden asks, his eyes narrowing.

I shake my head fiercely. "Not the time, Caden. I'll explain later."

Cale wants us to turn on each other. We can't afford to start breaking apart, especially not with Sebba slinking around trying to access our secrets. I'd guessed early on that Aenoh had come here to kill Danton—his control over the Vectors, and me, is too much of a threat. Once the Reptiles are contained with his weapon and his daughter comes into the Neospes crown, it makes sense that Aenoh would want to depose Caden, too. It's a neatly packaged scheme.

Inka must have been aware of her father's motives. She'd tried to warn me in Avaria, and she'd given me her word that she would defend Caden with her life, which had seemed counterintuitive. Or maybe she's been playing us, too.

Right now, we have bigger things to worry about. I'll deal with the Avarians later.

I turn back to Cale. "What's your point?"

"None of them care about *you*, not even your king, or he'd have chosen you." Cale shrugs, and I can't help sliding my gaze to Caden, whose face remains shadowed. "Hey, at least I'm upfront about why I want you." His voice hardens. "Now get to work disabling that grid, or you'll get a taste of just how heartless I can be."

"Why do you want to get into Danton's lab so badly?"

"He has something I want."

I think back to the Reptile working in the medical facility. My eyes flit to Bass, and he nods. I study the flickering screens and frown. Cale sees my expression. "We control the entire Neospes network except for that lab."

"What makes you think I can get in?"

Cale arches an eyebrow. "You have always been Danton's Achilles' heel. He sees you as his greatest strength when, in fact, you are his greatest weakness. If anyone can get into that facility, it's you." Cale flicks a wrist and the Reptiles surround Caden and the others. "No more delaying or I'll start giving you an incentive to cooperate."

Engaging my suit, I log into the computer. I feel Sebba's ghostly telepathic presence hovering over me, making my blood crawl. Sebba is monitoring my every stroke. Cale's right—Sebba is everywhere, in every pocket of the Neospes network but my father's lab. My gaze slides to the pulsing exposed human brain behind me.

Wires weave in, out, and between the throbbing layers of spongy tissue. I've never seen anything like it. Not only is Sebba a telepath, he's the mastermind behind this whole coup.

He is the true Reptile king.

"How come your mini-me super clone over there couldn't hack the grid?" I ask, trying to bypass the wireless encryption by executing a packet sniffing application and analyzing the data. "The decoding process is simple enough."

"You'll see."

Danton would have reprogrammed all the security protocols, particularly in Sector Two. It'd take far too long for me to hack the network and bring down the grid. I make sure that the connection between my suit and me is secure before proceeding. Sebba will try to crack my security, but he won't be able to.

Can you execute simultaneous secure network commands? I ask the suit.

Yes.

Without being detected by Mr. Super Brain over there?

Yes.

Bring the ship into the hangar on the West Quadrant, near Sector Two. Engage camouflage mode and make sure you bypass all systems upon entry. They are monitoring everything in every sector.

Confirm command—Execute?

Execute.

I take a breath and release a replay packet application, attempting to gather more data. I can feel Sebba scrutinizing my every move, so I have to make it appear that what I'm doing is accurate or he'll see right through it. I blink, and suddenly I'm kicked out of the network. It must be a protocol designed to respond to replay attacks. I re-access the system and after completing a port scan, locate a foothold in a running application and try to use it as a backdoor to access the main database server.

Sebba's robotic voice echoes through the microphone. "I tried that already."

I nearly jump out of my seat. He hasn't said anything since bidding me welcome. "Yes, but did you become an internal user and create a remote command shell for the server?"

"Yes."

"And then what did you do?"

"Port redirection and a Trojan horse application."

I almost laugh out loud at the Trojan horse metaphor. "Did the tool send you secure authentication data?"

Sebba's tinny voice takes a moment before responding. "Yes. But it disappears. The entire security structure compresses and rebuilds from the ground up each time."

"That must be frustrating."

Cale interrupts. "Can you get past it or not?"

"Yes."

"Then do it. Or I start killing your friends."

I itch to get my hands on my ninjatas and get to work on Cale. "How is killing anyone going to get you what you want? You're just going to piss me off, and then I'll go berserker on you and your little mini-me bitch over there. And you'll have nothing."

Cale leers at me. "So much you don't know . . . so much about those closest to—"

"Yes, yes. Danton has always been out for himself. Things will never change."

The ship is in the hangar as requested. The message from my suit couldn't have come at a better time.

Instruct Danton to drop the grid. Tell him his daughter is here to rescue him from a slow death by starvation and dehydration. My suit relays my father's response. **He says, "As opposed to a swift death?"**

We all have to die. He can meet his end by actually doing something good for once . . . saving the remaining citizens of Neospes and the people we love. I glance at my mother, who is standing beside Caden, her face blank. *If not me, then his wife.*

I run another aggressive packet attack. Suddenly, a response comes up—a susceptible port via an unpoliced server. I run a few scripts, knowing that the information has to be from my father. This network is far too secure for a random, unrestricted port to just show up out of the blue. I wait for a few moments before accessing the system via the vulnerable port. "I'm in."

I feel Sebba shadowing my every move as I enter each command, running script after script. I shake my head. "I can bring down the electromagnetic grid protecting the perimeter, but there's another layer of security that's on-site, which can only be accessed with a biometric scan."

"Bring it down," Cale says coldly.

"It's down," I say after a few intense minutes. "Let's go. We don't have much time before the system restores its default security settings once it finds the breach." I nod to where my mother and Caden are standing. "Some of them should stay here."

Cale sees right through my ploy. "Not a chance. See how well you got the job done with a bit of incentive? They come along for the ride."

I keep my satisfaction under wraps—the last thing I want is for us to be separated. Bad things happen when we split up. But if Cale knew that's what I truly wanted, he would have commanded them to remain here.

Outside the castle walls, Reptiles crowd the streets, vandalizing the places where we'd had the Summer and Winter Solstice games. I force myself not to react. The last time I'd seen this courtyard it'd been filled with people dressed in their best, laughing and celebrating. Now, it's like a graveyard, taken over by bloody bodies and scrap metal.

The trip to Sector Two is short. Cale doesn't trust that I've actually bypassed the grid, even though Sebba has confirmed it, and he sends two Reptiles in first. They pass through the Sector line unscathed.

"Satisfied?" I ask.

"Get us through the next security checkpoint and I'll let you know."

I grin widely as we arrive at the elevator that leads to my father's subterranean bunker. "You know it's underground, right? I seem to recall you having a fear of spaces deep within the earth. Something to do with being buried alive? Does that idea still give you nightmares? Or does your new . . . form make you invincible?"

Cale had never passed his fear tests. As heir to the throne, he'd been granted a pass after spending ten minutes hyperventilating in a shallow subterranean passage. He insisted the experience had allowed him to conquer his fear. And no one ever contradicted him, not even me.

I see the beads of sweat forming on his forehead. "This elevator goes way, *way* down. Are you sure you're ready?" I ask.

"Yes." But the word is a half growl.

We crowd into the massive elevator, and I face the scanner, trying not to move while the biometric laser passes over my entire body. There's a slight chance that my father could have taken away my clearance and the security breach lasers will chop us all into tiny little pieces. I hold my breath.

The elevator dips, making Cale's skin go a little gray. I let myself enjoy a brief twinge of satisfaction at his distress before loudly announcing our arrival on floor seventeen—seventeen floors beneath surface level. If possible, Cale pales even more.

"We're here, princess," I tell him and he shoots me a dark look. "Maybe you should actually have taken the fear tests."

"I did take them."

"Then why are you shaking like a leaf? We both know you never passed. I was there, remember?"

"I passed them at a later date."

Cale is deathly afraid, and even if I can't be one hundred percent sure, my suit can. According to his biometric readings, his fear levels are off the charts. That makes him vulnerable.

Inside my father's lab, a thin shimmering wall—cutting-edge laser technology—separates us from him. "Danton," Cale salutes. "Good to see you again."

My father finds my face, and then my mother's before answering. Something like relief flashes across his eyes, unnerving me. "You, too."

"Why don't we drop the pretense and you give me what I want? The nanotech you've been secretly developing."

Danton's gaze slides to me before retraining on Cale. "I don't know what you're talking about."

The lights in the room flicker and then dim, all of the screens go blank, and the laser barrier fizzles and winks out. Cale smiles. "That's Sebba. He's in control of every sector now."

"Sebba?" My father's eyes widen in delayed, horrified understanding. He lurches toward us, his hand splayed wide. I can't quite determine if it's to protect or to harm, but I step in front of Aurela just in case.

"Riven, you have to get her to—"

He's not able to finish the sentence before the entire lab is plunged into darkness.

24

BURIED UNDERGROUND

SOMETHING HEAVY SMASHES into my back, sending me careening to the floor. The air is filled with shouting and sparks. Staying down, I slide my weapons from their sheaths and lie flat on my stomach, scrabbling backward until I come up against a wall and engage my infrared vision. My heartbeat trips over itself at the bodies littering the floor. I run facial recognition for Caden and heave a sigh of relief that he's not there. Most of the fallen are scientists who attempted to run past the Reptiles the minute the lights went out. With all the doors sealed, Sebba controls the only way in and out of this bunker, which means we'll be swarmed by more Reptiles at any moment.

Encircled by his Reptile guards, Cale is intent on finding whatever it is he came to retrieve from my father—searching through the glassed-in shelves and tossing aside vials in frustration. His six Reptiles have night vision, so I wedge myself between the wall and a cabinet for extra cover. My suit shimmers into camouflage mode. In the darkness I've become just another shadow. I sweep the room searching for Caden, relieved to find him hunkered beneath a table with Sauer. Inka and Enola are crouched near them. I can't see Aenoh or Matias, or either of my parents.

Scanning the area, my eyes focus on someone lying motionless on the far side of the room—Bass. I can't tell if he's dead or unconscious. I calculate the odds of getting across the room undetected, and exhale a sigh of relief when I see his arm move.

Can you lock Sebba out of the network? I ask the suit's computer.

Yes.

Then do it. I feel disconnected, as though the suit is considering my request. For a second, my stomach sinks. If this suit turns on me now, I'm screwed. I glance down at the wrist pad, prepared to power down when the response comes back in the affirmative.

Do you have any problem executing my commands? Loyalty to Sebba, or to anyone else?

No. My operating system is linked to your DNA.

Good. Break Sebba's signal if you have to. Just get these lights back on and lock down the perimeter. Tell the Vectors to engage the Reptiles on all fronts and ready my ship for immediate evac.

Done.

Now, engage all offensive and defensive modes. We're going into battle. The lights flicker as my suit tries valiantly to kick Sebba off the network. It's only a matter of time before the security runs its usual algorithm and resets all defaults, including network access and privileges. The beauty is that since the system self-repairs from the ground up after detecting any intrusions, it erases any backdoors that Sebba or any intruder may have built. But for the moment, we remain at Sebba's mercy.

Cale and his Reptiles move deeper into the lab. Once they are out of sight, I stoop down and crawl over to Bass. Dull emergency floor lighting comes on giving the room a pale, eerie glow. "You hit?" I ask him.

"Flesh wound," he gasps, cradling his palm against his side. "One of the Reptiles. Hurts like hell."

I pull apart the material of his shirt. He's been stabbed in the side. Putting pressure on the blossoming red spot, I grab a numbing salve from the medkit pocket of his gear. "Put this on. Find the others and see if you can get them to safety."

"Where are you going?"

"I need to find Danton and my mother. And figure out what Cale wants so badly." I don't miss the look that flashes across Bass's face. "Wait, you know what it is, don't you? What were you working on before you left to come on the mission?"

He hesitates, but then nods. "Danton's research was twofold. He wanted to create other super soldiers like you, but he also wanted to study your genes because of their healing properties. What if you could heal any internal injury? Or prevent an organ from failing?" Conflicted emotions work across Bass's face before he continues. "We were able to synthesize a workable genetic strain from your DNA." We both crouch down as something rustles nearby. "But it doesn't last more than a day. The host human tissue accepts the strain at first, but later, the immune system starts attacking the nano-antigens like a bacteria or virus, causing acute and chronic rejection."

"So it doesn't work?"

"It works. Just not long term yet. That's why Charisma wanted Danton's help so badly. We were about to conduct trials, but then things changed."

My conversation with Charisma seems so long ago. But it makes sense—Cale would want the strain both to rebuild his failing organs and to create soldiers like me.

"What about the vaccine to boost our immunity in the Otherworld, did Danton complete that?"

"Yes."

I shake my head as the rustling turns into a heavy, metallic scraping. Something large—and unfriendly—is headed our way. "Then we have a huge problem. Cale hasn't quite given up on his dream of ruling two universes. He wants to make himself a superior life form so he can have his cake and eat it, too. That's why he needs that vaccine." I help Bass to his feet. "Do you remember someone named Sebba working for my father?"

Bass glances at me sharply. "You mean the thing in Sector One? No, why?"

"It's just that my—"

Before I can finish explaining, an explosion shakes the foundations and Reptiles storm the hall beyond the lab. A small group breaches the space before the door panel slides shut in accordance with emergency parameters. I half-drag, half-carry Bass to where Caden and Sauer are hiding, and twist to face the creatures swarming my way.

The first two fall with a swipe of my ninjatas. I slide to the ground and spear my blades backward to get rid of another. I'm so wired that it feels like they're moving in slow motion.

Scissoring the head of a viper-looking Reptile, commotion at the far end of the room distracts me.

"Don't you dare open that door," I yell loudly. I can feel the counterattack commands flying out to the network. As fast as Sebba is trying to reenter, my suit is denying access. It's a game of cat and mouse, with the advantage changing every second. "Good," I tell it, "keep blocking him."

"Who are you talking to?" Sauer asks, confused.

"This suit has a built-in computer synced to me. It's online. Sebba is trying to get in, and we're trying to keep him out."

Caden's eyes narrow. "Riven, your father built that suit. Do you think you can trust anything it does?"

"What choice do we have? Now, come on. Let's find the others. I'm not sure how long we can keep Sebba—and the rest of those Reptiles—out. Sauer, you and I will take point. Inka and Enola, cover the rear. Let's move."

We push toward the rear of the room where I thought I'd seen Cale disappear. To my surprise, Aenoh's in the narrow hallway, and he has my father in a brutal headlock. Matias is standing beside them, watching the action play out, his gun pointed at my mother's head. He raises a second one toward me and shakes his head in warning.

"What the hell are you doing, Matias? Get that gun away from her!"

He eyes me coolly. "One move, you both die."

My mind is racing. I feel Sauer stiffen beside me, but I sheathe my ninjatas and show Matias my bare hands. "We have worse things to worry about," I say urgently. "Like the thousand Reptiles waiting to bust in here and kill all of us. Stop this,

Aenoh. We need Danton. Do you understand? We need him to get out."

Aenoh loosens his grip, and my father takes the opportunity to smash him in the side of the head. As he shuffles in our direction, Danton's lip is split, his chin covered in blood, but other than that, he looks no worse for the wear. He backs behind Sauer. I eye Matias, daring him to pull the trigger, and he slowly lowers both hands at his chief's nod.

My gaze shifts to the Avarian ruler. "I know exactly what your endgame is, Aenoh. Threaten any of my people and you'll be dealing with me. We're not in Avaria." Aenoh remains silent, his mouth puckering. "And keep your man in line," I glance over my shoulder, giving Matias a dark look. "If he crosses me, I will take him out."

"General!" I whirl at the sound of Arven's panicked voice. He's racing toward us, a group of Reptiles hot on his heels. "They're everywhere."

"Let's move. Danton, what's the best way out?" I look for my father, but he's vanished. Trust him to try to save his own skin. I scan the area. A door is to the left of Sauer, and another to the left of that. Danton could have scuttled out through either, but if I had to guess, I'd choose the first. Someone would have noticed him moving halfway across the room.

I can help you to locate Danton.

Yes, find him.

A hologram blazes before my eyes, tracking my father's position as he races through the maze of underground floors. "There!" I say, pointing to the door. "Go."

We take off running. Crashing sounds and the smell of burnt rubber trail behind us. The Reptiles are ripping the lab apart. It's full of technology and materials for them to snap up, but scavenging won't distract them for long. We race down a narrow hallway, following the dot on the holo in my head. I had no idea the subterranean level stretched this wide.

At the entrance to a large chamber, I stop short, and the others nearly crash into me. It's the Vector bunker—rows and rows of blue-veined bodies awaiting initiation and instruction. I swing around to Bass who is back on his feet.

"Are all of these ready?"

He frowns. "Yes, but the programming hasn't been tested in simulated combat. There could be rogue Vectors in there."

I blanch, but grit my teeth. Every so often, the programming doesn't take. The risk is low, but a rogue Vector can cause more than its share of trouble. I shake my head decisively. "This is the test."

Centering myself, I use the suit to connect remotely to the Vectors, and within seconds, I feel hundreds of them come online and sync to me. It's overwhelming, like a rush of cognitive awareness, the Vectors connecting back to my core as if they're extra limbs. I realize that, like the ship, they are, and I'm a little freaked out at the immense power at my fingertips.

Launch Vector Initiative—Execute?

Execute.

"Eliminate the Reptiles." I order most of the Vectors in the room. I issue a different command to a small group: "Follow Cale and hold him until I come to you. Do *not* terminate." I turn to another cluster: "You seven, defend these people with your life. Protect your king. You two, come with me."

"Wait, Riven, where are you going?" Caden asks.

I don't answer. Instead, I sync the hologram tracking my father to Sauer's wrist pad. "Follow Danton. He clearly knows an alternate way to get aboveground. I need to find Cale. He can't get his hands on Danton's research."

"I'm coming with you," Caden says in an urgent voice.

"You and Lady Inka need to be safe on the ship." I glance at Sauer. "I'll send you coordinates. It's close."

But before we can move, a massive explosion rips through the ground, throwing us all to the floor. The lights flicker and fade as Inka crawls to her feet, coughing. I engage night vision, but it's too hazy. The shadowy darkness makes it hard to see, but as the dust settles, what happened becomes clear. And it's not good. Half our group has been cut off by the internal collapse.

"What the hell was that?" Bass says, shaking debris out of his hair. His eyes widen as he stares at the caved in ceiling. Sparking wires protrude from the rubble, emitting sharp bursts of deadly color.

"Sauer?" I shout through the pile of stones. "Count off. I have Inka and Bass."

"Lady Aurela, Enola, Arven, and Aenoh." He pauses, his voice muffled. "And five out of your seven Vectors."

"Where's Caden?" I ask desperately. "Caden!"

"We're over here," Matias says, rising like a specter from the dust behind us, with Caden limping at his side.

"Got pinned in the leg by a flying desk," Caden gasps. "I don't think it's broken."

Another violent detonation shakes the building, and I fall to my knees again. "Sounds like there's a war going on up there," I shout to Sauer. "You need to get the others to the ship—I don't know how long the structure will hold now that the ceiling's collapsing this far down. Follow Danton's tracks."

"What about you guys?" Sauer yells.

"We'll find a way around. Now, go."

"Wind at your back." Aurela's voice is low, but I still hear it. It's meant to give me strength, and it does. If anyone can get them out of here, she can.

"And at yours."

I study the people standing beside me, their faces somber. I crook a finger at the two bulky Vectors. It's funny how I used to see them as hideous, with their milky eyes and translucent bodies. Now, I only see extensions of myself. "You two on the Lord King at all times. Bass, you take the rear. I've got point."

"What about me?" Inka says, bow in hand.

"Stay near Caden. Anything comes at you, shoot to kill. Do not hesitate." She nods fiercely and notches an arrow.

Find us an egress, I command the suit. *But first, locate Cale and transfer data to the Vectors.*

Within seconds, I see Cale's position register. He's two floors above us. The suit sends me the coordinates of the nearest staircase and I take off running, the others close behind me. There's wreckage everywhere. We have to reroute twice before we can reach the staircase. I'm not sure what I'm going to find or whether we'll be able to access it. Luckily, the staircase seems to have escaped structural damage. At least, on the surface. The suit confirms my suspicions.

Sixty percent secure. Severe fundamental damage detected.

Great. We have no alternative. There's another staircase, but it's on the other side of the facility. And it could be as compromised, if not worse. We'll have to take our chances.

"Be careful," I say over my shoulder. "Move fast. Don't stop for anything . . . or anyone." I hold my breath the entire way up, expecting the construction to collapse beneath our feet. The landing is damaged—barely a thin sliver of metal attached to the next flight. I hop carefully over it, followed by a Vector. He helps Inka to safety as I peek around the door.

"How does it look?" Bass whispers, peering around me.

"Clear." I turn back, glancing over my shoulder and to do a quick count. "Where's Caden?"

"He was right here," Bass says.

All of a sudden, I hear his voice coming from inside the staircase a few feet above us. "There's someone here. They're stuck."

"Caden, I told you to—"

"I know what you told me. I couldn't very well leave her here. She's only a trainee. The Vectors are with me. It'll be fine. Just hang on a sec."

I grit my teeth and shoot a dark look at Bass. We don't have time to waste. I told him to take the rear and make sure everyone was safe. Caden rounds the corner, a slight figure cradled in his arms. He hands the barely conscious girl to the first Vector as they both navigate the treacherous landing.

More rubble crumbles to the hallway below as the second Vector steps onto the rickety segment. I hold my breath as the metal sways precariously. Caden starts inching gingerly past the waiting Vector and steps away from the door when the landing suddenly drops out from beneath them both. I scream and sink to my knees, watching as Caden plummets, his eyes frozen in shock.

The falling Vector flails wildly. He grabs the ledge with the fingertips of one hand and, with the other, catches Caden's sleeve. I flatten my belly to the ground, reaching out a hand. "Quick, help me get them up!"

Do not lean forward, the suit warns. **The ledge is no longer structurally sound.**

What do I do? I can't just leave him to die. He's the king. You're the supercomputer genius, come up with something!

Options are limited—suggest mooring from a safer position.

"Bass, find a rope, chains, wire. Anything that can help!" But even as he and Matias disappear around the door, I feel a slow rumble beneath my stomach winding its way up the stairwell.

No, no, no. Not now.

I watch in horror as the stairs below us crumble like dominos, the metal lip dipping as the entire structure crumples inward. I scrabble forward to grab the Vector's fingers. My suit responds immediately, anchoring me to the floor with tiny inverted hooks. It's not much leverage, but it's enough for me to get a better hold.

The Vector wraps his fingers around my wrist just before the metal ledge rips out and I'm dangling over the edge, held in place by nothing but a few well-constructed hooks. Someone flings his weight on top my feet, but the Vector's grip starts to slip from mine in cruel slow motion. Several feet below,

Caden's eyes meet mine and a smile forms across his lips—lips mouthing three words I don't want to see or hear.

Tears burn my eyes. A voice inside me screams at me to say it back. Say the words. But I can't. I can't lose him. I refuse to lose him right now.

"Protect your king!" I scream at the tumbling Vector just as our fingers part. Acknowledgment shimmers in his milky eyes and I see the muscles in his shoulders tense, corded veins bulging in his neck. With a roar, he heaves the arm holding on to Caden upward—a feat of pure programmed, inhuman strength.

Caden lands on top of me, and strong arms haul us back to safety. For a moment, I meet the eyes of the Vector as he falls into the abyss. I don't know if *thank you* means anything to them, but I send the message anyway.

Briefly, I imagine something like satisfaction flaring in those milky irises, and then his eyes close as he disappears from view.

25

PROTOTYPE

THE GIRL CADEN saved is young, around twelve. She's dressed in military gear, odd if she's a trainee in my father's lab, but maybe she's a soldier and was here on rotation.

"Are you hurt?" I ask Caden.

"No," he says, giving me a crooked grin. "My life flashed before my eyes, but what's new, right?"

I don't smile back. "That was close . . . *too* close, and for what? A girl who probably won't survive, anyway? We can't afford to lose you. Neospes is too vulnerable without its king."

"I know, Riv, but I couldn't just leave her. What kind of king would that make me? Everyone matters." Caden pushes the light-colored hair from the girl's face and offers her a sip of water from his pouch. She sits up, disoriented.

"Where am I?" the girl asks, staring at us with wide, blue eyes.

She looks more like a doll than a soldier. I frown at her. "What's your name? Your rank?"

"Rila," she says. "I don't have a rank. I was trying to get out when the floors started collapsing. A piece of rock must have hit me on the head." She touches her hand to her temple and winces.

"Where is everyone else?" I ask.

"They were evacuated to the Peaks," she says slowly. "Danton only kept a skeleton crew here after the Reptiles breached the dome."

"Why? Why were you here?"

"I was on patrol duty with someone else, my CO." She pauses, her voice cracking slightly. "He didn't make it."

"You're coming with us," Caden says decisively. "Do you have anything to defend yourself with?"

Rila opens her jacket to show a line of thin, weighted darts—all lethal, I expect—along with a selection of spindly blades. She's a throwing expert. I look at her with new respect—it's one of the toughest weapons skills. Most soldiers choose other specialties. Shae had been an excellent thrower and even she had squeaked through the final evaluation.

"Let's move." I stop just inside the door, expecting to see Bass and Matias clearing the way, but no one is in the room. "Where are Bass and Matias?"

Inka shakes her head. "They went to look for rope. Neither came back."

"Maybe they're scouting up ahead," I say, but I don't have high hopes. Matias has his own agenda, and none of us, not even Inka, are part of it. Bass probably went after him because he's a hothead. "Let's go find them before they kill each other."

Pull them up on the holo, I tell the suit and breathe a sigh of relief when I see that they're only a few hundred feet in front of us. But the relief is short-lived. Their images on the holo are engaged in a deadly dance.

We take off at a run, dodging falling cables and mountains of overturned, broken furniture. Rila keeps up well despite her injury. It's kind of sweet watching Caden's solicitous manner with her, and a bit humorous, because she could probably kick his ass. Still, it makes me smile. Times of war almost always entail a loss of humanity. It's nice to see that Caden hasn't lost his.

By the time we reach the other side of the room, we can hear the sounds of a vicious scuffle. Matias is on top of Bass, pummeling his face with both fists. They're both covered in blood and breathing harshly. I run toward them just as Bass kicks Matias off with an upward lunge and staggers to his feet. Matias turns to me, a desperate expression on his face, and starts to say, "You must—"

Bass's backhand catches Matias squarely in the jaw, making him spit crimson onto a nearby wall. He growls and rushes his opponent, producing a knife out of nowhere and pressing the blade into Bass's throat.

"Matias, no!" I shout, but I'm already calculating the odds of getting there in time to stop that strike—they're not good. A thin seam of blood appears, and Bass's eyes go wide. Any movement will end the same—a slashed-open throat. "Matias, please."

He glares at me, his hands firm against Bass's throat. "You don't understand. They're—"

Suddenly mid-speech, Matias's fingers separate from the knife, the severed ends falling to the floor as he lurches back, keening and clutching his spurting hand. I look over my shoulder just in time to see a second dagger fly past to embed itself into Matias's forehead, right between the eyes.

Rila's face is troubled. "He wasn't going to stop."

"He wasn't yours to kill," I snarl. "I wanted to know what he was going to say, and now he's dead because of you."

"Riv," Caden says. "She was only trying to help."

"Well, she shouldn't have." I glance at Inka, who also had her bow notched, trained on her fellow Avarian. She hadn't trusted him, either.

"She saved my life." Bass's words are quiet. I look at him and see the crusting red line across his neck. I nod, swallowing hard. If the price of Matias's intel is Bass's life, it's not a cost that any of us would willingly pay. Least of all, me.

"Next time, kid," I say in a grudging whisper, "wait for my order."

"Copy."

I shake my head and toss Bass a medkit from my pocket. "What happened? You took off after him, and he attacked you?"

"Yes." Bass grimaces as he spreads the salve across his wound. "You know how shifty Matias was all the time. When he saw I was following him, he came at me."

I throw my arm around him. "No more taking off on your own. From now on, we stick together. We have no idea what we're up against, and I don't want to lose anyone else, not even shifty, weird Avarians. No offense, Inka."

"Got it," Bass says with a smile.

Inka inclines her head gracefully, and replaces her arrow in the harness on her back. She's a woman of few words, and yet, for some reason, I trust her . . . in battle, anyway. I swallow hard. At least Caden will be in good hands.

A sour feeling fills me at the thought of her hands anywhere near him.

"Come on, let's keep moving," I say in a sharper voice than I intend. "Cale is up here." When we come to the wide titanium doors at the far end of the next hallway, my breath hitches, and Inka's sharp inhale breaks the silence.

"What is this place?" she asks wide-eyed, taking in the vast, icy gallery with its glistening metal tables stretching before us like a horror landscape.

"It's where they decontaminate the Vectors before they're prepped for the nanobes," I say. The space is empty now since all the Vectors are reanimated and fighting up top, but it's still disturbing. "My father's research lab is over there in the left corner." Right where I'd seen a Vector get decontaminated up close for the first time. Bass and I exchange a look. He remembers, too. "That's where Cale is, and he's not alone."

The room is beyond freezing. Inka looks confused. "It's for the bodies," I explain, bringing up the holo on my wrist sensor. I switch to camera mode, showing a feed from the office. Cale is sitting in my father's chair, staring intently at something—or someone—on the other side of the desk.

Suddenly, something else comes up on the holo—six figures hustling along the right side of the structure. "That's Sauer," I say.

"We should split up," Bass suggests. "I'll get Cale and you take the Lord King to Sauer and the others. Inka and Rila can come with me. He's safer with you."

I shake my head. I'll have no leverage with Cale, not if I have to protect Caden. "No, you take Caden. The Vectors will go with you. Get him to Sauer, and keep the Lord King covered."

Bass nods. "Will do."

"Inka, you and Rila go with them," I say.

Inka frowns. "If it's all the same, I will stay."

"Me, too," Rila says. "I know these floors—you'll need my help."

I nod, surprised. "I'm grateful." I don't watch Bass and Caden as they disappear around a low wall—the less I let emotion in, the better. I inhale sharply. "We go in hard and fast. I need Cale alive. Or as alive as he is these days. Destroy any Reptiles."

We move swiftly down the corridor until we're crouched outside Danton's office. I hear low, angry voices, but I can't quite decipher what's being said. Without preamble, I lunge into the room, decapitating the Reptile stationed there. Inka takes out two more with her arrows. The stars and darts that Rila's throwing are a blur as Reptile after Reptile fall at her deadly strikes. Scowling, I dispatch a couple more, bringing me closer to the desk . . . and closer to the despicable person sitting opposite Cale.

Closer to Danton Quinn.

"You goddamned traitor!" I seethe. "Is there anything that you won't bargain away to save your own skin? Illegal vaccines, AI tech, robotics research? *Me?*"

"Everything has its price," he says in a gravelly voice. "And Cale, too, has his."

I tighten my fists around the hilts of my blades. "If you give Cale what he wants, the Reptiles will take over Neospes. Is that what you want?"

Danton shrugs. "I find that I'm better suited to the climate of the Otherworld. I care little what Cale decides to do with this one."

"And me?"

A haunted expression crosses his face. "A man should always have a few regrets, shouldn't he? Sadly, you are one of my very, very few."

"You'd bargain me away to Aenoh, just like that?"

Danton laughs hollowly, making the hairs on my neck stand at attention. "I gave you the suit, didn't I? Aenoh was simply a means to an end." I can feel Inka bristling beside me. She's new to my father's chess game and the clever, insidious way he plays people like pawns. I should know—I've been one all my life. But now it's time for the pawn to make a move to challenge the king.

I rush forward, only to hear gurgling beside me that halts me in my tracks. Despite her diminutive size, Rila has Inka on her knees in a choke hold. A garrote dangles loosely from one of her knives, looping around the princess's neck.

"What are you doing?" I snap.

"What she's programmed to do," Cale says coolly.

Rila's eyes flare blue and I take a step back, realization dawning as the light flickers down her arm. No wonder she's so fast with knives—no human could be that fast or that accurate. My eyes narrow at the flush in her cheeks and the brilliant blue, distinctly *not* milky irises. She's no Vector, which makes her . . .

"No," I whisper, turning to my father. "She's your test subject for my DNA strain," I say in a dull voice. Caden hadn't just stumbled upon her in the stairwell—we'd been meant to find her. "You couldn't just leave it alone, could you?"

"Riven, you have to understand what I'm trying to accomplish here."

"What? Mass genocide?"

He sighs. "Of course you would see it that way."

"What other way is there to see it?"

"She's the future. *You* are the future."

"She's a thing," I snarl. "One you tried to make into me. I'll kill her if I have to, and then you'll have nothing."

Danton stares at me, a hint of madness glimmering in his eyes. "And what would that achieve? The testing is already complete. There's nothing you can do to stop any of this. Killing her would be futile. You never understood, did you, Riven? This was always about you—everything I have ever done has been for you. Did you notice her name? I named her for you and your mother."

I hadn't noticed, and if he intends to make it more difficult for me to take her out, it's not working. It wouldn't make one iota of difference if he had named her *Riven II*. "Release her," I command Rila. "Or you will regret it, I promise you."

In response, she wraps the wire around her wrist, pulling it tighter against Inka's throat. I nod just once and raise my ninjatas in fighting stance. In a blur of motion, Inka head-butts Rila in the hip, forcing her to loosen the wire enough so that she can roll out of the way. I don't even have time to think before four darts come flying toward me. I easily flick them away with my ninjatas, then lift the blades, daring Rila to toss more my way.

"No matter how fast my DNA makes you, I will always be faster," I say.

A cold, doll-like, smile graces her lips as she pockets her garrote nonchalantly, but Rila's more than ready—I recognize it in the set of her shoulders and the tension around her mouth. Her hand flutters above the lethal display of knives, throwing stars, and darts at her waist.

My father and Cale are mesmerized as if seated in the front row at the Winter Games. I grit my teeth. If they want a show, they're going to get one. I exhale slowly and sink into a crouch. To my right, Inka notches her arrow and releases it, but it's not meant for Rila. It flies directly at Cale, who ducks in surprise, the arrow missing him by inches.

Inka sets another arrow and fires it at Rila, but the girl catches it in her hand and snaps it in two. There's no denying her skill. Inka's bow is loaded before I can blink, and then I'm rushing forward, fending off dart after dart, with my blades producing a shower of sparks as I get closer to Rila.

I'm inches away from reaching her when a huge aftershock rips through the building, causing plaster to fall in large chunks. Danton and Cale dive for cover under the large metal desk as I flatten myself against a central wall. When the dust settles, I scan the space. Rila has been trapped for the moment beneath one of the structural columns, and there's no sign of Cale. I find Inka covered in debris, but otherwise unharmed. She nods and we advance together, weapons drawn.

Squinting through the thick cloud, I catch sight of a pair of steel doors sliding shut. I should have remembered my father's private elevator. But as another violent tremor rocks the foundation, I shake my head. There's a good chance that the elevator will go into shut-down mode, if it hasn't already, and I'd rather be stuck out here than in there. It'll take a miracle for Cale, or any of us, for that matter, to make it to the surface alive.

I turn to Inka. "We need to go."

"What about her?" she says, staring at Rila's slight, pinned form.

I shrug. "She's a casualty of war."

Inka frowns. "But she's human."

"*Mostly* human. And she'll kill us the minute we help her. Her loyalties are to my father and Cale. Not us."

"So, change her loyalties. It's your DNA, after all."

My eyes meet Inka's and I pause, considering her suggestion. *Can it be done?* I ask the suit.

Yes. It's simple reprogramming.

It's worth a shot. And if it doesn't work, we can always leave her behind. Squatting beside Rila, I feel her cold eyes focus on me, and I take a breath. Engaging my suit, I use it as a conductor and place my fingers against her temple. Pushing forward, I connect to the nanobes firing in her system. They feel like foreign entities, but eventually, I force them to comply with the process synchronization.

You must reboot for the changes to apply.

Reboot? How do I reboot a human?

Partial human. For a second, I wonder if my suit is mocking my earlier words, but then it speaks again. **Reboot the nanobes and when they confirm the sync, you can shut them down.**

It won't hurt her?

The odds of her survival are fifty percent.

Wonderful. But it's the only option I've got. Focusing carefully, I shut down the robotics in her system. Rila's body jerks wildly as her human organs start failing. I hold her head so she doesn't injure herself.

"What's happening to her?" Inka whispers urgently.

"I'm shutting down the nanobes. They aren't part of her genetic code, like they are with mine. They're an accelerator—an artificial transfusion to give her an extra boost. My suit says she has fifty percent odds of survival."

Inka crouches beside me. "We don't have much time," she says as ominous cracks start forming along the walls.

It's not working!

Please stand by. After a few seconds, the suit instructs: **Place your hand on her chest and defibrillate.**

Inka helps me to remove the pillar laying over Rila's inert body. The nanobes had done well to protect the girl when it fell—if she were a normal human, she would have been crushed. I do as my suit commands, and flash an electric pulse into her, jumpstarting her heart. It takes a couple of tries before Rila sits up, gasping. Her eyes, so brilliant before, are now a shade of pale, unassuming blue.

"Are you all right?" I ask.

"Yes."

"What did you do?" she asks, flexing her fingers as I pull her to her feet.

"I deprogrammed you," I say. Then in a gentler voice, "Stay close. The nanobes don't define how strong you are. That's in here." I point to my chest, and then my temple. "And in here." I pause, handing her a few fallen darts. "One more thing. Don't mistake my help for weakness. You mean nothing to me, and I won't hesitate to kill you next time. In fact, you owe your life to Inka. If it were my choice, I would have left you." Rila nods, swallowing, and I continue. "Once we are out of here, you're free to go."

The building is unstable. Evacuate now.

The elevator?

Sebba has deactivated it, but there is a staircase a few feet to your right.

I'm starting to really hate that clone.

"Over here," I yell to Inka and Rila as I take off racing in the direction of the stairs. I check carefully—it seems intact, but appearances can be deceiving. "Run, and whatever you do, don't look back. Inka, you take point—I'll follow behind Rila."

We take the stairs two and three at a time, our breathing harsh. "Not far now," I pant. "We have a few more flights to go. Looks like we are coming up to the fifth floor."

"Riven," Inka says, halting. "It's blocked up ahead. Completely caved in."

"Let's see what's past that door. Maybe this floor has another way through."

We enter the access door to Five. Acrid smoke is thick in the air. I pull my visor over my head and tell Inka and Rila to do the same. What good is getting this far if we die of asphyxiation?

"Be careful," I warn as we inch around the perimeter of the burned-out room. "We don't know how stable this floor is."

Structural foundation is at fifteen percent.

Thanks for the good news. Where's the other staircase?

But before my suit can respond, a massive explosion at the center of the room blasts a wave of heat toward us. I crouch, feeling the hot blaze on my cheeks as a wall of flame flares up to the ceiling, completely encircling us. We can't go back and we can't go forward.

We're well and truly trapped.

2b

MASTER OF THE GAME

RILA STARTS COUGHING as the smoke thickens.

Think, Riven! "Maybe we can turn back and go down a floor," I say, but Inka shakes her head.

"Too dangerous. That staircase is not going to hold much longer."

The last thing I want is to die down here, but maybe that's exactly what will happen. Maybe it's just my time.

Is Caden safe? I ask the suit.

Yes. The Lord King is en route to the hangar. They are clear of the building.

I feel a wave of relief—one that's eclipsed by a sharp realization that I may never see him, or hear him laugh, or kiss him again. I close my eyes and feel the strong pull of him, deep in my center where I've buried all my feelings. They rise up to take hold of every part of me. And I realize that I want to survive. I don't want to die here today. Even if Caden *is* bound to Inka, I'd rather have a part of him than none at all. I want to live.

Give me all my options.

Running analysis.

As the suit prepares a list of alternative routes, I scan the room, calculating odds of escape. The fire is creeping closer, and Rila's coughing has gone from bad to worse. Suddenly, my eyes stop on the barely visible indented space in the wall— the shaft to my father's elevator. The doors can't be opened from any other floor, but the access panels are there in case of emergency.

Does that shaft go directly to the top?

Yes.

"Inka, help me wedge these panels open!" I pry my ninjata into the narrow seam, grateful for the strength of the Artok-forged blade. We work together, digging our fingers into the gap, widening it until I can fit my head inside. I look up and down, locating the service ladder. I can't see the elevator car anywhere so Cale must have made it out. "We're going to have to climb. Let's move."

Inka and I drag the panels apart. Sending Rila first, we pull ourselves through, and start climbing just as the entire floor explodes, sending a blast of heat into the shaft beneath us. Fire licks at my calves and back.

"Climb!" I urge Inka.

The ascent seems like it will never end, but we can't stop. My arms and lungs are burning. Suddenly, Rila coughs, a violent spasm wracking her body so hard that she loses her grip, slamming into Inka who falls past me, arms flailing. Gasping, I reach out and grab her wrist. My body bends backward and I lock my knees between the rungs, holding her fast as her body dangles in open space.

"Don't let go," she tells me, her dark eyes panicked.

As if I would. Although, a tiny part of me wonders what would happen if I did—there'd be no alliance, and Caden would belong to me.

Our hands are slick with sweat. It would be so easy to slacken my grip. My fingers relax, and Inka's eyes widen, but the move is only so I can get a better grasp as I swing her to the ladder beneath me.

"For a second there, I thought you were going to let go."

My frank answer surprises us both. "Me, too."

We start climbing again in silence, each occupied with the weight of our own thoughts, until Inka taps at my boot.

"What's wrong?"

"So," Inka says, her breathing echoing in the shaft as she peers up at me. "I hate to be the bearer of bad news . . . again . . . but, well, the elevator is moving. Toward us."

I frown—there's no one in the building, but to my horror, I look down and see that she's right. The elevator is heading straight for us, and ascending fast. It has to be Sebba. I hiss angrily. I really, *really* hate that clone. There's no way there will be enough space for the compartment and us, but I've come too far to be beaten now.

I engage the suit. *I don't care what you have to do. Stop that thing. Fry the entire network. Just do it.*

I will no longer have access to the Neospes network if I bring it down.

Do it!

We wait a few seconds before the elevator halts a few feet away and the shaft is drowned in complete darkness. "Climb."

"How much farther?" Rila wheezes.

"Almost there."

We stop at the final egress panels and I swing across, my toes barely gripping the edge as my body teeters for a moment. With a deep breath, I stabilize myself and wedge apart the doors. I shimmy my body through, using my back and feet as leverage. Rila and Inka follow me to the surface level of Sector Two.

It's a complete war zone.

I press a finger to my lips, pointing to the horde of clashing bodies—Vectors and Reptiles alike—a stone's throw away. A Reptile grabs my foot, and I stab it in the head before skirting past two decapitated Vectors that have slick blue fluid pooling beneath them. The last thing we need to do is attract unnecessary attention.

"Stay close to the buildings," I say in a low voice. "When we get out in the open, run." I glance at Rila. "I gave you my word. You can go."

"I'd rather stay, if it's all the same to you." Her eyes are huge. For a second, I see myself at that same age. I sigh. This is no time to get sentimental. She'll probably stab me in the back and I'll regret this for the rest of my life.

"Fine. Keep up." Inka gives me a look of approval, which I ignore.

Staying close to crumbling buildings, we move toward the hangar where I hope Caden is waiting. Twice, we run into Reptiles, but we dispatch them quickly and quietly.

Inka grabs my arm just before we enter the cavernous vaulted building, which has its own exit out of the dome.

"Riven, before we go in, I have to tell you that I did not know my father's army was not coming." She draws a long breath. "I told you that I would protect Caden with my life, and I will."

"I know." I hate the sound of his name on her lips.

"And, about the whole—"

Her words make my stomach clench and I cut her off. There's nothing she can say, short of breaking the agreement that will make a difference. She is as much a pawn as I am. "Inka, it's fine, just forget it."

"But, I don't want—" Her eyes grow round like saucers, staring at something behind me. The biggest Reptile I have ever seen barrels toward us.

"What the hell is that?" she says.

"Whatever it is, it's ugly. And huge." I hold my ninjatas at the ready and Inka notches her bow, but the beast is quickly swarmed by a few dozen Vectors, which take it to the ground. I exhale in relief. I have no doubt in my abilities, but getting close to a Reptile the size of a small house is nothing short of daunting. "We may not be that lucky again. Come on."

Being extra careful to avoid further detection, we sidle along the edge of the hangar. I enter the code and step into the shadowy space, the doors gliding shut behind us. The silence is oppressive, and a spidery sensation settles around my neck. We aren't alone. "Sauer? Caden? Anyone in here?"

"Welcome, General!" Cale's voice booms. I freeze, turning toward the sounds and lights coming to life along the hangar track. "What took you so long? Feel free to leave your weapons at the door."

Sauer, my mother, and Aenoh, are strung up on one side of the hangar, directly in front of our ship. Inka tenses when she sees Enola, also secured. There's no sign of Caden or Bass. I engage my suit. *Can you access their location?*

The network is rebooting from the manual override. It must complete all the security algorithms.

How much longer?

Fifteen minutes.

There's going to be a bloodbath in five.

I force my feet forward and paste a blank look on my face. Inka trails a half step behind me, and I notice that Rila remains behind in the shadows.

"Where is Rila?" Cale asks lightly. "I'm sure Danton will want to know whether his replacement spawn has survived."

"Where is he?"

Cale snorts. "He outlived his usefulness. He's over there with the rest of the undesirables." Only then do I see my father's lanky form, bound and gagged on the floor.

"You really have no concept of loyalty, do you?"

"To Danton?" Cale sneers. "The man who tried to play us all? He didn't have the stomach to see things through. He was intent on saving you, you see. First, he thought he could send you to Avaria where you'd be safe from me." Cale shudders, glancing at Aenoh. "Not sure that was his *best* idea. Then, desperate for his own daughter's love, he built Rila as a stand-in. He tried to use her to destroy the lab and all his research, but you see, we have our secrets, too." Cale laughs, making the hairs rise on my skin. "No, darling, my loyalty lies elsewhere."

"To the Reptiles?" I scoff. "Please."

"No, Riven. Not to the Reptiles."

His cryptic smile makes me want to smash his face in with the flat end of my blade. "I'm done playing your games, Cale. This time, you have nowhere to run. You are no match for me, and you know it. Release my friends, and leave Neospes."

"Or what?" He laughs. "We have everything we want. A nano-tech serum, an immunity vaccine, and an army. No one can stop us."

"Us? What are you talking about? You and your Reptile army? The Faction will never allow it. Remember what happened last time?"

"Not if the Faction is no more," he says smugly.

"You're deluding yourself, Cale."

"Am I?"

Have you located Bass and Caden yet? I ask the suit, knowing that the cat and mouse game with Cale will wear thin soon.

The system will be live in two minutes.

Every possible scenario races through my mind in quick succession. Had they gotten separated from Sauer? Had they seen what happened and decided to hide until we got here? What if they'd been attacked and overcome by Reptiles? What if . . .

I take a deep breath. I need to keep Cale talking, at least until I can locate them. Then I can figure out a counter move. Right now, our odds of success aren't great. "So, what? You're telling me you killed the entire Faction?"

"All but one, and she's going to destroy herself."

Now he has my attention. Era Taylor couldn't withstand an attack, not in her physical state. "What have you done?"

"Replaced an old, uncooperative regime with another."

My suit flickers against my body. **We are back online. The Lord King is in the hangar with you. Behind the ship.**

I stare past Cale, trying to see beyond the Reptiles to find Caden. A patch of red hair catches my eye, and I huff a victorious breath as I spot both Bass *and* Caden. They're hidden behind the landing gear. I signal to Bass, and he winks, pointing at the cannon on the top of the ship, then pressing a finger to his lips. If he can get up there, we could have a chance at turning the odds around.

"Be ready," he mouths, gesticulating at the engines as he swings himself up and over the landing gear like a cat. No one seems to be wise to his presence, which gives us a slight advantage. I need to buy us more time.

Tell me when the ship's weapons are online.

"Why don't you tell me what you did to Era?"

Cale grins. "Remember when she got taken by Vectors?"

"That was you?"

He nods, smirking smugly. "Suffice it to say that we sent her home with a little present—an imbedded bug. We've been privy to all Faction discussions and the whereabouts of all members. It was easy to pick them off. We've left the best for last."

"You're bluffing," I say horrified. "Cristobal is still alive."

"Is he?" Cale tilts his head in a birdlike motion.

Cristobal had been alive hours before we'd left, and no one knew the coordinates to Avaria but the Avarians. We've had a spy in our midst all along.

I open my mouth to confront Aenoh, but Inka beats me to the punch. "It was you," she hisses at her father. "You snake.

You betrayed us all. No wonder you wanted to kill Danton."
Aenoh shakes his head wildly as his daughter notches her bow
and points it directly at him. Her body is shaking with rage.
"You are a disgrace to Avaria."

Weapons are online. The message couldn't have come at a
more welcome time, but first I need to talk Inka off the ledge.
Killing Aenoh is not the answer.

"Inka, don't," I say gently.

"He deserves to die."

"You don't want his blood on your hands. Trust me, I know
about guilt. It'll eat you alive."

A loud, drawn-out groan draws everyone's attention. "Oh,
for fuck's sake, get it over with already," Bass shouts from his
position behind the cannon. "Just shoot him."

Well, okay, we're going to play it like that. Honestly, Bass is
like a bull in a china shop. He must have felt the plasma cannon
come online, and he has always been one for flair. I shake my
head at him, biting back a laugh. Holding my gaze, he reaches
to his side, pulls out a gun and shoots Aenoh in the head. Inka
screams and falls to her knees.

"See?" he says. My eyes snap back to his in shock. "It's easy
to kill a traitor. That was for you, Riven. We both know about
his foul plans for you. Seriously, it made me want to barf."

"Bass, what are you doing?"

"Having fun?" he says, gesturing theatrically with his side-
arm.

"Are you on something?"

He studies me, stroking the nose of the cannon. "The
only thing I am drunk on is power. Lots and lots of power."

A fake-regretful smile settles on his lips as he turns his attention to Inka, who is kneeling and keening beside Aenoh's body. "Sorry about your dad. He was a piece of work, and I've wanted to kill him for weeks. Only . . . I hate to break it to you, he isn't the one you're looking for." Bass rises to stand along the cannon's nose as if he's walking a tightrope. He vaults off, dropping into a quirky bow on the ship's top deck. "That would be me."

"You?" Inka whispers, confusion and doubt flitting across her face.

Understanding hits me like a punch to the gut. The spy isn't Aenoh . . . it's *Bass*. The suit flutters against me as the pieces come together in dizzying, unbelievable succession. Bass is the snake in our midst. He's been playing everyone—my father, my mother—and most of all, me.

I shake my head. "You? But why?"

"Why not?"

"You told me you wanted revenge on my father for your family. Was that a lie?"

He shrugs. "I took liberties with the truth. It wasn't an accident. I killed them because they were holding me back. They said I was one screw short of a set. They never got me. Danton took me in, trained me, taught me. Opened up a world of amazing possibilities. I was a particularly driven learner." Bass shoots a disparaging glance at my father's bound form. "But no matter how much I learned and how much I did, I could never measure up to you."

"Wait, why is this about *me*?"

"It's always about you, Riven. You are the only one of your kind, and no matter how much we wish to create others, what

Danton achieved was an exceptional anomaly." He takes a breath. "I convinced him to take your DNA, to try to replicate his best mistake. I was the one who made the initial nano-tech serum work. But then he got soft. He didn't want to go through clinical trials. We were at the end, success was so near I could taste it, and he wanted to quit. I had no choice but to give him an incentive."

"I don't understand. Why would you want to be anything like me?"

Bass laughs. It's an empty, humorless sound. "I was born with a severe learning disability. My father looked down on me, called me names, never tired of telling me how ashamed of me he was. I couldn't learn in the training sessions like the other children, so I figured out how to teach myself. And how to defend myself against those who didn't . . . understand me." His laugh takes on a wild, desperate edge. "Despite my limitations, I developed an aptitude for genetics and robotics. I watched and I learned, and then I cloned a new brain to fix the holes in mine. My first try was adequate, but I wanted to build a super-brain, and I did. When I first met you, I knew you were the future. Perfect, strong, invincible—the key to creating a super species free of flaws. Full of strength." He scowls at me, his nostrils flaring. "You never could see how special you are."

Something clicks in my head and I almost can't believe it. I remember my father's reaction in the lab when Cale mentioned Sebba, the horrified look on his face.

I engage the suit, shaking. *Is Sebba physically in this room? The one who made you?* I ask the suit.

Yes.

It feels like the floor has disappeared beneath me, even though I think a part of me already knew.

"You're Sebba," I say slowly. "You built the super-brain in Sector One."

"Can't get anything past you, can I," he says. "My name is Sebastian—Sebba when I was a child, Bass as an adult. Reinventing yourself can be so liberating. You should try it. And Sebba is a two-part process—Cale's body, *my* brain."

A distant memory of Era Taylor calling Bass *Sebastian* flits through my mind. Caden had, too, after the scuffle in the Outers. How had I missed it? I frown, staring down, as something else registers. "You built this suit."

"No," he says with a wry smile. "That was all Daddy Dearest. I let him. It was kind of sweet seeing him trying to make up for everything he's done to you, trying so desperately to atone for the past. Not up for the Father of the Year award, is he?"

I shake my head, my eyes flicking to Danton's motionless form. "Bass, you're wrong about me. I'm the furthest thing from perfect."

"You don't appreciate your gifts. You never have. I watched you, leading the Vectors at fourteen. You were a natural. I saw you in the Outers and beyond . . . the way you fought, the way you flew this ship. You are flawless. The suit was one of Danton's best creations, only I made a few adjustments. Couldn't let him have all the fun, could I?" He waves theatrically. "Imagine a suit modeled on the Vectors, designed to work only with your own DNA, enhancing all of your strengths and allowing you to communicate, to focus. It made you better. Stronger. More *you*. Less like them."

Now I understand my lack of emotion over the last few days. The suit doesn't just enhance my robotic abilities—it suppresses my basic human ones. "Neither of us is better than they are, Bass. Humans deserve to live, too. To live and love as they wish."

"And what about the reverse? To hate and ridicule as they wish?"

"We can't choose our parents. We can only choose who we want to be, and I know deep down, this isn't you."

Bass walks over, sliding his fingers down my face. My fingers twitch on the hilts of my blades, and I fight the desire to use them. "You don't know me at all," he murmurs.

"Don't I? It was all an act then? Everything on the ship? Our friendship?"

He stares at me, a smile playing on his lips, saying words he's said before. "I'm good at what I do, Riven." Of course he is—he's an assassin with a brilliant, engineered mind. My gaze flicks to Cale and I remember what he'd said about the Faction.

"Did you kill Cristobal?"

"Cristobal met an unfortunate end over that lovely precipice in the jungle. You remember the one, don't you?"

"I trusted you. We all trusted you."

"As you said—I am a master of deception." He gestures at his injured side. "All it takes for you to believe are a few well-chosen words and a few well-placed wounds."

"You stabbed yourself in the lab?" I deduce slowly, and Bass nods. I remember how in awe I'd been when I'd complimented him on his ability to blend in. He's right—I hadn't exactly made it difficult for him to fool me. "Why do you need him anyway?" I jerk my head toward Cale. "I don't see the connection."

Bass spreads his palms wide. "Cale, like me, tries to make something out of his very unfortunate circumstances. I respect that. He is a means to an end. He had an army at his disposal, and I needed one to breach Neospes."

"And the Avarians?" I glance at Inka, who hasn't moved from the floor. I'm not sure what she's doing—meditating or mourning—but I'm going to need her help if we're going to get out of this situation that's worsening by the second.

"Danton had something Aenoh wanted. When Aenoh told the Faction that he'd offer his aid in return for Danton, it was a no-brainer. And then, of course, your father jumped at the chance to trade his life for yours. I planted the idea of an alliance to strengthen the deal. The rest took on an eerie life of its own. And here we all are."

"What about Caden?"

"What about him?"

"You plan to kill him, too?"

With a flick of his finger, one of the Reptiles walks forward, holding a lethargic Caden by the scruff of the neck. "No, I made a different deal with Cale for him. You know the drill . . . everyone has to pay the piper. And the Reptile piper wants his due." Cale's face ripples with pleasure as Caden is thrust toward him. I have no doubt what he's going to do to Caden. The thought makes me sick.

"Bass, this is insanity. You cannot mean to create a cyborg species. It's unnatural. *I* am unnatural. What my father did was wrong. I shouldn't exist."

"But you *do* exist, and I am so close to re-creating your genetic strain."

"Is that why you needed Rila?"

"Rila was your father's pet. He'd always wanted to re-create the daughter he'd lost, but never had the guts. Until I came along." Bass leaps off the ship to land confidently on the floor of the hangar. My eyes grow wide as understanding registers scant seconds before his revelation.

"Rila was test subject number one." Bass's irises flare acid green. "*I* am test subject number two."

27

COUP DE GRACE

BASS CIRCLES ME, pulling his staff from its holster and twirling it over his hands. That's why he's so fast. I should have seen it earlier, but I'd wanted—no, *needed*—to trust him so badly that I'd been blind to all the signs. If Bass is anything like Rila—artificially modified—then he is not to be underestimated.

"I'm not going to fight you."

"I'm afraid you don't have a choice. I'll be gentle and we'll stick to standard sparring rules. Every strike you get on me, you get to save one hostage."

"And if you get a strike?"

"I kill one."

He spins his staff, and crouches into fighting stance. I don't move. I'm not going to play this game, not when there are so many lives at stake. Bass's eyebrows shoot to his hairline and he grins crookedly before lunging with a powerful strike to my stomach. The breath whooshes out of me and I stagger back. Without hesitation, he spins away and puts a bullet in the head of the closest Vector, the one standing trussed next to Sauer.

"Next time, it will be a human. Fight back."

"I don't want to fight you. Can't you see what you're doing? You're going to murder people based on injustices you *think* you suffered as a child. We all have our demons. Mine was him for a long time"—I jerk my head to my father, whose open eyes are now glued to us—"but he doesn't define me. My actions define me."

"Brave words from someone who is already genetically superior. Now fight, Riven. I want to see just how good you are."

"You already did, remember? In the bone yard." He blanches a little, but the look is quickly erased by an overconfident expression. Bass lunges again, catching me on the shoulder. I don't even try to deflect the hit. "I'm not fighting you."

Before I can blink, he swings around and shoots Arven right between the eyes. My mother's scream is agonizing, as is Sauer's groan. "See what you made me do?" said Bass. "You could've saved him. You chose not to. What were you saying before about actions?"

The swell of rage is overwhelming. I know Bass is pushing my buttons, but I don't care. He wants to play, so we'll play. I swing my ninjatas and wait, watching him. He shifts the weapon mode on his staff, turning both ends into triple-pronged machetes. Guess he means to draw blood. He lunges, his blade swinging dangerously close to my ear. I drop to my knees and roll, slicing one of my ninjatas through a well-muscled thigh.

"Aurela," I say and swoop back in, my blade nicking up the side of his cheek, and then down the other. "Sauer, Enola. Want me to keep going? I can go all day."

"I really enjoy when you get all feisty." He swipes at the lines of blood on his cheeks, and studies the fluid. I can see the injected nanobes doing what they're meant to—healing his broken skin.

Bass swings his staff, the playful expression on his face gone. He's all business now, and we start sparring in earnest, ducking and weaving out of each other's way in a blinding blur. He's good—more than good—and I have to work to keep up with him. It's like battling a version of myself—one that can make decisions on the fly and be unpredictable. After several intense minutes, we're both breathing hard.

Inka has worked her way back toward Sauer and the others. Out of the corner of my eye, I see a shadow creeping against the wall. But the moment of distraction costs me as Bass gets in a blow to the side of my head that makes me see stars.

"Aurela."

I narrow my eyes. "I already took her out."

"And I put her back in."

"You're changing the rules."

"It's my game."

I grit my teeth as he comes at me again, but this time I sidestep him neatly, bringing the hilt of my ninjata up into the soft rear part of his skull. I sweep my foot out, and he goes down hard onto his back. "Double hit. Aurela *and* Caden."

"Caden's not in the game," Cale screeches from the periphery.

I glare at him. "If he can change the rules, so can I, and I choose Caden."

Bass stands, rubbing the back of his head and wincing. "Cale's right. The lovely Lord King is not an option. I made a promise, you see. And it's *my* game."

This game of Bass's is all for sport, I see that now, a twisted way to punish me for being the cyborg he wants to be. He's not going to give me any hostages, and with him changing the rules, I'm not going to have any advantage. I don't know how I missed the signs—Bass's cruelty or the rocket-sized chip on his shoulder. Maybe I'd wanted to focus so badly on someone other than Caden that I'd had blinders on all along.

Truth is, I'd liked Bass's attention. I liked it so much that I refused to see what was right in front of my face. The clues were there—his presence in the Otherworld, showing up with my father at Charisma's, everting to escape the moss monster when he should have died, his derisive thoughts about the Otherworlders. None of that had registered. I'd fallen for his lies the minute he'd told me that sob story about his parents.

A sour, cold feeling settles in my stomach. "You said you were there when . . . with Shae. Were you the one to make her into a Vector?"

Bass's smile is pure, vengeful victory. "She was one of my greatest works."

"I'm going to end you."

With a hiss, I spin between Bass and Cale, ninjatas flying out and meeting my mark on each of their torsos. They stagger back at the same time, and I signal to Inka who releases three arrows into the Reptile ranks. Cale melts back into the darkness, coward that he is, and Bass wheels on me with a roar. I kick him in the mouth, wiping that smile off for good, my ninjatas a blur as my rage takes over. Bass can barely fend off my manic blows with his staff. Inka fires more arrows as Reptiles rush me from all corners—no doubt summoned by Sebba. A shower of darts follows, felling four more assailants, and I send a grateful look to the slight figure in the shadows.

"Rila!" Bass bellows, recognizing the weapons. "Get out here and do what you're programmed to do."

Inka dispatches the last of the Reptiles as Rila slinks past Sauer and the others and appears behind an unsuspecting Cale, who's hiding on the far side of the hangar.

"Hi," she says, her blade tipped into the vulnerable still-human side of his temple. Cale's hands go wide in surrender. He knows exactly what she's capable of.

Out of the corner of my eye, I see Sauer cutting his bonds loose with a knife that Rila must have slipped him on her way to Cale's side. Sauer gets to work on freeing the others, before rushing over to Caden. He looks anxious as he checks Caden's vitals, but I can't let worry distract me. Not now. The noise has drawn more Reptiles, and they're swarming the door.

It's my turn to taunt Bass. "I forgot to tell you. Rila's on my side, now."

His face contorts as studded pikes appear on the ends of his staff, and he swings it viciously at me. I dance back until we're by the far side of the hangar, away from the others. I let Bass get close and he hefts the pike again. I duck easily, squatting down and kicking out in a sweep that catches him in the ankles. Bass topples, and I waste no time jumping on top of him, my ninja-tas scissored at his neck.

"Sebba!" Bass thunders, his throat bobbing beneath my blades. His cold eyes don't leave mine for a second. "Summon all the Reptiles. Now. And you . . . you are mine." He pushes up against the blades until welts appear on his neck from the sharp edges. "You can't kill me. Deep down you know we are the same. You are mine."

"You're insane," I say, trying to press down. But instead, my arms fall limp to my sides and I keel over.

What's happening? I ask the suit, which suddenly seems to be going rogue, holding me immobile.

Secure Sebba program script operational. Shutting down DNA sync.

That sneaky bastard. He'd programmed parameters into the suit—ones that become operational if I ever come close to killing him.

Override. Now!

Negative.

Then shut down. I swipe at the neck of the suit, trying to disconnect it from my brain and body, but it only cinches tighter like a full-body noose. Something cool slithers into my spine—the suit's injecting some kind of paralyzing agent into my bloodstream. Fighting with every ounce of strength, it isn't long before I am unable to move an inch. I'm imprisoned in an inescapable casing, my brain the only thing functioning. I glance around, taking a desperate count. Sauer's still with Caden, Aurela, and Enola. Cale is lying in a crumpled heap on the ground. Rila is nowhere in sight.

Bass pulls himself up to leer over me. "I told you once. Always be prepared for the inevitable. I knew you'd be the one to try to stop me. I had to build you something that would make you feel invincible, and then take it away at the very last moment, just as you realize how much you've depended on it." He leans down to press a kiss to my forehead. "Watch, sweet warrior. Watch while I kill every last member of your family. When this is over, you'll be the queen you always wanted to be." He laughs. "Oh, I know all your secrets—how badly you wanted the Lord King to choose you. It's pathetic."

I try to talk—try to tell him that I'll do anything he wants—but my lips are glued together. Bass walks away. I watch in slow motion as hundreds of Reptiles pour in like a foul river of broken metal and bones, barricading the entrance to the hangar. They surround Bass like a god, and I can only stare helplessly when Inka's bow is wrenched from her grip and they force her to the ground. Only the slight twist of Bass's fingers stops them from ripping her to shreds.

"Slowly now, I want the General to watch every excruciating moment. How could this human be more worthy than you?" he asks. "To *you*? All because of a boy you think you're in love with? Love is nothing, and has no place in this world. You are flawed because of it. It taints you with its promises, and then discards you when it sees fit." Bass's voice becomes gentler as his fingers brush Inka's bronze skin. She doesn't even flinch. "I'll save this one for last." He stands. "Bring me the other Avarian."

Inka struggles against the hold of the Reptiles, fear flashing across her face. Bass is quick to notice. "Figured she means something to you after you went all crazy against your father. This should be interesting."

Bass nods to one of the nearby Reptiles, which has a soldering laser for an arm. I want to scream as they hold Enola down, but my body is unresponsive. She doesn't make a sound, not even when they burn the top layer of skin from her arms. Her dark lips turn white and a single tear slips from the corner of her eye. The tissue puckers and blisters, the scent of scorched flesh saturating the air. Inka screams, thrashing against the Reptiles holding her in place, as the laser moves to Enola's chest.

"Stop." The voice is weak but authoritative, and my eyes fly to Caden's form. He's standing, half-leaning on Sauer.

Bass sneers. "The Lord King awakens."

"Stop this, Bass."

"May I remind you that you have no authority here?"

"I'm asking you. Just take me. Do what you will with me, but let them go. The Avarians have done nothing to you."

"Nothing?" Bass scoffs. "Look at everything they've hoarded and hidden. They're more than selfish. And they, too, will pay."

"That's not Inka's fault. That was her father's choice. You already dealt with him. Let them go. Show mercy, I'm begging you."

Listening to Caden's desperate plea, I'm so focused on what he's saying that I suddenly realize a person is lying flat next to me on her stomach. Rila shimmies closer.

"I know you can hear me," she whispers. "I'm going to try to disconnect the suit. It may hurt."

I wince as she wrenches the connectors out of my body. Even with the paralysis agent, I can feel the sharp sting as the suit tries to hang on to me like a leech. Rila tugs each plug out, careful not to make any noise or draw attention. Blood rushes into my numb limbs as the suit powers down, flaking off my body like a discarded snakeskin. I'm in underclothes, but I don't care. I can move.

I study the slight girl stretched out beside me, suddenly grateful I hadn't left her to die in the lab. "Thank you, Rila."

She nods and leans in. "You should trust them, you know, the nanobes. They're yours. I know what you said about them not defining me, but they *are* part of *you*."

I stare at her for a moment, then take off at a mad run toward the ship, leaping over bodies and slashing with my ninjatas. My entire body glows blue. I'm a bright neon streak across the hangar. Bass stares at the spot where his suit is lying in a crumpled heap, and he turns back to me, howling.

"Stop her!"

He lunges at me as dozens of Reptiles converge, but I push myself faster, vaulting off one of them at the last moment to propel myself in a flying somersault to the top of the ship. Bass is fast, but not fast enough. I don't hesitate, slipping through the hatch and powering up the ship with a mental command. I don't need the suit to be an accelerator. The ship is already attuned to me—I feel it locking on.

"Shields!"

The ship is already taking a beating. I power up and point the cannon into the middle of the fray and fire. The shock makes part of the hangar explode outward. A wave of waiting Vectors surges through the opening, engaging the Reptiles as if possessed. I switch to guns, and start picking off the Reptiles closest to Sauer one by one. He, Caden, Aurela, and Inka are pressed into a tight circle with Enola and Danton lying between them and a ring of Reptiles closing in. I shoot faster.

Bass jumps off the ship and the Reptiles clear a path for him. He swats off a couple Vectors like gnats, and melts into the mass of clashing bodies. I lose sight of him when a few rogue Reptiles break forward to attack Caden's group.

The Reptiles press in on the circle, obscuring it from view. I contemplate shooting the plasma weapon again, but Caden and the others could be in the blast radius, so I keep picking off individual Reptiles.

"Locate Bass," I tell the ship, paying close attention as it runs its facial analysis program. I finally see him. He's holding the Lord King in a choke hold, the edge of his staff now a sharp sword and pressed against Caden's stomach. Sauer, Aurela, and Inka have lowered their weapons, surrendering.

Bass looks directly at me, his face, large and ferocious on screen. "You're clever, Riven. I'll give you that. But I know your weakness and I will gut your lover from navel to nose if you don't get off that ship."

"Don't do it, Riven!" Caden shouts and earns a vicious stab to the belly. I can see the blood flowering through the shallow wound.

"The next one will be much deeper, I promise," Bass growls.

I press the communicator. "Don't hurt him. I'm coming out."

But instead of exiting the ship, I swing myself down through the hatch to the engine room, and retrieve the weapon Arven had hidden inside the shell of the magnetic rings. I wonder why Bass didn't destroy it, but then realize that he meant to use it against the Reptiles. He needed them to attack Neospes, but he despised them the same way he scorned humans. Once they'd done their jobs, eliminating them would have been easy.

I exhale slowly, hefting the weapon in my hands. This could be the end of me, but I know what I have to do. I open the hatch as promised. As the door slides open, my eyes find Caden's and

I communicate my good-byes with a painful sigh. I look to my mother who nods once, touching her fingers to her lips in silent acknowledgment.

"Riven," Caden whispers, his face stricken as his eyes dart from my face to the metal cylinder in my arms. "No . . ."

I glare at Bass. "Game over, assclown."

Bass lifts his staff in a rage, but he doesn't complete the strike. Not when I fire the weapon and everything goes black.

20

LIFE, DEATH, AND
SECOND CHANCES

THE SUN IS hot on my face as I float on the softest surface imaginable. I'm lying in a pool of water, lights dancing off the top like joyful sprites. I've never felt so at peace.

"Do you miss home?" I ask my sister, who is floating beside me. Shae flicks a few droplets toward me, and I let my feet submerge, to tread water.

"Sometimes. I miss you and mom." Her arms moving gently beneath the surface. "And Sauer. It's not really about the place—it's about the people you leave behind."

I study my sister's perfect features—the clear blue eyes and the wet, blond dreadlocks plastered to her glowing cheeks. "Did it hurt?"

"Dying?" she asks. "Not really. It hurt to separate from the life I knew and loved, but this one isn't so bad. You can be anywhere you choose to be. Like here." She waves a hand, sending a shower of gold-tinged droplets flying in a shimmery arc above us. "Death, like anything else, is a state of mind."

I hesitate before asking the question that's making my stomach churn. "What if your state of mind isn't . . . like this? What if you think you deserve less?" *Much less.*

Shae smiles sadly, her fingers reaching out to me. I stretch forward to take her hand, but she fades and disappears. The water grows cold and dark and, suddenly, I'm locked in a damp, musty cave. My fingers curl around the rusty bars caging me within the rock. I cry out, but no sound escapes my lips.

A shadow flickers in the darkness beyond the metal slats. It's a girl, one who looks so familiar. My brain is fuzzy, but I think I used to have that face. Maybe I even used to be her once. She has burning yellow eyes. Large, glowing orbs that scorch into mine. She approaches the bars, humming softly, and when her fingers push past to close around my throat, I welcome the pain.

"Hold her down; she's coming out of it!" I hear someone yell from far away. It sounds like my voice, but I know it can't be. I don't have a voice.

"She's going into cardiac arrest!" another person shouts.

I scream until my throat is sore. Air is forced through my lungs and something heavy is pressing onto my chest. I jerk upward, trying to buck it off, but the pressure is relentless. It feels like I'm covered in fire ants, each taking hungry bites from my flesh. My entire body feels like it's coming apart, bones and blood crumbling into tiny fragments. My eyes flutter open, drawing me out of my nightmares.

Shae was wrong. Death isn't a state of mind. It's all-consuming and unending. It's agony.

When I open my eyes, I'm in a sterile white room, and I'm not alone. There's a boy in the corner lying on a cot, his hair falling into his face. I recognize him immediately, or something deep inside me does. There's a chemistry between us, something intangible linking me to him. I wonder if I'm still dreaming.

I take a breath, feeling a sharp ache radiate through my body. I look down and start to hyperventilate. I'm encased within a silver capsule from neck to toe. I close my eyes and reopen them—the capsule is still there. I take in my surroundings bit by bit. The capsule is suspended inside a glass box cut off from the rest of the white room—quarantine—with monitoring screens everywhere. I flex my fingers. Pain stabs up through my hand and into my chest. Everything hurts, even breathing. I inhale slowly, focusing on each breath before releasing it slowly. It hurts a little less. But at least the pain tells me one thing—I am alive. And I'm not dreaming.

Someone comes into the room and I feel a tear leak from my eyelid at the sight of her face. She enters a second, smaller glassed-in room off of the main area, and then enters my room once the decontamination process is complete. Harsh lines etch the corners of her eyes and her mouth, making her look far older than when I last saw her. Her lip wobbles a little as we make eye contact.

"Mom," I murmur. The syllable scorches a path up my throat, making me wince.

"Easy," she whispers gently, holding a container up to my lips. "Here, sip some of this. You're still healing."

"Wh-at happened?" I croak. A wave of dizziness hits me. I want to ask so many questions about the capsule and why I feel like I've been dragged naked across the Outers by a hoverbike. "Feel . . . funny. Caden . . . okay?"

She presses a hand to my forehead, consulting a tablet, before entering something on the monitor above my bed. Something cool floods my body and the sharp edge of pain recedes into something more bearable. "You need to rest, darling. You've been through an ordeal, one that most of us would never have survived. Caden is fine. He's slept in here for the past few weeks, refusing to leave."

Weeks? I swallow hard. Images flicker through my brain— Cale, Bass, Caden, the hangar, Reptiles, Vectors—but I can't make sense of them. They're too chaotic, out of sequence. "Tell . . . me."

Aurela pulls a stool from under the capsule and sits beside me, her hands fluttering against my hair. Her soft touch is comforting and I want to lean into it. I close my eyes, and breathe in her scent instead. "What you did was so very brave, and so very foolish. Detonating that weapon when you didn't know what it would do to you . . ."

I remember the last moments—the look on Caden's face and the one on hers—before I pressed that button. And then there was only darkness. "Every . . . body safe?"

"Yes. The weapon worked as the Avarians said it would. Everything electronic shut down—all the Reptiles, all the Vectors, and all of our systems. Including you. Your heart shut down. So did Bass's. But you were our priority. You and Rila."

I'm glad she's safe. I'm alive because of her. I remember how I'd had to restart her heart. She'd had a fifty percent chance of survival. The odds would have been the same for Bass. "Is Bass . . . dead?"

Aurela smiles a little sadly. "Yes. Sebba and Cale, too."

I feel a brief spurt of remorse for the two boys who had once been my friends. In the end, they'd become monsters. It's funny how something small can twist you until you break inside. They'd both been damaged beyond repair. "And Enola?"

"She suffered severe burns, but she's going to make it. And Inka is fine. They're all asking about you."

I blink and swallow hard, wanting to ask the question, but not wanting to at the same time. I don't want to care about him, but I do. "Danton?"

"Your father is gone."

"To . . . Otherworld?"

My mother nods. She looks like she has more to say, but offers me the cool drink instead. I sip it gratefully, feeling it soothe the sting from the effort of speaking. I'm not surprised that my father took off—he has always been about self-preservation. Unless, that was the old Danton. Aurela was right—maybe he changed. "Why?"

"He said he had unfinished business."

Something clicks in my brain. "Era Taylor safe?"

Aurela's fingers close over mine. "Era Taylor died two weeks ago, Riven. Her body couldn't handle the stress any longer. Her son, Philip, is now the Chancellor. He's rebuilding from the ground up, as are we."

Philip? I want to laugh, but I know it'll hurt something fierce. Philip is better than nothing, and hopefully he'll have

Charisma at his side. At least she has a brain. Era Taylor wouldn't have gone quietly. Once she realized what the Vectors had done, she would have taken measures so that she couldn't hurt anyone else. It's the hallmark of a true leader. I say as much to my mother, and she nods. "That is what I believe, too."

I shake my head, flinching. "Philip . . . asshat."

She laughs. "He's not so bad. Sometimes people need a little challenge to rise to their full potential." Her hand finds mine and squeezes gently.

"So what's"—I gasp through the words and stare pointedly at my metal housing—"with my new outfit?"

Aurela smiles, stroking my fingers. "You're sure you want to hear this now?" I nod and she continues. "When you set off the weapon, you were in bad shape. After the nanobes were deactivated, your entire body shut down for several minutes. For all intents and purposes, you *died*. When we resuscitated you, your body went into massive shock. Unlike Rila, the nanobes are bonded to your DNA, so when they failed, your body tried to repair itself and couldn't.

"We forced you into an induced coma to keep you alive. Week after week, we tried all we could to rebuild your cells. Everything failed. Your father"—she rakes a hand through her hair, her expression conflicted—"he was the one who saved you."

"You said he left? How?"

"He was here the whole time. He left the minute you started responding to the genetic therapy. He built this," she says, waving a hand at the contraption holding me in place. "It's an advanced auto-transfusion machine. It was something he was working on in secret with Rila. It salvages your living blood cells and recycles them back into you."

I stare at the capsule. I'm not sure what it means, or why I'm not healing as I normally do. I frown, missing the connection between what I know and what my mother is explaining. "So, the nanobes aren't rebooting?"

Aurela stares at me. "There's nothing to reboot. The weapon destroyed them. This machine is teaching your body to self-repair and survive without the nanobes."

My mouth drops open. "I thought that wasn't possible."

"We learned a lot from the Vectors."

"Vectors?"

"It was a collaborative effort," she says. "We stripped you down and reverse engineered your DNA sequencing with specific nano-gene targeting. It was part of Sebastian's research, and how he was able to synthesize your DNA."

"Sebastian," I repeat dumbly.

"Bass," she corrects. "He isolated your nanobes like a mutation, making them inoperative, and was able to knock in and knock out specific variations to develop a strain that was compatible with regular human DNA. We did the same with an artificial DNA construct, introducing new self-replicating gene technology to replace what we took out."

My brain is working, trying to keep up. "You cloned me? My blood, I mean?"

"Yes. We used artificial plasmids as a vector in your molecular reconstruction."

"Are you saying that . . . I'm human? Like *full* human?"

"The short answer is *yes*, for now. The long answer is we don't really know."

My mind is racing. It feels weird not to have the nanobes rushing around inside of me, responding to my every thought. I feel . . . strangely vulnerable.

I tell my mother and she smiles gently. "Welcome to being human."

I swallow hard. "When do I get out of this tin coffin?"

"Soon," she promises. "Now, you really do need to rest. Your stress levels are skyrocketing, probably because you're trying to process all of this information. Perhaps I should have waited until you were stronger."

"No, I needed to know. Thank you."

Aurela stands and types in a sequence on the monitor. This time, a different colored liquid fills the plastic tubing and dissolves into the metal cylinder. I watch my mother's face until it fades into a soft palette of rosy color. My eyelids droop heavily, and I give in to a deep, dreamless sleep.

When I wake again, I'm in a different room, this time without the glass box. My body is wrapped in sterile cloth, but I'm in a bed and no longer confined by the silver capsule. My ever-faithful roommate is slumped in a chair by my side. Caden looks as haggard as I feel. His head is resting on the bed near my hand and I thread my fingers through the soft strands of his hair. He shifts and looks sleepily at me, his head snapping up when he realizes that I'm staring back at him.

"Hey," I say. Brilliant green eyes catch and hold mine, making something like butterflies take flight in my stomach.

"You're awake."

"When did I get out of the tin can?" I say with a half smile.

"A few days ago."

"I was asleep the whole time?"

Caden turns his face and presses his lips into my open palm. The soft, warm sensation makes a host of tingles take off in my chest. "It was safer to keep you sedated during the transition. Plus, I like watching you sleep." I snort. "You know, it's my special brand of creepy-sweet. You're kind of like my own Sleeping Beauty."

My breath hitches at the tender look on his face. "Doesn't Prince Charming get to kiss her awake?"

Caden's eyes flare at my words, but he shakes his head with a quick look at the doorway. "I'm not sure I'm allowed."

"You're the Lord King; you make the rules. Plus, if you don't, I'm not going to be accountable for my actions."

He leans over and brushes his lips over mine in a kiss so tender that it makes my toes curl. I want more, but he pulls away, and looks at the door again. "Your mother's out there, and she can be really fierce where you're concerned."

"Wimp."

"When it's Aurela? Totally. Your mom scares the bejeezus out of me."

I laugh and stare at him, drinking in his features—the way his eyes catch the light, the stern lines bracketing his lips, his half-crooked smile. "She said you stayed with me the whole time."

"It was touch and go for a while there. I thought I was going to lose you, but your father . . . he simply refused to let you go."

Caden pauses, pulling a slim tablet from his pocket, his expression growing serious. "Speaking of Danton, this is for you. You should know that he turned himself in to the Faction."

"He did what?" I say, dumbfounded, staring at the device. "What is that?"

"A message. Want me to read it to you?" Caden asks, and I nod as he clicks on the device. "It says, 'Riven, I had one promise to fulfill before I destroyed the synthesized strain of your DNA Sebastian created. The nanobes had one more purpose—to help your friend's sister. I hope you understand that in my own way I do care for you deeply. You were never my weakness. You were always my greatest achievement. A flawed, hopeful father, Danton Quinn.'" Caden re-pockets the tablet and looks at me. "That's it."

Truth is, I don't know what to feel about my father's message or what he's done.

I'm mostly grateful that he helped Charisma's sister, knowing that he broke all kinds of Faction laws to do it, but maybe Charisma and Philip will cut him some slack now that he's in their custody. Danton will find a way to survive. He always does.

I guess I was wrong—some people can change. I don't know if I'll ever be able to forgive him, but maybe that's something I can work on, too.

"How are you feeling?" Caden asks. "Now that you're almost back to yourself?"

I shrug. "Not totally. I don't have special abilities anymore, you know. I won't be able to protect you as well. You could probably beat me in a sword fight now."

Caden laughs, the sound bright. "Are you kidding? I've been waiting forever to be able to do that. Finally, a silver lining."

"Cade, I'm serious. I'm ordinary now."

Caden leans over, pressing his lips to each cheek, my nose, and then my lips. "For the record, you are not, and will never be, ordinary. You will always be extraordinary whether you have a body full of tiny little nanobes or are made of flesh and blood. Surely you know that by now."

I lick my lips, seeing his eyes darken, marveling at the power we hold over each other. I swallow hard and decide to tackle the eight-hundred-pound gorilla in the room. "What about the alliance? Inka? You're kind of engaged."

My question is eclipsed by a sudden commotion. "You have visitors," Aurela announces. She smiles at us before warning Sauer, Inka, and Enola not to overexcite me. I bite my lips to stop from laughing at Caden's mock terrified I-told-you-so look.

"Hi," I say to them.

"Hey, yourself." Sauer grins. He's dressed in his commander uniform. "Welcome back."

"Thanks. You look official."

"Supervising the rebuilding of the city. It's insane how much damage rogue Reptiles and Vectors on a mission can do. But, not to worry. We citizens of Neospes are tough and it'll take a lot more than that to bring us down."

"What about the people hiding in the Peaks?"

"Safe and sound," Sauer says. "Thanks to you."

"Not all me," I murmur.

I look at the other visitors, Inka and Enola, and force a smile. Caden hadn't responded about the alliance. The Avarians are dressed in Neospes gear, but they still look as intimidating—and stunning—as they did in their own city. The scars along Enola's arms and neck are raised and angry looking, but she wears them proudly, like badges of honor.

"So, when's the wedding?" I joke weakly, staring from Inka to Caden.

Inka laughs. "That's what I tried to tell you when we were outside the hangar. I don't *want* to marry your king."

"You don't?"

"No," she says, linking hands with Enola. They share an intimate look, and everything makes sense. *Oh.* Inka smiles. "I see you understand. Enola is . . . my other half. My father never understood this. He saw her as a slave, as someone common born. But she was always so much more to me."

I let her words sink in. "You're not marrying Caden?"

"I would have for my people, but no, I would not want to marry him when my heart is elsewhere." She smiles gently. "Plus, I think it's obvious that he is in love with someone else." Inka smiles fondly as Caden tugs on my hair. "I wish you both well. Neospes will always have Avaria's help whenever she needs it. And your people can come to us for sanctuary at anytime. I offered this to your king, but he refused."

Caden nods. "I choose to rebuild. Our city is a great one, too. With Avaria's help, we can become strong again."

"Riven," Inka says, bowing to me as if I'm the queen and she's the servant. "It has been an honor, and I do not say this lightly. You are truly one of a kind."

I laugh weakly. "Not anymore."

Inka approaches me, her face stern. "Not because you were a cyborg, but because you are *you* . . . always putting others before yourself, always doing what needs to be done. Even with me, I knew you were predestined to hate me, yet you still put my life above your own. That's not technology, that's *heart*, and you have more of that than most humans." She leans in to embrace me, kissing both my cheeks. "I am in your debt for saving Enola's life."

"Thank you." Overwhelmed, it's all I can manage to say.

"You must visit us again," Inka says brightly. "We will have a feast to end all feasts. I will see you again, my sister."

The sound of the word doesn't cause the pain I expect. In a strange way, I do see some of my own sister, Shae, in her—I see it in the proud strength of her shoulders, in her gentle touch with Enola, in the fierce determination of her eyes. I accept her gift in the way in which it was offered . . . in love and friendship and sisterhood.

"I will see you soon . . . my sister," I agree.

After they take their leave, Caden sits beside me on the bed. I study him, a smile playing on my lips. "Are you relieved not to have to trade your virtue to save Neospes?"

"My virtue?" he sputters, and then realizes that I'm joking.

"You aren't the first royal to be married off, you know," I tease. Caden silences me with his lips, kissing me until I'm breathless. When we pull apart, we're both flushed and panting hard. I touch his face, my thumb memorizing the curve of his cheeks and the sweet arch of his lips.

"What are you thinking?" he whispers against my fingers, kissing them.

That I love you.

"That I want to see the sunrise," I say as the first light of Neospes dawn creeps through the windows of my room. "Will you take me over there?"

Caden is careful, hooking one arm under my knees and the other bracing beneath my shoulders. I wrap both my arms around his and bury my face in the crook of his neck as we walk to the window. We are on the top floor of the medical facility, one of the only buildings that remains standing. Instead of taking in the still-smoking rubble inside the dome, I look beyond it. I look to the sun rising in the distance.

The brilliant red sphere peeks above the horizon, setting the Outers awash in hazy, dazzling waves. Its gold-tinged crimson fingers reach everywhere, chasing away the shadows in the darkness, and bringing radiant light to everything in its path. I thread my fingers through Caden's hair as we watch the Neospes sunrise together, setting everything in its reach on fire. His lips find my temple as another day begins fresh, beautiful, and unsullied.

My name is Riven.

And I live in a world of infinite possibility.

ACKNOWLEDGMENTS

To Julie Matysik, whom I cannot thank enough for being such a huge champion of my books, thank you for believing in me and in the Riven Chronicles series. *The Almost Girl* and *The Fallen Prince* would not have found a home at Sky Pony Press without you. To Alison Weiss, editor extraordinaire, working with you has been everything an author/editor relationship should be—fun, challenging, and instructive. *The Fallen Prince* wouldn't be the book it is without your insightful notes. Thank you. To my longtime friend and agent, Liza Fleissig, you know I have nothing but mad love for you. Thank you for saving the orphans and for being such a tenacious, passionate advocate of mine for so many years. To Angie Frazier, thanks for reading and blurbing both books in this series! I am so grateful for your friendship. To all the bloggers, booksellers, librarians, conference leaders, educators, and readers who spread the word about my books and humble me with your unwavering enthusiasm, thank you so much for doing all that you do. To my extended family, and all my wonderful friends and fans—

online and off—so much gratitude goes out to you for being so generous with your love and friendship. I'm thankful to have you in my corner.

Lastly, to my wonderful family—Cameron, Connor, Noah, and Olivia—thanks for all the hugs and the love and the never-ending encouragement. You are my heart.